The
VALLEY
of the
ANCIENTS

Praise for *The Promised One*

'Utterly enthralling for any child with an interest in animals.' *Daily Telegraph*

'I am writing to say how much I enjoyed your book, *The Promised One*. I read it a few weeks ago and could not put it down at all it was so exciting. The story is amazing and one of the best I have ever read.' Natascha Mathews, aged 11

'I have just finished reading *The Promised One* for the second time and I love it.' Thea Pope, aged 11

'I have recently read your book *The Promised One*. I think it is really good and I feel I'm just like Lucy (apart from the special powers!) because I love animals too . . . My friend Isabelle has also read the book and loves it too.' Alexandra Gibbs

The VALLEY of the ANCIENTS

DAVID ALRIC

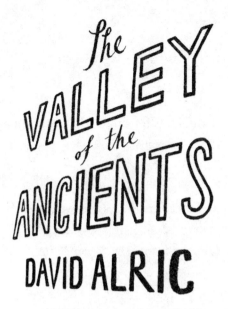

Illustrated by

David Dean

Acme Press

First published in 2008
by Faber and Faber Limited
3 Queen Square London WC1N 3AU

This edition published in 2011 by
Acme Press
PO Box 65725, London, N21 9AY

Design by Mandy Norman
Printed and bound by CPI Group (UK) Ltd, Croydon, CR0 4YY

British Library Cataloguing in Publication Data. A catalogue record for this book is
available from the British Library.

ISBN 978-0-9568356-2-8

To Derry

Acknowledgements

The author wishes to thank his wife, children and grandchildren for their help and encouragement during the writing of this book, especially Catherine for her suggestions concerning the preliminary drafts. He greatly valued the advice he received from his three young advisers, Sadhbha Cockburn, Jonathan Jackson and Georgie Hill, all of whom made comments that influenced the final text.

Finally, his grateful thanks are due to Julia Wells, Lucie Ewin and Mandy Norman for their help and patience and to Faber & Faber Ltd for permission to reproduce their original design and typography in this edition.

Contents

	Preface	ix
	Prologue	1
1	The Adventure Begins	3
2	A Hidden Message	10
3	Living in a Greenhouse	22
4	A Miscellany of Miscreants	39
5	An Invisible Surprise	54
6	A Voice in the Dark	73
7	Chopper Takes A Break	80
8	Plots and Plans	84
9	Aerial Combat	88
10	Walking on Eggshells	100
11	An Eye-opener for Tina	112
12	Clio gets a Head Start	125
13	Biggles Blunders into a Bog	145
14	A Helping Hoof from a Hosenose	161

15	Perfidious Plans and Pleistocene Post	169
16	The Horror of the Hollow Hills	183
17	More Monkey Mail	196
18	Hoodwinking Hungry Hunters!	209
19	Vanishing Villains	227
20	Spider Speak	247
21	Search for a Subterranean Slitherkin	260
22	The Mighty Ones Get Stuck In	279
23	Another Invisible Surprise	293
24	A Final Surprise	311
	Epilogue	318
	Appendix: Coping with Carbon:	322
	Lucy's Lexicon	329
	Notes on the names in the book	333
	An Anthology of the Animals of Antiquity	341
	Glossary	348
	Unit conversion table	425

Preface

This book is a sequel to the first book in the series, *The Promised One*, which recounted the extraordinary adventures of the Bonaventure and Fossfinder families in the remote jungles of the Amazon river.

The glossary of difficult and unusual words that was included in the first book proved to be so popular that I have repeated and expanded it. There are new versions of 'Lucy's Lexicon' and 'Notes on the names in the book' so that readers can again have some fun guessing the meanings of neologisms and names, and I have included 'An Anthology of the Animals of Antiquity', which gives factual information about the creatures mentioned in the book.

The situation with regard to the factual knowledge contained in the book is a little complicated by the fact that the story contains some elements of fantasy. These provide, after all, the principal sources of excitement in the tale. Those facts and figures that *do* pertain to reality, however – subjects such as geography; the flora and fauna of current and prehistoric epochs; global warming and the greenhouse effect – are, to the best of my knowledge, accurate.

Concerning invisibility, the achievement of this, to the extent described in the story, still belongs to the realm of science fiction. The underlying physical concepts discussed by Dr Angstrom are, however, based upon orthodox science. I depart from reality only in permitting the doctor to succeed in actually accomplishing at a macroscopic level that which is only currently theoretically possible at a molecular level.

The contentious issue of units of measurement is one that I have addressed by using the same compromise as in *The Promised One*. Heights and distances are usually expressed in imperial units, particularly by the older characters in the book for whom such usage would be everyday speech. I have used metric units or SI units for specific anatomical dimensions and scientific measurements. These 'rules' have not been rigidly applied and I have endeavoured to use those units which would come most naturally to an English-speaking person in the particular situation being described. I have included a short unit conversion table at the end of the glossary.

I make no apology for having included in the book some discussions on the greenhouse effect, global warming and the issue of future energy resources. These topics are arguably the most important that the children reading this book will have to face in their lifetimes, and they seem to merit inclusion in a tale about nature and the world's greatest rainforest.

Serious matters, however, can intrude upon the flow and enjoyment of an adventure story and I have attempted to get round the problem by moving some of this material from the text into an appendix. I trust that this compromise provides a satisfactory solution to the problem; if it does not I can only apologize.

All that now remains is for me to wish you a happy and exciting journey into the Valley of the Ancients.

David Alric
London, 2007

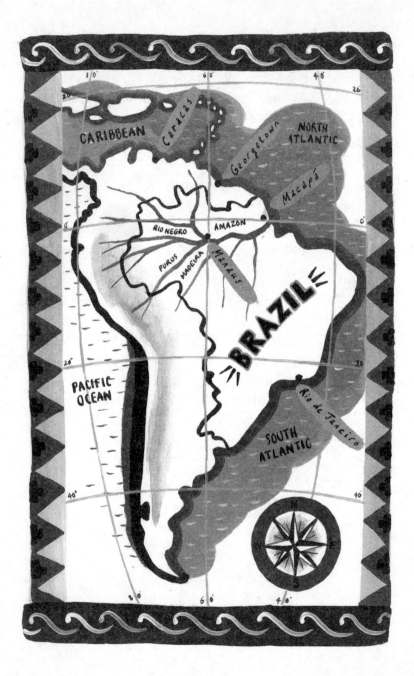

Prologue

In a London suburb two families guarding an extraordinary secret plan an epic journey to a lost crater in the Amazon jungle. Their mission: to discover whether dinosaurs still exist on earth.

Thousands of miles away, in a Brazilian high-security prison, a gang of ruthless criminals hatch plans of escape and murder.

In a nearby university laboratory a brilliant but evil professor becomes obsessed by one of the most incredible inventions in human history.

Soon, all their destinies become inextricably linked in a violent and mortal struggle. The outcome will affect the lives of countless people, all over the world.

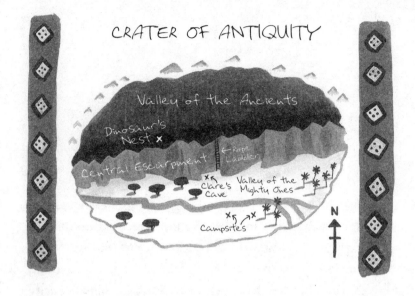

CRATER OF ANTIQUITY

Valley of the Ancients

Dinosaur's Nest ✕

Central Escarpment

← Rope Ladder

✕ Clare's Cave

Valley of the Mighty Ones

✕ ✕ Campsites

N

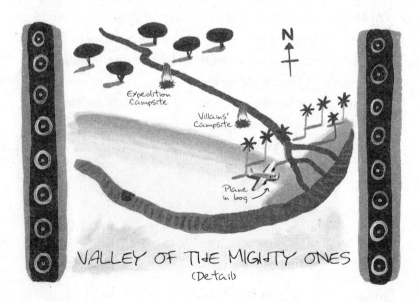

N

Expedition Campsite

Villains' Campsite

Plane in bog

VALLEY OF THE MIGHTY ONES
(Detail)

1

The Adventure Begins

Clare Bonaventure woke early. It was mid-July; the summer sun was already streaming into her bedroom through the crack between the curtains, and the birds were singing loudly in the garden and the woodland beyond. Her alarm clock had not yet gone off and she lay for a few moments thinking happily about the exciting holiday that lay ahead. She had just finished her first year at medical school and today she would be setting off for South America with her family and their friends, the Fossfinders.

As she contemplated the plans for the trip her thoughts went back, inevitably, over the extraordinary events that had led to the forthcoming adventure. Even now, almost two years since her younger sister's accident, she still had to remind herself that she wasn't in a continuous dream and that all that had taken place, incredible as it seemed, had really happened. Lucy was now thirteen, six years younger than Clare, and on her first day at secondary school she had been run over by a car. After an operation on her brain she had discovered that she could speak to animals and that all creatures held her in high regard. She was the 'Promised

One', a human being whom the animal kingdom had been expecting for hundreds of thousands of years and whose destiny was to restore harmony between humans and animals and to correct the harm being done to the environment and the planet by human activities. Lucy had been kidnapped and taken to the Amazon jungle in South America where, with the help of the animals, she had escaped from her captors and rescued her father. He was Richard Bonaventure, a botanist who had become trapped in a prehistoric valley with two other scientists, a husband-and-wife team called the Fossfinders.

After returning to England Richard had invited the Fossfinders and their two sons – Clive, who was a year older than Clare, and his younger brother Mark – to come and meet the rest of the family. The two families had decided to revisit the Amazon one day and explore the valley adjacent to the one in which they had been trapped, for they believed it might be inhabited by dinosaurs.

The forthcoming trip to South America had been planned as a combined family holiday and scientific expedition. Richard worked for a timber company based in Brazil, spending half the year there and the other half doing related research at his university in England. He was working in Brazil at the moment and the trip would be a holiday to mark the end of his current tour of duty. Both families were flying to Rio de Janeiro to join him; then the dinosaur hunters were heading off up the Amazon while the remainder spent a few days in Rio before going to the Pantanal, a wonderful nature reserve in the centre of Brazil.

Clare gave a little jump as her alarm clock went off. Seven o'clock: now, at last, the long-awaited adventure was about to start. Their flight didn't leave until the evening so she had most of the day to get herself ready and pack one or two final bits and pieces in her hand luggage. She jumped out of bed and drew back the curtains. It was going to be a fine day. Lucy's bedroom was next to hers and she could see various birds and a squirrel already gathering on the tiled half-roof below their bedroom windows. They came every morning to greet the Promised One and report to the entire animal kingdom that she was safe and well. They did this through what Lucy called the 'animanet', a form of universal communication that animals could use to talk to other animals, even those of different species. As they saw Clare, a robin and two blue tits fluttered up to her window as if to say good morning. As she was Lucy's sister, animals held her in high regard and were, of course, completely fearless of her. She opened the main window, stroked the birds in turn with her forefinger and then gave them some seeds from a packet she kept for the purpose on her windowsill, despite her mother's protestations. The squirrel immediately scampered over for the same treatment and Clare laughed as she gently stopped him from stealing the whole packet. Soon she heard Lucy's window open and there were chirrups and squeaks of excitement around the garden as she appeared. Clare called hello to her sister from her window and then turned to find her slippers. She knew her sister would now be talking to her animal friends.

'This day I fly with my kin in the thunderquill across the Great Salt . . .'

'Greetings all who have come to see me,' said Lucy to the little group that had assembled. The small garden birds had been joined by a jay, two magpies, a wood pigeon and a passing seagull. A badger from the copse that lay beyond the garden had squeezed under a gap in the fence, followed soon after by a fox. They now sat on the lawn below next to Lucy's tortoise, two hedgehogs and a stoat. As Lucy spoke she saw a rabbit peeping under the fence, too nervous to come in at the sight of the predators on the lawn.

'Come nigh, O coneyhop,' she called, reassuringly. 'The coneybane and the henbane shall do thee no harm in here. See, the hedgiquill and the shieldkin sit with the stripeybrock, yet have no fear.' The rabbit, obviously on its first visit to the daily ceremony, crept cautiously under the fence and sat near the flowerbed, as far as possible from the stoat and the fox.

'This day I fly with my kin in the thunderquill across the Great Salt to the land of the Great River where the junglefang dwell. Fare ye all well; I will return before the Great Silver One grows large again.'

When she spoke to the animals she often found herself slipping into the old-fashioned words and phrases that most of them used when speaking to her. She had forgotten the explanation her grandpa had once given for this, and she kept meaning to ask him again. Suddenly the birds and smaller animals fled for cover.

'Why do the little ones flee?' Lucy asked the badger.

'The forkiquill comes nigh,' was the simple reply. Lucy looked up and there, soaring effortlessly above was a magnificent red kite.

'*Come down, O master of the wind and skies,*' Lucy called, '*but spare the little creatures that bide here with me.*' At her words the magnificent raptor came down and settled on the roof. The animals that had hidden from the predator gradually re-emerged, reassured by Lucy's words.

While she had been speaking, Tibbles, her cat, had jumped up to sit on the windowsill. She always accompanied Lucy on this little morning ritual. They had an arrangement that Tibbles did not chase or threaten any animals in the garden but was a free agent elsewhere. The cat benefited from her association with Lucy in many ways and leaving the birds and mice alone in the house and garden was part of the deal. While the family were away in Brazil a neighbour was going to come in to feed Tibbles and check that everything was all right. Lucy stroked the cat and then turned back to her audience:

'*While I am away Black Furriclaws will remain here but you will be safe from her, as always, inside the fences and the wall. Beware, however, of the new furriclaws that is red like the Brilliant One when sunsleep is nigh.*' Their next-door neighbours had just acquired a ginger tom, but Lucy didn't feel it was fair to impose rules on cats other than her own.

The morning news about Lucy would spread from animal to animal, and within the space of a few hours an untold number of creatures in countries far and wide would know that all was well with the Promised One. In particular, the animals of South America would know that she was returning to their land.

Later in the morning Lucy went to the cupboard under the stairs and lifted up a section of loose floor board near the gas meter. She thought her mother didn't know about the place she talked to the mice. This greatly amused Joanna who was perfectly aware of her daughter's activities but turned a blind eye to them. *'Greetings, O scurripods,'* she said. Soon several mice appeared and greeted her with squeaks of delight. *'Have you heard what I am doing this day?'* she asked.

'Many have spoken to us: the dreykin, the velvetkin, the sleepikin and the minikin have all been to tell us of the journey that thou must make across the Great Salt,' said the eldest mouse, *'and we are very sad to be bereft of thee.'*

'I will return soon,' said Lucy, *'and before I go I will leave you food in the House for Little Tailless Ones; you are not to come in here while I am away. Another Tailless One comes to feed Black Furriclaws and she must not see you at any time. She greatly fears all scurripods.'*

'It is strange indeed that one so mighty can fear those that are so small,' said the mouse in wonderment, *'but it shall be as thou commandest.'*

At ten past nine that evening British Airways flight 247 left the runway at Heathrow Airport with the Bonaventures and Fossfinders safely on board. They were all happy and excited that their adventure was about to begin; it was just as well that none of them knew that their precious, secret crater was already occupied by some extremely unpleasant characters.

2

A Hidden Message

Three days later the members of the dinosaur expedition arrived in Macapá at the mouth of the mighty Amazon river. After a great deal of discussion it had been decided that the dinosaur party should number six, Helen and Julian Fossfinder with their elder son, Clive, and Richard Bonaventure with Clare and Lucy who, everybody hoped, might be able to talk to any dinosaurs they met. Helen and Julian were palaeontologists who studied ancient fossils and were now fascinated by the possibility of discovering living dinosaurs. Clive was studying to be a doctor and was in the year above Clare at medical school.

Lucy's grandpa, who had originally hoped to go on the trip to the mysterious valley, was becoming increasingly affected by arthritis and had decided that it would be unfair of him to hold up the younger, fitter members of the expedition on their explorations. Mark, who had his leg in plaster following a serious sports fracture, was also excluded; he and Grandpa would be going with Joanna Bonaventure, her youngest daughter Sarah and cousins

Ben, Henry and Christopher, on a less arduous sight-seeing holiday.

The dinosaur hunters were met at Macapá airport by José Verdade, the senior executive of Richard's company. He was a man of great integrity who had taken charge of the company after its previous corrupt owner, Chopper, had been imprisoned. José had invited them all to stay at his home for a couple of days before they flew inland into the rainforest. There they all received a warm welcome from José's wife Francesca and their son Rio, particularly Richard and Lucy who had stayed there on their previous trip. Rio was the same age as Lucy and they were firm pen pals.

After dinner they discussed their plans for the forthcoming expedition. José and Francesca already knew of the existence of the crater because in the previous adventure they had been involved in a rescue operation for Helen and Julian, but they were unaware of Lucy's special power – for Lucy's own protection her family and the Fossfinders had resolved that her secret should never be revealed to any outsider.

'What we are going to do is rather complicated,' Richard said, 'so I'll just remind you about the exact details of what we know so far. The giant crater discovered by Helen and Julian has sides so high and steep that no creature can climb out of it into the surrounding rainforest and nothing can get into it. There are unusual air currents around the rim, so birds are reluctant to fly near it. The crater, known as the Crater of Antiquity by the animals, contains two valleys, separated from each other by a central mountain range which is so steep that no animals can pass from one valley to the other.

'The three of us were trapped in one of these valleys, and found it to be a "lost world" containing creatures from the Pliocene and Pleistocene epochs, that means animals that existed from five million years ago down to about ten thousand years ago. These include sabre-tooth tigers, giant ground sloths which give the valley its name, and other weird and wonderful creatures. Because of the central escarpment we were never able to explore the other valley in the crater – which the animals call the Valley of the Ancients. And now it's really for Helen and Julian to tell you why we're all here today. It was their idea, after all.' He smiled at Helen who took over the tale.

'The day that you . . .' she looked at José, '. . . kindly arranged for a plane to rescue us, Julian and I found a small animal at the base of the central escarpment. It had obviously fallen down from the top and we think it must have climbed over from the other side.'

'Why?' asked José.

'Because we're pretty certain it was a dinosaur. That means it lived at least sixty-five mya and probably much more.'

'What is mya?' asked Francesca.

'Sorry. Million years ago,' laughed Helen. 'Nothing complicated – just palaeontologists' shorthand jargon.'

'So now,' said Julian, taking up the story, 'we're going back to see if the other valley is another lost world, only one that is much, much older than the one we stayed in before.

'And that brings us to something we need to discuss with you. The only people who know that the crater is special are our three families, and we all agreed that it should remain secret.' José and Francesca nodded. They knew that the three scientists were worried about the possible destruction of the unique plants and animals that lived in the crater by commercial exploitation or as a result of contamination by modern-day species.

'The three of us,' Julian indicated to include Richard and Helen as he continued, 'have now reluctantly decided that we can't keep our secret for ever so we've got a plan for breaking the news to the world in a way that we think will minimize any ecological risks. The first thing to do is to establish for certain whether or not there really are dinosaurs in the other valley and that's the purpose of this trip. Then, with unassailable video and photographic evidence, and physical items such as eggs, horns and hides, we'll present all our findings in the utmost secrecy to an international environmental committee. That committee can then set in place appropriate safeguards for the protection of both the valleys of the crater, before the stupendous news of its existence is revealed to the international scientific community and the world media.'

José looked at Francesca who smiled and nodded. He turned back to the others.

'We think it's a great plan,' he said. 'In fact, before you came we had already been wondering how long it was going to be possible to keep such an incredible discovery secret. But,' he continued, 'from your description of the crater and the impenetrable jungle surrounding it, how on earth can you find anywhere safe to land your plane? Especially as,' he added, looking at Julian, 'without meaning to be rude, you're not an experienced pilot and you've never even seen into the dinosaur valley – the terrain might be impossible to land on.'

Julian laughed. 'You're not rude at all – it's a very good question, though I have put in hundreds of hours of practice in the last few months; the flying club say I've flown as much in the last year as most amateurs do in five years.

'Ideally,' he continued, 'we would have a helicopter, but the distances involved are really too great and there is simply no way in which I could have learned to fly one safely in the time available. No, we have a different plan, which may sound crazy but it's the best we can do. You may or may not know that Richard here,' he nodded in Richard's direction, 'in addition to all his other talents, is something of an expert mountaineer. It was his hobby as a young man and proved incredibly useful in his career as a botanist looking for rare and exotic plants on mountain ranges and inaccessible cliffs.

'Clive is also a keen climber and he's just been elected captain of his university climbing club.' He looked over at Clive who blushed slightly with embarrassment but nodded in agreement. 'Anyway,' Julian continued, 'this is our crazy plan. I will land the plane in the original valley –

the one we know, on the landing strip Helen and I prepared for our rescue last time.'

He didn't mention that, at the time, Helen had been suffering from an infected leg which meant that she could barely walk, never mind prepare an air strip. The landing strip had actually been prepared, under Lucy's instructions, by four giant ground sloths, each as big as an elephant.

'I can remember the geography exactly,' he went on, '– we did live there for six months after all – and I have been practising steep-approach landings for weeks at my flying club; I explained to my instructor that we might have to land in some pretty confined spaces for our fieldwork and he's helped me to develop a safe technique.'

'But I thought you said that the valley you now want to explore is separated by a steep escarpment from the one you're going to land in,' said José. 'How will you get into it?'

Julian grinned. 'That's where Richard and Clive come in. We've brought all their climbing kit with us – ropes and all kinds of stuff. And some of the new lightweight rope ladders used for escaping from fires in tall buildings. Richard and Clive are going to climb the cliff at its lowest point and fix rope ladders for the rest of us to get from one valley to the other. It sounds complicated but it will be far safer than either trying to land in the dense jungle surrounding the crater, or attempting to land directly in the dinosaur valley about which, as you correctly pointed out, we know nothing. To hit a hidden rock or a crevice in the ground that was invisible from the air would be disastrous.'

'It sounds as though you've thought of everything,' said José, 'I only wish we could go with you – it sounds like the adventure of a lifetime. But I've got too much on at work and Rio goes to summer school in a couple of days.' The others all breathed silent sighs of relief. They really couldn't cope with the complications of having expedition members who didn't know about Lucy's power.

Julian then spoke to José about back-up plans for the rescue of the expedition should their plane break down or some other disaster befall them.

'We'll have our radio of course, so if there's a problem we'll give you a call. We can also give you the GPS coordinates for the crater, but if you do have to send somebody out to us the best person would be the pilot who rescued Helen and me last time. He knows exactly where the crater is and he seemed pretty expert at flying. He did some kind of ballasting job with rocks which was a great help as we took off.' José frowned and shook his head.

'It would have been a great idea to use him but we can't. After what happened to him the company's policy has been only to use company pilots for this kind of job. We don't use any outside contractors any more.'

'What happened?' asked Richard. 'Did he have an accident?' He knew about the company's new policy but hadn't realized it was anything to do with the pilot who had rescued Julian and Helen.

'No, he's in jail. He was using his plane to fly drugs

across the border and got trapped in a police operation. Our company was exonerated of course, we only used him for occasional jobs when our own pilots were too busy, but we decided we couldn't risk any dealings with dodgy contractors and there's no real way we can check up on them. Don't worry though, we've got some expert pilots in the company who are experienced in rainforest flying. If you have a probl———— "" get you out.'

With the discussion over, Francesca suggested that they sat outside on the patio while she made coffee and they all wandered out into the balmy evening air. While the others were chatting, Lucy drew Richard further down the garden to where there was a cane seat lit by garden lamps.

'Wait here a minute,' she said, 'I need your help.' Richard was intrigued and sat down obediently while she disappeared upstairs and returned a few minutes later with a hard, plastic spectacle case.

'What's that for?' he said, curiously. 'I saw you buying it at Heathrow, but I thought you already had a case for your spare specs.'

'I have. This isn't for glasses – it's for your letter.'

'What letter?'

Lucy laughed. 'The one you're going to write for me.'

'To whom?'

'To José, saying we are trapped in the crater and we need rescuing. You're to tell him we'll light a bonfire as a beacon at midday every day so they can find us.'

'But . . .' Richard was utterly bewildered, '. . . we'll have a radio with us and, in any case, what's the use of giving him a letter now when we're not even lost?'

'We're not giving it to him now.' Lucy chuckled at his bemused expression.

'Anything might happen to our radio – you of all people should know that after what happened to you last time – and we're not giving him the letter now, we're giving it to Cerberus. Now, are you going to write it, or shall I ask Helen or Julian?'

Richard looked even more mystified but by now he was used to his daughter and her extraordinary ways. He gave a puzzled smile and wrote a note along the lines she had suggested. When he had finished she read it, nodded approvingly, and put it in the spectacle case. Then she stood and a faraway expression came over her face – the one that meant she was talking to an animal. A few seconds later the Verdades' dog Cerberus came bounding up, tail wagging and then sat at Lucy's feet while she fondled his ears and, Richard knew, spoke to him, even though she just appeared to be gazing silently into space.

'*Greetings, O wolfkin,*' said Lucy.

'*Greetings to thee, O Promised One,*' replied the dog. '*It was known that thou wouldst come to the Great River but I am honoured that thou art here in my home. How might I serve thee?*'

'*I have a small task for thee, but the help of another is required. Is there another wolfkin to assist thee?*'

'*There is another within my ken,*' the dog sounded slightly guarded. *'He lives close by. He . . . he likes me not, but will undoubtedly serve thee in the common cause. What wouldst thou have us do?'*

Lucy then explained what she wanted him to do.

At that moment Francesca appeared down the path from the house with a coffee tray.

'We wondered where you two had got to,' she said, smiling. 'I thought you'd like a cup of . . .' She stopped in surprise as she saw Lucy and the dog.

'Well!' she exclaimed, 'that's a first! He's not really a bad dog but he isn't very sociable, I'm afraid. We adopted him from the kennels to save him being put down. He was treated very badly when he was young and has never really got over it. He's OK with the family and is a reliable guard dog, but he really isn't good with strangers and he's never let *anyone* stroke him like that before. You must really have a way with animals, Lucy!'

'Yes, I suppose I do,' said Lucy, with a little grin to her father. 'It comes in useful now and then.'

After Francesca had returned to the house Lucy spoke once more to the dog which then stood up, wagged its tail, took the spectacle case and bounded off into the bushes at the end of José's garden.

Richard looked enquiringly at Lucy.

'He's going to bury it. If he ever gets a message from me through the animanet he's going to dig it up and give it to José. He's also going to tell the dog next door, as a back-up. José won't have the faintest idea how it got here but he'll know it's genuine and assume you managed to get it out with the help of some remote tribe in the Amazon. We'll almost certainly never need it, but it could save our lives and after what happened last time I'm not taking any chances. Oh,' she added with a chuckle, 'and after what Francesca said I told him to try and wag his tail a bit more often!'

Richard shook his head in admiration as he experienced an intense sense of déjà-vu. During their last adventure he had been impressed by Lucy's resourcefulness and organizing ability but for the last eighteen months she had just been an ordinary schoolgirl. Now that they were back in action she was clearly once again mistress of the situation. For her father, used to being in charge or, at least imagining himself to be, it was strangely comforting to feel once again the sensation of security that existed within the umbrella of his   power.

The next morning José took Richard and Julian to the small company airfield, which was situated a few miles outside the city.

'I think you're going to like what you see,' he said confidently as they pulled into the airfield. 'Your new plane was delivered two weeks ago and, even though it's brand-new, our mechanics have checked everything just to be on the safe side. They've also fitted the long-range tanks you wanted. I'll send you the bill for the work and parts you requested.' He paused. 'I'm afraid it's not going to be cheap

'. . . how . . .?' His voice tailed off and Julian rescued him.

'Don't worry, José, the whole expedition is being paid for by the United Nations scientific committee that funded our original research trip.' He explained that the committee had been so impressed with the evidence brought back from the prehistoric valley that they had readily agreed to support another visit to the crater. They hadn't realized, of course, that the extraordinarily detailed knowledge that had been given to them had been based on observations on living animals rather than fossils.

'There was a bit of a problem when it came to getting a new plane,' Julian continued with a smile. 'We could hardly tell them that the old one had been destroyed by giant ground sloths but, as luck would have it, the insurance company agreed to cough up. I described what had happened in true but deliberately vague terms to a rather bewildered official who said we were covered, even though they had no previous record of a plane being torn to pieces by wild animals.'

José looked relieved at this news and pointed across the airfield. There at the edge of the runway was a gleaming white plane with large extra fuel tanks under each wing to increase its range across the vast stretches of jungle they would have to traverse. Julian's eyes lit up at the sight. He spent the rest of the morning familiarizing himself with the controls of the aircraft and making a test flight while José talked to Richard about company business. In the afternoon the three of them packed the plane with all the equipment and supplies that would be needed on the trip.

3

Living in a Greenhouse

The plane flew in a cloudless sky across the apparently interminable jungle. Clare and Clive, for whom this was a new experience, gazed out in awe at the immense green canopy of the rainforest, stretching as far as the eye could see in every direction. Clare had been eagerly looking forward to the expedition. It was her first visit to South America, and she had been fascinated by Lucy's stories about the Amazon jungle and her amazing adventures there with animals and villains. She was also looking forward to spending some time with Clive. He was at the same medical school and, though they met occasionally there, they were both extremely busy on their separate courses and he was shy and quiet by nature. She hoped she might get to know him better on the forthcoming trip – she little knew that her wish would be more than fulfilled; soon they would face mortal danger together and need all their reserves of courage and resourcefulness to survive.

Early that morning they had taken off from Manaus and, after a brief refuelling stop at a small private airfield, were now heading along a remote tributary of the Rio Negro to Cayman Creek, the logging camp at which Lucy had been held captive during her kidnap.

The previous day they had flown up the Amazon from Macapá to Manaus and had been spellbound by the sight of the mighty river, pouring the water from over seven million square kilometres of the South American continent into the Atlantic Ocean. Rising high in the mountains of Peru on the other side of the South American continent, and in places reaching up to sixty-five kilometres in width, the Amazon was by far the largest river in the world, and along its sprawling tributaries lay the greatest remaining areas of rainforest on the planet. During their long flight they had seen numerous examples of the destruction of the rainforest by logging and burning and Richard had told Clare and Clive some of the grim statistics relating to the rate at which this vast natural resource, with its abundance and diversity of animals and plants, many unique, was steadily disappearing.

An area of forest equivalent to the size of several football fields was being destroyed every minute of every day, he explained, and much of this land contained species of flora and fauna as yet unknown to science, doomed to extinction before being discovered, with their possible benefits to mankind as food or medicine unexplored. As the plane headed north and west the settlements and signs of human activity became fewer and fewer until, eventually, it seemed as though they were flying over a world uninhabited by anything but forest and the river below, itself growing narrower and more tortuous as they followed it towards their destination. Eventually Helen, who was navigating, said they must be very nearly there and Richard, who had seen the creek twice before from the air, suddenly pointed out the little airstrip. Richard's timber company had now closed down its operations at Cayman Creek as part of its ecofriendly policy of only using renewable resources, but the airstrip had remained in operation during the dismantling of the camp and was still usable. The landing area looked terrifyingly small from the air and Julian knew he was facing his first big challenge. His months of practice stood him in good stead, however, and he brought the plane down in a perfectly executed landing, which brought him a chorus of congratulations from his relieved passengers.

'Look!' said Lucy, pointing to the side of the airstrip. 'That's the drugs plane the animals trapped, and you can still see the mounds of earth dug out by the armadillos . . . just in case,' she added with a broad grin, 'you thought me and Dad were exaggerating.'

Sure enough, the wrecked remains of the abandoned drugs plane were still visible, its wheels sunk into the trenches dug by the animals, the tail charred from a lightning strike and the fuselage now becoming overgrown with creepers and seedlings.

The camp huts had been dismantled, so they erected their tents on the airstrip near the plane and sat round a campfire for their evening meal. It was a fine evening with a full moon and they sat chatting late into the night against a background of never-ending noise from the surrounding jungle as the creatures of the night played out their eternal drama of survival of the fittest.

As Clive looked at the dying embers of the fire he was reminded of the forest burning and the other forms of deforestation they had witnessed on their flights.

'If the forests are disappearing at this rate,' said Clive, 'then how long can they last?'

'Not long,' said Richard. 'An area the size of a small country is being destroyed every year and if that carries on, the bulk of the Amazon jungle will have disappeared within the next generation or two. This has serious implications for the future of the planet because of global warming. We are sitting in the middle of the greatest rainforest on earth and, as you know, trees remove carbon dioxide from the air and produce oxygen.'

He paused and looked at the young people. 'Do you all know about the greenhouse effect?'

'Well . . . yes – but remind us about it,' said Clare and the others nodded.

'As you all know, a greenhouse is a house made of glass for growing plants,' Richard began. 'The glass lets light in from the sun, but stops much of the heat from escaping. This means the greenhouse gets warmer than the outside world, so you can grow plants in it that would die in colder conditions. The situation with the earth is much more complicated than this, but the term "greenhouse effect" has been used to try and give a general idea of what's going on. The earth is surrounded by its atmosphere and some of the gases in the atmosphere, especially water vapour, carbon dioxide, methane, nitrous oxide and ozone, make it act in the same way as the glass in a greenhouse. Light and other short-wave energy coming in from the sun passes through it easily, but when some of this energy is radiated back from the earth as longer-wave infra-red radiation, only some of it can get through into space. Most of it is reflected back to the earth as heat, making the surface of the earth warmer than space. The so-called "greenhouse" gases act like valves; they let light in but they don't let all the heat out. Without this greenhouse effect, evolution, at least as we know it, would never have occurred and the world would be too cold for humans ever to have existed.'

'So, isn't it a good thing?' asked Lucy. 'Why is there a problem then?'

'The problem,' Richard continued, 'is that for a very long time the concentrations of greenhouse gases have remained reasonably constant or changed only very slowly, and life on earth has developed and adapted to suit the conditions that have existed during this period. Human activity, however, has increased the amounts of several of these gases in the atmosphere, one of which is carbon dioxide, and most scientists think that because of this the earth is getting warmer – that's the global warming you hear so much about. This may have serious effects on the climate, on the sea-level, and on plants and animals throughout the world, some of which may not be able to adapt to a warmer environment.'

'But surely,' asked Clive, 'if the trees absorb the carbon

dioxide when they grow and then release it again when they die and rot down the whole thing is in balance? The actual *amount* of carbon in the atmosphere isn't changing.'

'True,' said Richard, 'but there are two important things to bear in mind. The first is that, as you say, if trees die and are replaced at the same rate throughout the world then, on average, the total amount of carbon "locked up" in the trees remains the same and that vast quantity – billions and billions of tons – is not getting into the atmosphere. The trouble is that we are destroying trees faster than they are being replaced, so less and less carbon is safely tucked away in the biomass and more and more is escaping into the atmosphere. As the Amazon rainforest is by far the largest on the planet, its destruction will release untold quantities of carbon dioxide. The second point, however, is even more serious. Massive quantities of carbon trapped within trees and other living things over millions of years *in the past* never got back into the atmosphere when they died. It got buried in the earth and, as a result of different geological influences over vast periods of time, turned into different kinds of combustible materials – coal, peat, gas and oil. We actually call them "fossil fuels" as if they were created for our benefit to use for heating, lighting, transport and all the other things we do. The atmosphere as we know it is in a balance that formed while all this carbon was safely tucked away under the earth. We are now burning coal and oil at a prodigious rate and releasing carbon dioxide back into the atmosphere as a greenhouse gas, which is disturbing that balance. And it's not just coal and oil,' he added. 'Peat was formed from trees that lived 26,000 years ago. At the Royal Geographical Society's recent international meeting it was announced that burning peat bogs in Indonesia, set alight by farmers clearing land, are producing almost one seventh of the world's total fossil fuel emissions. That isn't even *benefiting* anyone and I think it's nothing short of criminal.'

They all sat in silence for a while thinking about what he had said.

'The animals believe that I am going to help them,' said Lucy eventually, 'and from what you're saying it sounds as if the most important thing I could do would be to sort all this out. But it's all so incredibly complicated. Where would anyone begin?'

Richard smiled. 'I think you're certainly right about it's being one of the most important ways in which you could help your animals, but how you go about it is something that a great many scientists and politicians would dearly love to know. What's important is that you're focusing on it and nobody knows yet how you might be able to use your extraordinary power in the future. And now, I think, we've done enough of setting the world to rights for one day. We've a big day ahead of us tomorrow and it's time to turn in.'

The tents were equipped with mosquito netting, but to be sure of an undisturbed night Lucy instructed all the scurripods and crawlipods in the locality to leave everybody alone during the night. It had been a busy and exciting day for them all and soon they were all fast asleep, secure in the protection from all creatures afforded them by Lucy's unique gift.

In the morning Lucy announced that she would organize breakfast. Clare and Clive looked puzzled – especially Clare, who couldn't remember Lucy ever actually getting a meal ready in her life. Richard, Helen and Julian grinned; they had seen Lucy in action before and sure enough, she soon stood gazing silently into the forest with the faraway look in her eyes that they all knew to mean that she was 'talking' to the animals.

Within a moment or two, there was a crashing sound in the nearby trees and a troop of spider monkeys swung to the ground and scampered towards Lucy.

Clare and Clive stepped back in alarm – the large black monkeys looked quite threatening as they boldly approached the humans. One of them had a baby on her back, its tail wound firmly round her. Then one of the animals suddenly raced ahead of the others and leapt into Lucy's arms. To Clare's utter astonishment, she saw that the creature was wearing a pair of green spectacles.

After a few moments the monkeys disappeared and Lucy turned to the others.

'They've gone to get our breakfast and will be back shortly – it'll only be fruit and nuts, if that's OK.'

Clare, still recovering from the shock of what she had seen, eventually managed to stammer: 'What . . . what was that monkey doing giving you a hug – and how on earth did it come to be wearing spectacles?'

Lucy laughed. 'I'm so pleased she's still alive. That's

Queenie, the monkey who helped me to find Daddy in the lost crater and those are the specs I told you about at home – she always wanted to wear mine, so when I left I gave her a pair of her own. I never thought, though, that I would ever see her again. She must wear them all the time – did you notice that she had little marks on the side of her nose where the fur has got rubbed away?'

'Actually, no,' said Clare with a smile. 'My attention was focused more on your hugging a monkey with glasses than whether she had marks on her nose!'

They all laughed and then sat down on some logs to await the return of the monkeys while Helen started to brew some coffee over the campfire.

'And now,' Lucy announced as they all settled down, 'I have a favour to ask you all.'

Everybody waited expectantly and Richard eventually prompted her.

'Well, go on; what is it?'

'I've been thinking about this a lot,' said Lucy, 'and I'm sure it's the right thing to do. I don't know if the animals in the valley will remember me, and none of us knows whether the animals in the *other* valley will have ever heard of me or even be able to speak to me. I think it would be really useful for us to have some animals with us that can help us and if it's OK, I'd like to ask Queenie and her daughters to come with us to the crater – if Sophie's fit to fly that is; she was the one with that cute little baby.'

The others looked somewhat taken aback.

'You mean . . .' Julian eventually stammered, 'that we

take them in the plane as part of the group?'

'That's exactly what I mean,' said Lucy with a grin. 'The only downside for you all is that they'll have to squash in the back of the plane, but once we're there, they won't affect you at all – they'll look after themselves and could be very helpful.'

'Well, I think it's a great idea – if the monkeys don't mind being squeezed up next to us,' said Richard, to everybody's amusement. He had seen first-hand on their previous adventure the wonderful symbiotic relationship that existed between Lucy and the monkeys and he trusted implicitly her instinct to make them part of the expedition.

'Is everybody happy then?' asked Lucy, looking around. Just at that moment the monkeys returned, laden with the most delicious fruits imaginable and went to each member of the party in turn, offering them whatever they wished.

'I think the answer to your question is a definite yes,' said Clare, munching into a succulent yellow fruit that looked like nothing she had ever seen before, 'if only to get a breakfast like this every day!'

But Lucy was looking again into the bushes, oblivious to human conversation. Soon a small rodent appeared and started to crack the nuts that the monkeys had brought.

'It's an agouti,' said Lucy. 'Lots of them helped me last time and when I got home I looked them up in my animal book. The animals call them scurridents and they seem to be able to crack any nut on the planet with a single bite!'

Clive shook his head in admiration. 'You've certainly got everything worked out, Lucy, and I think everybody agrees that you should invite the monkeys along. Go for it!'

During breakfast the younger monkeys had disappeared to play in the trees but Queenie remained, sitting contentedly at the side of the Promised One she had never expected to see again. Lucy now turned to her and the others watched in wonder as they communicated.

'*I have a great boon to ask of thee,*' said Lucy. To the other humans she appeared to be completely silent.

'*Speak thy will, O Promised One,*' replied Queenie.

'*This is a great favour I request. The paterpromise, my sister and my other companions, some of whom you already know, now set forth to seek the creatures that live in the Valley of the Ancients. I would dearly love to have thee, thy daughters and thy daughter's baby by my side on this quest. It means that you would have to fly near the Brilliant One in the thunderquill.*'

The monkey did not pause, nor did she call back her daughters to consult them.

'*To have served thee once was a privilege bestowed upon few animals in creation. To serve thee twice would be an honour beyond all description for me and my kin. Sophiekin can come for the arboribabe no longer clings underneath her; he is now large enough to sit on her back and will be no trouble.*' Queenie hesitated, then continued a little nervously.

'*Speaking of this little one, I now have a boon to ask of thee in turn. Sophiekin would be greatly honoured if thou wouldst bestow a name upon him. He would be the first of his generation to feel thy favour and would be revered among all arborikin till the end of his days.*'

Lucy smiled. '*Of course he should have a name. I shall call* him Kai *for that is the name of a toy arborikin that belongs to my own sister, Sarah.'*

'Thank you, O Promised One, Sophiekin will be forever in thy debt.' She paused for a moment, then continued. *'But now to other things: when do we depart? For there is a small task I must complete before we leave this place.'*

'Soon,' said Lucy, *'but there is still some time and we will wait until you return.'*

She turned to the others as the monkey scampered off into the trees.

'They're on,' she said and continued with a grin, 'their only stipulation is that, as Sophie and Clio are a bit shy, they don't want to sit next to any of the men on the plane.'

Everybody laughed and they set to work breaking camp and loading the little plane for the final leg of their journey. As they did so Lucy walked to the edge of the forest and called:

'Hear me, O great arboribane! I seek thy help!' Soon a dark shape swept out of the trees and came to perch on a nearby log.

'Speak thy will, O Promised One. It is many moons since thou departed hence.'

Lucy realized with delight that this was the very eagle that had guided her to the crater on her previous expedition. That made life much simpler. *'I go now with my kin to the Crater of Antiquity and I would like you also to go there.'* She remembered that the eagle had been reluctant to fly into the crater because of the powerful and unusual air currents around its rim and hurried to reassure him. *'I* know that it is dangerous for you to fly into that place and ask only that you come to its edge, at the place I climbed down.'

'I know it well,' replied the eagle. 'What wouldst thou have me do?'

'Only to come for a short while each day as the Brilliant One rises from his sleep. If I have need I will call up to thee with a message to take to all those creatures who live where the Great River passes into the Great Salt. This should be done by many fledgiquills in turn for it is many leagues away. There is a wolfkin there who will heed this message. If I need thee not I will come before I depart from the crater and bid thee farewell.'

'It shall be done as thou bid.' The eagle was a creature of few words but Lucy trusted him absolutely. His great wings clattered as he rose and flew west towards the crater.

When Lucy returned to the others they had almost finished loading and Clare was just teasing her for bunking off, when Queenie reappeared. She was carrying what looked like a small bundle and, as she approached, Lucy suddenly gave a squeak of joy and rushed to meet her. As the others watched, the little bundle leapt from Queenie into Lucy's arms and then climbed on to her shoulder and started to lick her ear. Richard saw Clare and Clive's mystified expressions and smiled.

'It's Michelle, her pygmy marmoset. We never thought to see her again; no wonder Lucy's so happy – she absolutely adored her.' When Lucy rejoined them, Clare could see why. She had never seen such a cute little creature before and as the tiny monkey hopped from Lucy into her outstretched hands she was astonished at how light it was. She closed her hands round it for a few seconds and laughed in delight as the tiny face, surrounded by a little mane like a miniature lion, peeped out through her fingers.

'Oh, I wish she had a twin sister who'd come and sit on my shoulder,' she said as the monkey sprang effortlessly back to her usual perch on Lucy.

'I expect she has,' laughed Lucy, 'but Michelle's very friendly and I'm sure we can share her attention.'

Seeing the marmoset reminded Richard of Lucy's other special forest friends and he asked her about Melanie, the black panther, and Katy, the coatimundi. Lucy's face fell a little.

'Queenie says she's called Katy but there's no answer. She hasn't seen her for months and thinks she may be dead. She does see Melanie from time to time – in fact she saved Queenie's life on one occasion when Queenie was being chased by a puma, but she goes away now and then and isn't around at the moment. I suppose I should just count myself lucky even to see the big monkeys and Michelle again when you think about how dangerous all their lives are.' As she spoke Queenie tugged at her shorts.

'*If the thunderquill can wait a little longer there are three others who would greet thee: the Dreadful Ones who pulled thee along the Flowing One and the hippophant who bore thee for many leagues through the forest.*' She led Lucy towards the river. Clare and Clive were curious and followed the pair, but stayed a few steps in the rear, slightly apprehensive at what the next surprise would turn out to be. To their astonishment a tapir was waiting at the edge of the bushes near the river bank. On seeing Lucy approaching it hurried towards her and nuzzled her affectionately. Lucy then climbed on its back and it carried her for the remaining few yards to the river's edge. Clare and Clive started back in horror as the surface of the water suddenly boiled, thrashed into a white foam by gigantic black tails.

'Lucy, look out!' Clare called. She couldn't help her instinctive reaction but realized immediately that this was just another dramatic scene in the 'Lucy Show'. Soon she was utterly absorbed at the sight of two caymans emerging from the swirling waters and lumbering up the mud to Lucy's feet.

'Your sister really is something else,' murmured Clive as he shook his head in disbelief at the sight of Lucy gently patting the fearsome monsters on their snouts.

'Time to leave,' called Julian briskly. 'Let's get the entire menagerie aboard and we'll make the most of this perfect weather while it lasts.' Lucy said goodbye to the caymans and then rode back in style on her unusual mount, Queenie now sitting behind her and Clare and Clive hurrying to keep up with the tapir as it trotted back to the plane. On a nod from Lucy the big monkeys scrambled into the back of the plane on top of all the equipment; then the explorers got in, Michelle glued to Lucy's shoulder. Julian started up the engine and they all felt a thrill of excitement at the thought that at last, after months of planning, they would soon be in the 'lost world' of the crater.

Lucy greets the Dreadful Ones.

Little did they suspect that, before the day was out, their happy group would be split up and they would be facing the greatest challenge of their lives.

4

A Miscellany of Miscreants

Six months before the dinosaur hunters set off on their expedition to the Amazon a meeting took place in a jail near Rio de Janeiro; a meeting that was destined to change all their lives. It is a curious fact that the origins of the most profound events are often to be found in the most trivial of circumstances, and in this case the course of history depended on the fact that on a particular day, early in January, the jail was full to capacity and a cell that was usually reserved for one man had to accommodate two.

On that day Alf 'Chopper' Sawyer lay on his hard narrow bunk with his hands behind his head and stared up disconsolately at the filthy ceiling. Flies buzzed in and out of the tiny barred window of his cell, attracted by the all-pervading stench of the inside of the jail and, in particular, the massive, recumbent and unwashed lump of humanity lying there.

Things, Chopper thought to himself, had come to a pretty pass. He had been the director of a large timber company which, under the guise of legitimate operations, had made enormous profits from illegal mining and drug peddling. With his extravagant wife Nandita, he had lived an opulent lifestyle and moved in Rio's highest social circles – a man respected and feared by all who knew him. And now . . . his thoughts wandered back to that dreadful day, just over a year ago, when some wretched girl had somehow drawn him into a police trap.

It had been New Year's Day – the day he should have made millions of pounds from the largest drug deal in his entire criminal career. Instead, his brother Sam had disappeared – almost certainly eaten by crocodiles, the police had informed him with barely concealed satisfaction; his site manager Pollard had been blown to pieces; and he and the two remaining members of his gang, tiny Bert Shortshanks and the massive 'Crack' Barker, had been charged with kidnap and drug peddling. Because of the gravity of the case it had been dealt with in the highest court in the land and Chopper and associates had been stripped of their illegal assets and then sent to this dreadful prison, one of the largest in the country and notorious for the violence and depravity of its inmates.

Chopper had realized from his first day in the place that he was in a situation where it was a question of the survival of the fittest and that, if his life wasn't going to be sheer hell for the next ten years, he had to establish his place in the prison pecking order from day one. He had quickly learnt that there were two or three gang leaders who virtually ruled the institution. They controlled the supplies of drugs and alcohol within the prison and punished any who failed to cooperate with the utmost brutality, bribing the prison officers to turn a blind eye to their activities. Never one for half measures, and frightened of nobody, Chopper had picked arguments with the most feared and formidable of these felons and beaten him to a pulp. Slow to learn from example, two other gang leaders had formed a temporary alliance with each other and cornered Chopper in the latrines. They only narrowly escaped with their lives: one had to have a cistern removed from his head by the fire brigade who found as they cut it off that the toilet chain had gone through one of his cheeks and out of his mouth; the other suffered a particularly unpleasant form of acute water intoxication after being forced to drink a massive but unknown quantity of toilet water. As Barker had later remarked to Shortshanks: 'I knew Chopper had finally settled in when they started building an extension to the prison hospital.'

Chopper's thoughts now turned once again to the police raid on his jungle camp. His younger brothers Sid and Fred, identical twins, had also been arrested in the police operation but had only been charged with the lesser offences of illegally trapping and mistreating wild animals. They had spent three months in a small local prison and on their release had visited Chopper in jail and told him they were off to Africa to 'start up a new business'. He had little doubt that soon the big cats of Africa would be suffering a fate similar to that which his vile brothers had already inflicted on Asian tigers and Amazonian jaguars.

He decided that his troubles had really started when a young schoolgirl, who had turned out to be the daughter of a treacherous employee, had started to poke her nose into the twins' jaguar business. Chopper had kidnapped her but, by an amazing sequence of unfortunate events which he still couldn't fathom, she had eventually destroyed his camp and his business deals, and cost him his freedom. Chopper wasn't a superstitious man, but he couldn't rid himself of the feeling that there was something almost *supernatural* about the way the girl had frustrated his plans at every turn. If he ever laid hands on her again . . .

His musings on his misfortunes were rudely interrupted as his cell door opened with a clang and a new prisoner was pushed into the cell. James Bigglesworth, known universally by his nickname Biggles, was small and apprehensive and as his eyes fell on his future cell-mate his apprehension turned to frank terror. Chopper was never a prospect to gladden a man's heart and the sight of him lying there, unshaven, scarred, malodorous and morose, with his massive frame bulging over the side of the narrow prison bed, would have intimidated the most hardened of criminals. This was Biggles's first time in jail and as he sat on the other bed and contemplated his awful situation he felt physically sick with fear.

The guard turned to Chopper. He spoke in English; everybody spoke in English to Chopper. He had no patience with 'foreign lingos' as he called all other languages, and those who ignored this soon lived to regret it.

'Ze guv'nor want see you – now.'

Chopper sullenly heaved himself up and put his sandals

on. He gave a contemptuous glance at Biggles, who stammered out his name by way of introducing himself. Chopper nodded curtly in response and then left with the guard. The door slammed shut behind them, leaving Biggles to his tormented thoughts.

Soon Chopper passed into the carpeted luxury of the governor's quarters and was ushered into his office. He stood in front of the governor's desk with the guard behind him. Just in case he didn't know where he was there was a gleaming brass nameplate on the desk mounted on a polished hardwood stand:

CONSTANTE SUBORNOS
GOVERNOR AND GENERAL DIRECTOR

'I don't share my cell with anyone,' said Chopper, before the governor could speak. As the undisputed 'king' of the prison Chopper now led a reasonably trouble-free life, unmolested by the other prisoners and given favours by the governor and the guards who knew he could exert a controlling influence over the other inmates and keep trouble to a minimum.

'I know, I'm sorry,' said the governor. 'The prison's full. We'll move him as soon as possible. We'll step up your secret booze and fags allowance in the meantime.' He paused briefly for thought and then continued. 'I wanted to see you because there have been rumours about a possible riot. The ringleaders seem to be a couple of unsavoury characters called Barker and Shortshanks. See what you can do, will you?'

'I'll sort them out tonight,' said Chopper. 'No problem. I presume it will be under the usual terms of our . . . ahem . . .' he glanced back at the guard who was gazing aimlessly into space, clearly not following the conversation, and Chopper continued, '. . . arrangement.'

'Of course,' said the governor with a wink.

'And Boggles, or whatever he's called, gets shifted as soon as possible,' added Chopper.

'Understood,' said the governor.

They were both happy. The governor had averted a riot and when Chopper returned to his cell from the exercise yard the next day a package of drugs would have mysteriously appeared under his bed. These he could sell, convert into bribes, or use to pay the informers and lackeys he had working for him throughout the massive prison. What the governor didn't know was that Chopper was in league with Barker and Shortshanks. On arrival in jail they had decided that for many reasons it would be better if no one knew they were associated, and the arrangement had proved to be extremely useful. The present case was a perfect example: at Chopper's suggestion Barker and Shortshanks had spread false rumours about a possible riot, making sure through informants that news of it reached the ears of the prison authorities. Chopper had been summoned to try to suppress it, and the three of them would now end up splitting the governor's bounty.

Back in the cell Biggles lay quivering on his bed. He couldn't believe how stupid he had been, as his thoughts ran over the events that had led up to his present dreadful situation. He was a pilot who had formerly worked for one of the large airlines but he had wanted to be his own boss, so had gone into business with a partner called Algy. They had rented a private airstrip near his home in Fonte Boa where they had two small planes, a hangar and a workshop. For several years they had run a successful charter business undertaking flights for logging companies but Biggles had eventually been unable to resist the temptation of making an easy living by smuggling drugs from various neighbouring countries. One of his last 'straight' jobs before turning to drugs had been for a logging company called the Ecocidal Timber Company. The job had involved flying to a remote crater deep in the Amazon jungle to rescue two scientists who had been trapped there for several months.

The crater and surrounding area were unmapped, but he had been given very specific instructions about its location by a third scientist who had managed to escape and reach a camp owned by the logging company. He had found the crater without too much difficulty and, after experiencing serious and unusual turbulence while crossing the rim, had landed on a strip cleared, apparently, by the scientists.

After the scientists had climbed aboard the four-seater aircraft, he had decided that he should stabilize the plane by having an even distribution of weight. He was terrified of encountering further turbulence as he undertook the tricky flight out of the crater. Apologizing to his new companions for the delay he had gathered a large bag of rocks, equivalent in weight to another person, and put it in the empty co-pilot's seat next to him.

His precautions were fully vindicated for they had narrowly escaped hitting the lip of the crater as the little plane was thrown about by gusts of rising air currents, but they had eventually reached calmer air and had then flown over the rainforest to the pilot's home airfield. It was dark as they landed and, after his passengers had thanked him and disembarked from the plane he had hauled out the bag of rocks and tipped it into the grass by the side of the runway. The scientists had been picked up by a company plane the next day and, for the next few weeks, he had thought no more about the trip.

Shortly after this job Biggles had been approached by a drugs cartel and offered a monthly salary more than three times what he earned from his charter work with the logging companies. The drug dealers had recently lost a plane in a police operation and were anxious to resume their cross-border smuggling activities as soon as possible. Since all their activities took place in the remote border country between Colombia and Brazil, Biggles's jungle-flying experience was invaluable so, in addition to the inflated salary, they offered him a generous percentage on each successful drug delivery. The temptation had proved irresistible and for several weeks Biggles had undertaken a series of lucrative flights across the border. One evening when landing at dusk he had noticed an eerie glow coming from the grass, which, at first, he thought must be due to glow-worms. As he walked away, however, the glow abruptly ceased. Intrigued, he walked back and the glow reappeared. On close inspection he found that it came from the pile of rocks he had used as ballast when rescuing the two scientists. The glow intensified as he approached the rocks but disappeared again as soon as he was more than a few feet away. This phenomenon made him both apprehensive and curious. He was fearful that the rocks might be radioactive, though he wasn't sure if this made things glow in the dark; whatever the cause, however, it seemed likely that the rocks might be valuable – his mind ran on to the possibility of having discovered an open seam of uranium, unknown to the rest of the world. It was odd that the two scientists he had picked up had made no mention of funny glowing rocks, but then he remembered that they had said that they never ventured out after dusk.

He put a small rock fragment in an old biscuit tin and hid the remainder under a nearby fallen tree.

The next day he had phoned his local university about the rocks but they had suggested he contact one of the leading universities in the country, near Rio de Janeiro, where there was a specialist geology department. Not wishing to trust his sample to the post, or to anybody else, he had made the long trip to Rio, left his plane in a bay at the airport, and given the sample to a young geologist who had been extremely interested in the whole story. Now, four dreadful weeks later, he was here in jail. The airport authority in Rio had identified his plane from a police surveillance video of a drugs delivery. When he had returned to the aircraft he had been arrested. The evidence against him had been overwhelming – there were still some drugs in the plane – and he had been sentenced to five years in prison.

He had been appalled at the severity of his sentence; it had been his misfortune that the government was having a crackdown on drug dealing, but only now, shut in this awful cell awaiting the return of his fearsome cell-mate, had the true horror of his predicament come home to him.

His dismal reverie came to an abrupt end as the door swung open and Chopper entered. Much to Biggles's relief he seemed in a better mood after his talk with the governor and even shook hands with Biggles as he introduced himself. As it happened, Chopper and Biggles got on quite well together, despite the pilot's initial forebodings. Biggles was an intelligent and interesting man and Chopper actually found it a pleasant change to have a companion in the cell. A few days later when, at the governor's behest, a guard came to shift Biggles into a different cell, Chopper requested that he stayed.

Biggles woke up one day with a severe attack of vomiting. It was so bad that he was admitted to the prison sick bay and while he was there he read in the newspapers of the death in London of a Russian spy from radiation poisoning. His blood ran cold as he read of the man's initial symptoms – identical to his own – and realized that, with all the turmoil of being arrested and imprisoned, he had not been able to find out about the nature of his rock samples. He mentioned this fact to the prison doctor, who had just finished examining him, whereupon the doctor turned a little pale and hurried away. After washing his hands several times and changing all his clothes and shoes, he then rang the university with Biggles's details and enquired about the rock analysis.

The doctor returned within minutes to tell Biggles that there had been no evidence of radioactivity in the rocks and that the cause of his problem was, almost certainly, the state of the prison kitchens. He was visibly relieved as he gave Biggles the news and the pilot was touched by the doctor's concern for his welfare. As he said to Chopper the next day, 'It's good to know that there are still some completely unselfish people about.'

Biggles was one of the few literate individuals in the institution and, as he also spoke fluent Portuguese, he began to help many of the inmates to read and reply to the letters they received from their families and lawyers. Over the weeks, as Chopper observed his cell-mate handling the queries of dozens of prisoners, it dawned on him that information could be gleaned from these sources that might be put to very good use in the future, and a curious, mutually convenient relationship began to develop between the two men. Biggles was a small and timid individual and, as his friend and cell-mate, Chopper protected him from the predations of some of the more malignant prisoners – in that jail there were some truly awful individuals. In return for this protection, the pilot allowed Chopper to read the letters that came through his hands, translating them as necessary.

The correspondence between the villains in jail and their outside contacts revealed an astonishing amount of significant information. Although individual letters contained little in the way of detail, the information built up over a prolonged period of time and pieced together from sequences of letters to and from the same prisoner gave Chopper details of crooked lawyers, corrupt policemen, criminals who were associates of the prison inmates but still at large, and fences, who handled and disposed of stolen goods. Even better were the names and addresses of relatives of the inmates, for in many cases these families knew the whereabouts of caches of stolen goods. Chopper, with an eye to the future, kept detailed notes on all these characters and planned to have a very busy time when released from jail. Not only would he have considerable scope for the blackmail of various lawyers and police officers, but he intended to pay courtesy visits to the families of several of his 'old friends' in jail. He had little doubt that his powers of physical persuasion would yield the location of more than one hidden hoard of stolen goods that would never be subsequently enjoyed by its *un*rightful owner in jail.

One morning, about three months after Biggles had arrived, a prison warder told Chopper that he had a visitor. Chopper racked his brains to think who it might be. His wife, Nandita, had not been heard of since his arrest. His villa had been appropriated by the authorities under new anti-drug dealing laws but Nandita had apparently disappeared only hours before the police had appeared, taking with her almost every removable object of value in the house.

None of Chopper's criminal colleagues ever came to see him for fear of being recognized by the prison authorities, and his only visitors during his year in prison had been his twin brothers before they left for Africa. He was, therefore, somewhat mystified as he went down to the visiting hall. There, to his astonishment, was his brother Sam.

When Chopper and the twins had been arrested during a drugs raid on their remote jungle camp, Sam had managed to escape. They had all assumed that he was dead. Nobody believed that without weapons, food or water he could possibly have survived the perilous journey back to civilization through the greatest jungle on earth.

Chopper gaped at his brother. Sam looked self-satisfied and fatter than ever, and sat fingering a large new gold stud in the side of his nose.

'Sam!' Chopper spluttered, '. . . Where? . . . How? . . . What?' It wasn't often that he was lost for words.

'Hi, Chopper,' said Sam. 'How's tricks?'

Chopper recovered rapidly from his initial surprise. He knew that their conversation would be monitored and recorded by the prison authorities and that neither of them must give anything away.

'Hi, Sam, thanks for visiting. How did you get on after I last . . . er, saw you leaving?'

'Well, as you may remember, I had an urgent

appointment and had to leave the meeting in a bit of a hurry,' Sam replied. 'I nearly had a very nasty accident shortly afterwards but luckily avoided any harm and eventually made it back to some friends.' Chopper knew that Sam's house would have been under surveillance by the police and he must have contacted some other criminal friends after escaping from the jungle.

'I then visited a spot that we both fell in love with some time ago but haven't visited since,' Sam continued, 'and that turned out to be very helpful.'

Chopper knew that his brother was talking about a large stash of cash that they had hidden together after a spectacular bank robbery and decided to leave as an emergency reserve until interest in finding the stolen currency had died down.

'I've ordered some new machinery for the farm,' Sam went on, 'but I'm a bit worried about the pigs. The new tractor is very big, in fact it will only just fit through the gate. As you know, their enclosure is right next to the front gate and if the new tractor bumps into it some of the animals might get out.' Chopper sat forward intently. The 'pig enclosure' must be the prison ('pigs' was what the prisoners called police and prison officers) and Sam was clearly planning a break-in to get his brother out. He tried to sound as casual as possible for the benefit of the microphone he knew must be hidden in the grating that separated them.

'Er, when's the new tractor arriving?'

'It looks like Tuesday next,' said Sam, equally casually,

'but it's the last delivery of the day so it probably won't be until the evening. That's part of the problem: if any of the animals escape they could be tricky to find in the dark. I think, to be on the safe side, it would be best if I drove the last few yards myself.'

'I think that's a good plan,' said Chopper, 'and I can't wait to see the new tractor.'

'Well, you never know what's round the corner in life,' said Sam, with the merest suggestion of a wink. 'Let's just hope your sentence is unexpectedly shortened and you get to see it sooner than you think.'

They talked a little longer of Sam's plans for the farm and then he got up to leave.

'I'm sorry it's been such a long time since we met, I promise to come and see you again soon – but it won't be until after a short break.'

He gave Chopper a warm smile, and the guards scrutinizing the CCTV images were touched to witness this display of brotherly affection by an honest, hardworking farmer for his criminal brother.

5

An Invisible Surprise

Professor Lucius Strahlung, Luke to his very few friends, drove his immaculate, ageing, green Jaguar XJ12 carefully through the traffic towards the university. The early-morning rush in Rio de Janeiro was appalling and the brash owners of other imported cars such as BMWs and Mercedes, flashed at him, hooted at him and overtook him under entirely inappropriate circumstances, but he completely ignored them. He regarded them, and indeed, most other people, as being fundamentally inferior members of society and to prove his case he would, this very day, close a deal that would enable him, at the tender age of fifty, to retire to a life of luxury in Hawaii; a life in a beach mansion interrupted only by occasional trips to London when he felt in need of some culture in his life. Rome, New York, and Paris were other possibilities, if he became desperate.

Professor Strahlung was a scientist and the head of a department studying the physics of light at one of the leading universities in the country. His late father had been a scientist who had fled from Europe to South America at the end of the Second World War to escape accusations of war crimes. He had built a new life under an assumed name and had passed on to his son a number of qualities including scientific aptitude, apparent respectability, insatiable greed for money and a ruthless criminal streak.

Luke was internationally renowned for his work on laser beams, but had been unable to resist the temptation to share his knowledge with criminals prepared to pay a great deal for his discoveries. He had recently made a breakthrough in laser science that would revolutionize the ability of the police and armed services to protect the public against terrorists. The leader of a group of terrorists based in neighbouring Bolivia was coming to see him that day to discuss the purchase of this secret device which would then be available to terrorist groups around the world, and enable them to take countermeasures against the authorities.

Luke arrived at the university early, well before most of the other staff. He wanted to download his secret information onto computer disks before other members of his team arrived. As he walked to his office he had to pass one of the light research laboratories and noticed that he was not the only one to make an unusually early start that day. Through the half-open door of the laboratory his attention was caught by a young scientist called Lucinda Angstrom. He knew that though she was only a relatively junior member of his department she was already beginning to cause a stir in the scientific world with her innovative ideas. He was intrigued by her current behaviour and stepped back a little so she wouldn't see him. She was walking sideways and moving slowly towards a large machine while looking at herself in a very wide mirror that covered the whole of the adjacent wall. At first Luke thought she was admiring herself in a new outfit; he vaguely remembered that there was a Faculty Ball that evening. Suddenly, however, she disappeared. Luke rubbed his eyes in astonishment and pushed open the door to get a better view. She was nowhere to be seen in either the room or the mirror. Then, as he watched in disbelief, the young woman gradually reappeared, first a hand and an arm, then her entire body. Suddenly she became aware of his presence and turned. As she did so she flicked a switch on the wall and something that looked like a blanket hanging on a washing line appeared behind her. She recognized her head of the department immediately but was clearly very upset about having been observed.

'I . . . Did you? . . . Was I?' she stuttered in confusion.

'Did I see you disappear? Yes, I most certainly did.' He walked over and pointed to the blanket which was suspended from a rope between two stands, resembling a high jump. 'And I presume that this is some kind of invisibility cloak?'

'Yes,' she said simply. The professor's heart was pounding with excitement.

'Why am I able to see it?' he asked.

'At present I have to energize it to get the full effect.' She pointed to the machine and the nearby switch on the wall. 'That's obviously a serious problem – you can't cart a giant machine around. But I'm in the process of developing a portable energizer which will work off a torch battery and fit into a pocket.'

Luke turned to look at her. His expression was stern.

'This is a major development. As head of department, I think I should have known about it a little earlier, don't you?'

He saw her dismayed expression and hurriedly continued. In his mind he was feverishly assessing the implications of what he had just witnessed and he needed her total cooperation. He relaxed his expression a little to reassure her.

' . . . But let's not worry too much about scientific protocol. You've clearly made a significant breakthrough and I need to know all about it. You're going to need advice and funding to take this further and . . .' he paused almost imperceptibly, 'your instincts to keep this discovery secret were absolutely right. For the moment you shouldn't discuss it with anyone else. Now I think it's best if you come to my office, have some coffee, and *enlighten* me.' She relaxed on hearing his little pun and followed him to his office.

'Now,' said the professor once they were settled down with cups of coffee and he had flicked on a switch under his desk activating the DO NOT DISTURB UNDER ANY CIRCUMSTANCES sign outside his office door, 'tell me all.' He could be a charming man when he chose and he gave her a disarming smile. 'They all told me that you had brains as well as beauty and I'm beginning to realize that it's true.'

The young doctor blushed and hurriedly started to talk to cover her embarrassment – just as Luke had intended.

'One of my first childhood memories was of playing with a kaleidoscope and whenever we did drawing or painting at playschool I always did a rainbow while the others were drawing animals and cars. At secondary school my classmates were astonished to learn that my favourite subject was physics – the one they all hated – mainly, I think, because nobody taught it properly, but that's another matter. Although I was born in Brazil my parents travelled a great deal and I went to university in the UK. At St Andrews in Scotland I became fascinated by some research going on into ways of making things invisible and I was lucky enough to win a scholarship to Duke University in North Carolina where I was able to specialize in this field. As you know, we are talking about one of the Holy Grails of physics; for centuries men have dreamed of becoming invisible with all that it implies in terms of power and riches, and I saw an opportunity of combining my childhood interest in light with a fascinating field of research in modern physics.'

'How does it work?' asked the professor with barely concealed impatience.

'At present we know of several possible theoretical ways to make something invisible. These include the use of active camouflage; plasmons – electron configurations that can cancel light; super lenses which create local areas of resonance that affect light; and metamaterials. The last of these methods is the one I found most exciting and which I believed had the greatest potential for achieving invisibility in practice. Basically it depends on surrounding an object with a cover made of a special material that can bend light around it. As you know when we see something we are actually seeing light that has reflected off it. If the light never touches the object but simply flows around it like water round a fish in a stream, or air streaming round a rocket then we won't see the object. For several years we have known theoretically that metamaterials could do this. They can change the direction of electromagnetic radiation in a manner similar to that described by Einstein in his theory of general relativity almost one hundred years ago.'

'If we've known about it for years, how come nobody can become invisible?' asked the professor.

'Until now, the calculations suggesting it should be possible only apply to tiny molecules. We didn't in any case have metamaterials of the right sort that we could construct into a sheet or cloth. These materials aren't found in nature. That's where I was extraordinarily lucky.'

The professor leant forward, listening intently.

'A few months after I started work here I started going out with Peter Flint, one of the geologists.'

The professor nodded. Flint was a lecturer in the geology department on the floor below and the departments shared a common room and canteen.

'One day he brought me a most unusual rock that had been sent to him for analysis. It had been picked up by a pilot who had found it in a remote crater in the Amazon and who noticed that it glowed in dim light. Peter thinks it was a mixture of fear and greed that brought him to the university: fear that he may have been in contact with radioactivity, and greed in that if he had discovered a secret source of uranium he might become rich.

'The geology department soon established that the glowing in the dark was not radioactivity, nor was it some type of natural phosphorescence which had been Peter's first thought. It was a curious effect produced by the concentration of light round the edges of the material. The substance itself is a completely unknown metallic crystal and is the first naturally occurring metamaterial ever discovered in significant quantities. I've called it photogyraspar. It's impure of course, in an ore, which is why it only produces unusual light effects rather than total invisibility. The metamaterial distorts the light passing near it and concentrates it. This happens all the time of course but the effect is invisible in broad daylight. At dusk, the concentration of rays makes it appear to glow, and at night it disappears completely because there are no light rays to concentrate. It means that the glow is only visible for a very limited critical time at dusk. The pilot said he had passed the same spot for weeks without noticing it.

'Knowing my special interest, Peter bought all the remaining rocks from the pilot and I have now created the world's first invisibility blanket. When you came in just now I was testing it out in front of a mirror for the first time. As you saw, it works!' she added, with a shy smile.

The professor was stunned at what he had heard and his mind was racing ahead.

'Where's the pilot?' he asked.

'Unfortunately he's in jail. Before we could ask him the exact location of the crater in which he'd found the rocks he was arrested for drug trafficking and got five years. I was going to approach you once I'd finished my preliminary experiments and ask if you could use your influence with the Vice-Chancellor to try and get his sentence commuted – apparently it's his first offence and the whole future of light science depends on our getting more of this material. If the crater is situated in remote jungle there'll be no way of finding it without the pilot. We know exactly where he is because the prison doctor was worried that he might be radioactive and rang us to get the results of the rock analysis.'

The professor was relieved, though he didn't show it. If the pilot was in jail, at least nobody else could be finding out the whereabouts of this mysterious crater. As Lucinda continued he casually scribbled on the pad in front of him, apparently doodling, but in reality making a note: *'Find out which gaol from Peter Flint in geology.'*

When their discussion was over and Dr Angstrom had finally returned to her lab, Luke leaned back in his chair with his hands behind his head, gazed out of the window and went over in his mind what he had just heard.

It was almost unbelievable. One of man's greatest desires now seemed to be actually achievable. He knew that many of the major technological advances seen in the past century or so had all seemed like magic when they had first appeared: the telephone, radio, television, space travel, the prodigious power of computers, had all enabled mankind to achieve feats that had previously been regarded as impossible, but this – the ability to become invisible – was surely one of the most astounding discoveries of all time. And, if Luke had anything to do with it, its very first practical use would be to make him the richest man on earth – the richest man, in fact, who had ever lived. He felt almost euphoric with elation as he turned over in his mind the limitless criminal possibilities created by the power to become invisible: robbery of all kinds, including theft from the most secure establishments on earth; fraud; access to any information being received by anyone whether in their own home, their business or their bank; the ability to use information gained in this way to blackmail the richest people in the world or to blackmail governments over commercial, political or military secrets; the extortion of unlimited funds from banks and businesses; the list of possibilities was endless . . . and he and one young, somewhat naïve scientist, were the only people on earth to know about it.

Well, that would soon change, he mused; soon there would only be *one* person who knew about it. She would have to suffer a fatal accident, which he would arrange as soon as he was certain he could fully understand and apply the technological principles of the discovery. His thoughts were interrupted by a call from the terrorist he was due to meet later that day. Using the language code they always employed on the phone the Bolivian said he wanted to postpone their meeting because he thought he might be under police surveillance. Luke was relieved; the last thing he wanted was the police taking an interest in him. The laser deal suddenly seemed much less important than it had done a few hours ago: he now had much bigger fish to fry!

For the next month Luke stole every scrap of information relating to his discovery. Under the guise of making Lucinda's computer more secure in order to protect their secret, he actually inserted an advanced bugging device into it which transmitted the entire content of her hard drive to his own computer. He kindly allowed her to store all her notes and files relating to the project in his own safe. This had been made particularly secure by government agents because it contained details of his confidential laser defence research, and nobody but himself had access to it. He consoled her when her personal laptop mysteriously disappeared from her office one day, and she counted herself fortunate to have such a kind and understanding head of department. He sacked her technician, Ray, after the professor's wallet mysteriously disappeared and was later found in Ray's locker. He copied all the information he gathered onto CDs and, as a precaution against ever being found out, stored them in the safe deposit boxes of a bank originally recommended to him by his father as being an institution that did not go out of its way to cooperate with police enquiries about the assets of criminals.

At last, Lucinda announced that the mobile energizer was ready for testing. The timing was perfect for the professor, who had now acquired all the information he needed to continue the project on his own and was looking for an opportunity to arrange a freak accident for his junior colleague. He had already bought a new dark suit to wear at her funeral.

Lucinda was anxious to test the cloak in natural daylight, for all her experiments up until now had been in the artificial light of the laboratory and she was terrified that the invisibility device might somehow be less effective in full natural light. The mobile energizer now made it possible to use the cloak outside and one afternoon she and the professor went to a deserted spot for the trial. She was a keen scuba diver and knew of a suitable cliff top above the bay where she and fellow club members practised their underwater skills. The professor kindly offered to drive and after lunch he packed her cameras and specialist equipment into the boot of the Jag and they drove out to the coast.

There was no shade at the location she had chosen and the cliff top was bathed in brilliant sunshine. Far below, the Atlantic breakers pounded against the base of the cliff. Before they got out of the car to begin their ground-breaking experiment, the professor reached into his pocket, took out a small parcel and gave it to Lucinda.

'For you my dear,' he said with a fatherly smile. 'A token of good luck for what I'm sure is going to be the most momentous day of your life.'

Lucinda took the parcel and opened it. Inside was a velvet-covered box emblazoned with the name of an exclusive jeweller:

Gyges of Lydia.

In the box, nestling in silk, was a lucky clover, exquisitely chased in solid gold and mounted on a ring.

She was lost for words at the touching gesture.

'Why . . . it's . . . it's . . . beautiful,' she eventually stammered as she slipped it on to her finger. 'I shall always treasure it as a memory of this day and your kindness to me over all these weeks.'

She leaned over and kissed the professor on the cheek and he blushed faintly with embarrassment, as well he might.

Lucinda had readily agreed to the professor's suggestion that he should be the one to don the invisibility cloak so that she could do her experiments with various light meters and cameras from different angles. The cloak was basically a large cape shaped like a poncho with Velcro slits inserted in the sides so that the arms could be poked out if necessary. There was a Velcro hem to adjust the length of the cloak precisely so it hung just clear of the ground. The portable energizer fitted into a pocket inside the cloak. There was a separate invisibility helmet with two tiny eyeholes cut in it that the professor referred to as 'Hades' cap', for some reason that Lucinda couldn't discern. As she helped the professor to put everything on she noticed his hands were trembling and felt touched that he was so excited about the outcome of her experiment. Her interpretation of his excited state was, of course, completely wrong, as she was soon to discover. With the

'I'm sorry about the Nobel prize, my dear, but I think it's about time I received one myself!'

robe in place Lucinda set up her instruments and cameras at different angles and then instructed the professor to switch on the energizer. To her delight he instantly disappeared.

'Does it work?' she heard his disembodied voice ask, eerily, out of apparently empty space.

'Yes, it's fantastic,' she replied. 'Nobel Prize, here I come!'

'Just walk completely round me and check I'm invisible from every angle,' said the voice. Lucinda obediently walked round the spot where she knew him to be standing. She couldn't even see the flattened grass beneath his shoes, for the light simply flowed around the robe down to the ground. It was truly as though he didn't exist. As she passed between the invisible man and the cliff top she suddenly

saw a disembodied hand appear in midair; as it moved towards her a wrist and a forearm appeared, followed by an elbow.

'I'm sorry about the Nobel Prize, my dear, but I think it's about time I received one myself!'

As he spoke, the midair arm emerged completely from the slit in the robe and pushed her off the edge of the cliff.

Even up to the last second she did not suspect what he was about to do and as she tumbled backwards into space her terror was mingled with an overwhelming sense of injustice and betrayal. As she fell she took a deep breath in mid-air and struggled to twist her body into the semblance of a dive; she knew that at all costs she mustn't be struck unconscious by the impact with the water and prayed she would avoid the vicious rocks at the base of the cliff.

The shock of hitting the water was unbelievable and stunned her for a second or two but she had protected her head with her hands and remained conscious. From her scuba diving she had an intimate knowledge of this section of coastline – her diving club was only half a mile along the bay – and, still under water, she swam down and towards the rocks where she knew there was an overhang. If she could reach this area where the sea had cut in under the rocks she knew she would be invisible from above. She resisted the temptation to break surface and look up. She wouldn't be able to see her invisible assailant, but he might see her and know she had survived. At last, with her lungs almost bursting and her heartbeat drumming in her ears, she surfaced under the rocky overhang, bruised, frightened, but alive.

As she sat on a ledge, gasping for breath and recovering her strength, her eyes fell upon the ring the professor had given her just an hour before. From being a token of luck and affection from one had she believed to be a true friend and mentor, it had now became a symbol of hatred and betrayal. She wrenched it off her finger and hurled it out into the ocean.

Back on the top of the cliffs the professor congratulated himself on how smoothly his little plan had gone. He was afraid of heights so he lay on the ground and crawled to the edge of the cliff.

Staring down over the brink at the waves smashing themselves against the jagged rocks below he gave a smirk of satisfaction – it was inconceivable that anyone could have survived that fall. But just to be sure . . . he struggled out of the invisibility robe and ran to the car. In the boot was a box that he had left behind while unloading Lucinda's other equipment. A wire ran from the box to the car aerial leads which ran down inside the boot. Now he flipped back the lid of the box and inspected a flat-screen computer monitor.

His face fell for an instant as he saw the trace of a heartbeat coming across the screen. The gold ring he had given Lucinda was more than an exquisite piece of jewellery: it was a masterpiece of electronic engineering that was recording the pulse in her finger and transmitting it to the car aerial. But even as he watched, the pulse flattened and stopped. A flat line traced across the screen. She was dead. Fame and fortune awaited him!

Lucinda rang the police from her diving club. She had changed into a set of dry clothes she always kept there in her locker and was now clutching a cup of hot chocolate and telling her story to a policeman. On hearing that her accusation was attempted murder a senior detective called Poirot had come in person to interview her and they now sat in a quiet corner of the locker room. The detective had originally intended to inspect the scene of the crime, but on hearing Lucinda's story he changed his mind in case the professor should see him and realize that she had survived. Lucinda told him that she thought the professor was trying to steal her research, but didn't say what it was about.

'We've had our eye on the professor for some time now,'

the detective divulged to Lucinda. He did not tell her that at that very moment a captured Bolivian terrorist was 'helping them with their enquiries' and had already been persuaded to reveal Luke's identity.

'I can't say any more at present,' the inspector continued, 'but he's involved in a serious matter concerning state security and we now know that he's prepared to commit murder. If he discovers you are still alive he'll stop at nothing to do the job properly the second time. If you agree, I think you should tell only your closest relatives that you are OK and go away on extended leave. I will have a quiet word with the Vice-Chancellor of the university – I need to tell him anyway about the professor – so your job will be secure. In the meantime we will let the public know that a body has been washed up and that it seems that a young woman was involved in a tragic cliff fall. That should keep you safe from the professor while we continue to observe him and tighten the net around all his terrorist contacts.'

Lucinda readily agreed to this plan and was only too happy to hear that the professor would not only eventually get the justice he deserved but would never be able to steal the credit for her wonderful discovery. She rang up her older sister Maria, a widow with two children who adored their Aunt Lucie and were delighted to hear that she was coming to stay for an indefinite period. Two days later the Dean called an emergency meeting of the senior university staff and announced that, tragically, the body of the young woman that had been reported in the news that morning as having been washed ashore was almost certainly that of Dr Angstrom.

The professor appeared to be devastated by the news.

'Oh my God!' he exclaimed, striking his forehead in an histrionic gesture. 'I simply can't believe this!' The Dean's secretary couldn't help thinking that he looked just like an actor overplaying a dramatic scene, but then immediately felt guilty at letting such an uncharitable thought cross her mind about the poor man. She gave him some strong coffee and a large brandy before helping him back to his office as he dabbed his eyes with a large handkerchief.

Beneath the professor's outward show of grief his obsession with the invisibility suit now made it essential for him to obtain further supplies of metamaterial. Without this it would be impossible to create more suits using the stolen know-how. Lucinda had been uncertain how long the cloak would remain effective, as she had no idea whether or not its metamaterial coating might start to deteriorate and the professor was terrified that it might do so before he had the chance to obtain more of the precious ore from which it came. He had to track down the pilot who had first brought the mystery rocks to the university. He had already obtained the name of the prison from Lucinda's boyfriend and now, using his extraordinary IT skills, he hacked into the confidential computer prison records and learnt all he could about the man who held the answers to the knowledge he was so desperate to acquire; in particular, he found the exact location of the man's cell within the immense prison.

The professor thought about his strategy in great detail. The first thing was to make sure that the pilot could take him back to where he had found the rocks and was willing to do so. He might have to let him in on the secret at some point to gain his cooperation, but as long as he alone possessed the invisibility suit he could always dispose of the pilot when it suited him. It would be no more difficult than getting rid of the girl had been. Next, he had to get the pilot out of jail. It would be easy for the professor to get in to jail, but much more difficult to get the pilot out. That was something he would have to give some thought to but, with his new-found power, the problem should not be insuperable.

6

A Voice in the Dark

Biggles awoke with a start. He thought he had felt a hand on his shoulder, but decided he must have been dreaming. Chopper was snoring like a pig on his bunk on the opposite side of the cell and though the cell was narrow he couldn't possibly have reached the pilot. The cell was dimly illuminated from the corridor lights shining through the barred door and as Biggles became fully awake he was puzzled to see that the shadows of the bars on the floor, which he had observed through countless sleepless nights in jail, had changed position. He sat up in bewilderment and then saw, to his astonishment, that the cell door was slightly ajar. Then he heard the voice. He broke out in a cold sweat as childish fears of ghosts and other supernatural entities flooded through his imagination.

'Ssh. Don't be alarmed. Listen.'

The voice in his ear sounded real enough but what on earth was going on?

'Who are you? Where are you? What the hell's happening?' Biggles' voice was hoarse with fear.

'Never mind that for the moment,' the voice replied. 'Are you interested in making a great deal of money – enough to keep you in luxury for the rest of your life?'

'Yes . . . but . . .' the pilot stammered, 'how can I get it or spend it while I'm in this hell-hole?'

'Just tell me the answer to one question and I can sort everything,' came the reply. 'You took some rocks to the university a few weeks ago. Can you remember where you found them and could you take me there?'

The pilot swallowed hard as he cast his mind back to the crater. Could he find it again? He was sure he could; he assiduously kept records and map references of all his flights with notes about any special circumstances or problems he had encountered. Over the years this record had proved invaluable in his dangerous flights over the remote rainforest and had saved his life on more than one occasion.

'Yeah, I can get you there OK. There's just this little problem of getting out of here.'

'Leave that to me. I'll be back in touch soon,' said the voice.

'Who are you?' asked the pilot.

'Just call me X for the moment. I'll be back.'

The cell door closed and there was a quiet click as it was relocked.

'Who the hell were you talking to?' demanded Chopper. He had clearly been woken by the disturbance, but Biggles wasn't sure how much he had heard or whether he had seen the door move.

'Sorry,' he said quickly. 'Just a nightmare. I'm OK now.'

Chopper grunted, turned over and within a few moments was snoring again.

The pilot lay awake on his back staring at the ceiling in the dim light. Common sense began to reassert itself. The hand on his shoulder must have been a dream. The voice must somehow have been transmitted to him electronically. The guard must have left the door open during a final inspection after he and Chopper were asleep and he must have come back and relocked it without Biggles catching sight of him. But what about the message he had received? Clearly the rocks contained some valuable ore and somebody at the university intended to make himself a little fortune out of it. Well, that was OK with Biggles as long as he got a fair share. But how was he going to get out of jail? He didn't sleep any more that night as he went over and over in his mind what had happened.

The next day Chopper sat opposite Biggles at lunch. Chopper ate greedily despite the appalling food – his massive frame needed every calorie it could get to keep going. When he had scraped his bowl clean he looked across at Biggles, having made sure that nobody else was in earshot.

'Now,' he said, 'tell me what was really going on last night. I heard another voice whispering and I'm sure I saw the door being shut. Have you got a scam going on with one of the guards, 'cos if you have, I'm in on it, OK?'

Biggles thought quickly. Despite the friendship that he had formed with Chopper, he was, like everyone else in the jail, intimidated by the big man and knew he could expect the worst if Chopper thought he was trying to deceive him. The only safe course of action was to tell him the truth.

He told Chopper everything that had happened and explained that he had made up his story about a nightmare simply because he didn't understand what was going on and didn't want Chopper to think he was going mad. Chopper listened to the whole story without interrupting. An inveterate liar himself, he recognized the truth when he heard it and he knew that the pilot was being completely honest with him. He was, as always, calculating his best way of exploiting the situation. It sounded as though a previously undiscovered gold or uranium mine could provide a fortune for several people, not just the pilot and his unknown conspirator. Chopper had already been considering including the pilot in his forthcoming escape – he had, after all, formed a close working relationship with the man – and now he saw how this unexpected turn of events could benefit everyone. He leant towards Biggles, who had now finished his tale and was watching Chopper with some trepidation.

'Let's make sure I've got this right. You know where some fancy rocks come from. This guy says they're worth a fortune if you can get out and show him where they are. You need him because he knows what's special about them, and he needs you 'cos he doesn't know where they are. He's got some way of talking to you in here, but you don't know what it is. Is that it?'

The pilot was relieved beyond measure at Chopper's reaction.

'Yeah, you've got it in one,' he replied, his voice trembling with relief.

Chopper fell silent and gazed into space for a few moments. Then he turned back to the pilot.

'Right,' he said, 'here's the deal. My brother is going to get me and my mates out of here on Tuesday night – I don't know how he's going to do it yet but I'm pretty certain he will. If you cut us all in on your little arrangement with the mystery voice I'll take you out with us.'

Biggles thought for a moment. He really had nothing to lose as he certainly wasn't going to make any money staying in jail, and a fortune was a fortune however it was divided up. And he was still anxious to stay on the right side of Chopper.

'OK,' he said, 'but there's a problem. I can't talk to this bloke – I have to wait 'til he talks to me again and we've only got two more nights before Tuesday.'

'Well,' said Chopper grimly, 'you'd just better hope that your mystery mate gets in touch soon or you'll be enjoying these prison lunches for another five years.'

Chopper didn't know whether putting pressure on the man would make any difference but it certainly couldn't do any harm.

That night Biggles lay awake, hoping against hope that he would hear the voice once again. But the night passed with no sound other than Chopper's snoring and occasional laughter from the guards' coffee room. He felt sick with fear that he had truly dreamt the events of the previous night and was doomed to spend years in prison but, after Tuesday, without the protection of Chopper.

He spent the next day in a state of continuous anxiety and foreboding. From time to time during the prison routine Chopper caught his eye and looked enquiringly at him and he shook his head despondently in reply.

That evening, exhausted by his previous sleepless night, he fell into a fitful sleep and was woken in the early hours by the mystery voice.

'I have a plan,' said the professor. 'I am going to steal all the keys necessary for you to make your escape and get them copied. I'll bring you the copies as soon as I can and you can escape whenever a suitable opportunity arises.'

Biggles then told the professor about Chopper's deal. For Luke it was like an answer to a prayer; he knew that his own plan could easily fail if any of the guards saw the pilot escaping. He didn't care how many people were supposedly in on the deal; all he was interested in was getting the pilot out. When the time came to exterminate the pilot he would dispose of them all.

'OK,' the voice whispered, 'it's a deal. We are all going to be rich beyond our wildest dreams.'

They arranged to meet in the city on Tuesday night, and the voice said goodbye.

On this occasion the professor had been more careful. He had shut the cell door behind him before waking the pilot and now he waited until he was sure the man was asleep before quietly slipping out and making his way past the many guard points situated between the pilot's cell and the outer gates. He rejoiced in his power as, completely invisible, he strolled nonchalantly between several guards, pausing only to remove their wallets as he passed. At the main gate he went into the porter's lodge and pressed the emergency red button that would wake the prison governor in his home adjacent to the prison, and activate a riot squad from the city police station. A few moments later, as a bewildered guard opened the door to a furious governor in pyjamas, the professor slipped quietly between them and disappeared into the night.

7

Chopper Takes a Break

Situated next to the prison was a large municipal refuse dump. As the outspoken mayor of the city had said, when approving planning permission for the site to be so close to the prison, putting all the city's rubbish in the same place made good sense.

Shortly before 6 p.m. on Tuesday Sam drove up to the dump in a large, old American car. He had connections with all elements of the criminal underworld and car mechanics were no exception. Outwardly decrepit, this car had a souped-up engine that could outpace any regulation police car and inside the darkened windows there was more than enough space for the extra people Sam anticipated would be occupying it on its return journey from the prison. At the flick of a switch underneath the dashboard, furthermore, the number plates, back and front, rotated to show any one of three different sets of numbers; these had been chosen by Sam, with an unusual turn of wit, to correspond with the private car numbers of the Chief of Police, the Mayor and the Bishop of Rio.

Sam had been observing the dump for several days and

knew precisely the routine of the dump operators. Shortly before six in the evening they parked their massive JCBs near the gate, locked the gate and left in a council van which presumably dropped them off near their homes or at a central railway or bus station. He backed his getaway car into some bushes near the gate and waited until the operators had driven off. He then cut the gate lock with a hacksaw and went to the largest of the JCBs. It was a truly massive machine, capable of shifting tons of rubbish with its shovel and scoop. Sam climbed into the cabin. Since the age of seven he had been stealing vehicles and there was nothing from a moped to a steamroller that he couldn't start with a length of electric cable, a screwdriver and a pair of pliers. He did a test start on the bulldozer, and spent a few moments practising with various knobs and levers to make sure he could manipulate the hydraulic shovel and scoop, then switched off and waited.

To the casual onlooker the prison looked impregnable. The entire complex was surrounded by an electric fence, ten feet high. At each corner of this fence was a forty-foot tower built of steel girders, at the top of which was a guard manning a machine-gun. Five yards inside this outer fence was a thirty-foot wall surmounted by barbed wire. Inside the section of this wall that faced the municipal rubbish dump was the prisoners' recreation area, with pool tables, table-tennis tables and pinball machines. Chopper, Barker, Shortshanks and Biggles were now in this area, playing snooker at the table furthest from the outside wall.

Shortly after seven Sam saw the day guards emerging

from the prison gates and exchanging jokes and greetings with the incoming night shift. When all was quiet again he pulled a balaclava over his head and started up the massive machine. It rumbled through the rubbish site gates as though they were matchwood and headed first for the governor's house which was adjacent to the prison, just outside the electrified fence. The governor's Mercedes-Benz R-class Grand Sports Tourer, his pride and joy and the fruit of many bribes from both criminals and police officers, stood in the drive, sparkling from the daily wash and polish it received from prisoners on parole. Sam picked it up effortlessly in the JCB's giant shovel and, raising it high in the air, tipped it onto the electric fence. Amidst a thunderous crackling and flashing of sparks the fence short-circuited and, as an unexpected bonus for Sam, there was a minor explosion in the prison electricity substation which reduced the entire prison to darkness.

The previous night Sam had fixed a massive steel hawser to one of the legs of the nearest lookout tower. He had done this unobserved by the guards whose attention was always focused on prisoners trying to get out rather than on intruders trying to get in. The hawser lay coiled and hidden in the long grass and Sam now attached it to the rear of the JCB and set off at speed. Either the back of the JCB would come off or the guard tower would collapse, and having seen the rusting plates and screws holding the tower together, Sam was entirely confident of the outcome.

Before the dust had settled around the crumpled tower

Sam manoeuvred the JCB through the remains of the electric fence and, still dragging a rusty tower leg behind him, drove straight through the prison wall into the prisoners' recreation area. There was already a considerable level of excitement in the prison as a result of the power cut but this reached a new peak as the massive JCB appeared, framed by an archway of broken bricks and with a table-tennis table now sitting on its shovel.

Chopper and his companions sprang into action and, struggling against the prisoners rushing for safety in the opposite direction, removed the table-tennis table from the JCB's shovel and clambered in. Sam was already backing out as Chopper threw a snooker ball at the recreation room guard, his least favourite warder, hitting him in the eye.

'What colour was the ball?' Barker shouted over the din of the JCB's motor.

'Black,' replied Chopper. 'Why?'

'I just wondered what colour his eye was going to be tomorrow!' They all laughed, slightly hysterical with excitement at their dramatic escape.

Within minutes the escaped villains were in Sam's getaway car and roaring off to the city to meet the professor. The great game was on at last.

8

Plots and Plans

'You mean an invisibility cloak, like in Harry Potter?' exclaimed Chopper, wiping the remains of a triple monstaburger and chips from his mouth with the back of his arm. He had never read a Harry Potter book – or anything else much – but he had seen a Harry Potter film in prison. Barker and Shortshanks, who had neither read the books nor seen the films, but had played the video games, both nodded sagely. The villains were sitting with the professor in a sleazy nightclub – the rendezvous arranged by the pilot – and he had just told them about 'his' discovery. He had decided, wisely, that the best way of getting total cooperation from these rogues was to tell them the truth and appeal to their greed. When the time came, he would eliminate them all, just like Lucinda.

'Yes,' replied the professor modestly, 'I have made what is probably the greatest discovery in history. I can now make myself completely invisible.'

'So *that's* how you got into the prison!' Biggles muttered, as the events of the last few days began to make sense at last.

'But . . .' the professor continued, hurriedly. He knew that if these thugs thought an invisibility cloak in full working order already existed his life expectancy would be very short indeed. He had to blind them with science and appear indispensable to the continuation of the project. 'But I only have a primitive prototype at the moment. It doesn't work for more than a few moments unless I continually recalculate the appropriate field strengths for the ambient conditions of luminescence.'

The villains looked suitably impressed, but also somewhat crestfallen. Barker asked the question that was in all their minds.

'So, like . . . it don't work proper yet, is that it?'

'Oh it works all right,' replied Luke. 'It's just that, until I've perfected the technology, I'm the only person who can use it. That's just a detail though; fundamentally, one of man's most ancient dreams has now become a reality. And,' he added to encourage them, '. . . I'm sure I don't need to tell you that it will make us all extremely rich.' He certainly didn't. Chopper's fertile imagination was already racing through all the countless scams and criminal possibilities that the invention offered. He knew instantly that this was the greatest opportunity that had ever come his way. He leant forward, his piggy eyes gleaming avidly, ignoring the excited babble of his companions, as the professor spoke again.

'I must say that things couldn't be turning out better for all of us. Meeting you interesting fellows has been pure serendipity.' His ironic delivery was completely lost on Chopper.

'Yeah, that's it, sendippity,' agreed Chopper eagerly. 'Just what I was going to say myself. Now, tell us what you need, prof, and we'll arrange it. Whatever it is, it's as good as done.'

The professor pretended to ponder for a moment, quite unnecessarily for he had already worked out his strategy in great detail.

'Basically I need the raw materials to create more invisibility cloaks – enough for all of us – and the time and facilities to refine the design so that you can all use them. In practice this means Biggles has to find the crater where photogyraspar comes from, and we have to find a safe place where I can work and experiment in secret for at least three months.'

'What's photowhatnot?' asked Chopper.

'It's the name I've given to a unique crystalline ore which was first discovered by Biggles in a remote crater,' explained the professor. 'So far as anyone knows, that's the only place on earth where it exists and it's essential for the creation of invisibility robes.'

'It would presumably be useful if your laboratory were near the mineral source,' said the pilot thoughtfully. 'How elaborate are the facilities you need for your experiments?'

'Very basic,' said the professor. 'The problems are mostly mathematical, but I do need a small rock crusher and various extraction and impregnation chemicals.'

'What about a loom for weaving the robe material?'

'Not necessary,' said the professor. 'I'm pretty certain I can impregnate linen cloth with a layer of metamaterial – it only needs to be a few molecules thick.'

'In that case I think I have the solution to your requirements,' said the pilot. He turned to Chopper. 'I presume you guys can build a cabin and power it from a portable electric generator?'

'No problem,' said Chopper, 'we must've built half a dozen lumber camps from scratch during the past few years.'

'I thought as much,' continued the pilot. 'In that case I think we *all* go to the secret crater. I've already checked my flying journal and think I can locate it without too much difficulty. I'll have to make several trips to get all the stuff there that we need. You and your men, Chopper, can build a lab for the professor and some cabins for us to live in and then we all disappear for a crater holiday for three months, out of sight, out of mind, while the prof works out how to make us the richest men on earth.'

Chopper looked at his brother and the rest of his little group enquiringly. He wasn't used to somebody else organizing his life but everything the pilot said made perfect sense. The others all nodded encouragingly.

'OK,' said Chopper, 'let's get started. What do we do first?'

Biggles couldn't believe his good fortune as he looked in turn at Chopper and the professor. The rare conjunction of two ruthless criminal minds, one avowedly streetwise, the other unswervingly academic, promised to be a uniquely potent combination. With every minute that passed he felt more confident that they would all make their fortunes.

9

Aerial Combat

Just three months after Biggles and his co-conspirators had flown over the seemingly boundless immensity of the rainforest, another small plane heading for the same destination was floating high above the jungle, following an ever-shrinking tributary of the Rio Negro towards its origins in the remote jungle. Richard was reminded poignantly of the last time he had made this journey – a journey that had ended in the death of his pilot and the destruction of his plane in the depths of the jungle.

As he gazed out across the green forest canopy he saw some hills coming into view on the far horizon and pointed to them.

'That's where the crater is, I'm sure,' he said to Julian, who nodded in agreement as he consulted a document on his knee.

'I think you're right. It agrees with my GPS co-ordinates. We approached it from a slightly different angle on our first visit, but there can't be two plateaux like that sticking out from the forest in this region.'

Soon they swept over the rim of the crater and were

above what Lucy called the Valley of the Mighty Ones. She explained to Clare and Clive that this was the name given to the valley by the animals in the surrounding jungle to whom the giant ground sloths – the Mighty Ones – were clearly visible because of their immense size.

Julian cursed as he struggled to control the plane through the unusual air currents at the edge of the cliff, but then they were floating serenely above the floor of the valley.

'Look!' shouted Clare suddenly, pointing down to the ground. 'Aren't those bits of a plane?'

Richard looked to where she was pointing.

'Yes, they're the remnants of Helen and Julian's plane and next to it is the cleared strip where we're going to land.' Clare then remembered Lucy telling her how she had asked the giant ground sloths to clear an airstrip for the plane that came to rescue Helen and Julian and couldn't really believe that, at last, she was now going to land on that very spot.

Julian flew almost to the end of the valley and then, with the sun behind him, he turned into the wind and brought the plane down in a perfect landing on the little landing strip. The hours of practice he had put in at his flying club had been richly rewarded.

There was a babble of congratulations for Julian from his relieved passengers, all of whom felt that the most dangerous part of the expedition was now behind them. How wrong they were!

They all got out and stretched their legs. Helen, Julian

and Richard looked about them with a curious nostalgia as the memories of their months trapped in the valley came flooding back to them. They had spent some of the most fearful and depressing moments of their lives in this place and yet now, in the bright sunshine with Lucy by their side to protect them, and the prospect of an exciting scientific expedition ahead of them, the valley seemed much less forbidding than it had during the time they were marooned within its walls.

They unpacked the plane and were starting to erect their tents when Clive stopped. 'I've got an idea,' he said. 'Visibility is perfect today and we might have to wait for days before the conditions for flying to the other valley are as good as this again. If you're not too tired, Dad,' he looked enquiringly at Julian, 'I suggest we reload the ropes – we can leave the rest of the climbing gear here – and while the others set up camp, some of us should fly to the central escarpment and try to chuck a rope over. Then, whatever the weather's like tomorrow, we can at least make a start on the climbing.'

They all looked at Julian.

'Well, I'm game,' he said. 'I think it's a great idea if it's OK with everyone else. I'll take Clive and Richard and the rest of you can start setting up camp – and getting a nice supper ready,' he added with a grin.

'No!' said Lucy.

They all looked at her in surprise. Clare and Clive had never seen her in this authoritative mood, but the others had seen it before and knew that whatever she was about to say was probably worth listening to.

'I don't think all the men should go. At least one should stay here just in case something goes wrong. A mixed group will have a much better chance of survival. Also, I think that, after I've told the animals here to look after you, I should go in the plane; in that way if we have to come down somewhere else, I can protect the plane party. Oh – and I think we should split the monkeys – in that way we can keep in communication whatever happens.'

The others looked at each other, but nobody argued. Everything she said was obviously true.

'OK,' said Julian. 'I'll take Lucy, Richard and a monkey and the rest of you can set up camp. Though I do think . . .' he smiled at Lucy, 'you're being a little pessimistic. We've got a radio in the plane and flying conditions are perfect.'

And so it was agreed. Lucy called into the bush and within a few seconds Clare and Clive were horrified to see a sabre-toothed tiger* sauntering towards them, its giant fangs glistening in the sunshine. Richard put a comforting hand on Clare's arm and Julian did the same to Clive.

'It's OK,' Richard said. 'It's alarming but these creatures will do anything she tells them.' They watched open-mouthed as Lucy, in complete silence, communed with the great cat.

'*Greetings to thee with the fangs that put all others to shame!*' said Lucy.

'*Greetings, O Promised One. My kin spoke of thy return but this is sooner than any of us thought. Many of those who served*

* Author's note: not a true tiger. See Animal Anthology.

thee many moons ago are still here and will be greatly honoured to see thee once again.'

'Thank you,' said Lucy, 'and I shall speak further to thee anon. I now leave in the thunderquill for a short time and, for the moment, ask only that while I am away you protect my kin and the arborikin who serve me.'

'It shall be so,' replied the sabre-tooth, 'as it was with the others.'

At the time Lucy thought that 'the others' referred to by the cat were Helen and Julian, whom she had left under the protection of the animals on her previous adventure while she and Richard had gone for help. She would have been horrified if she had known that the sabre-tooth was referring to the villains who had now been living in the valley for three months. The animals had simply assumed that Lucy's instructions applied to any humans coming into the valley and had left the villains unmolested.

She turned and spoke to the monkeys. 'I fly once again in the thunderquill and desire that one of you accompanies me. We shall return before sunsleep. I think it best . . .' She paused, for fear of insulting Queenie. She would rather take one of the younger, more active monkeys, just in case there was a problem with the plane but the monkey was ahead of her and interrupted:

' . . . it is best if Clio goes with thee, O Promised One; I am getting old and Sophie is with Kai. Henceforth, we will stay and serve thy kin until the thunderquill returns. If needs be, I can talk to the greatfang in the common tongue.'*

---

* Author's note: the common tongue is an ancient and primitive language which all animals understand, even though each species also has its own particular language or dialect.

'Let's go, while we've still got a few hours of daylight,' said Julian impatiently. He was worried about the flight but immediately felt slightly ashamed when Lucy explained that she had been ensuring the safety of the others and apologized for his impatience. The three of them then got back into the plane. Michelle, as always, was clinging to Lucy's shoulder, and Clio hopped in behind them, now looking forward to another magical trip high above her native canopy. Before setting off Richard coiled three ropes by the sliding door. They were slender and immensely strong, being made of woven polyamide, and each had a grappling hook at one end. Richard and Clive had discussed at length the best method for scaling the central escarpment into the neighbouring valley. They had decided that the best strategy was to drop a rope from the plane so that its grapples would secure it to the top of the ridge, with the rope extending down into their 'home' valley. The two climbers would use the rope to scale the steep cliff and then lower rope ladders on either side of the escarpment so that the entire party could move freely between the valleys.

As the plane took off Richard felt a pang of apprehension. They only had three grappling hooks, and if he couldn't get one to catch securely on the cliff top he couldn't bear the thought of Clive's expression when he had to confess he had failed. Lucy saw his expression and squeezed his arm.

'It'll be OK, Dad. You can do it.'

He was grateful for her encouragement but knew that he

still faced a serious challenge that could affect the entire success of the mission.

After taking off, Julian flew to the edge of the valley and then turned to fly right across the middle, parallel to the central escarpment so that Richard could identify the lowest point along the ridge. Like Richard he faced a technical challenge unlike any he had met before in his limited flying experience. He and Richard had practised their technique along cliff tops in England but this seemed very different. He had to fly slowly and as low as possible alongside the ridge while Richard and Lucy examined the terrain.

The top of the ridge consisted of sharp, jagged serrations thrusting up to the sky. For most of its length it would be impossible for anything to pass along it and it was now readily apparent why nothing had been able to survive an attempt to get on to it at the edge of the crater from the surrounding jungle.

'That's the place!' Richard exclaimed, pointing to the cliff. He couldn't believe their good luck. They were flying past a major geological fault in the ridge about half a mile long where a rock slippage had resulted in the crest plunging down to a wider ridge within about two hundred feet of the valley floor. He and Clive had discussed at length how high a cliff they might have to climb, and to have now found a point at which the precipice was far less than half the height of the main ridge was an unexpected bonus. Julian turned the plane in a wide circle and then positioned it to fly transversely from one valley to the other across the gap in the summit.

Richard slid back the door. He was immediately taken aback by the rushing wind and the speed with which they crossed the ridge, even though Julian was flying as slowly as he dared without putting the plane at risk. Richard threw down the first rope and was dismayed to see it disappear behind him in a flash, spiralling down at least a hundred yards away from the escarpment. He suddenly realized that he faced an almost impossible task.

'Can you fly along the cliff instead of across it?' he shouted to Julian over the roar of the engine and the rushing wind through the open door. 'The bit I'm aiming at will be further down but the timing won't be so critical.'

Julian nodded. He flew to the end of the valley and then turned the plane for a run along the top of the cliff. As they flew over the gap in the crest Richard made a second attempt. His throw was perfect but, by the greatest ill-fortune, the hook bounced off a very smooth piece of rock and disappeared from view into the valley below.

'We're not going to be able to do this,' he said to Lucy in despair. 'There's only one rope left.'

'Yes, we are, Dad, and it's not your last chance. *We* could never find those lost ropes down there but the animals will easily find them for us and we can come out for another go if necessary. Now, go on, have another go.'

Richard had forgotten about their animal helpers and, much relieved by Lucy's reassurance that this wasn't his last and only chance, he relaxed and concentrated completely on the job in hand.

Julian swung the plane round again at the end of the valleys and commenced another run along the ridge that separated them. He flew even more slowly than before and prayed that the plane would remain under control.

Richard waited until they once again reached the place where the crest fell away, breathed a fervent prayer, and flung the final grapnel out of the plane, its attached coil of rope starting to stream out behind it like the tail of a kite. As the plane sped on he and Lucy looked back and saw the hook bounce once, twice and then, unbelievably, catch tight on a rough stony outcrop. As Julian turned the plane back once again, they could see the rope unfurling itself to the floor of their valley.

Julian grinned and gave them both the thumbs-up sign as Richard hauled the door shut and shut out the noise of the rushing wind.

'Brilliant, Dad!' Lucy exclaimed, '– and Julian,' she added quickly, for the success of the manoeuvre had undoubtedly depended as much on the skill of the pilot as on the throwing of the rope.

'And for my next trick,' said Julian, 'we'll have a quick look for a dinosaur before flying home for the large supper I hope they've got ready for us.' And so saying he banked steeply and flew straight out across the unknown territory that Lucy called the Valley of the Ancients. To their intense disappointment, however, banks of mist were now rolling across the valley and its floor was becoming rapidly obscured from view. As they tried to peer down, the gathering gloom made the strange valley seem ever more mysterious – as if it were determined forever to protect its ancient secrets from the prying eyes of an alien species.

'I'm sorry but we've got to get out of here – fast,' said Julian, a worried frown on his face. 'If this gets any worse I may lose my bearings and the compass is going crazy.' As he spoke he pointed to the instrument panel where the compass needle was spinning jerkily, first one way and then the other. But Richard was looking past him out of the windscreen.

'Good God!' he exclaimed, 'another plane – and it's coming straight for us!'

Julian spun round and gripped the controls as he looked ahead at the dark shape that had emerged from the swirling mists. 'Planes don't flap their wings, Richard,' he said grimly, as he put the plane into a steep climb. 'It's a giant pterodactyl and . . .' as he spoke the creature also changed course to meet them '. . . it's attacking us!'

Julian wrenched at the controls to bank away but, with astonishing aerobatic ability for such a large creature, the giant reptile twisted to keep them on target. It flew straight at the front of the plane, its prodigious beak poised like a lance to strike through the windscreen which it obviously took to be the face of a rival invading its territory. It did not, of course, see the rapidly spinning blades of the propeller and there was a juddering crash as the creature was turned into mincemeat, the windscreen becoming instantly opaque as it became covered in gore and pulverized remains. The windscreen wipers were useless, their mechanisms clogged with skin and guts.

'Planes don't flap their wings, Richard,' he siad grimly . . .

Julian had retained a mental image of his last clear view of the landscape; a savannah-like plain stretching back towards the heavily forested base of the central escarpment. He realized instantly that he couldn't make it over the escarpment and attempt a blind landing back in their own valley. The engine was racing but he knew that this was only because the propeller blades must be shattered and that the engine was meeting no resistance. He had no power. All he could do was to try and glide down to a savannah landing. He fought to keep the little plane steady as some of the pterodactyl's blended remains gradually slid off the starboard wing into the slipstream. Then they were down, bouncing and bumping along the uneven plain. The terrified passengers waited for the final fatal crash into a rock or tree but it never came. The plane gradually slowed in its jarring progress across the ground and then, after a tremendous final jolt that skewed the plane steeply to port, it came to rest amidst a crackling of branches and twigs in what seemed to be a giant springy bush.

10

Walking on Eggshells

The motor had finally cut out and after some creaks and twangs as the plane settled, there was silence apart from a steady hissing from a broken hose in the engine.

The whole incident had lasted no more than a few moments but they all felt as if they had lived through a lifetime of terror. None of them could really believe they were still alive and unharmed.

Julian released his hands from the controls. They had been clenched so tightly that they were white and bloodless and as he turned to his white-faced passengers there were beads of sweat on his brow. 'Sorry about that, folks,' he said. 'A bit of a cock-up by crater air traffic control!'

Richard spoke – with some difficulty for his mouth was still dry with fear.

'This is becoming a bit of a habit,' he eventually croaked. 'There's something about me and small planes and jungles. I have a distinct sense of déjà vu about all this.' The others remembered that his previous trip to the crater had also ended with a crash in the jungle.

'It's going to take a lot ever to get me into one of these things again,' he continued. 'I've walked back to civilization once before through the jungle and I think I'm prepared to do it again.'

'Well, nobody's going to fly in *this* plane again,' said Julian. 'I'm afraid it's a complete write-off. It would be cheaper to buy a new one than to attempt to get this one out and repair . . .' His voice tailed off. In the danger and the excitement of the crash his sole concern had been their immediate survival, but now the full implications of their plight began to dawn on him. '. . . Which brings me to the next question,' he continued grimly. 'How on earth are we going to get home without a plane?'

'And even more urgent than that,' said Lucy, as Michelle emerged from hiding in her lap and resumed her usual position, 'is how on earth we're going to get back to the others? Remember, the rope you dropped is on the other side of the escarpment; it was intended to help us get *into* this crater from that side – not *out* of it from this side.'

They all fell silent again as they contemplated their situation. Not only were they now deprived of their means of returning to civilization but they were separated from the rest of the group by a formidable escarpment.

'Where's the radio?' said Julian. 'Let's at least tell the others what's happened.'

Richard retrieved the radio from his rucksack. It was, fortunately, undamaged but when he tried to communicate with the others there was no response.

'I'm just not sending or receiving any signals,' he said

angrily. 'What the hell's the matter with it?'

There was a pause as Julian cast his mind back to his own experience with the radio on their previous visit to the crater.

'I think I told you,' he said thoughtfully, 'that our pilot couldn't get the radio to work because we were too near the cliff for decent reception. You know how your mobile phone doesn't work sometimes near tall buildings. Our pilot lost his life because he was trying to find a spot away from the cliff where he could establish a successful radio transmission.' Richard nodded in agreement.

'We-ell,' Julian continued slowly, 'We never actually got the radio back so we were never able to see if it *did* work further away from the cliff. Even if we'd had the radio we couldn't leave the safety of the cliff because of the danger from animals. It never crossed my mind that there would be any problem on this trip because I assumed, with Lucy's power over the animals, that we could walk freely anywhere in the crater to get good reception. I'm now beginning to think that the problem wasn't just our proximity to the cliff. It seems to have been caused by something that affects the whole crater. There must be something funny about the metallic ores in the rocks which makes them interfere with electromagnetic impulses.'

'Could that be why the compass was going funny?' asked Lucy.

'Of course!' Julian exclaimed. 'Clever girl. That's exactly what was going on.' He paused and frowned. 'And I'm afraid it confirms my suspicion that the radio will be useless wherever we try to use it.'

There was a tense silence as they all absorbed the full implications of this remark. It was eventually broken by Richard.

'What the hell are we going to do? We're trapped.'

'It seems pretty clear to me what we have to do.' Julian and Richard turned to look at Lucy. She spoke once again with a tone of authority.

'The first thing to do is to find out if I can speak to dinosaurs. If I can we're relatively safe – at least for the time being. If I can't, we've got a problem – a serious problem. Then we've got to get in touch with the others, though quite how I haven't yet worked out. Thank goodness we brought Clio with us; she's probably going to be our best chance of communication.'

Richard and Julian had both forgotten the monkey and now looked at her. She had just recovered from the shock of the crash and crept out from behind Lucy's seat. When she saw everyone looking she became embarrassed and crept back again. Lucy laughed and spoke to her kindly.

'Do not hide, O little one. We speak only in your praise and are glad you are here to help us in our quest. The thunderquill has died in this place and we talk now of how to escape without it. Soon I will tell you of our plans.'

The monkey appeared comforted by her words and came out of hiding once again.

The plane was tilted at a steep angle but the door, fortunately, was uppermost. Before opening it Lucy peeped out of the window. The sky was clearing of mist and visibility at ground level was normal.

'Wow!' she exclaimed. No wonder we had a soft landing!'

The others pressed against the windows.

'Oh no,' Richard groaned as he looked down. 'How can we possibly have been so unlucky!'

Julian looked and his face, just recovering its colour after the crash, went pale again.

'My God,' he whispered eventually. 'I'm so sorry. I thought a trip over the valley would be interesting and look at us now. I've not only crashed the plane but landed in a bloody dinosaur's nest!'

They all stared down in stunned silence at the clutch of giant eggs surrounding the plane. The silence was eventually broken by another groan from Richard.

'Well, here's the really bad news; it wasn't going to take long, but I'm afraid Mum is already on the way.' He pointed to a nearby copse and, sure enough, an enormous shape was looming in the thicket. As it emerged into the open its size was truly awe-inspiring. It was as high as a six-storey building and as long as three buses.

Julian gazed at the monster. His mouth fell open. His expression was a curious mixture of profound terror and professional fascination. 'Good heavens,' he said. 'A real . . . live . . . Argentinosaurus!'

'And what's that?' asked Richard, '– apart from being something that's awfully big.'

'Well, to start with, it's a herbivore – though with something so large, that doesn't seem much of a consolation. On current evidence it was – is – probably the largest and heaviest animal ever to have lived on land. It weighs over a hundred tons.'

'So, out of all the creatures on earth whose home we could choose to wreck,' said Richard bitterly, 'we went and picked the biggest one that ever existed in the history of the planet. Trust us!'

After stopping and looking uncertainly at the plane for a moment or two the giant reptile came to inspect her eggs and nest. She was so close they could see every detail of her skin and could have touched her if the door had been open. The monkey whimpered and cowered once again behind Lucy's seat.

'Look!' Lucy exclaimed. She pointed. 'Look, she's been hurt!' And sure enough, there was a giant gash across the creature's head, passing just below the left eye which was closed. The injury was obviously very recent, for the wound itself glistened in the sun and rivulets of congealed blood could be seen where they had coursed down over the irregular wrinkles of her leathery skin. The dinosaur sniffed at her eggs in turn and seemed unperturbed by the presence of the plane.

'She's ignoring us,' said Richard, in relief and astonishment.

'Yes, thank goodness,' said Julian. 'It's the same phenomenon we noticed with the animals in the other valley – and with big game in Africa when we were out in a Land-Rover. Once the animals think an object is inanimate they ignore it. I suppose as far as she's concerned it's no different from a tree falling on her nest. We wouldn't expect her to start attacking a tree trunk and it's just the same with us. If we got out, though, it would be a very different matter.'

'Well, what are we going to do?' said Richard. 'We're trapped here with no food, a few bottles of water, and no radio.'

'There's only one thing *to* do,' said Lucy slowly. She looked very worried. 'I'm going to have to get out and see if I can talk to her.'

'But you can't possibly –' her father started to protest.

'She's right, Richard,' Julian interrupted. 'There's nothing else for it. Either she makes contact or we're doomed. It's as simple – and as awful – as that.'

They discussed the matter for a while and eventually Richard accepted that there was no other possible course of action. He kissed his daughter and hugged her.

'You're incredibly brave and I'm so proud of you. Good luck.' And with that he pulled back the door as gently as possible so as not to alarm the dinosaur with a sudden noise. The heat outside was incredible and their senses were overwhelmed with all kinds of strange sights and sounds from this alien world. There was a great variety of smells, dominant among which was a very strong smell of compost which, Julian later explained, was from the leaves and ferns that the dinosaur had put in the nest to keep her eggs warm. Clio retreated back behind her chair.

Lucy moved to the open hatch, undecided as to whether to leave the plane or stay in the doorway. The decision was taken out of her hands for, aware of either the door opening or the unfamiliar scent of a human being, the dinosaur looked up from her eggs and glared straight at Lucy and Michelle with her remaining good eye. Lucy froze, motionless in the doorway. Then she spoke:

'*Greetings, O Prodigious One!*'

There was a long, breathless pause, punctuated only by the harsh and outlandish cries of the myriad creatures of the air, bush and swamp that belonged to a long-lost age. Lucy became progressively more nervous, but then suddenly had a feeling that the dinosaur's expression had changed a fraction. Was the creature beginning to look slightly puzzled or was it just her imagination? There seemed nothing to lose, so she repeated her greeting:

'*Greetings, O Prodigious One!*'

Suddenly she heard a voice. A voice unlike any she had ever heard before. It was deep and resonant and had an echo-like quality, as though it were reverberating around some cold and desolate canyon. Most of all, it sounded as though it had somehow travelled on an endless journey through space and time; as though it had started on a far-distant world and come across an immeasurable void to reach her. To hear it gave her a strange and spooky sensation as though she were crossing some unseen boundary in history that nothing had ever been intended or expected to cross.

'*What . . . art . . . thou?*'

The monster spoke incredibly slowly. Her question was entirely reasonable but Lucy found it a difficult one to answer. Suddenly she didn't feel frightened any more. Instead she was filled with excitement and anticipation, for she knew that she had now crossed a threshold of unimaginable significance in the history of the planet.

'I am The Promised One.' Lucy knew, even as she spoke, that what she had said would mean nothing and, as she expected, the dinosaur simply waited for her to say something that it could understand. She changed tack:

'I have come with my kin from across the great rock. We mean no harm.'

What a joke, she thought to herself, as if we could do any harm to this thing.

Richard momentarily took his eyes off the immense creature in front of them to glance at Lucy and, to his partial relief, recognized the expression she always bore when communing with animals. Something was happening. Frantic to know what was being said, but desperate not to distract her from her critical task, he and Julian could only watch and wait in impatient silence.

'The . . . Great . . . Pterokin . . . has . . . slain . . . the . . . Savage . . . One . . . who . . . sought . . . to . . . eat . . . my . . . eggs.'

Lucy looked round and to her astonishment saw a massive dinosaur that looked like a tyrannosaurus, lying on the ground several yards behind the plane. Its neck was twisted at an angle that could only mean it was broken and it had obviously been killed by the plane. As she turned back to the dinosaur she glanced at Richard and Julian, waiting in agonized anticipation for some news.

'Sorry about this,' she hurriedly muttered to them. 'She's, like, *really* slow! Tell you more soon.' The men relaxed slightly. At least she was able to talk to the monster. At that point Clio crept out again to sit by Lucy, which gave them further encouragement; she was presumably listening in on the conversation.

Lucy now seized upon the opening the dinosuar had given her:

'The pterokin is with me and does as I bid, but it is now injured and cannot move. It will not hurt thine eggs.'

'I . . . am . . . indebted . . . to . . . thee . . . and . . . thy . . . pterokin . . . for . . . ye . . . have . . . saved . . . my . . . future . . . babykin.' Lucy felt a surge of optimism at this development.

Lucy turned once again to her rapt audience. To the men it seemed like an age since she had last spoken to them but, in reality, it had only been a few minutes.

'Do you want the good news or the bad news?' she asked. There was a look of immense relief on her face.

'Just get on with it, love,' said Richard, somewhat impatiently. He was in no mood for flippancy. 'Are we going to survive or not?'

'Well, the good news is that she understands the common tongue, so at least we can speak. The bad news,' she continued, 'is that she's obviously never heard of the Promised One, so I'm just any other animal so far as she's concerned.'

'And . . .?' said Julian. He knew there must be more from the look of relief on Lucy's face.

'And . . .' her face broke into a grin. 'If you want the

really good news look carefully at the nest. You'll see that we haven't actually broken any eggs – we ended up on the edge of the nest – but we did flatten that tyrannosaurus thing that had just attacked her and was about to eat her entire clutch of eggs.' She pointed back. The men rushed to the rear window through which they could just see the mountainous carcass of the predator. It was already being sniffed at eagerly by some small scavenging dinosaurs, while a small, bird-like creature was busy pecking its eyes out.

'That –' breathed Julian, '*that* was the final bump before we ended up being cushioned by the nest.'

Richard nodded in agreement.

'What an extraordinary sequence of events,' he mused. 'We hit a flying dinosaur, do a blind crash landing and kill a tyrannosaurus that was about to destroy an entire family of Argentiwhatnots. Does this mean . . .?' He turned back to Lucy with a hopeful expression on his face.

'Oh yes, no doubt about it – we're the good guys as far as she's concerned. We're OK.' She glanced at Clio – clearly talking to her – and the monkey leapt past Julian into the open air, thrilled to stretch her limbs and investigate the extraordinary sights, sounds and smells of this new world. Richard noticed that she was careful to avoid the giant leathery eggs as she leapt over the nest and immediately started to investigate a fig-like fruit growing on a nearby tree. Michelle watched her, then jumped down from Lucy's shoulder and hopped into the nest where she started grubbing about for insects between the eggs and amongst the rotting stalks and leaves that partially covered them. Lucy turned to Julian.

'What did you say she was – an Argentisomething? I want to give her a proper name.'

'An Argentinosaurus.' said Julian with a smile.

'Right. I shall call her "Tina" then.'

Lucy clambered down from the plane and picked her way gingerly to the edge of the nest. There she sat and started speaking once again to the dinosaur.

Julian and Richard looked at each other in amazement and Julian said: 'Tell me this isn't a dream. Are we actually watching your daughter talking to an animal that should have disappeared over ninety million years ago?'

Richard put his arm round the other as though his physical contact would emphasize the reality of their experience.

'No, it isn't a dream – it is simply one of the most incredible sights that can ever have been witnessed by anyone, anytime, anywhere, in the entire history of the world.'

11

An Eye-opener for Tina

Lucy sat on the edge of the dinosaur's nest. As she looked at the dinosaur's dreadful injury she felt sorry for her and decided to talk about it:

'*Thou art gravely injured, O Prodigious One.*'

'*Yea, the Brilliant One has faded in half the world.*'

The dinosaur was now speaking slightly less ponderously and less hesitantly and Lucy decided that she must be recovering from her initial bewilderment, though she subsequently found that the dinosaurs always spoke more slowly than other creatures.

In what Richard would later describe as a rash moment, Lucy decided to try and help.

'*One of my kin can make the Brilliant One return, but I alone can tell him for he speaks not the common tongue.*'

Richard and Julian watched this conversation from the door hatch of the plane, both still in a state of stupefaction at the sight they were witnessing. To their alarm, the gargantuan creature suddenly twisted its seemingly endless neck into a gentle curve and lowered its head towards Lucy but they were relieved to see that this was only to let Lucy inspect her wound. Richard's relief was to be short-lived, however. Soon Lucy stood up and called over to him.

'Well, she's certain we saved her brood so we're definitely in her good books for the moment. There is just one thing, Dad. You've got to get up on top of the plane – I want you to look at her face. She says that since that other thing bit her she can't see properly. I've told her you'll fix it.' Richard had originally qualified as a doctor before taking up a career in botany and though his practical medical experience was extremely limited, Lucy seemed to imagine he could do anything.

'You've what?' exclaimed Richard. 'Don't be so ridiculous – she might have any kind of injury . . .' But he was wasting his breath. Lucy completely ignored his protests as she interrupted:

'. . . C'mon, Dad, she's waiting; get up on top of the plane.' Richard looked: sure enough, the great beast was standing expectantly by the plane.

He got out of the door and clambered up on top of the plane, using the wing as a support. On Lucy's instructions the dinosaur bent down so he could examine her face. It was a daunting yet fascinating experience looking at a living prehistoric beast at close quarters. Even though she was a herbivore, one snap of those jaws would be enough to finish him, yet here he was leaning against her nose and cheek to examine the terrible wound, already absorbed by professional interest in the exact nature of her injury. As he expected from seeing it at a distance, there was a terrible laceration that would undoubtedly have been fatal for a smaller creature. Inspecting the wound more closely, however, he saw something else; something that was yellow and glistening embedded in the depths of the wound. It had penetrated her face just below the eye, and the distortion and swelling it had created in the flesh around it had pushed up the lower eyelid and shut the eye completely. It looked like a piece of bone, but he didn't think it could be hers; as he gently explored with his hands her skull and facial structures seemed intact and he was mystified as to what it was.

'Warn her it may hurt,' he called to Lucy, and after she had done so he stretched out and touched the object of his attention. It was jagged and discoloured at the top but, as he slid his fingers round it, he realized its sides were smooth and hard. Light suddenly dawned.

'It's a tooth!' he called to the others. 'She's got a tooth stuck under her eye. I'm hoping it's missed the actual eyeball but the swelling round it has squashed the eye shut. It must have belonged to the predator that attacked her, and got broken off in the struggle.'

He looked at it. He had brought a few ampoules of local anaesthetic on the trip in case one of the party needed stitches, but there wasn't remotely enough to anaesthetize a dinosaur, and he had no proper surgical instruments – certainly none suitable for this job. On the other hand, if he left it he was certain the animal would die of blood poisoning.

He recalled that, on one of his field trips looking at rare trees on the islands of Indonesia, he had seen several of the

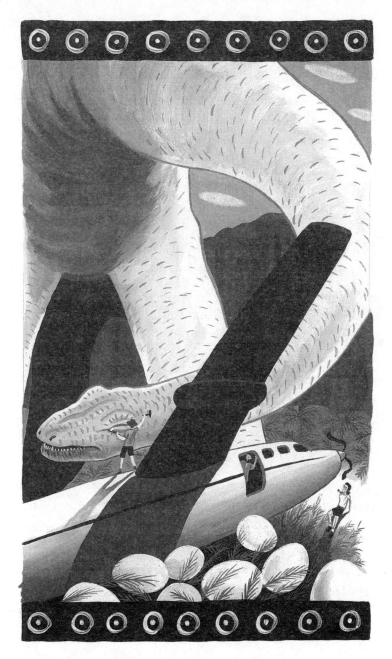

He gently tapped the tooth with the hammer . . .

largest species of lizard in the world – the Komodo dragon. These animals – three metres in length and weighing ninety kilos – are fierce predators and they have such virulent bacteria in their mouths and teeth that any creature they bite is almost certain to become infected and die of septicaemia. It seemed all too likely that the bite of a giant reptilian cousin such as the owner of this tooth might be equally pernicious.

He called to Julian who was still standing in the doorway.

'I'm going to try and get it out – I'll need some stuff from the toolbox.' He thought quickly. 'A mole wrench, a claw-hammer, the biggest screwdriver and pliers you can find – oh – and a can of that spirit you use for cleaning engine parts, some squirty liquid soap and a bottle of water.' He broke off and looked enquiringly at Lucy about using up their precious water, but she nodded encouragingly; she was sure they could now find fresh water with the help of the monkey.

Julian found the various items and passed them up to Richard who laid them out on the wing as if preparing for a surgical operation. He spoke again to Lucy. 'Say this is going to hurt – a lot. But if I don't do it she'll die.'

He gently tapped the tooth with the hammer but, to his intense dismay, it didn't budge an inch. The dinosaur, on the other hand, didn't seem to notice this manoeuvre, which he felt was at least a good start. Maybe the whole area was already so painful or so numb from the injury that she didn't notice a bit of extra discomfort, or maybe her entire pain system was less highly developed than that of a modern creature. Heartened by this Richard tried to get hold of the tooth with the wrench, but couldn't get a proper grip. He took up the hammer again and, inserting it deep into the wound, just managed to wedge its metal claws around the stump of tooth. Breathing a silent prayer he then gradually levered the hammer against the creature's cheek bone. As he exerted his full strength the animal let out a roar of pain – a small roar for the dinosaur but big enough almost to deafen Richard at such close quarters, and he was engulfed by a draught of foetid breath that made him retch. As the animal flinched, the movement of her head finally dislodged the tooth and to Richard's relief he extracted it intact, still firmly gripped in the hammer claw. It was fully four inches long and razor sharp. The base of the tooth where it had snapped off was blackened with decay and gave off a disgusting smell. Richard couldn't help thinking that its former owner must have had frightful breath.

'Tell her I've nearly finished,' he told Lucy, 'but the next bit's going to be painful again.'

He then squirted the entire bottle of liquid soap into the wound and flushed it out with the water. Then he poured the can of spirit into the wound and once again the beast groaned and winced. Already, however, the eye was slightly open and Richard could now see that it was unharmed.

Richard passed the tools down to Julian and clambered back into the plane. He used another bottle of water to wash his hands which were covered in blood and gore.

'Well, let's keep our fingers crossed. If it doesn't get too badly infected she should be OK and when the oedema – that's the swelling – settles down I think she'll be able to see perfectly again.'

Soon they were all standing outside the great nest. They were actually very close to the escarpment and Clio had already found a rivulet of clear water running down from the rocks above, from which they drank their fill and replenished the empty bottles. She had now gone off to forage for food while the human trio reviewed their situation.

They decided it would be safest to live in the plane for the time being – just as Julian and Helen had done on their previous adventure and, with the help of the dinosaur, the men hauled the plane off the edge of the nest so that they could get in and out without harming the eggs. While Julian took photographs and video recordings, scribbled notes, took specimens and made detailed measurements of the dinosaur eggs, the nest and the dead predator, Richard and Lucy sat down on a rock and discussed their plan of action.

'It's going to be very dangerous to move above,' said Lucy, 'because the animals don't know I'm the Promised One. We're OK here because Tina will protect us, but going anywhere out of sight of the plane and nest is going to be very dodgy. If only we knew exactly where the rope was, I might be able to think of a way to get Clio up to the top on this side and she could then climb down the rope into the other valley and take a message to the others.' She frowned. 'It's going to be difficult getting her up though; the reason that this valley's so special is that nothing can get out of it. Still, we'll have to meet that problem when we get to it: the first job is to find where the rope is.'

The mist had now completely cleared and they looked towards the central cliff. They had thought it would be easy to identify the place where they had successfully anchored the rope; it had, after all, been the only place where there was a significant break in the mountain crest. The cliffs in this valley, however, jutted in and out from the main range, masking from view the gap in the ridge that had been so obvious from the air. From the ground where they stood it was quite impossible to locate the point from which the rope was hanging down the other side of the cliff.

They looked over to the nearby escarpment. It was a forbidding sight with an almost sheer face rising hundreds of feet into the air.

Richard began to speak but fell silent as he saw that Lucy had on her 'communing' face. While she was talking to the dinosaur Julian returned to the plane, clearly excited by his zoological investigations but, before he could speak, Lucy turned back to report on her conversation.

'Tina says there's a place not too far away that's different from the rest. She says the dinosaurs go there to eat the rocks – whatever that means – but I think we should check it out; as it's different it might be the place we fixed the rope. She says she can leave her eggs for a short time as long as the sun is shining on the nest.'

They all looked west; the sinking sun, brilliant red and

giant in the sky, was already touching the horizon.

'We'd better leave it till tomorrow,' said Julian. 'I know the others will be desperately worried but there is nothing we can do. She can't leave her eggs to get cold and we can't risk such a dangerous journey at dusk – especially as we need to get a good look at the cliff in daylight.'

They all reluctantly agreed and sat down on the wing of the plane to eat the strange but delicious fruits that Clio had collected.

While they were eating Richard asked Julian what he had discovered on his preliminary scientific studies.

'The first thing is that I've got bad news for you, Lucy,' he replied with a half-smile. 'I'm afraid your "tyrannosaurus" is nothing of the sort. I half suspected it might not be when I saw the herbivore you've christened Tina. As far as we know, the argentinosaurus lived millions of years earlier than the famous T. rex and it would have been strange to find them together – though I admit anything's possible in this unique place. No, the predator we killed is a carnotaurus, a most unusual dinosaur that has got horns like a bull – hence its name. It was a fierce and vicious animal and I sincerely hope we don't meet any of its mates when we go walkabout tomorrow. I think from what I've seen so far the dinosaurs in this valley date from about ninety to a hundred million years ago, which puts them in the middle Cretaceous period. The valley was obviously cut off then from the further dinosaur development going on in the outside world and, though evolution must have carried on inside the valley, the dinosaurs haven't changed much. The conditions in the valley must have been pretty well perfect for the species we can see here.'

'So I won't see a T. rex after all?' said Lucy.

'Probably not,' Julian replied.

'And what about all those other dinosaurs you see in books and films; things like triceratops and stegosaurus?'

'Well, triceratops, like T. rex, lived millions of years later than the creatures you see here and, I suspect, never did appear in this valley. Stegosaurus, on the other hand lived millions of years earlier and was long extinct by the time this valley became isolated. We sometimes forget just how long the dinosaurs ruled the earth. Stegosaurus lived about one hundred and fifty million years ago – that's about seventy million years earlier than T. rex, which means that T. rex lived closer in time to you and me than it did to stegosaurus! Books and films about dinosaurs can be misleading because they sometimes give the impression that all the different dinosaurs lived at the same time.'

'Look!' said Lucy suddenly, as a flock of birds flew down. 'I thought nothing from outside could get into the crater,' she said, '– or have they been here as long as all the dinosaurs?'

Julian grinned as he turned to Lucy and gave her his binoculars. 'Look at your birds again.'

Puzzled, she took the glasses and looked intently at the flock then her jaw dropped in surprise. '. . . but they've got . . .'

'Yes,' said Julian, 'they've got four wings. A big one and a little one on each side – just like butterflies.'

'But surely,' said Richard, 'even with millions of years to play with, a new *limb* can't have appeared can it? Didn't evolution have to work on the basic structure that was already here in the animals of the valley when it became isolated?'

'Good point,' Julian replied. 'And I suspect when we get a closer look at these birds we'll find that the extra "wing" is a split-off from the main wing or some other such adaptation of the basic form. Even that must have taken ages to happen; it's easy to forget that if this valley has somehow, incredibly, existed intact and isolated for nearly a hundred million years, then life within it obviously didn't stand still. It has undergone its own private evolution. The creatures we are looking at now are the result of evolution in a unique world in which dinosaurs didn't get annihilated. They were obviously even more successful than anyone thought; they had, after all, been the dominant species on earth for nearly two hundred million years and when they didn't get wiped out in this valley they simply remained on top. The insects, birds and mammals here could only expand into the few developmental niches left to them by the dinosaurs – and they were very few indeed. Just think of our modern large herbivores for example: how could our cattle, antelopes, rhinos, hippos and elephants have the room to evolve as long as things like those existed?' He pointed to nearby Tina who, while they had been speaking, had casually consumed as much as a modern cow might eat in an entire day. 'And have you noticed,' he continued, 'that there are virtually no monkey-like mammals? That guy,' he pointed to a chameleon-like dinosaur the size of a large cat sitting in a fork of a nearby tree, 'is slower and more stupid than any monkey we know in our world.'

As he pointed Clio became alert, thinking they wanted a favour from the creature.

'*Shall I speak to the changekin?*' she asked. She added, somewhat doubtfully, '*He is very large.*'

Lucy laughed. '*No, fear not. We only speak of him and his kin.*' She told the others what had been said and Julian smiled.

'As I was saying,' he continued, 'he is much more stupid than a monkey but, because he existed, the small mammals living in this valley that might have developed into monkeys could never evolve further into his space. He was eating the food they wanted and he was bigger than them – so their modern descendants simply never happened here.' He paused, thoughtfully. 'And those, of course, include us. There are no large monkeys or primates here, so we're not going to find any hominids either, which is probably a very good thing. Quite how we would deal with a caveman, or even more worrying, a superhuman, I don't know, but fortunately we don't have to. In this little world the dinosaurs have continued to reign supreme; their absolute physical supremacy has effectively suppressed the development of any species with a superior intellect.'

Lucy and Richard both remained silent for a while, thinking over what Julian had said. He was absolutely right. The thought of meeting a human being who had evolved to a state superior to *Homo sapiens* was positively spooky – and meeting one who hadn't, who was still the equivalent of a Neanderthal or something similar, was equally problematic: should they regard such a creature as human, or potentially human, or as an animal? As it happened, it looked as if they didn't have to face a problem of this nature and on this slightly reassuring note they decided it was time to bed down for an uncomfortable and scary night in the plane. Before they settled down Julian produced some mosquito repellent for them to rub on and he sprayed the inside of the cabin for good measure.

'Mosquitoes were already alive and biting at this period in history,' he said with a rueful grin. 'We don't know what they think of Lucy and we don't want to catch some alien disease against which we have no protection whatsoever in our body defence systems.'

And with this unsettling thought in mind they all drifted off to sleep.

12

Clio gets a Head Start

The next day dawned bright and clear after a night of heavy rain. The first to wake was Clio. She scampered off in search of breakfast and by the time the others were awake there was already a pile of fruit and nuts waiting for them on the floor of the cabin. Richard was relieved to see that Tina's eye was now completely open and her wound looked satisfactory, with no signs of serious inflammation. Lucy chatted with her for a while and then turned to Richard.

'She hero-worships you, Dad. You'd better make the most of it because she must be the only thing on the planet that does!' She ducked as her father threw a fruit stone at her, and they all laughed as Clio jumped down to find it and give it back to him.

After breakfast, Clio went, on her own initiative, to collect more vegetation to strew over the nest and keep all the eggs well covered. Tina's giant feet were useless for any intricate task and trying to cover the eggs just using her jaws was a difficult and time-consuming job. She was immensely grateful to the monkey for her help; something that was later to prove very useful. While Clio was away gathering some stalks and leaves Michelle scampered over to the nearest tree, gouged a hole in the bark and stuck her nose into the cavity. Julian was intrigued.

'What's she doing?' he asked. 'Catching insects?'

'No,' said Lucy. 'I read all about marmosets after I got home last time. They are gumivores, which means they love to eat tree saps and gums. But she loves spiders and insects as well.' No sooner had she spoken than Clio returned with an armful of vegetation and Michelle immediately returned to the nest to snatch up the insects and creepy-crawlies disturbed by the larger monkey's activities. Suddenly Michelle gave a squeak and dashed back into the safety of the plane and Lucy's arms. Lucy looked round in alarm but Clio seemed unconcerned. Seeing Lucy's anxiety she explained: *There is much food here that the Little One loves. There are crawlipods, arachnopods, raspihops and creepipods, but she is very frightened of the buzzibane. He comes here only to catch the buzzikin and the squitohums but she fears his great size and speed.*

Lucy looked down to see a large and fierce-looking lizard crouching at the edge of the nest picking off insects. She tried to reassure Michelle but the marmoset decided that breakfast in the nest had definitely lost some of its attraction and climbed instead to her usual perch on Lucy's shoulder.

'The Little One is wise,' added Clio, suddenly, *'for look, another approaches! He looks like a Malevolent One but I have never seen his like before.'*

Lucy followed the monkey's gaze and saw that a snake had emerged from a burrow and was heading for the edge of the nest. But it was no ordinary snake; it half crawled and half slithered along the ground and to her astonishment she saw that it had two hind legs with which, even as she watched, it started scrabbling to gain a foothold on the twigs at the base of the nest. She called to Julian who took one look and then grabbed his camcorder before the chimera disappeared. After he had recorded his precious footage he turned to Lucy and Richard who had joined them at the hatch to see what they were peering at with such interest.

'This is absolutely incredible,' Julian said. 'I only read about this creature for the first time last month and now I'm actually looking at one. They found a fossilized specimen in Argentina recently and reported it in *Nature*. Its scientific name is *Najash rionegrina* and it's believed to be a 'missing link' between lizards and snakes. Snakes gradually lost their legs as they evolved from lizards and this creature is a sort of halfway house.' Even as he finished speaking there was a flurry of activity as a pterosaur the size of a buzzard swept out of the sky towards the nest. The lizard disappeared under the nest in a flash but the snake/lizard hybrid was too late and after a brief struggle its still-wriggling form was borne away in the grip of the predator's powerful claws. Julian, whose camcorder had already been in his hand, had managed to catch most of the episode on video and started eagerly reviewing the images.

'We've just *got* to escape from here,' he murmured, as he

gazed in fascination at the stunning sequence. 'Otherwise all this will be lost to science.'

Richard smiled and shook his head at Lucy.

'Yes, that's very dedicated of you, Julian, but I think there are two of us here who want to escape for somewhat less noble reasons than the advancement of science!'

Once the nest was fully bathed in sunshine, they set off towards the escarpment. A more incongruous party would have been difficult to imagine. Three humans from the Old World, a large and a small modern monkey from the New World, and a seventy-foot-high dinosaur trekking through a Cretaceous landscape. On their two-mile journey along the base of the escarpment, free at last from the all-pervading stench of compost, they passed sights that palaeontologists could only dream about: herds of massive herbivores browsing on giant ferns and trees; pterosaurs of every description gliding and fluttering through the trees and diving for prey into the lakes and marshes; bizarre mammals and birds completely unknown to science which were the product of the valley's internal evolution since its isolation unimaginable aeons ago; giant insects of every description and, most terrifying of all, predators of all shapes and sizes: at every turn they saw cat-sized individual dinosaurs or mammals roaming in search of prey, and in the distance they occasionally glimpsed herds of much larger hunters chasing prey remorselessly to the death in a manner similar to packs of wolves or wild dogs.

The scenery was stunning – a mixture of the completely unknown and the surprisingly familiar – the latter looking strangely out of place in this outlandish setting. Richard as a botanist was fascinated by the vegetation through which they passed. Trees such as fig, plane and conifer he instantly recognized, and the sight of a beautiful magnolia in full bloom reminded him of his own garden at home. Ferns and cycads flourished, and horsetail looked as healthy here as it did in his own garden – the worst weed in a Surrey suburb one hundred million years later. He was particularly interested in the variety and structure of the flowering plants they came across, for he knew that they and their dependent feeders and pollinators such as bees and butterflies had co-evolved during the Cretaceous period.

Guided by Tina they threaded their way along the base of the escarpment, stopping and hiding behind rocks or trees at the slightest intimation of danger by the dinosaur or the monkey. Julian commented on the fact that the monkey's eyesight seemed to be far superior to that of the dinosaur but that the dinosaur had an amazing sense of smell. Most of the smaller predators, even when in large packs, paid no attention to them in the presence of Tina. Even though a herbivore she was obviously a formidable opponent and they concentrated on easier prey. Without her presence, Lucy felt, it would have been a very different story and she doubted if their journey would ever have been possible. Julian and Richard were unarmed, but even guns would probably have been useless against a determined pack of carnivores.

At one point both Clio and Tina stopped and looked north towards the centre of the valley. The humans

'... the huge carcass collapsed before its ruthless foe.'

followed the direction of their gaze and saw a sight none of them would ever forget. A hundred yards away a titanic struggle was in progress. An immense predator almost fifty feet in height was attacking a long-necked herbivorous dinosaur on the shore of the swamp. The victim was part of a herd, the other members of which had scattered and now stood at a safe distance, watching impassively as their unfortunate relative was torn to pieces.

'It's a giganotosaurus,' whispered Julian to the others. There was no need for him to whisper – the anguished bellows and shrieks of the sauropod and the terrifying roars of the predator drowned out every noise in the vicinity – but he couldn't help obeying his instinct to do nothing that could possibly attract the attention of the awful creature.

'It's the big brother of T. rex,' he continued. 'It weighs about eight tons – against five for tyrannosaurus – and is probably the largest land predator that ever lived. It's the scariest of them all.'

The others needed no convincing as, before their very eyes, the monster ripped a chunk of flesh the size of Lucy from its victim's shoulder with its razor-like teeth. As the doomed creature stumbled, the predator bit through its neck with a single bite and even from the distance at which they stood the observers could feel the ground vibrate beneath them like a minor earthquake as the huge carcass collapsed before its ruthless foe.

Tina seemed unconcerned. She was utterly indifferent to the fate of the other sauropod and clearly knew that while the ferocious predator was otherwise occupied, she and her companions were not in danger. As Lucy looked at her in alarm she spoke some words of reassurance:

'The Implacable One is our greatest foe, but now he heeds us not.'

Julian had shot the entire scene on his camcorder and was beside himself with excitement at the scientific value of his recording.

'Can you imagine what that sequence is going to do to the world of science?' he said. 'The colours alone are mind-blowing.'

And it was true. Lucy remembered the dull grey skin of most of the dinosaurs she had seen in books and museums and looked once again at the stunning black and yellow stripes on the back of the giganotosaurus and its spotted underbelly; it looked for all the world like a giant lizard as it gorged on its prey, the brilliant purple, blotchy skin of which was now in bloody tatters. Even as she watched, scavenging dinosaurs were creeping to the edge of the kill, and pterosaurs and strange birds with tails were landing in preparation for a free meal.

The giganotosaurus ignored the smaller scavengers but, as one or two larger dinosaurs approached, he grunted savagely and lunged to keep them at their distance. Suddenly he stood erect and stiffened. Two other, smaller, giganotosaurs were approaching and as they drew near they separated to approach on different sides. Their giant quarry looked from one to the other and let out the most amazing roar that could possibly be imagined. Undeterred, the others drew closer.

Julian spoke. 'Much as I would love to stay and watch the match of the century, I think we should move on while they're all occupied.' He looked at the others enquiringly as he somewhat reluctantly put his camcorder away and zipped up the case. 'This has got to be our best time to go.'

They all agreed, and Lucy looked up to instruct their giant guide. A moment later they were once again on the move.

As they walked they discussed the fact that the dinosaurs knew the common tongue but had never heard of Lucy.

'If you think about it,' said Richard, 'it makes perfect sense. The common tongue is obviously incredibly old and existed before this valley became isolated. The legend of the Promised One, on the other hand, must have arisen at some time during the age of the mammals, long after the dinosaurs had become extinct in the outside world. The animals trapped in this valley would never have got to know about her. I'm surprised that Grandpa didn't think of that when we discussed it.'

'Well, I think it's mean to blame him when he's not here to defend himself,' interrupted Lucy.

'Pax!' said Richard, laughing. 'I might have known better than to criticize your precious Grandpa in your hearing.'

'And while we're on the subject,' said Lucy, 'I must tell you something really fascinating. Talking to the dinosaur reminded me of what Grandpa told me about speaking to the animals. He said that when they 'speak' I am really hearing their thoughts which my brain then turns into my own words. Tina obviously thinks the plane is a kind of giant pterodactyl so I hear her say *Great pterokin*; in the other valley the animals think it's a loud bird so I hear them say *thunderquill*. I can't wait to tell Grandpa – he'll be so pleased he's right.'

As they moved out of some trees into a small glade they came across two small dinosaurs with parrot-like beaks, pecking at some nuts on the ground. There was a primitive nest nearby, the eggs partially covered with sticks and ferns.

Suddenly Tina stopped and raised her head. As they watched, the small dinosaurs stood erect on their hind legs, sniffed the air, and then scampered towards a large crevice in the rocks at the base of the cliff.

'*Did we frighten them?*' asked Lucy looking up at Tina. It was an eerie sensation, for the dinosaur's head was in front of her but her colossal body was more than forty feet behind. The great dinosaur was also sniffing the air.

'*It is not you they fear, but great danger that comes hither. I am safe because of my great size but you must hide where the little peckosaurs have hidden. Those who come cannot enter there. You must make haste!*' Her voice became urgent and Clio and Michelle, who had been listening, were already scampering after the small dinosaurs. Lucy lost no time.

'Run!' she shouted to the others, and fled after Clio. She squeezed through the crack without a problem but the men only just managed to fit. As Julian twisted sideways to force himself through he saw a herd of dinosaurs streaming into the glade pursuing a smaller creature that was clearly exhausted and terrified. The pursuers were about three metres long, running on their hind legs like giant birds, with sharp teeth and large claws and Julian immediately recognized them as being similar to dromaeosaurs; ferocious, fast, meat-eating predators. He hurriedly squeezed out of sight through the gap as he heard the screams, followed by rending and crunching noises, that signalled the end of the hapless victim.

He found himself in a small enclosed space among the rocks at the back of which the cliff face soared into the sky.

'Phew, that was a close one!' he said to Richard as he sat down next to him on a rock. Lucy looked across to the parrot-beaked dinosaurs huddled fearfully together in the opposite corner of the little den. They gazed in astonishment as she began to speak:

'*Fear not little ones,*' she said. '*We intend you no harm. We seek sanctuary, as ye do, from those that pursue us. The Prodigious One is our friend and she will guard your nest.*' She paused at the sounds of frantic scrabbling and blood-curdling snarls from the entrance to their refuge.

'*Are we safe in this place?*' she asked anxiously.

'*Yes,*' said the male, to her great relief. '*The Relentless Ones roam hither and thither in search of prey, but they cannot enter herein. Only once,*' he continued, with more than a hint of pride, '*did one of their young manage to squeeze in, and I chased him out again.*'

Lucy turned to the others. 'They say that those horrid bounding things can't get in. I've told them we won't hurt them and that Tina will guard their nest – so they think we're OK. What on earth are they, Julian?'

Julian managed to crack a nervous smile. 'Which ones, these or the hunters?'

'These – tell me about the others next.'

'Well, these are very interesting. Can you ask one to come over?'

Lucy looked a little uncertain but did so and soon the larger of the two came over cautiously and sat at Julian's feet.

Julian looked intently at the creature. After a moment it glanced nervously at Lucy and then seemed to relax.

'These are the same species as the creature I found in the other valley which had fallen over the cliff. I was never really able to really examine that one because, if you remember, a scavenger pinched it before I had the chance.' Richard and Lucy nodded. 'In fact, the place where we cast the rope yesterday I recognized as being the spot where we found it. That can't be far from here on the other side of the escarpment.' He paused. 'Good Lord!' he breathed, 'the one we found must almost certainly have come from this colony. A dead cousin of these little creatures in front of us is the reason we are all here in the first place.' It was an extraordinary thought and they all fell silent for a moment, pondering over the curious turns of fate that had brought them to be sitting here.

Julian examined the animal with renewed interest, then continued: 'Helen and I thought then that it was a psittacosaurus because of its parrot's beak but I was puzzled because the only fossils so far found of that species have been in Asia. I think this is actually a bit different; it's obviously in the same group of dinosaurs – they're called ceratopsians or "horned lizards" – but, as you can see, this one has got a little frill round its head.' He pointed and they all peered at it.

'I think it is a different species from psittacosaurs and is a forerunner of a bigger, frilled dinosaur that we do know lived in South America – the notoceratops.'

'Well, if we ever get out of here, you can call it *Notoceratops fossfinderi*,' said Richard as Julian took photographs and measurements of the little dinosaur while Lucy continued to reassure it.

'This is becoming a familiar theme,' he continued bitterly, 'our making incredible scientific discoveries and then not being able to tell anyone about them!'

'What were the things we escaped from?' said Lucy to change the subject. She hated seeing her father looking so gloomy.

'Well, they're interesting too – do you remember *Jurassic Park*?'

'Who could forget?' she said, nodding vigorously.

'Well these creatures are like the animals they called velociraptors in the film. The things chasing us belong to a different and earlier genus than so-called velociraptors, but are very similar in appearance and behaviour. They are also, fortunately, much larger, otherwise we wouldn't be here now. Some of the *Jurassic Park* animals would have had no trouble getting through that gap.' He looked back at the crevice. 'So we owe a lot to the knowledge and experience of our newly described specimens of *Notoceratops fossfinderi* –' he smiled at his own egotism. 'It seems to have become fashionable in popular literature,' he added, 'to call predatory dinosaurs "raptors", but proper zoologists still reserve this term for predatory birds such as hawks and eagles.'

Suddenly the two little dinosaurs came hurrying over to Lucy and tried to hide behind her feet. She looked round in alarm and then saw a movement at the base of the rocks opposite where one of the snake/lizard creatures they had seen earlier was emerging from a gap. Julian saw it as well and, picking up a large piece of broken rock, got up and moved towards it. As it saw him it returned immediately into its crevice and they all relaxed.

'As you know, I don't normally go round thumping animals with rocks,' he said, 'but the last thing any of us needs at this stage is to get bitten by a snake. I've no idea whether it's poisonous or not, but it wasn't worth taking a chance on.' The others nodded vigorously in agreement.

'The malevopod fears thy kinsman will smite him,' said the female dinosaur, the first time she had spoken. *'I am glad, for he sometimes steals my eggs and I cannot stop him since his bite brings doom to all small creatures.'*

As she spoke, Clio, who had been peering through the rock gap, turned and said something to Lucy.

'It looks as if the coast is clear,' said Lucy, and just at that moment she heard Tina, also calling to say that all was safe. She trusted the judgement of the monkey and the dinosaur implicitly and without further ado she scrambled through the gap and back out into the glade.

As they moved on it became apparent that the broken rock formation that had provided a safe haven for them was simply one end of a massive slippage from the cliff face. And it was now clear that this was indeed the same place on the other side of which they had secured their rope. It was the only major fault visible in the entire central range of hills. Julian was almost certainly correct in his conclusion about the little dinosaur he had found on his previous visit being from the same colony as their recent companions. At the base of the cliff various herbivores were wandering about foraging among the fallen rocks. There was no obvious vegetation and it was not clear what the animals were looking for.

Julian looked at the cliff formation with a geologist's eye. The cliff face was still a sheer precipice up to a height of about eighty feet where there was a ledge. Above this major ledge a succession of smaller ledges led to the very top of the escarpment which, at this point, was about two hundred feet above them. The ledges must have been formed by successive slides of rock because of a geological fault at this point in the cliff. If the process continued for another few thousand years the valleys, which had been isolated from each other for countless millions of years, would be separate no longer.

He turned to the others who were looking at the cliff with mounting excitement.

'This is the place,' he said simply, and as they nodded in agreement he continued:

'We've just got to get Clio up the first eighty feet.'

'Just . . .' said Richard, laughing, and Lucy was relieved to see him cheerful again. 'Just to get up a sheer face as high as a six-storey building with no equipment – a piece of cake.'

But Lucy was busy listening to Tina.

'Many, great and small, come to this place to eat the hard ones,' said the dinosaur. Lucy looked more closely at the various animals among the rocks and, to her astonishment, saw that the browsing herbivores were not seeking out ferns and greenery but were actually swallowing stones and small rocks.

'The best ones only I and my kin can reach,' Tina continued and Lucy followed the dinosaur's gaze to the first ledge above the smooth cliff face. It was covered in a scree of loose rocks and stones.

'But why do you eat rocks?' asked Lucy. *'Is it their taste?'* She had read how the game in Africa concentrated on salt-licks to obtain the minerals they lacked in their diet and wondered if the dinosaurs did the same.

'I know not why,' replied Tina. *'The hard ones do not taste pleasant like the trees, but I am driven to swallow them. I am told my kin have done this since time immemorial and will always do so.'*

Lucy turned back to the others, eyes sparkling. 'You're not going to believe this but the animals come here to eat stones and rocks. And guess where Tina gets the best ones?' As she spoke, Tina put her forefeet on the mound of fallen rocks, and stretching her enormous neck to the utmost she could just reach the first ledge above the smooth cliff face. 'All Clio has to do is climb up Tina's neck and then she can get to the top. But I still don't know why Tina eats the stones. I asked her if they were salty but she didn't really understand.'

'It's gastroliths!' exclaimed Julian.

'Gastro what?' asked Lucy.

'Gastroliths. They're gizzard or stomach stones. Many herbivorous animals swallow stones which help to grind up the food in their stomach. Modern hens eat grit for this purpose and stones up to ten centimetres long are found in ostrich stomachs. Other modern animals such as crocodiles and sea-lions seem to use them as a kind of ballast. Zoologists think that the weight of the stones helps crocs to sink more easily under the water. Palaeontologists have found stones several kilograms in weight in the fossils of dinosaurs. They think that, as the dinosaurs eat massive amounts of fibrous vegetation but don't have proper grinding teeth, they need the stones to digest their food. Over time the stones are worn smooth in the stomach by their constant grinding, and they often come from rock strata miles away which helps in working out the migration patterns of the animals.'

He looked to see if Lucy was interested but she was already talking to Clio and Tina. He looked at Richard who shrugged his shoulders and smiled. 'I found it interesting, even if nobody else did, Julian.'

Lucy turned back to them. 'Sorry, what were you saying, Julian? Oh yes, stomach stones; fascinating. Now, can you write a note to send back with Clio to the others?'

Julian obediently flipped his scientific notebook open to a fresh page. After they had agreed on the contents of the note Julian taped it firmly to a Velcro strap from his rucksack which Lucy then fixed gently round Clio's neck before looking up to Tina.

'The arborikin who helped thee with thy nest now goes on a quest over the great rock. Canst thou lift her up on high?'

Tina didn't answer. She simply lowered her great head almost to the ground and Clio sprang nimbly onto it, carefully avoiding the dreadful gash on the dinosaur's face. As the monkey clung on, her prehensile tail now wrapped firmly around the top of Tina's neck, the dinosaur slowly extended her immense length against the side of the cliff and stretched her neck up to the ledge. Clio bounded onto the ledge and then, with an alacrity that amazed the excited onlookers, romped effortlessly from ledge to ledge up the precipitous face of the cliff. She reached the top in a couple of minutes, stood erect to look around, sniffed the air, and set off to the west along the high ridge. Soon she was lost to view among the jagged peaks and crags along the crest.

The three looked at each other with relief.

'What an achievement,' said Julian. He put his arm round Lucy and hugged her. 'Thank God you thought of bringing the monkey – it looks as if you've saved our lives once again!'

Lucy blushed but was saved from any further embarrassment by Tina who leaned down to attract her attention.

'The little Agile One is safely gone but there is always danger near this place. The Merciless Ones know that the Timid Ones come here to eat the hard food and they often attack us. You must return to the safe place where you sought refuge before.'

Lucy explained this to the others and they started to move back towards their small rocky sanctuary. As they did so Lucy stopped and said something else to Tina, then joined the others as the dinosaur moved to some nearby trees. When they had sat down in their refuge Richard asked Lucy what she had said. Before answering she grinned and pointed. To Richard's astonishment he saw the dinosaur returning with an enormous mouthful of fruit-laden foliage which she lowered into their little retreat, looking for all the world like a crane manoeuvring materials into a building site.

'We don't know how long we might have to wait here till Clio gets back with some news. We've got water . . .' she gestured to the rivulets running down the cliff face and across the ground at their feet . . . 'but without Clio we can't easily get food. As we don't know what's safe to eat I've asked Tina only to get us the same things that Clio brought.'

The men exchanged amused glances at her organization and foresight, then set to work stripping the branches. The parrot-like dinosaurs, attracted by the smell of delicacies they could never normally reach, reappeared through the entrance fissure and Lucy gave them some fruit. She sat with one dinosaur on either side, their forefeet resting on her lap, and Michelle leaning forward from her shoulder perch to share in the feast. Julian got out his camcorder and filmed her giving succulent morsels in turn to the three eager little creatures.

'When we get back,' he said to Richard, who was watching the little scene with a disbelieving smile, 'we're going to make the most fascinating nature film of all time!'

13
Biggles Blunders into a Bog

The night before the dinosaur hunters arrived in the Valley of the Mighty Ones the six villains had been discussing the progress of their project to create new invisibility suits from the special ore in the crater. Chopper, desperately eager to get his hands on a suit he could work himself, had suggested to the professor that he should tell the group how many suits he had now made and demonstrate how to use one. He pointed out that it was important to maintain enthusiasm in the team and reassure them that a fortune was now just round the corner. Somewhat reluctantly, Luke had agreed – he could hardly refuse – and he had explained to the men that he had completed two suits and helmets, complete with portable energizers. He had now mastered the technology and could make a new suit every couple of days. He had then shown Chopper how to don one of the suits and energize it and the villains had been truly amazed to see their leader disappear into thin air before their very eyes. The meeting had been a great success and all had gone to bed dreaming of the riches that would soon be within their evil grasp;

once four more suits were made they would each be in possession of a unique criminal tool.

The next day the professor sat after lunch in the shade of a tree sipping coffee and mulling over his situation. He knew that Chopper was now in a position to kill him if he chose to do so. He knew how to work the suit and, with the professor out of the way, would have access to all his research data. That meant that, should he ever need more suits, he could hire, blackmail or intimidate some other scientist into creating them. That scientist would then undoubtedly mysteriously disappear – probably into the foundations of a new motorway – never to be seen or heard of again.

As it happened, the professor was also in a position to dispense with Chopper. It was now just a question of who got in first. He had never had any intention of making six suits, one for everyone: all he had needed was to ascertain the source of the ore and refine the technique for turning it into a robe. That he had done and all the scientific information he needed was now recorded on a single CD. At any time from now on, and the sooner the better, Chopper and his gang could meet with an unfortunate and tragic accident and Biggles and Luke would fly back to a fortune. It was important that the pilot didn't suspect that Luke was in any way involved in the deaths of the other villains. Luke would dispose of him once they were safely back in civilization.

As he sat planning the details for the demise of the gang the professor looked across the valley and saw, in the far distance, a giant ground sloth stripping a tree. He had been aware from his first day in the crater that there were special animals here and had discussed it with Biggles. They had surmised, correctly, that they were in a unique environment and their observations only strengthened the professor's conviction that this was probably the only place on earth where photogyraspar might be found; surely otherwise, in the countless geological surveys for oil and precious minerals and all the archaeological diggings that had taken place over the years, all over the world, somebody, somewhere, would have come across this extraordinary crystal. Chopper and his gang had never noticed the unusual fauna. They had no interest whatsoever in anything other than making money from criminal activities and provided the animals kept their distance, as they did, they completely ignored them. Luke decided that when he killed the others he would avoid arousing Biggles's suspicions by making it look as though their deaths had been due to an unexpected attack by the unusual animals. His musings were interrupted by a distant drone. At first he thought it was a swarm of bees but he suddenly realized that it was an aero engine. At the same instant Chopper leapt out of his camp chair and gazed into the distance, scanning the horizon above the crater rim. Not for nothing was he a leader; he went straight into action shouting commands:

'It's a plane. Could be cops. Biggles, you hide the plane in the trees – quickly before they see it. Prof, go to the lab and put on your suit – could be useful. Sam, switch off the generator – they'll hear the humming. Bert and Crack – take guns, binoculars, food and water and go and hide as far as possible – over at that cliff.' He pointed to the distant central escarpment. 'They may search this whole area and if there's trouble we'll need you to come back later and rescue us.' Chopper himself cleared away the camp chairs, then hurried to get binoculars and watch the incoming plane.

Biggles climbed into his plane and started the engine as the others did Chopper's bidding. He taxied into the bush, carefully choosing a route that avoided shrubs and trees that were large enough to damage the wings.

The best cover seemed to be near the crater wall and he headed in that direction, the thickening undergrowth obscuring his view of the ground. Suddenly he felt the plane lurch forward and to his horror he saw that it had run over the edge of a steep gully, until then completely invisible from the cockpit. He shut down the motor but it was too late. The plane plunged down the steep rocky slope and with a final lurch ended up in a marsh with the wings resting on the surface of the bog and the nose facing the cliff.

He scrambled along the wing, jumped on to dry ground then turned to review the situation. The full horror of what had happened began to dawn on him. Although the engine was just clear of the water there was no way he could use the plane's own power to get it out; it was facing the cliff and stuck firmly in the marsh. It would have to be hauled backwards from the marsh and back up the steep rocky slope before it could be turned round, and that would take a large tractor or a crane. They were stranded. As he stumbled back with leaden feet to confess to Chopper he had a sickening thought. Up until now the only reason for his continued existence was the fact that Chopper needed him to fly the plane back to civilization. If that reason no longer existed, then Chopper would see no particular reason why the pilot should have a share in their criminal profits, assuming they were eventually rescued. He was now dispensable and the thought struck fear into his heart.

Eventually he reached Chopper who had now been rejoined by Sam. The new plane was parked about two hundred yards away. Chopper and Sam were lying hidden from view behind an outcrop of rock, scrutinizing the scene before them through binoculars.

There were six newcomers and, Sam maintained, three or four monkeys, but Chopper said he had drunk too much beer with his lunch. For the past half-hour they had been busy unloading supplies and were now engaged in erecting two large tents. They were still unaware of the fact that the valley was already occupied. The collection of huts comprising the villains' camp nestled among the trees at the edge of the open plain. This not only meant that they were shaded from the equatorial sun but that they were invisible from the air and relatively inconspicuous even from the ground. Chopper had not wanted to risk the camp being visible to a passing plane or a police search, however unlikely that eventuality might be in this remote area.

As he approached the others Biggles coughed nervously and Chopper and Sam turned round.

'Get down,' Chopper hissed – then his brow darkened as he saw the pilot's face. 'What's up?'

The pilot explained and, as he had feared, Chopper went totally berserk.

'Get back there,' he eventually hissed, 'and think of some way of getting the bloody plane out. How can you possibly screw everything up when we're just on the point of getting out and,' he jerked a thumb back to the new plane, 'we've got this lot to deal with.'

The pilot mumbled an apology and escaped back to the gully. There was nothing he could do, but at least he was out of Chopper's range.

In his laboratory Luke watched events carefully through the window. He had seen the pilot return and observed Chopper's reaction to whatever it was that the pilot had told him. He decided that he had to find out what was going on. He was already in his invisibility robe as Chopper had suggested – a precaution in case the police had arrived – and now he slipped out of the cabin and walked silently over to where Chopper and Sam lay in hiding.

'. . . so I've sent Biggles back to check,' Chopper was saying as Luke crept up and stood behind him, 'but it sounds as if the plane is stuck in a bog – he says it would take fifty men to pull it out. That makes it all the more important to see what these characters are up to – they don't look like cops and we're going to need their plane to get out of here.'

'It could actually be better than we thought,' said Sam as they both watched the new arrivals unpacking their plane. 'Cos if we use their pilot to get out we can dispose of Biggles along with all the rest. Then there'll just be the two of us to share the proceeds. Have we everything we need?'

'Yep, the prof keeps the robes and a back-up data disk in a tin box in the lab. We now know how to use the suits so we just pick everything up when we leave.'

As they watched, three of the party under scrutiny got back into the plane and the engine started up.

'What the hell?' said Sam. He started to get up, but Chopper pulled him down.

'Don't let them see you, you fool. Wherever they're going they'll have to come back for the others. Meanwhile let's turn on the charm.' His mind was working rapidly. 'We'll pretend to be a secret government scientific expedition. They can't check up on us as no radios seem to work in this place. Where's the prof?' He looked round. 'We need him as our scientific front man.'

'You sent him back to the lab,' said Sam. 'I'll get him.' He waited until the plane had disappeared towards the central escarpment and then started to get up. Luke was already hurrying to beat him back to the laboratory, his mind racing. What he had just overheard meant that he had to dispose of Chopper and his gang as soon as possible – before they disposed of him. He would now have to murder Biggles at the same time; the pilot was no longer of any use to him with the plane being out of action. The more he thought about it the more he saw that his best plan was to befriend the new arrivals and leave in their plane; he could deal with them later once he was out of this wretched place. He saw Sam approaching and was about to remove his invisibility robe when he remembered, just in time, that he was meant to have it on.

Sam appeared in the doorway.

'Hi, prof,' he said, looking round, 'where are you?'

'I'm here,' said a disembodied voice from the side of the cabin.

'My God, that thing really is incredible,' said Sam, awestruck yet again by the effectiveness of the technology. 'Anyway, time to become visible again and meet the new arrivals. Chopper wants you to pretend to be a senior government scientist, here with your team on a secret mission.'

They joined Chopper just as Biggles reappeared and confirmed that the plane was irretrievably stuck. It didn't improve Chopper's humour but it confirmed his resolve to steal the other plane. He explained to the pilot his plan about their being government scientists and the four of them then started to make their way over to the tents that Helen, Clare and Clive had erected half a mile away.

Meanwhile Barker and Shortshanks were cautiously emerging from the bushes into which they had flung themselves on hearing the plane start up again and take off. They were still a long way from the escarpment where the plane was now flying up and down and Barker watched it with a scowl.

'It's the ******* cops,' he swore. 'They're really

searching the place. We'll have to wait here a bit till they shove off somewhere else – and when we get to them hills we'll have to find a cave or something. Can't risk being out in the open with that lot snooping around.'

Back at the camp, Queenie tugged at Clare's shorts and pointed to the oncoming figures of Chopper and his group; she then disappeared quietly into the bush. Clare and the others gazed in astonishment and some apprehension at the sight of the four strangers approaching them in this, supposedly isolated, lost world.

'Hi there,' called Chopper cheerfully, exuding bonhomie. He attempted a jovial smile but only succeeded in looking as if he had severe toothache. 'Welcome to our crater.' He introduced himself and his companions and Helen did the same. As she shook hands with the pilot she suddenly paused and her brow furrowed. Then she remembered where she had seen him before.

'Do you come here often?' she said with a smile.

The pilot looked puzzled for a moment, then he remembered who she was. She had looked very different then: somewhat unkempt, with long, tangled hair, unwashed, and ill with an infected leg. He was very disconcerted to have been recognized, but then told himself that there was no reason whatsoever why Helen should know he had been in jail. As far as she was concerned this could be a routine, legitimate flying mission. He managed a fake smile.

'Oh, hello again. What a coincidence!' he said. 'My second job involving this crater. Getting quite an expert at it.' Seeing the bewildered expressions on the faces of his companions he explained that the rescue of Helen and Julian had been the purpose of his original visit to the crater.

When he had finished, Chopper turned back to the others.

'Well,' he said, 'what a coincidence, as Biggles says. And I suppose you're all wondering what we're doing here?'

They nodded. He dropped his voice conspiratorially as though they were surrounded by spooks and microphones.

'The distinguished professor here –' he nodded deferentially towards Luke – 'is conducting a scientific experiment for the government. His laboratory is based here because this area is believed to be completely uninhabited and the research has to take place under conditions of absolute secrecy. Under the circumstances we obviously can't ask you to leave, but I must request that none of you comes near our camp and that no photographs are taken in the immediate locality.'

'And who are you?' asked Helen.

'Ah, you guessed I wasn't a scientist,' said Chopper.

'I did suspect that you weren't,' said Helen, trying to keep a straight face and avoiding looking at Clare and Clive.

'I'm here with a small team of government . . . experts, let's call them, to make sure that the prof isn't disturbed by unwanted visitors – not people like you, of course,' he added hastily, 'but there are foreign powers who would very much like to know what is going on here.'

As he was speaking, Chopper noticed the pile of climbing gear and rope ladders and the horrifying thought struck him that there might be others who were interested in the same rocks as the professor. His eyes narrowed as he continued.

'Well, that's us. Sorry I can't be more specific but I'm sure you get the picture.' He looked straight at Helen and tried to smile again. As usual the effect was to produce a leer that disconcerted rather than reassured. 'What about you guys? There must be something very special here for you to pay a return visit – and I see,' he gestured to the equipment behind Clive, 'that you've come prepared to do some climbing.'

'We're palaeontologists,' said Helen. She didn't explain, much to Clive and Clare's amusement.

'Ah yes,' said Chopper. 'Pal . . . palli . . .' The professor stepped in to save him.

'Fossil hunters,' he said in his most charming voice. 'How fascinating – and I presume you found good pickings here on your previous visit?'

'Very,' said Helen, 'and we've returned with some more refined equipment this time. We're hoping to find some Cretaceous deposits here – that's the period I specialize in. We'll probably be focusing on the escarpment –' she pointed to the central cliff in the distance – 'so we won't have any reason to disturb your privacy.'

While she was speaking Queenie had wandered up.

'Interesting pets you've got,' said Chopper putting his hand out to her. Queenie looked at Helen who nodded imperceptibly and the monkey snarled and revealed a formidable set of sharp white teeth. Chopper snatched his hand away in surprise. 'Bit touchy, isn't he,' he snapped.

'It's a she, and she's cautious of strangers. We've got two with us here at the moment and I feel safer with them than a couple of Alsatians.' She somehow felt there was no harm in Chopper knowing that it would be impossible for anyone to approach their tents unobserved.

They chatted for a few more minutes and then the villains returned to their camp. After they had gone Clare turned to the others. She made a grimace.

'What rotten luck,' she said. 'Of all places to pick, they're here in our precious valley. The only good thing is that at least they're on official government business and not here to start illegal mining or something.'

'True,' said Clive, 'but when you ask yourself what it is that governments do in secret, the answer isn't any more reassuring.'

'Like what?' asked Clare.

'Like things to do with defence, oil, gold, uranium. You name it. And that could mean all kinds of things, none of which would be very good for the crater; a new defence satellite tracking station, a giant new telescope drilling for oil or minerals, a missile silo, a new nerve gas to try out on the animals – the list goes on for ever. Our best hope is that they are just using it as a remote place to conduct some secret research that is going to be applied elsewhere and doesn't have any bad implications for the crater.'

Clare looked depressed and turned to Helen who was looking pensive.

'What do you think?' she asked.

'It's good and it's bad,' she replied. 'While you've been talking I've recalled a conversation José had with Julian over dinner last week. They were talking about back-up rescue plans and I was only half listening, but I'm pretty sure that José said the pilot who rescued us was in jail.'

'But,' said Clive, 'he can't be – we just met him, didn't we?'

'Exactly,' agreed Helen. 'That means he's just been released or has escaped. Either way it is quite impossible that he could have any involvement whatsoever with a top-secret government project. They would have exhaustive checking and vetting procedures for such a crucial member of the support team.'

'So that means . . .' began Clive.

'It means,' Clare interrupted, 'that they're not going to do any of those horrid experimental government things you just mentioned, but they're probably a bunch of crooks up to no good.'

'Exactly,' said Helen, 'that's what I meant when I said it's good and it's bad. Just what they're up to is anyone's guess. I do think the professor is genuinely a distinguished scientist – I've met a few in my career as you know, and there is something about him that fits the mould. What on earth he's doing here though, with a bunch of thugs and a jail-bird, is a mystery. What could they possibly find to attract them in a remote and dangerous crater?'

'I'd forgotten it was dangerous,' said Clare, a puzzled look on her face, 'but now you mention it, Helen, I thought you and Julian had a terrible time here because of all the ferocious animals. I haven't seen one and why on earth haven't they attacked the crooks?'

'I suppose they might have shot them,' said Clive. 'That Chopper thug and his minders would shoot anything on sight. But I agree, it's odd they didn't mention it – and they didn't warn us, come to that; they were pretending to be as nice as possible.'

'Well, they wouldn't need to warn us,' said Helen, 'because they knew we'd been here before. But your question, Clare, is very interesting and I think I know the answer.'

She then told them that, on their previous visit, Lucy and Richard had left her and Julian behind in the crater because of her bad foot and then arranged for a plane to rescue them later.

'Before Lucy left, however,' she explained, 'she instructed the animals to help us and protect us. She also told them – and this, I think, is crucial to what we are now discussing – that if ever another plane came they were to make themselves scarce.'

'Why?' asked Clive.

'Because of the unique animals here. We knew a pilot would be coming to rescue us – the pilot you've just met as it happens – and we wanted to ensure that he didn't see any bizarre animals that would alert him to the fact that this was a special place. When he came, the animals disappeared, as instructed, and everything worked as planned. The really interesting thing,' she continued, 'is that I think the animals remembered her instructions and when the so-called government plane arrived,' she nodded to the other camp, 'the animals moved away. They probably even think,' she speculated, 'that these people are somehow *connected* to Lucy – as we were – so they have effectively been under her protection all the time they've been here.'

'Wow,' said Clive, 'that must be the explanation. They don't know how lucky they are!'

' . . . and, annoyingly, they never will,' said Clare, casting a baleful look towards their camp. 'They're the last people on earth we'd let into our secret.'

Helen followed Clare's gaze. 'I'd really love to know what they've got over there,' she mused. 'They obviously don't want us anywhere near the place.'

'Well, I'd be happy if they just leave us well alone,' said Clare, 'and I'll feel a lot happier when the others are back. Talking of which,' she said looking with a frown at the sun, rapidly getting lower in the sky, 'shouldn't they be back by now?'

They all looked north to the central escarpment. The plane, which had still been buzzing to and fro along the range at the start of their conversation with Chopper, was nowhere to be seen.

'Maybe they've seen somewhere to land in the other valley and are stealing a march on us,' said Clive.

'Maybe,' said Helen doubtfully, but none of them really thought it likely and as dusk fell they grew progressively more worried. Eventually Clare spoke.

'Don't you think,' she said hesitantly, 'that we should tell them what's happened?' She nodded to the other camp. 'And ask for their help? They must have a plane.'

Helen thought hard.

'I know it's awful not to do anything,' she said at length, 'but I think we should wait until tomorrow before we decide anything. It will be dark in a few minutes – the sun sets very quickly on the equator – so they can't use their plane anyway and now we're fairly certain that they're lying to us my instinct is not to reveal to them that we are helpless and vulnerable.'

And on this depressing note they went to bed, to spend a night frantic with worry about their loved ones.

14
A Helping Hoof from a Hosenose

In the morning Clare was up at dawn. She had been thinking overnight and had a plan to share with the others. As they ate breakfast in the pink morning light she suggested that she and Clive went to the escarpment with the climbing equipment and rope ladders and looked to see if the lost group had managed to fix a rope onto the cliff before they went missing.

'It's a pity I can't speak to Sophie,' she said, 'because she could help enormously, but she may twig we're looking for something and help anyway. You should stay here, Helen – if you agree,' she added somewhat apologetically, thinking she was sounding rather bossy, 'in case the others try to contact us through the animals, and Queenie should stay with you. I'll take a pencil and paper and send a message back with Sophie if there's any news and you can send a message to us using Queenie if you have any news. Lucy's told them to do whatever they think we want, and they're pretty quick on the uptake.'

'You sound just like your sister,' said Helen, laughing, 'but everything you say makes good sense and we should get on with it as soon as possible. Oh – and don't forget to take your survival packs.' When planning the expedition Helen had insisted that each member of the team should be equipped with a rucksack with a knife, torch, spare batteries, water, iron rations, anti-malarial drugs, antibiotics and other survival items, and she now gave a pack each to Clare and Clive.

The most problematic items were the rope ladders. Richard had realized that to get into the other valley they would have to climb up and over a cliff that was at least two hundred feet high and so they had brought sixteen 25-foot ladders, enough when fixed together to see the non-mountaineers up the escarpment and down the other side. Each ladder weighed about 12 pounds, however and, though Clive was big and strong, he had his other climbing gear to carry – boots, ropes and pitons as well as his survival kit. He had always envisaged having Richard as his companion to assist him with the ladders. He immediately decided to take only half the ladders, a total of two hundred feet when tied together. The same ladder would have to be pulled up when they got to the top and used to get them down the other side. Even so, the load was going to be considerable.

'Do you think you can carry some of these?' he said to Clare, showing her the packs.

'I'll have to,' she said simply.

Helen helped them both to load up and then bade them a somewhat tearful farewell. As she trudged into the bush and looked at the distant escarpment Clare began to regret her bravado; her pack seemed to be growing heavier by the moment and she was wondering just how far she could manage to go without ditching something. At that moment Sophie, who had scampered off ahead with Kai on her back, returned accompanied by one of the strangest animals Clare and Clive had ever seen. It was a female, the size of a small camel with a body like a horse, a long neck and a long nose like a shortened elephant's trunk. The macrauchenia knelt in front of the travellers. Her intention was unmistakable and the overburdened pair needed no further persuasion. They carefully strapped most of their equipment onto their willing beast of burden and then set off at twice their previous speed towards the cliff, which looked more formidable and menacing with every step they took.

Suddenly the macrauchenia stopped and sniffed the air, her head raised, flanks trembling and muscles taut, ready to spring into action. Clare followed her gaze and at first could see nothing; then, to her horror she saw a sabre-toothed cat prowling towards them through the sparse bush. She was followed at a distance by two small cubs. As Clare watched the animal stopped, and dropped low to the ground in an unmistakable stalking stance, her actions immediately copied by her young. She heard an anguished snort from the macrauchenia and glanced at the terrified creature. She was obviously torn between her duty to the Promised One and her natural instincts which were telling her to flee for her life. Sophie sprang in front of Clare and started to approach the fearful predator. Clare saw that the brave monkey was trembling with fear and her tail was coiled forward round the baby on her back.

'*Greetings, O thee of the mighty fangs,*' Sophie said in the common tongue. '*The gentle one with the three toes serves the sister of the Promised One. See, she flees not from thee.*'

'*The nosekin shall be spared this day,*' the smilodon replied, '*and my daughters shall one day tell their own daughters of the honour of this meeting.*' She turned to speak to her cubs who then bounded up like playful kittens to an astonished and somewhat apprehensive Clare, and started licking her and tugging at the laces of her trainers. She saw that Sophie and the macrauchenia were relaxed and guessed, correctly, that the mother cat would not harm them and was now gaining tribal kudos for her cubs. After stroking and cuddling the little creatures she reluctantly tore herself away and the party continued its trek towards the looming crags of the central range.

They crossed the central river using as a bridge the same fallen tree that Clive's mother and father had used on their journey to the escarpment eighteen months earlier, and reached the cliff just before midday. Sophie went to fetch them fresh fruit and they drank crystal-clear water from a rivulet flowing down the cliff face. As luck would have it the central escarpment on their left, the west, curved gently round to the south so they had a clear view for a considerable distance. Scanning it with his binoculars Clive could see no rope so decided that, if the flying team had been successful in securing a rope to the escarpment, it must be to their right where the cliff face was hidden from view at several points.

Soon Sophie returned with the food and they sat in the shade of a tree and had their lunch. They were about to set off when Clive suddenly had an idea. Lucy had said the monkeys were both intelligent and helpful, and this seemed a perfect opportunity to use Sophie's skills. He reached up on to the back of the macrauchenia who had been patiently grazing during the rest stop and unhitched a coil of rope from his climbing equipment. He showed it to Sophie who held it in her paws and sniffed at it with interest. Clive took the rope back and held it at shoulder height against the cliff, letting a loop unravel and fall vertically to the ground while Clare watched the little pantomime with an amused smile. Clive then pointed east along the cliff, pointed back to the hanging rope and then gestured to Sophie to go along the cliff. She looked at him, at the rope, and along the cliff several times, then suddenly she gave a little squeak and scampered off.

'Good Lord!' said Clive, 'I really think she's twigged!'

Sophie found the rope a few hundred yards along the cliff and turned to rejoin the others. As she did so she was confronted by a large monkey, a male who was at least twice her size and who looked rather fierce. Behind him she could discern the shapes of others in the trees and bushes and knew it was useless to attempt to escape. She sat down submissively and spoke to the stranger.

'*Greetings,*' she started somewhat timorously. She spoke in the common tongue in case he didn't use the same dialect as modern monkeys. '*I am here at the behest of the*

Promised One.' The other monkey was taken aback.

'*And greetings to thee and thy young!'* he eventually replied in true monkey speech. To Sophie's ears it sounded old-fashioned and rough but she could understand it. As he spoke, the other monkeys emerged and gathered round to listen. There was a chatter of excitement as the news spread through the troop that an emissary of the Promised One was present.

'*We will assist thee in any way thou desirest,'* he continued gravely, *'for it is said that hitherto others in the valley have done so and now the time has come for our kin to be so honoured. Whither goest thou?'*

'*Thank you!'* replied Sophie with great relief. '*On this quest I serve the kin of the Promised One and we think that she and others of her kin lie beyond the mighty rock.'* She pointed to the escarpment. '*Is there a passage through to the other side?'*

'*There is a cave in the cliff back along to where the Brilliant One sleeps,'* the other replied. '*Within that dark place there are two ways. One leads up inside to the top of the mountain whence, it is said, one can see as far as the fledgiquill flies in every direction to the skysill. If the Promised One is on the other side, thou wilt surely see her from that high place!'*

'*And the other?'* asked Sophie. '*The other path; does that go through?'*

'*It might,'* said the monkey, *'but no one knows, for no creature that has entered therein has ever come out again. If thou takest the kin of the Promised One into that cave thou must take care to choose the right path lest ye both perish.'*

Sophie thanked him and was turning to leave when he

spoke again.

'*One other thing. We came to this place because we saw the liana on the great rock.*' He indicated the rope hanging down the cliff face. '*And as we drew nigh near we saw one of thine own kin – an arborikin – climbing down. By the time we reached her she had gone.*'

Sophie was in a quandary. Clio must be on her way back to the camp. Should she follow her and learn what had become of Lucy and the others? No, she decided, her first duty was to assist the kin of the Promised One. She sped back to the others, who were sitting in the shade of a tree eagerly awaiting her return. She was then faced with a second dilemma: should she just forget about the rope and take them to the cave? She was intensely frustrated that neither of them could speak in the common tongue. She decided that she must tell Clive where the rope was; that, after all, was the reason she had been sent on her mission. She would take Clare to the cave.

She first went to Clive and gently pulled him until he stood up, then she tugged him to the east in the direction from which she had just come. She looked excited and he had little doubt that she had located the rope. As Clare got up to join him and they started to move off, however, Sophie clutched at her shorts and tried to pull her in the opposite direction.

'What do you want, Sophie?' Clare asked with a bemused smile, but of course the monkey couldn't reply; she just tugged harder for Clare to follow her.

'She seems very determined,' Clare said to Clive, now

with a slightly worried frown on her face. 'What should we do? Everything Lucy and Dad have told me about the monkeys makes me feel we should take her advice.'

'I think you're right,' said Clive. 'Much as I hate splitting up, I think I should go to the rope – she's obviously found it – and get the rope ladders in place. Whatever has happened, that must be a good thing to do. You go with Sophie who, I'm sure, will keep you safe and she can lead you back to the rope after you've seen what she wants you to see.' And so it was agreed.

Clive trekked off to find the rope, the macrauchenia following him burdened with the rope ladders and climbing equipment. Clare picked up the survival rucksack that Helen had insisted she took and went west in the opposite direction, following Sophie.

Soon they came to a cave which was, as far as Clare could see, the only interruption in the smooth cliff face. The monkey led her unhesitatingly towards it. It was pitch black and very scary but she reassured herself with the thought that in this valley, as the sister of the Promised One, she was safe from all creatures.

How dreadfully wrong she was.

15

Perfidious Plans and Pleistocene Post

After Clare and Clive had left, Helen began to feel very nervous. She had agreed to Clare's plan, which made good sense, but now that she was alone the situation she was in seemed much more threatening. Although she had put on a brave face for the young ones she knew in her heart of hearts that Julian and the others were almost certainly dead, and now she began to wonder if she would ever see any of them again. She sat down and began to weep. Queenie looked very perturbed and came and stroked Helen's hand as if to console her. Helen smiled through her tears and gave the animal a hug.

'You're right, Queenie,' she said. 'I've got to carry on, however black things seem.' And she got up and started to tidy up the tents.

Over in the other camp the villains were just starting their breakfast. When they had finished the professor went to his laboratory as usual, ostensibly to make more suits but in reality to set in action a plan he had devised a long time ago for just this situation. First he opened the tin box that Chopper had referred to. He had made no secret of it and they had fallen neatly into his trap. He carefully attached minute direction finders inside the energizer units of each suit and switched them on. He had made them himself and they would continue emitting signals for at least three months. He wasn't sure if they would operate in this strange valley where radios didn't work, but it couldn't do any harm to have an extra possible way of checking on what Chopper might get up to, and the devices would certainly be effective if anyone ever took a suit out of the valley. Then, he removed the disk from the tin box, put it in the computer and modified it. He was too clever to wipe it completely: although he regarded Chopper and Sam as complete buffoons, he had considerable respect for the intellectual abilities of the pilot. He simply changed the data in such a way that nobody could ever use it to succeed in making an invisibility suit and then replaced it in the tin box. Next, he transferred all the information on his hard drive onto back-up disks which he then took back to his cabin. There, he shifted the packing case that served as a makeshift table, took up a floorboard and removed a box. Emblazoned boldly on the front and sides was the international symbol for radioactivity. There was nothing radioactive in the box but, over the years, the professor had found that there was no surer technique than this of preventing people from looking into places that he did not want them to look. He opened the box, removed his own invisibility suit, and put the disks in next to the gun nestling there. A few seconds later, invisible, he slipped out and went to sit on a log near the other three who were sitting outside on camp chairs drinking coffee and smoking.

As he rejoined them Chopper was pointing to the other camp where, in the distance, Helen could be seen rolling up the tent sides. On his face was an expression that, Luke now knew, meant that Chopper's unerring primitive survival instincts had been aroused.

'Where are the kids?' he exclaimed. The others looked, and Sam got out a pair of binoculars.

'They've gone!' he said. 'There's just that older bird and a monkey – you know, one of those things you said I was imagining until it nearly bit your hand off.' Even Chopper had to give a shamefaced grin; Sam was the only person on earth who could speak to Chopper like that and live to tell the tale. He looked again, more intently. 'You're really not going to believe this,' he said, slowly, 'but it's wearing bloody glasses!'

But Chopper didn't answer. He was now deep in thought. He reached over for the binoculars and peered intently at the site.

'And they've taken most of the climbing stuff with them,' he murmured. 'Sam,' he said suddenly, 'get your gun and binoculars and get after them. They can't have got far carrying all that gear and they may be taking it to the others. It's our best lead for finding the plane and our free ticket out of here.' Sam downed his coffee in a gulp, and went to get ready. A few minutes later he disappeared into the bush, choosing a route that meant he wouldn't be seen by Helen.

After Sam's departure Chopper and Biggles discussed the situation. To the relief of the pilot Chopper seemed calmer after his angry outburst the previous day and had apparently accepted that the disaster with the plane had been an unfortunate accident.

'What the hell are they playing at?' said Chopper, 'and where's their plane?'

The pilot drew on his cigarette and thought for a few moments before speaking.

'There are three possibilities,' he said eventually. Chopper leaned forward. Despite the unfortunate accident with the plane the day before he had come to respect the pilot's judgement and wanted to hear what he thought.

'First of all, the plane group may have just dropped the others off and will come back for them in a few days, or whatever. They may have even gone on to another site.'

'Hmm, that would be bad for us,' interrupted Chopper. 'It means we'll have to watch them all the time to make sure we're ready to grab the plane when it lands – and it might not be for weeks.'

Biggles nodded in agreement and continued.

'The second possibility is that they landed here because from the air this landing strip looks safe and easy, and it's a good camping site because of the nearby shade and the river. They arrived in the afternoon and would obviously have wanted to get their tents up before nightfall, even though it's not convenient for the rocks and fossils in the escarpment, which is what they've come for.'

'So where's the plane now?' asked Chopper.

'Well, I'm only guessing, but once some of the group got cracking setting up camp the others went off on a recce.'

Chopper looked puzzled.

'Sorry, pilots' slang. They went to reconnoitre, to look for whatever it is they're interested in. While they were flying over the escarpment they saw the type of rocks they were looking for. They saw a suitable landing place nearby and they haven't come back because they've decided to leave the plane near the rocks. Their specimens will be heavy and they can put them straight in the plane instead of lugging them back here.'

'And what about their camp here?' said Chopper.

'Well, it's only a couple of tents. They'll either move them to a new site near the plane, or simply use this as a base – sleeping here at night and working near the plane during the day. On the last day they'll fly the plane back here to pick up the tents and then go home.'

'You said there were three possibilities,' said Chopper. Biggles continued.

'The third possibility is that they've crashed, though that seems unlikely. Flying conditions were perfect yesterday afternoon and the plane looked brand new. A mid-air collision is out of the question – there's nothing here to hit!' They both looked up into the empty blue sky and Chopper chuckled. He thought over what he had heard. It all made good sense.

'How do we find out which of these theories is true?'

'Simple,' said Biggles. 'We watch the group here and see

if they are working on their own or joining the others. You've already done the right thing by sending Sam after the two kids. If they've gone to join the others he'll find out where the plane is in the next few hours.'

'So what you're saying,' said Chopper after a moment's thought, 'is that we don't need to do anything until Sam gets back.' The pilot agreed.

Chopper took a long final draw on the filthy-smelling black cheroot he was smoking and crushed it out in his plastic coffee cup. He looked at the pilot.

'You're a smart guy, Biggles. Maybe we should carry on working together when we get out of here – make those fat fortunes as a team, eh?' He smiled, revealing a set of broken, nicotine-stained teeth. It was not a particularly attractive sight and the pilot felt slightly ill. Off hand, he couldn't think of anybody on the planet he would rather not work with than the repulsive, belligerent oaf sitting opposite him, but he managed to conjure up a smile and nodded enthusiastically at Chopper's suggestion. His immediate concern was his own survival, and he was only too pleased to be back in Chopper's favour.

Chopper was still thinking over the conversation.

'One more thing,' he said. He jerked his thumb towards the other camp where, in the distance, Helen had rigged a rope between two trees behind the tents and was now hanging all the sleeping bags out to air. 'If she leaves, we follow her. I don't ever want them and their plane all out of sight at the same time. If they decide to leave we're stranded.' He paused, '. . . and we take the invisibility suits and the prof's data disk with us. Everything's in that tin box in the lab. Then if we have to grab the plane we'll be all ready to go.'

'What about the others?' said the pilot.

'We'll top the professor before we go and pick up Sam on the way; the rest of them can have a long holiday here – a lifelong holiday. It's a very relaxing place and they all need a break. They've served their purpose. I think the proceeds from the invisibility suit divides better into three than six, don't you?'

Biggles suppressed a shudder. He was appalled by the man's casual brutality.

'Do we . . . er . . . *have* to kill the prof?' he asked, somewhat tentatively. Having got back into Chopper's good books he didn't want to get on the wrong side of him again.

'Well, no,' Chopper replied. 'If he's around when we have to leave we'll knock him off; if he's not around we'll just leave him, he looks in need of a holiday too. We'll just do whatever's convenient when the time comes.'

Luke had heard enough. He hurried back to his hut and tore off his suit. He quickly stuffed it into the specimen case he used to collect samples of ore then took his gun from its hiding place, checked it was loaded, and slipped it in his pocket. Meanwhile, Chopper had been having further thoughts.

'If she suddenly decides to leave,' he said to Biggles, 'we'll need to be ready to follow straight away; we can't risk losing her.' He paused. 'In fact, where's the prof now?

Maybe we should sort him out first so we can get the stuff out of the tin box.'

'I think he's in the lab – or his cabin,' said Biggles. 'I'll go and get him.' He started to get up hurriedly in case Chopper decided to go and catch Luke unawares. He was desperately trying to think how he could warn the professor without incurring Chopper's wrath.

'No!' said Chopper, confirming his worst fears. 'He's a clever bastard. We need to take him by surprise.'

Just at that moment, however, to Biggles's intense relief, the professor appeared from his cabin carrying his specimen box. His other hand was in the pocket of his shorts clutching the gun. He walked up to them, praying that neither would notice the extra bulge of the weapon.

'I'm just going to collect some more ore,' he said casually. 'See you guys later.' He turned and walked away, his entire body tingling at the thought that at any second a bullet might come crashing into his back. He began to breathe more easily with every yard that put him further away from Chopper and eventually, sweating with fear, reached the safety of the trees.

'Well, that solves that,' said Chopper with a chuckle. 'He seems to have opted for a long holiday rather than an unmarked grave – at least for the moment. What happens next is up to her.'

As he spoke they both looked over to the tents just in time to see Clio running up to rejoin Helen and Queenie.

'What on earth is this thing they've got with monkeys?' muttered Chopper as he pushed back his chair and got up to go and check on the contents of the tin box. Biggles followed him to the lab and neither of them saw Helen stoop to remove a note from the monkey's collar. Nor did Luke who, at that moment, was hiding among the trees donning his invisibility suit. Helen tore open the package with trembling hands; at least one of them must be alive to have sent it but now visions of a sole survivor lying critically injured flashed through her mind. She sobbed in relief as she read the note and the reassuring capitals that jumped instantly out of the page at her.

Hi love, WE'RE ALL OK!
Plane bust up and unusable. Dinosaurs in valley. Lucy can talk to them but they don't know she is the PO, so v. dangerous to move about. We will wait near rope till you can get ladder over. Clio will tell Queenie where rope is and can bring reply back.
Hope all OK with you,
Love to all there from all here.

She sat down at the camp table to scribble a reply when she saw Queenie and Clio sniffing the air. She looked around but could see nothing unusual, so turned back to her task. As she did so the professor crept up behind the sleeping bags hanging on the line and struggled out of his suit. The monkeys came round and looked at him. Luke did a double take on Queenie's spectacles and, having reassured himself that he hadn't gone mad as a result of his recent encounter, called to Helen.

'Helen, don't be alarmed. It's me, Luke,' he called. Helen jumped. She got up to investigate as he spoke again. 'I'm in great danger. That's why I'm hiding from them.' He pointed over the line towards the villains. He was still deathly pale from his recent near-death experience with Chopper. Helen glanced over to the other camp but saw nobody. At that moment Chopper and Biggles were in the lab rifling through the professor's possessions.

'You look terrible!' she said sympathetically to the professor. 'Sit down and I'll make some coffee while you tell me what's going on.' As she spoke she passed him a camp chair, then went back to sweep the note from the table and pocket it. He sat down in relief, completely hidden from the view of the other camp.

'I'm afraid I'm going to have to tell you the whole story,' Luke began, 'even though it may put my family in mortal danger. First of all, we are not a government expedition. I am a university physicist. A few months ago I made a significant discovery. A discovery that is going to change the world. An . . . *incredible* discovery. Unfortunately, that gang of villains,' he jerked his thumb towards the other camp, 'got to know what I was doing, kidnapped me, and brought me here so that I could complete my research without anyone knowing. Their plan is to steal the finished product and use it to become immensely rich.' He stopped and sipped gratefully at the coffee Helen had given him.

'But how could they force you to complete your work? Surely they couldn't make you *think* clever thoughts if you didn't want to.'

'Ah, very easily,' the professor explained sadly. 'I had no option but to comply with their demands. They said that if I refused they would murder my daughter and grandson – and I'm certain that their threat was not an idle one.' He wiped a tear from his eye.

'And what's happened this morning to make you come here?' asked Helen. She was sitting in full view of the other camp and cast a nervous glance in that direction.

'Two things. The first is that they know my work is now complete. I fear I'm now of no further use to them and I've no doubt that they haven't the slightest intention of my ever leaving this valley alive. The second is something that could be disastrous for both of us, my dear. Their plane is out of action. The pilot tried to hide it when you all arrived yesterday – the villains thought you might be the police – and it got stuck in a bog. I think they are now planning to steal your plane. If they do, they can't take the risk of leaving you alive in case you get rescued later. I think we are all in terrible danger.'

Helen was in a quandary. His story was entirely plausible; there was no question that he had been terrified when he had appeared at the tent a few moments earlier, and it had been obvious from the start that Chopper and his gang were a bunch of thugs. On the other hand, something made her instinctively distrustful of the professor. She decided it couldn't do any harm to tell him about the fate of their own plane. If he was in collusion with the other villains and his visit was all part of an elaborate charade, it would buy them all a little time, for the thugs would then know that they were all trapped in the valley together and think that a rescue plan for the explorers might already have been set in motion.

'It so happens,' she said, 'that our own plane is out of action as well, so there's no point in anyone pinching it.' She didn't say where it was, to avoid any awkward questions about how she knew about it.

'Heavens!' said Luke. 'So we're all stuck here?'

She nodded. 'Yes, I think we were hoping to borrow *your* plane but that's obviously out of the question.' A thought struck her. 'Is it actually damaged?' she asked casually.

'I don't think so, but it's stuck tight. The pilot thinks it would take fifty men to get it out.'

'And just how many men *are* there?' If they were up against an enemy, she thought, the more she could find out the better.

'There are six of us altogether so we couldn't possibly get it out, even with your lot helping as well.' He paused, then added. 'There's just two of them over there at the moment, I think the others have gone to spy on your group.'

'What are you going to do now?' asked Helen.

'Make myself scarce for the time being. I can't risk staying with them and I don't want to put you in danger by being seen with you. I've got some grub out there,' he nodded vaguely towards the bushes, 'and I'll lie low until someone comes to rescue you – if that's OK with you?'

'Of course,' said Helen, 'the others should be back soon.' She felt the white lie was fully justified in the circumstances and the sooner he disappeared the sooner she could get a note to the others and think about what she should do. 'If you run out of food I'm sure we can find a way of getting some more to you. Good luck!'

Luke made good his escape, choosing a route to the trees that was completely obscured from the other camp by the sleeping bags hanging on the line. As it so happened someone *was* watching from the other camp but the bags served their purpose and he saw nothing of Luke. Chopper was pretending to sleep in a hammock but was furtively inspecting Helen's camp every so often through his binoculars. He also occasionally looked to the escarpment to see if there was any sign of Sam returning with news of the plane. Biggles was drinking coffee in the lab, reading an old aeronautical magazine and hoping against hope that Luke wouldn't return to a certain death.

After Luke had gone, Helen sat down and scribbled a note to the others. She was glad now that the professor had appeared before she had been able to write her reply, as his visit had dramatically changed the situation. She taped it to Clio, stroked her and then patted her gently on the back while pointing to the escarpment. The monkey raced off towards the cliffs and Helen knew that her note would soon be with the others. After Clio had gone she made herself another coffee and sat down to work out what to do next. The more she thought about it, the more she felt instinctively that she should try and join the others. She was very vulnerable here on her own and if the villains decided to take her as a hostage the entire group would be at their mercy. She glanced over to the other camp but saw no sign of movement. She got up unhurriedly so as not to attract attention and checked her survival rucksack. She had a long drink of water, applied some suncream and then called softly to Queenie. They crept behind the hanging sleeping bags, just as the professor had done, and used their cover to get to the trees. As they reached them Helen stopped in consternation as she saw a troop of wild monkeys, apparently lying in wait for them. Queenie pressed confidently towards them, however, and Helen realized with relief that Clio must have enlisted their services as guides to lead them to the rope.

As bad luck would have it, Chopper chose to make one of his intermittent scrutinies of the tents only a few seconds after Helen had disappeared. He stiffened when he saw she wasn't there, then sat up and peered intently round the whole tent site.

'I think we're on the move!' he shouted to Biggles. 'She may be just having a pee, but let's get the suits on so we're ready.' They scrambled into the suits and Chopper grabbed a revolver, a rifle, and a pair of binoculars while Biggles retrieved the professor's research disk from the tin box. By the time they were ready there was still no sign of Helen. They hurried over to the empty tent site and were just in time to see her through the trees in the far distance, heading towards the escarpment. Chopper gave a grunt of satisfaction and the pair started to follow her. They might easily have collided with Luke who was standing silently nearby, also invisible, but the professor was expecting them and managed to avoid them by watching the flattened grass springing back up from where they had trodden.

16

The Horror of the Hollow Hills

Back at the base of the forbidding escarpment, Clare followed Sophie to the mouth of the cave and peered in. It was a narrow entrance – just big enough for a human being but certainly nothing bigger. She now realized why it had been invisible from further along the cliff.

Inside it was pitch black. The monkey walked in a little way then turned back as if surprised at Clare's hesitation. She suddenly remembered Helen's survival kit and breathed a fervent prayer of thanks as she rummaged to find the torch in her rucksack. She tested it and a weak light came on. She looked to see if Clive was still in sight, but he was long gone. There was nothing for it but to follow Sophie and Kai. She gripped the torch tightly, stretched her other arm out in front of her face to feel for obstacles, and walked into the darkness.

To her relief, the torch seemed much more powerful inside than out in the bright sunlight. They were walking along a narrow natural corridor, effectively a cleft in the rock, and she soon became aware of a disgusting smell which got progressively stronger as she went deeper into the tunnel. Soon the monkey stopped and Clare shone the torch beam ahead on to the ground where it illuminated a snake. The monkey glanced at the snake and then continued, simply stepping over the reptile, and as Clare came up to it she saw that it was engrossed in swallowing a rat. The rat was twice the diameter of the snake which had its jaws wide open around the half-engulfed rodent and it took not the slightest interest in either the monkey or Clare. Soon she realized why the snake came here for a guaranteed meal, for as she walked further, one or two rats scuttled past her, all passing along on one side of the tunnel. The monkey ignored them and Clare kept close to the opposite wall on her right and tried to do the same. The rats seemed to have been running in a channel beside the wall and when Clare shone the torch on it she saw that there was indeed a groove, three or four inches deep, perfectly smooth. As she peered at it she remembered how Charles Darwin had been awed by the sight of a rocky path in the Galapagos islands which had been beaten by the tread of countless giant tortoises passing only infrequently along the same route for an unimaginably long period of time. It dawned on her that the rats had been running along this corridor for so long that she was seeing a groove worn in the solid rock by the wear and tear of untold numbers of rat paws. This sight, more than anything she had seen, or was yet to see, brought home to her the true magnitude of the time that had elapsed since this extraordinary crater had become isolated from the rest of the world. How many countless aeons did it take, she wondered, for tiny soft paws to wear a groove, inches deep, into the living rock? And, jerking her mind back to the present reality, just what was it that the rats were so interested in? That, she was about to discover.

After about thirty yards there was a sharp bend in the passageway then, twenty yards further on, it widened a little and there was an opening off the corridor into another cave. Clare could now see that this was the place into which the rat run led. As she approached it the foetid odour that she had smelt since entering the tunnel was now accompanied by an increasingly strong smell of ammonia. There was a heap of something spilling out of the entrance to this cave into the corridor and, as she shone the torch in, the first light ever to reach into that place in the thousands of millennia it must have existed, an extraordinary and repulsive sight met her eyes. The cavern was very large – as large as the school hall at Clare's old school, St Sapientia's. The ceiling was at least thirty feet high and as Clare shone the light around she saw that it was covered in bats, thousands upon thousands of them.

The room was filled with an immense pile of bat dung which rose almost to the ceiling at the far end of the great cave and sloped gradually down towards Clare; it was the end of this disgusting mound that spilt out into the passageway and was now at her very feet. The guano itself was surprisingly dry and she could feel its warmth through the soles of her trainers. She was now coughing and choking on the pungent smell of ammonia, and as she looked about with watering eyes she couldn't believe that so many bats could possibly exist in one place. What filled her with revulsion, however, was not the bats. It was the other denizens of the cave; creatures of the everlasting night that fed upon the guano, the creatures that fed upon them, and the creatures that fed upon the dead bats and the bat pups that fell into that dungheap of no return. There were worms, cockroaches, centipedes, spiders and dermestid beetles; she realized now why the cave had been an irresistible magnet for generation upon generation of valley rats. There were countless numbers of beetle larvae and, as she moved her feet, her footprints in the soft dung immediately started to be erased by their continuous activity. The air was filled with flying beetles and soon her hair and arms and shirt were covered in them. To her horror something stirred on the wall between the dung and the ceiling and she saw it was a snake. The sinister cave racer was waiting patiently with its innumerable cousins to snatch the living bats from the air as they flew out to feed at night in the valley and returned at dawn to roost once again in their hidden lair.

There was a flurry of activity among some of the dreadful creatures on the guano – those that were capable of detecting light – as they sensed the alien beam of the torch and, as a large and disgustingly pale centipede moved towards her foot, Clare moved hurriedly backwards. As she did so, Sophie darted forward and grabbed the loathsome creature and, to Clare's disgust, gave it to the baby on her back which crunched it up with every sign of satisfaction.

Soon the monkey turned and continued confidently

along the corridor. Clare began to follow her and while the beam of the torch was, for a second, still pointing sideways into the cavern, she thought she could see a suggestion of light ahead. She switched off the torch, even though it was a daunting experience standing in the dark next to that frightful cave, and saw that she had been right. Ahead there was a faint glimmer of daylight. Greatly heartened by the thought that she must be almost through to the other side, but slightly surprised that the escarpment was much narrower than she had imagined it to be, she switched the torch on again and hurried after Sophie. Soon the corridor opened out again and then divided into two paths, dim light coming from the one on the right. The monkey stopped abruptly at the bifurcation and sniffed cautiously into each opening. Then she turned decisively to the left and started off, looking round to make sure that Clare was following her. But Clare wasn't. Clare had seen something lying in the other path. Something quite extraordinary. Something that simply should not have been in that place. She went to get it. It was a gun and it was lying in a bed of what looked like cotton wool. Above it, criss-crossing the corridor and, in the dim light practically invisible until Clare shone the torch onto them, were strands of what looked like silken rope, about as thick as a pencil in diameter.

As Clare bent to pick up the gun, Sophie pushed frantically past her to try and stop her going any further. Then she yelped in fear. Clare shone the torch and saw that one of the pale strands was entangled around her foreleg.

As the monkey tried to bite at the tether it stuck to her cheek and as she grasped it with her other forepaw that got stuck to it as well.

Her struggles did not pass undetected by the dreadful owner of the silken trap and suddenly Sophie shrieked in terror as she felt the ropes tauten and she looked into the cave. A few seconds later than Sophie, Clare saw what she was looking at. Backlit as a ghostly silhouette by the eerie light in the cave, and partially illuminated by the torch now lying on the ground, the largest spider Clare had ever imagined could exist was approaching. The creature moved in very rapid darts forward and then paused at intervals as if assessing the situation of its victim – just as Clare had seen its smaller cousins do when approaching a struggling fly caught in a web in the garden at home. As she watched in stupefied horror the frightful creature darted forward again and was now only about a yard from Sophie. Its body was the size of a television set and its legs as long and thick as a man's, covered in bristles.

Clare's instinct was to pull Sophie back, but she had seen the monkey's completely ineffectual attempts to rid herself of the strands of web and knew that once she touched it herself she would be inextricably trapped. Sophie's only thought, in the face of what now seemed like certain death, was for her young one. She called frantic instructions to Kai and the little creature reluctantly clambered down from her back and hid behind Clare.

Clare looked at the gun. It had a long, black, cylindrical attachment at the end of the barrel that she recognized from countless films as being a silencer. There was no obvious safety catch; if there was one, she prayed that the previous owner had slipped it off in his final moments. She held the gun in both hands as she had seen detectives do on the telly and, fighting to stop them trembling too much, pointed the gun at the foul beast facing her. She pulled the trigger just as the spider began its final pounce on Sophie. Despite the silencer, the noise in that confined space was deafening. Clare had no idea that it could possibly be so loud, and the monkey cowered on the floor in petrified silence. The spider was thrown back several feet by the impact of the bullet and its crumpled remains dangled from the netting of the web where its corpse continued to bob up and down for a few seconds, as though suspended on some ghoulish trampoline.

As her eyes adjusted to the dim light Clare, her ears still ringing from the report of the gun, now saw in the gloom a large bundle of web nearby; a second bundle was visible further in, close to the remains of the spider. The bundles were each about the size of a man, though one was larger than the other, and as a result of the recent disturbance in the web, were now slowly twisting and untwisting in the air. As Clare looked more closely she saw something faintly glinting in the one that was nearer to her. Putting the gun down and picking up the torch she shone it at the object that had caught her eye and saw, to her amazement, that it was the face of a Rolex watch. With a thrill of horror she realized that she was looking at a giant food cocoon; a nightmarish bundle of silk that almost certainly contained

She pulled the trigger just as the spider began its final pounce on Sophie.

the previous owner of the gun that had just saved Sophie; the other, smaller bundle undoubtedly contained his diminutive companion.

Suddenly, she saw a distant movement in the depths of the cave and the silken strands began to quiver with a new set of vibrations. She tore the rucksack off her back. Inside was a hunter's knife. Clare had shuddered when she had first seen Helen packing it but now she knew that its sharp blade was all that could save Sophie. Careful not to touch the web with her hands she cut the tenacious strands binding the monkey. The large knife slid through the silken ropes with ease and soon Sophie was free. She called immediately to Kai who jumped up onto her back with a whimper of relief. With trembling hands Clare carefully put the knife and gun into the rucksack, snatched up the torch and hurried back to the main corridor. The monkey, still pulling and grimacing at the remnants of the web stuck to her fur tried once again to lead her into the other passageway, but Clare had had enough. She started to run back towards the valley. With Sophie's help she could soon find Clive, who should, by now, be climbing the cliff. Then, as she burst out, blinking in the dazzling sunshine, she stopped dead.

Sam was standing not twenty yards away looking straight at her, a revolver in his hand. As he had approached the escarpment looking for Barker and Shortshanks he had heard the muffled report of the gun inside the cave and assumed that it must be something to do with the pair. It was, of course, but not quite in the way he imagined.

He saw immediately that Clive was not with her and gave a sneering laugh. 'Looks as if my mates have taken a pop at your boyfriend,' he said, moving towards Clare. As he did so his face abruptly became grim once again.

'Well, I'd better go and see what they're still up to in there. They may need some help and, as I see you've conveniently got a torch, you can show me the way.'

As he approached Clare felt Sophie tugging hard at her shorts. She needed no second bidding – she and the monkey obviously had identical instincts about Sam; they turned and fled back into the passageway. At the bend in the tunnel Sophie glanced back. Sam was standing at the entrance, his massive frame almost filling the space and, without a torch, he was obviously uncertain as to whether to follow.

Clare didn't wait to see, and continued round the bend until he was out of sight. As they approached the point at which the passageway split Clare obediently followed Sophie into the passage that the monkey had tried to take her down previously, before she had been distracted by the sight of the gun. It was darker and narrower than the passage leading to the spiders' den and soon they came to a black chasm across their path. It was only a yard wide but seemed to disappear down into the bowels of the earth and Clare could just discern the sound of running water far below, presumably an underground river. The monkey jumped over the cleft and looked back anxiously until she was sure Clare was also safely across. The path, which was damp beyond the cleft, then turned steeply upwards and as they climbed, Clare saw light ahead. Soon, after a sharp bend, they emerged on to a wide ledge running around the top of a giant cavern. The roof of the cavern was split by a giant cleft through which daylight poured and as Clare looked up she could see blue sky, far above. This was a giant crack down the very middle of the mountain and she could see a succession of ledges along which she could climb up to the top. Looking down she saw the floor of the cave, far below. It looked as though it were covered in snow, but then, as she saw black shadows moving across it from the dark edges of the cave, she realized that she was now at the top of the spiders' den. Its entrance lay directly below her and was concealed from her view by the ledge upon which she stood and, as she strained forward for a better view she felt Sophie trying to restrain her from falling. She could just discern the shape of the dead spider below her, near one of the frightful cocoons. The spider looked larger than before, until the shape moved slightly and she realized that she was looking at two spiders; one of the dead creature's cannibalistic companions was already enjoying an unexpected meal. Even as she watched the grisly scene she heard Sam's boots thumping into the cave below. He, naturally, had followed what looked like the main passage, especially as it led to the cave that was partially lit by daylight.

'Don't!' she screamed down. 'Don't go in there, it's –' But it was too late. A giant black shape, the stuff of nightmares, emerged from one of the far recesses of the cave – bigger by far than any spider that had appeared so far. It moved at an incredible speed across the patchwork of silk webbing and Clare, repulsed though she was at the sight, could not tear herself away from the unfolding drama below. She strained even further forward, the monkey feverishly trying to restrain her, as she heard a roar of rage from Sam who had now just come into view.

There is a popular myth that all bullies are cowards, but all who know a true bully are aware that this is not always the case. Sam's reaction to his dreadful plight was not one of fear; it was one of total, primitive, aggression and, as Clare gazed down in fearful fascination she saw him actually rip two legs off the hideous creature before its giant fangs sank deep into his face. Even then, he fought with the ghastly creature, until the lethal toxins it had injected spread in his bloodstream throughout his body and he succumbed, inexorably, to his fate.

Clare's knees felt like jelly. She stumbled to the back of the ledge and collapsed against it. Sophie, completely indifferent to the appalling events that had taken place below, was simply relieved to see Clare, at last, removed from danger. She crouched next to Clare, took her hand somewhat hesitantly, and gave it a consoling lick. Clare, who was sobbing at the sight she had just witnessed, gave a weak smile through her tears and caressed Sophie behind the ears.

'You've been loyal and brave and kind,' she said to the monkey. 'And if I'd followed you in the first place none of this would have happened.'

Sophie couldn't understand the words that were spoken,

but she perfectly understood the sentiment. She came closer and gave Clare a hug. As she did so Clare gently removed the remnants of web that still stuck to the monkey's face. After a little while Sophie got up and tugged at her once again. Clare followed the monkey, who climbed confidently up ledge after ledge towards the light, Kai clinging to her back. The ledges were worn by grooves which were damp and obviously created by rainwater entering from the top. Clare now realized that they had climbed up a watercourse which took the rain entering at the top right down into the scary cleft she had crossed. It dawned on her that this was the reason that their route had not been colonized by the spiders. The climb was tiring but not difficult or dangerous, and eventually Clare scrambled out into the glorious sunshine. After breathing in the rank miasma below Clare gratefully sucked in lungfuls of the sweet, clean mountain air. She had survived the worst experience of her entire life and emerged unscathed.

17

More Monkey Mail

Clare looked about her and gasped at the stupendous view. She was standing on a ridge running along the top of the escarpment that separated the two valleys. The monkey was carefully cleaning the dust and insects of the cave from her baby, both of them oblivious to the breathtaking panorama. Clare was cut and bruised but she was safe, and the exhilaration of standing on that escarpment temporarily displaced from her mind the gruesome scene she had just witnessed.

On her right, as she stood facing east, was the Valley of the Mighty Ones that she had just left, now far below. For the first time she was truly aware of the immensity of its extent and the variety and number of animals that lived within it. Vast herds of herbivores roamed across its savannah-like plains looking just like the game herds she had seen in television documentaries about East Africa. She could just make out the detail of some of the herds and see that many were composed of animals like the one that had acted as a packhorse for her and Clive.

There were packs of wild dogs and wolves, birds like

ostriches with giant beaks strutting over the plains, and giant ground sloths. Not far away from the cliff was a group of sabre-tooths around a recent kill, jackals and other scavengers prowling around waiting for their chance.

Turning her gaze away from the stunning vista she looked north into the Valley of the Ancients and her jaw dropped. The scene was like one from *Jurassic Park* with herds of long-necked sauropods browsing from trees and wallowing in marshes. Pterodactyls swooped across the waters of a lake and plunged for prey into waters that teemed with strange and wonderful lifeforms. Herds of predatory dinosaurs pursued their prey across the plains and, in a tree-studded gorge, two giant tyrannosaurus-like creatures were prowling around a dinosaur larger than any she had ever seen in a book or film.

From her vantage point she could see that the two valleys did together form one immense crater, the rim of which she could just make out on the horizon in every direction. The rugged ridge she was standing on ran right across the middle of the crater and the valleys on either side of it were separated in evolutionary time by tens of millions of years. She was overwhelmed by the thought that she was probably the only person in history who had stood on this spot and experienced this unique spectacle.

As she gazed in wonderment she felt a tug on her shorts. Sophie was at work again – and encouraging her to walk east. For most of its length the ridge had a jagged and blade-like crest, but she was at the western end of a section that was lower and wider than the rest. This part was about ten yards wide and ran east for half a mile before rising once more to a point where the cliff resumed its former shape and height and was clearly impassable. If Clive were somewhere along this section she could probably get to him; if not, her only resort would be to retrace her route down through the cave, a prospect that filled her with dismay.

She followed the monkey who scampered ahead and turned round now and then like a dog to make sure that Clare was following. Keeping up with the monkey wasn't easy, for in places the ridge was reduced to only a few feet in width with a precipice on either side, and its surface was interrupted by deep cracks she had to circumvent or jump over.

As they progressed east with no sign of Clive, Clare began to get more and more worried. He might have fallen from the cliff face and be lying with broken limbs, or worse, at the foot of the rope. And what if the other villains had pursued him, just as Sam had chased her? He would have made an easy target clinging to the vertical rock face with no possible means of escape. Then, as she scrambled over a miniature crag, to her utter relief, she saw Clive. He was in the process of pulling himself up with one hand over the edge of the cliff and as she clambered towards him she saw him collapse in exhaustion after his arduous climb. He looked utterly distraught and immediately turned and peered back down into the valley out of which he had just climbed. He didn't see Clare until she was almost upon him.

'What kept you?' she said with a grin.

He looked up and as he saw her his expression changed from one of despair to utter relief. He scrambled awkwardly to his feet and she saw immediately that his left hand and wrist were bruised and swollen.

'I was so worried about you.' he blurted out. 'I was well over halfway up when I slipped. I think I've broken my wrist. I nearly fell but somehow just managed to hang on. I wasn't sure if I could carry on and looked down just in case you and Sophie were following me and I could call to you. You weren't, of course, but to my horror I saw that nasty piece of work – Sam – walking towards your cave. He looked as if he was carrying a gun and my heart sank. I tried to start coming down but it was quite impossible with my wrist. All I could do was struggle slowly upwards with one good hand by placing most of the weight on my toes against the cliff and looping my bad forearm round the rope. As it turns out I was incredibly lucky that the rope was so secure.' He pointed down and Clare saw that the prongs of the grapnel that Richard had thrown from the plane were wedged inextricably in a deep narrow cleft on top of the ridge. 'I felt so useless at being unable to help you,' he continued. 'If anything had happened to you . . .'

His voice broke slightly and tailed off and they stood looking at each other.

Neither seemed to move – though later each insisted it had been the other – but suddenly they were in each other's arms. After a long moment Clive said:

'Clare, there's something I've been wanting to . . .' He

was interrupted by a distant shout from below.

'Do something, Clive! Either kiss the girl or come and rescue us!'

They looked down. Julian, Richard and Lucy were standing in their rocky refuge in the valley below, gesticulating and laughing. They were a long way down but the wind was rising up the cliff face and they were clearly audible.

Clive blushed scarlet and released Clare immediately. She waved to the others, then cupped her hands round her mouth to shout.

'Hi there! Thank heavens you're safe,' she called down. But the wind whipped her voice away and the others shaped their hands behind their ears and shrugged their shoulders. She turned back and saw Clive's embarrassed expression. Her eyes were dancing as she gave him another hug.

'Just ignore them,' she laughed. 'If they haven't got anything better to do than act as peeping Toms they don't deserve to be rescued.'

Clive grinned and relaxed. He found himself suddenly feeling very happy despite the throbbing in his wrist. He waved cheerily to the others with his good hand then turned to Clare.

'And now, how on earth did you get up here, and what was Sam up to?'

'No,' said Clare, who was already opening her survival kit and taking out a bandage, a bottle of water and some paracetamol tablets, 'before we do anything else you're going to sit down and take some painkillers, and I'm going to put a splint on that arm.' She looked around for a suitable splint but, of course, there was no wood up on the ridge. She was touched to see Sophie looking around as well, even though she didn't know what they were looking for. Then she remembered Clive's climbing gear.

'Have you got one of those metal spike things you use to drive into rocks?' she asked.

'A piton! Good thinking.' She opened his rucksack for him and after rummaging with one hand he produced what she wanted.

'I'm so lucky to have another medic for a . . .' Clive paused and blushed, '. . . for a . . .' he tried frantically to think of a different word from the one he had nearly used, '. . . a companion,' he ended lamely.

Clare bent her head down, smiled to herself, and then started to recount her adventures in the cave as she deftly splinted his injured wrist. When she had finished she stood up.

'Right. Now. You stay sitting down for a while. What do I have to do to rescue the others?'

Clive smiled. 'It's kind of you to try and spare me but I'm afraid it's going to need both of us.' He leant over and patted the rope leading down over the rim of the cliff from the grappling hook. 'Before I started climbing,' he continued, 'I linked the rope ladder sections together and tied them to the bottom of this rope. They make a ladder 200 feet long – which is just about the height of this cliff. All we've got to do now is pray it's long enough, haul it up and let it down the other side, but with the state of my wrist it's going to take all our combined strength to do it.'

Under Clive's direction Clare drove several pitons into fissures in the rock on top of the cliff. Together they then pulled up the rope, winding loops around the pitons every now and then to take the strain of the load while they rested for a few seconds. At last the first rung of the ladder appeared over the rim and, having secured it, they took another little break to rest their aching arms.

'I've been thinking,' Clive said. 'Once we've let this down into the other valley we won't need to pull it up again. When the others are all safely up we can just ditch the ladder to preserve the isolation of the dinosaurs' valley and then return to our valley on foot down through the cave route you discovered.'

Clare shuddered at the thought of going down past that dreadful lair once again but she knew it made good sense: she didn't fancy an unnecessary ladder climb down two hundred feet of cliff, and at least this time she would have the company of the others.

Just at that moment there was an excited squeak from Sophie who had rushed to the top of the rope. Clare and Clive looked down to see Clio swarming up. In the distance they could just see some valley monkeys disappearing into the bush. Clio reached the top a few seconds later and exchanged some excited chatter with her sister; soon she came over and nuzzled Clare's hand in greeting, then pointed to a note taped to her Velcro collar.

Clare bent down and detached it.

'A note!' she exclaimed. She paused and a little crease appeared in her brow. 'Hang on, Clio went in the plane with the others, what's she doing coming up the rope ladder from *our* valley?'

'Have a look at the note,' said Clive. 'Maybe all will be revealed!' Clare unfolded the little package.

'It's from your mum.' She quickly scanned it. 'I see. Clio must somehow have managed to escape from the dinosaur valley with a note from Julian to your mum. This is her reply which we happen to have intercepted because Clio had to come back up the rope.'

'What's it say?' asked Clive.

'Oh, sorry!' She read it out:

> Dear All,
> Great to hear you're all OK. I'm now v. worried about Clive and Clare who went off to look for you this morning (with Sophie and Kai) but haven't returned. I think Sam followed them. The prof has told me that he was kidnapped by the others who are all villains. Their plane has broken and he thinks they're going to try and pinch ours. He says they'll stop at nothing and our lives may be in danger.
> I'm going to come and join you.

I'm sure Clio will have told Queenie where you are so I'll just follow her. There are two villains left at the camp but I don't know where the others are, so keep on your guard. After you get this please ask Clio to take it to Sophie if she can find her, so the others are warned as well.

See you soon (I hope!!)

Love,

Helen xxx

'Oh no!' Clive groaned. 'Just our luck to get mixed up with a bunch of thugs. The sooner we get the others up here the better – we need to work out a plan of action.' He paused as a thought struck him. 'I just hope the others brought the rifle with them from the plane. Otherwise we're completely at the villains' mercy if things get nasty.' As he spoke Clare was hurriedly scribbling an addition to the bottom of Helen's note:

We've seen this. Will rescue you asap.
Love, C&C.

She retaped the note to Clio's collar, led her to the edge, pointed down to the others and gave her a little pat on the rump. Soon the monkey was on her way, bounding confidently down the rocky ledges.

'I know I could have chucked it down wrapped round a stone,' Clare explained as she turned back across the ridge to help Clive carry on with their back-breaking task, 'but it could easily have got lost among all those rocks and they may want to send a reply.' If they had happened to look back into the other valley at that moment they would have had the shock of their lives, for Tina had just reappeared and, under Lucy's instructions, was stretching up so that the monkey could spring onto her head to be transported to the ground with her note. But the two were already concentrating once more on the rope ladder.

As soon as Clio had jumped off Tina's head, Lucy snatched the note from her collar and read it to the others.

'I don't like this at all,' said Julian as she finished. 'They're almost certainly armed and if they decide to grab Helen they'll have us at their mercy.'

'If you're thinking what I'm thinking,' said Richard, 'it might be a good thing if we had the rifle.' As part of their scientific equipment they had brought a rifle with tranquillizing darts for zoological research.

'That's exactly what I was thinking,' agreed Julian. 'We don't want to get involved in a shoot-out, but having some kind of weapon could conceivably get us out of a nasty situation at some point. Being able to put the bastards to sleep for a while could save our lives.' He glanced apologetically at Lucy for his language.

'Where is it?' asked Lucy.

'Unfortunately it's back in the plane,' said Julian. 'When we left this morning, wondering whether we could ever escape, zoological research wasn't exactly at the top of the list of things I had to do today. The gun's heavy and cumbersome and I thought it would just be a nuisance. Just shows how wrong you can be!' he added with a rueful smile. He paused for a moment, thinking about the dangers they had faced that morning on their trek from the plane. 'I don't think we can possibly take the risk of going back for it now.'

Lucy was thinking hard.

'Seeing Tina lifting up Clio has given me an idea,' she said slowly, 'and if you guys really think we should have the gun I think I know how we can get it.'

The men looked at her in bemusement.

'Go on,' said Richard. During their adventures in the last few years he had learned to treat Lucy's ideas with a great deal of respect.

'I think we should get Tina to carry us back to the plane. We'll be so high up we'll be safe from almost everything except those giganotowotnots, and she seems to be able to smell those a mile off. She'll also get us there jolly quickly – much quicker than we could walk.'

Richard and Julian exchanged glances.

'I think it's a great idea,' Julian started. He hesitated. 'But it's your call, Richard. You might feel Lucy's taken enough risks already.'

Richard was torn. The trip would undoubtedly involve further danger for his daughter, but having the tranquillizing gun might prove crucially important in the confrontation with the villains that he was certain lay ahead. It might save them all. His mind was made up.

'You're right. Let's go for it. And the quicker the better.' He continued more slowly, formulating his thoughts as he did so. 'I think just you and Lucy should go. You know all about the gun and its bits and pieces, and you need Lucy to talk to Tina. Oh, and you should take Clio. I should stay here. The others'll have the ladder down soon and I can fill them in. I'll also then have Sophie in case I need to get a message to you.'

'Sounds great,' said Julian. 'Let's move!'

Lucy called to Tina:

'We must return in haste to thy nest to find a thunderstick in the broken pterokin. Can we ride upon thee?' Even as she spoke, Lucy realized that Tina would never have seen or heard of a rifle, but if the creature was puzzled she didn't show it.

'Of course,' came the simple reply.

Lucy and Julian scrambled up on to the rocks surrounding their refuge and Tina lowered her body until they could clamber on to her massive shoulders. Her frame was so broad that it was difficult for them to sit in a stable position and they couldn't possibly risk a fall from that height. With Clio's agile help they looped some rope around the base of Tina's neck so that they could sit clutching onto the loop for support, Michelle as always on Lucy's shoulder. They set off and, as the incongruous party of two humans, two monkeys and a dinosaur lumbered out of view, Richard prayed that he had made the right decision and that he would soon get his daughter back, safe and sound.

Meanwhile, back on the cliff top, Clare and Clive were engaged on their next task with the rope ladder. Clive's judgement as to the height of the cliff had been astonishingly accurate; when completely unfurled, the rope ladder ended only about two feet off the ground. Clive had just started to continue to pull the ladder up, to let it down into the other valley, when Clare stopped him.

'No Clive. Don't do that. Your mum said she's coming to join us.'

'That's OK,' Clive replied, 'when she arrives we'll tell her to go and wait for us outside your cave.'

'That's not the point,' said Clare. 'She's got to be able to get up here to safety, *then* we pull the ladder up before the villains get here. They may follow her to find out where our plane is – they don't know it's busted up. Your mum's safe until they know where we are. Once they find out they'll probably try and take her hostage so they can dictate their terms to us. They may intend to leave us all stranded in the crater.'

'My God, you're right!' exclaimed Clive. He looked anxiously back towards their camp for any sign of Helen. 'Quick, help me fix the ladder.' Together they fixed the top rung firmly to the ledge with more pitons driven deep into the rock.

The next hour seemed the longest in Clive's life as he watched anxiously for the appearance of his mother.

18
Hoodwinking Hungry Hunters!

As Clive and Clare waited up on the cliff top for Helen, the dinosaur riders down in the Valley of the Ancients were making good progress. Lucy found the experience exhilarating and, as luck would have it, the journey back to the plane was uneventful. Tina's nest was undisturbed and Julian retrieved the rifle and tranquillizing darts without incident. The dinosaur's gigantic strides made short work of the return journey and soon Richard was hugging Lucy in immense relief; while they had been absent he had become progressively more certain that he had made a terrible miscalculation in risking her life for the sake of retrieving the gun. Now, however, with her and Julian safely back with the weapon, he felt greatly reassured by the fact that they could mount some kind of challenge to the villains should it prove necessary to do so.

Suddenly Lucy turned and looked at Tina. The dinosaur was standing outside their refuge but had lowered her head and clearly wished to say something.

'*You are now safe in this place. I must leave you for a little while for I must eat. I will return as soon as I can.*' She made off towards the trees and was soon out of sight. Lucy told the others what she had said.

'Of course!' exclaimed Julian. 'To keep that amazing bulk going she must normally eat practically all the time. A modern elephant has to eat one or two per cent of its body weight every day. If the same is true for her, and I'm sure it must be, she'd have to eat well over a ton of vegetation every twenty-four hours to keep going, and she's spent several hours today just looking after us. No wonder she needs to go and refuel!'

Up on the cliff top Clare and Clive were still gazing into the Valley of the Mighty Ones. It was Clare who first spotted a movement in the bushes and pointed.

'Look, she's there!'

'Thank heavens she's safe!' said Clive as Queenie led Helen out of the undergrowth towards the cliff. 'And there's no sign of the villains. As soon as she's up we'll pull the ladder up and let it down on the other side for the others.'

He leant over the ladder as Helen approached the base of the cliff, cupped his hands round his mouth and shouted down.

'Quick, Mum – go for it!'

Helen looked up, unable to hear him properly but, as Clive frantically beckoned, she gave an apprehensive smile, glanced back to the bushes to check she wasn't being followed, then scrambled up on to the ladder. As she began to climb she was surprised at how taut the ladder felt – almost as if Clive had secured it at the base. She knew that wasn't the case, for the end had been dangling free, well clear of the ground. It also vibrated in a way that seemed at times unrelated to her own climbing movements but she put this down to Queenie scampering up and down above her as she clambered up the rungs. The climb was exhausting and frightening. In the original plan it had always been envisaged that the non-mountaineers would be assisted and reassured by the experienced climbers, but now she had to face the formidable ascent on her own. She stopped for a rest now and then, clinging close to the rungs; she wanted to look down to see if she was being followed, but didn't dare do so for fear of vertigo. The vibrations in the ladder got worse as she climbed and she was disconcerted to notice that they continued, undiminished, even after Queenie had left the ladder altogether. She decided they must be due to the currents of wind swirling along the cliff face.

There was still no sign of any pursuers and Clive began to breathe more easily. Once Helen was up and the ladder pulled up behind her they would be temporarily safe from the villains and could devise a plan of action.

Eventually she reached the top, breathless from the gruelling climb, and hugged Clive and Clare.

'Well climbed, Mum,' said Clive. 'Are we glad to see you! We've been worried about you ever since we got your note. Were you followed?'

'Not as far as I know,' said Helen, 'but Queenie kept sniffing the air and looking back. It was frustrating because without Lucy I couldn't ask her what the problem was.'

Clare then told Helen how she had reached the crest of the escarpment through the roof of the cave and about the fate of Sam and his cronies.

Chopper and Biggles, who had been climbing the ladder some way behind Helen, reached the top at this point. They had found it impossible to climb without tucking their invisibility robes up around their waist to free their legs and took a chance that none of those on the cliff top would look down and see two pairs of legs climbing the ladder. In the event, those on top were too busy exchanging stories to pay any attention to the ladder and the villains eventually made it to the top undetected. Chopper, fat and out of condition, was utterly exhausted by the climb and would never have made it but for the driving power of his greed. On the top rung he let down his robe to its full length and clambered as silently as possible on to the ridge, followed closely by Biggles. Once the pair had more or less recovered their breath they moved invisibly to the edge of the cliff-top group and eavesdropped on the conversation.

' . . . and if Sam and the others are dead,' Helen was saying, 'there are only two of the thugs left, three if we count the professor – I'm still not sure about him.'

Chopper was stunned at what he heard. How on earth had his brother and the others died, and how did Helen know that he and his group were up to no good?

'Let's carry on with this later, Mum,' Clive interrupted. He had been looking back to the edge of the bushes with increasing concern that the remaining crooks might appear at any moment. 'The most important thing is to get this ladder up before they appear; if they're armed they may be able to keep us away from the top of the ladder.'

As they all set to pulling up the ladder, the pilot gave a jump as he felt a touch on his arm. Then he heard Chopper's hoarse whisper in his ear.

'There you are. I lost you for a moment. Come behind that rock.'

The two of them went behind a nearby rock. Queenie followed them, sniffing the air.

'What's that bloody monkey doing around all the time?' Chopper muttered and landed her a savage kick. She yelped, picked up her glasses and put them back on and limped back to the others.

'What's up, Queenie?' asked Clare, taking a hand off the ladder to stroke her head. But the monkey of course could say nothing. She licked Clare's hand and sat down.

'Probably stung by a wasp,' said Clive. 'She looks OK. Lucy can let us know for certain in a few minutes when we've shifted this ladder to the other side.'

The pilot asked Chopper why they needed to hide when they were already invisible.

'So they can't see these,' said Chopper and as he spoke a pair of powerful binoculars materialized in mid-air. Chopper had obviously just taken them from beneath his robe.

'They're pulling up the ladder,' Chopper continued, 'which means they've somehow twigged what we're doing and they're making a run for it. Sam and the others are dead' – his voice broke slightly as he said this; Chopper had been very close to Sam – 'and we'll never have a better chance than this to nick their plane. If we can see it from up here we don't need them to lead us to it – we can get to it before them and take off.'

While he was speaking Chopper was slowly scanning the dinosaur crater.

'There's some funny-looking animals around,' he muttered, then suddenly stopped and hissed.

'There it is.' He gestured with the binoculars and then handed them to the pilot. Biggles could just make out a tail fin through the trees.

'That's it OK,' he said, 'they must have landed on that open plain beyond the trees. The pilot must have a lot of guts – I'm not sure I'd have taken a chance on it. A lot of this marshy stuff' – he pointed to a large bog nearby, 'would look just like long grass from the air.'

'Well, he landed it, and it's our free ride home,' said Chopper tersely. He couldn't care less about the skill of some unknown pilot. 'Let's go for it. As soon as they lower that ladder we'll beat them down it and get to the plane first.' He paused and frowned. 'I presume you can hot-wire a plane without the keys or anything?'

The pilot laughed softly.

'Are you kidding? I could start any single-engined plane on earth, in the dark, with my eyes shut.'

'Good,' said Chopper. 'It will be a lot less messy than having to deal with them.'

Biggles felt his blood chill. He was in little doubt as to

what Chopper meant by 'messy', and he was more than relieved that they could now get to the plane and leave without any confrontation. It was one thing leaving the other party stranded – they would almost certainly have some contingency arrangements in place for their ultimate rescue – quite another to shoot innocent civilians, including a child, in cold blood. He also felt less guilty about the professor. He would now, almost certainly, eventually be rescued with the other group rather than being marooned alone in the crater for the rest of his natural life.

In the meantime, Helen, Clare and Clive had finished hauling the ladder to the top of the ridge and Clive started to look for a suitable place to fix it on the other side so they could lower it into the dinosaur valley. Lucy, Richard and Julian were still sitting patiently in their rocky refuge below. Unfortunately there was only smooth bare rock at the top of the ridge above where they waited, and Clive could find nowhere safe to fix the ladder. He walked along the cliff top, nearer to where Chopper and Biggles were waiting, and eventually found what he wanted – an irregular rocky surface onto which he could hook the top of the ladder, and deep narrow fissures in the underlying rock into which he could drive his supporting pitons.

One-handed, but with the help of the others, he dragged the ladder along the ridge, secured it at the top and then lowered it down into the dinosaur crater. It reached the ground with several feet to spare – the rocks at the base were higher than in the other valley – and the redundant ladder folded up on the ground. The place it ended up was separated by a small ravine from where Richard, Julian and Lucy were sitting. They had seen Clive and his companions moving along the ridge and clapped and cheered them as they lowered the ladder down the cliff.

'He obviously couldn't fix it safely anywhere nearer to us,' Richard said to the others. 'We'll have to get out of here to get to it. Let's just hope that those things that look like rottweiler kangaroos stay away for the next few minutes.' He paused, frowning, and peered at the cliff top more intently, shielding his eyes from the afternoon sun.

'What's up?' asked Lucy.

'I could have sworn I saw something glinting up on the cliff, just past where Clive is standing.'

'Probably the sun reflecting off something in the rock,' said Julian.

'No, said Richard,' mystified. 'It was up in the air – five or six feet from the ground. It must have been some curious effect from floating dust particles or something. Anyway, it's time we moved.'

They sidled through the narrow cleft that led out from their sanctuary, praying that, after all the dangers they had faced and survived, they wouldn't now fall prey to some hungry dinosaurs. It would be the ultimate irony to die in the gorge they now had to cross, only yards away from the waiting ladder.

Chopper was anxious to get to the plane well ahead of the group and as soon as the ladder had been fixed he and Biggles had hurried to clamber down it ahead of Clare,

Clive and Helen. Neither of them realized that the three standing on the ridge had no intention of descending the ladder, and that the real challenge was for them to get down before those on the ground started to climb up. Descending the ladder with their invisibility robes on was much easier than ascending it, and the pair were well clear of the ladder and already heading for the plane before Lucy, Richard, and Julian, the rifle slung across his back, reappeared from the gorge. As they approached the ladder Julian noticed a package on the ground and, puzzled, bent to pick it up. At that moment an unearthly yelping sound came from the edge of the little glade surrounding the gully they had just traversed. The three spun round at the blood-chilling sound to see a hunting pack of raptors streaming from the eastern edge of the forest towards them, as the horrified onlookers at the top of the cliff screamed at them to hurry.

'Quick, Lucy, get up the ladder!' said Richard, his first instinct being to save his daughter as Julian quickly slipped the package in the pocket of his bush jacket.

'No, Dad,' said Lucy firmly, 'you and Julian go while I try and delay them.'

It made sense, and Richard obeyed, pushing Julian ahead of him up the ladder. They scrambled up as fast as they could and when Lucy was on the bottom rung she turned and spoke to the oncoming beasts. They were terrifying to look at, razor-sharp teeth in their snarling mouths and vicious hooked claws outstretched to tear into their victims' flesh.

'We're poisonous!' Lucy shouted. *'If you eat us you will die.'* The pack stopped in their tracks just short of the ladder. No prey had ever spoken to them before. When Richard was at a safe height he turned and looked down to see what was going on. The pack had stopped and the leading dinosaur was looking at Lucy who was obviously speaking to him. As she spoke, Richard saw that she was gradually edging further up the ladder. Then the pack grew restless and the nearest animals gathered themselves to spring. Lucy was still not out of reach and realized further delaying tactics were necessary. It occurred to her that the animals had never been lied to before.

'Our mother is just behind you,' she said. *'She's vicious and as large as the trees and she will eat you all!'* The dinosaurs couldn't help but turn round and look into the trees behind them. In those few vital seconds Lucy scrambled up the ladder as fast as she could. When she was about fifteen feet from the ground the leading creature, realizing he had been fooled, suddenly twisted round, snarled and leapt at her. It was an astounding feat of agility for, from a stationary start, the dinosaur grasped her trailing foot without apparent effort as she tried to climb. To his surprise her foot, as he thought, came off in his mouth and he fell to the ground. This was the first interaction on earth between a dinosaur and a shoe. His teeth had sunk into the rubber sole of Lucy's trainer and for a few seconds he paused as he pawed and grappled to remove the shoe from his jaws. Soon, however, the other pack members tore it from his mouth and its remnants disappeared down a

'. . . the leading creature snarled and leapt at her.'

dozen throats.

By now Lucy was even higher up the ladder and the dinosaur changed his mode of attack, attempting to climb up the rungs of the ladder, using the giant claws on his forefeet as a climbing hooks. As he moved up towards Lucy, Richard delved frantically in his rucksack and produced his bush knife.

'Here,' he cried, thrusting the handle into her hand. 'Cut the ladder!'

She reached down and cut through the ladder stays. As she did so the voracious animal was almost within biting distance and she could smell the putrefactive odour of its breath as it snarled and snapped at her feet. As the bottom of the ladder fell to the ground with the dinosaur Lucy looked up and grinned at her father.

'Close one, Dad!' she said.

'Too close for my liking,' he called back down. 'What on earth did you say to them?'

'I'm afraid I had to tell them some fibs,' she joked, 'but it worked!'

When they were almost halfway up Clare, watching from above, suddenly clutched Clive's arm and pointed to the trees, a look of horror on her face.

'Look out, you lot – get up as quick as you can!' she shouted down to the climbers on the ladder.

The three on the ladder looked down again. The raptors below were still snarling and circling round the crumpled section of detached ladder on the ground. Some of them were fighting over the remnants of Julian's discarded rucksack while the remainder, at the periphery of the group, were looking up in case one of the climbers should fall.

'No, not down there. Back over there!' screamed Clare, pointing to the trees.

The climbers twisted round and looked back across the glade. Out of the trees was lumbering a giant dinosaur, four times as tall as a giraffe. As she let out a deafening roar the pack of dinosaurs turned to look at the monster. They were carnivores and she was a herbivore but they were the size of wallabies and she weighed one hundred tons. Her intentions were unmistakable as her prodigious bulk bore down on the marauders and their ferocious snarls and grunts soon turned to yelps of fear and alarm as they fled back the way they had come.

By now Richard and Julian were well on their way to the top of the ladder but, to everyone's bewilderment, Lucy was actually climbing down a little.

'What on earth's Lucy doing?' said Clare in distress. 'She's back in reach.' Sure enough, Lucy was now only about sixty feet from the ground and well within reach of the monster whose neck seemed interminably long. It headed straight for the ladder and extended its great head at Lucy.

As it did so Julian and Richard finally reached the top and scrambled over the edge to join the others.

Richard looked back for Lucy, saw what she was up to, and turned to see that Clare was white with fear for her sister.

'It's OK, love,' he said, giving her a comforting hug, 'she's not in the slightest danger. That's Tina! She's just given Lucy and Julian a ride to the plane and back.' He smiled and pointed to the rope around the dinosaur's neck. 'You don't think Julian would ride on one of the old-fashioned models without a safety strap fitted, do you?'

As he spoke, to Clare and Clive's astonishment, Lucy turned and stroked the dinosaur's head and that gargantuan animal nuzzled Lucy as gently as a Shetland pony.

'We saved her eggs and her life, actually,' added Richard in a matter-of-fact tone, 'and she's just come to say goodbye.'

'You what?' exclaimed Clare.

'Saved her eggs and saved her life,' repeated Richard nonchalantly. 'It's a long story – we'll tell you all about it later.'

'Many, many times I expect,' added Julian with a grin. 'Ad nauseam, in fact.'

As they looked down, Lucy was speaking her final words to Tina:

'*I must bid thee farewell O Prodigious One,*' she said. '*Thou hast rendered great service to me and my kin.*'

'*Thou and thy kin saved my young,*' replied the dinosaur, '*and I shall remain forever in thrall to thee and all of thine ilk. But now I must depart hence, for the Implacable One draws nigh. Fare thee well.*'

After this once-in-a-planet's-history scene had been enacted, the observers on the cliff-top watched as the behemoth turned away and Lucy, her face streaming with tears, started to climb up the ladder once more.

As Lucy clambered over the top, the monkeys all swarmed down into the valley.

'Where are they off to?' said Helen in alarm.

'It's OK, they'll soon be back,' said Lucy, smiling weakly through her tears. 'I think they prefer Cretaceous figs to Pleistocene figs and have gone back to stock up, but what they *don't* know is that we've just cut the bottom of the ladder off!'

She hugged her sister closely.

'I've got so much to tell you,' she said, out of breath from the climb.

'I've got one or two things to tell you too,' said Clare gently. 'Don't think you're the only one to have exciting adventures!'

At that moment, just as Lucy had predicted, the monkeys reappeared, looking somewhat crestfallen.

'It is as well that you cannot return to the valley,' Lucy said to them. *'The Prodigious One fears that her roar may have attracted the Implacable One; that is why she has left in haste.'*

Julian was looking very excited.

'Did you see that dromaeosaur trying to get up the ladder after Lucy?' he said. 'It was using its giant hooked claw to try and climb the ladder. That's fascinating because some scientists think their claws were adapted for climbing rather than for slashing or tearing. I must make a note.' He fumbled in his pocket for his notebook and then his face changed as he did so.

'I've just remembered something extraordinary,' he said,

and they all turned to look at him. He pulled the mystery package out of his pocket.

'I found this at the bottom of the ladder but haven't the faintest idea what it is. Maybe you dropped something to do with the ladder kit, Clive, as you lowered it.'

Clive looked puzzled and shook his head as Julian tore at the waterproof covering and pulled out a CD. He screwed up his eyes to read the tiny neat handwriting on the label.

'Professor . . . Luc . . . ius . . . Strah . . . lung,' he said. 'I can't read the next bit; looks like "invisibility data" or something.'

Helen stepped forward with a frown and snatched the CD from Julian.

'Let's see that,' she said urgently. 'I've got a horrible feeling that . . .' She peered at the label and Clive looked over her shoulder.

'It says "invisibility data", Mum – whatever that is. Sounds like something out of *Harry Potter* but what on earth is it doing here?'

Helen didn't answer. She was deep in thought.

'My God . . .' she eventually breathed slowly. '. . . my God, so *that's* what he's been up to. And that means . . .' She rushed to the northern edge of the ridge and looked down into the dinosaur crater.

'What in heaven's name are you up to?' asked Julian, looking completely bewildered.

Seeing nothing below, Helen turned and spoke in a low voice.

'Listen, all of you. This is going to sound crazy – really crazy, but I think I just might know what's going on. You know the professor warned me that Chopper and the pilot might try and pinch our plane because theirs is out of action?' The others nodded. Helen had mentioned this in her note. They all looked perplexed.

'Well, I didn't have time to tell you in the note but the professor said he has invented something absolutely incredible; something that would change the world. The villains brought him here to force him to complete his invention so they could then steal it. That CD must contain all the data about his invention.'

'But how did it get here?' asked Clare.

'That's the incredible bit. I think . . .' she spoke very deliberately, looking in turn round the group '. . . I think that what he's invented is a means of making things invisible –' she paused, '– including people.'

There was a stunned silence, broken only by the raucous cries and alien calls from the creatures of the Pleistocene wilderness behind them and the Cretaceous wilderness in front of them. Clare eventually spoke.

'That means,' she said slowly, 'that Chopper and the pilot . . .'

'The glinting we saw on the cliff!' interrupted Richard.

' . . . and the funny vibrations I felt on the ladder,' said Helen.

They all now looked down once again in the crater.

'They'll be well on their way to the plane by now,' said Julian. 'They must have seen it from up here.' He pointed to the tail fin, just visible to those who knew where it was, among the trees in the distance.

'Lot of bloody good it'll do them,' murmured Richard. He couldn't stop a faint smile crossing his face as he imagined the expressions on the villains' faces when they finally reached the plane they hoped would be their salvation, wrecked beyond repair and lying in the shadow of Tina guarding her eggs.

'Look,' said Lucy and pointed to the edge of the glade. The raptors had returned, but not to the ladder. They were sniffing and looking west along the route that Chopper and the pilot must have taken.

19
Vanishing Villains

Chopper and Biggles pushed their way through the ferns and horsetails in the direction of the plane. The pilot was leading the way with a compass.

'Funny vegetation,' remarked Biggles. 'Have you noticed there's no proper grass in this place and hundreds of weird lizards and things?'

Chopper only grunted in reply. The subtleties of tropical flora and fauna held no interest for him whatsoever. His only concern was to get to civilization and make a fortune.

'Hang on a minute,' said Biggles again. 'What's that?' He pointed through a gap in the trees to a giant herbivore wallowing in some marshy ground. The creature was the size of a house. 'Good grief,' he continued, unable to believe his own eyes, 'it's a dinosaur! We must be in some kind of Jurassic park. *That's* what those scientists are doing here. They must've created these things from long-lost DNA just like they did in that book.'

Chopper looked. He hadn't read that book – or any other, come to that – but even he was impressed by the creature. The invisibility robe was cumbersome and he had been about to remove it, but now thought better of it.

'Well, whatever it is, it can't see us; we'd better keep these suits on in case it's got any friends ahead.'

He hitched his rifle strap to sit more comfortably on his shoulder under the robe. As he did so he realized with horror he could no longer feel the professor's CD in his pocket. He cursed out loud and called to the pilot.

'We've got to go back, Biggles. I've lost the CD – must've dropped it coming down the ladder – I know I had it when we were looking for the plane with the binoculars.'

'Can't we do without it?' said Biggles. He was horrified at the thought of encountering the others.

'Of course we can't!' Chopper snarled. 'If anything happens to these robes we've got nothing to show for six months' sweat and graft. Our fortunes could depend on it.'

'But we're almost bound to meet the others on the way back,' faltered the pilot.

'I expect we are,' said Chopper grimly. 'Looks as if things might get a bit sticky for them after all.'

The pilot shuddered. He rather liked what he had seen of the two families and the thought of Chopper gunning them down didn't bear dwelling on. For a wild moment he thought about running away. His invisibility suit would conceal his movements from Chopper and he could then either beat Chopper to the plane and take off, or go back to the others and warn them. He was deeply frightened of Chopper, however, and knew that if anything went wrong

Chopper would be merciless. He also couldn't put out of his mind the certain fortune that awaited him once he got back to civilization and put the invisibility cloak to work. It had, after all, been his discovery in a way. If he hadn't found the precious ore any notion of an invisibility cloak would have remained strictly in the realm of children's fiction. Reluctantly, trapped by his fear and greed, he turned and followed Chopper. It would prove to be the worst decision of his life.

Somewhat to their surprise and to the great relief of Biggles, the pair did not meet the others. At one point on their journey back they saw a truly gargantuan beast approaching them, directly in their path. Biggles felt for Chopper's arm and pulled him aside to hide in the undergrowth. As the monster went by she paused and sniffed in their direction and Biggles's heart jumped into his mouth. What he didn't know was that Tina instantly recognized their alien human scent after her recent experiences, and she assumed that they must be linked to Lucy and moved on steadily back to her nest.

After the dinosaur had gone the invisible pair emerged from their hiding place and hurried back to the ladder. As they entered the clearing Chopper stopped and swore.

'They're all up at the top!' he exclaimed. Biggles gazed up at the ridge and sure enough there were six figures standing there accompanied by three black monkeys. 'What d'you think's going on?' Chopper continued.

Biggles thought for a moment.

'The three that were down here have gone up,' he said.

'We know they're interested in fossils as well as in living dinosaurs and that must be a rich spot. They're all collecting as much as they can before returning to the plane.' His eye fell on the rope ladder. 'And they've lost a few rungs of their ladder so they'll have to jump the last bit.' Chopper looked at the ladder, then at the figures above and his eyes narrowed inside his helmet.

He took out the binoculars.

'I . . . just . . . don't . . . believe . . . this,' said Chopper after focusing the lenses. 'That *bloody* girl and her father again. It's like having a never-ending bad dream.' The pilot felt a sinking sensation in his stomach. 'Well they won't be jumping just the last bit,' Chopper snarled in fury. 'If they want to get down I'll make sure they'll have to jump the whole damn distance. But first things first. Let's find the disk.'

He strode confidently into the glade. It was Biggles who first saw movement in the trees opposite but, before he could warn Chopper, the pack of raptors came out once again from the undergrowth. They couldn't see the invisible pair but after sniffing the air they bounded straight towards them. Chopper cursed and drew out his rifle from under his robe. He was a crack shot. The leading dinosaur crumpled in a heap, a bullet between the eyes as the crash of the heavy rifle shattered the air; the first time in all history that mankind's dreadful tool had ever been heard in that Cretaceous world. The remainder of the group fled and Chopper hurried to the base of the cliff. He rested the gun against the rock wall and started to rummage among the toils of the detached section of ladder.

As he did so he heard a call from above.

'Is this what you're looking for?'

The wind rising from the valley floor had dropped in the late afternoon and Julian's voice was clearly audible. Chopper stepped back and looked up. Julian stood high above him, waving the professor's CD.

'Come back, Julian,' said Helen, 'he might shoot you.'

'It's OK, I can see his arms and the gun,' said Julian, 'and we need to talk to them.'

'Chuck that down,' shouted Chopper, his disembodied voice echoing eerily against the cliff face. 'If you don't you'll never see your plane again!'

'As it so happens,' Julian murmured to the others, 'that doesn't bother me too much.' He turned to Helen. 'Is this disk unique, do you think?'

'I doubt it very much,' she replied. 'The professor must still have all his data on the hard drive of his computer.' She thought for a moment, then continued. 'You may as well give it to him. He can't go anywhere with it and agreeing to his conditions may stop him from shooting at us when we walk along the ridge to Clare's cave. We're sitting ducks up here at the moment.'

'Good thinking,' said Julian. He turned back to the crater. The rifle was still safely propped against the cliff wall. He called to Chopper. 'Here you are,' he called, and threw the disk down. 'Not that it'll do you much good without a plane to get home in.' The wind had now abated and his words were clearly audible to the pair below.

'Oh, we have a plane all right,' said Chopper. 'We've

decided to borrow yours for a while. For ever in fact. And just in case you get heroic ideas about coming down and arguing about it, I've decided to take out a small insurance policy.'

As he spoke the six on the cliff top saw the rifle rise up as if by magic.

'Down!' shouted Richard and they all threw themselves flat on the ridge top. Biggles watched aghast as Chopper raised the rifle and took careful aim at one side of the rope ladder just below the top rung. He fired and the ladder sagged to one side. He fired again and the whole ladder fell to the ground. Those hiding up on the ridge saw nothing but heard the whirring ricochet of the bullets off the cliff face.

'But now they're stranded!' said the horrified pilot. 'There's no food or water up there!'

'Yes,' said Chopper with a chuckle. 'A rather neat solution, don't you think? And if the prof gets lonely over in his camp he can come and wave to them. At least he'll have a bit of company – for a week or so.'

'It's all right, children,' Chopper called up in a mocking voice. 'You can stop playing hide and seek now. I'm not going to shoot you. Look, I'm putting the gun down.'

Lucy peeped over the edge and saw that the rifle was indeed lying on the ground. Then she saw the frayed ends of the rope at her feet.

'He's shot the ladder off!' she said to the others. They got up cautiously and looked.

'The stupid, stupid idiot!' exclaimed Richard. 'They're

stuck down there now.' Helen pushed forward and looked down. She cupped her hands round her mouth.

'Listen to me,' she called. 'You're now in terrible danger. There are dangerous animals – as you've seen. The valley you're in is different from the valley where your camp is. The animals here are much more dangerous and we can't . . . we can't protect you any longer.'

'Protect us!' Chopper gave a scornful laugh. 'What are you talking about, you stupid bitch? We're invisible, we've got a rifle, one of us is a pilot, and now we're going to fly away in the nice new aeroplane you thoughtfully donated to us. Give our love to the prof if he turns up to say hello before you all peg it.'

Then Lucy called down.

'You're not invisible to the animals, you silly man. They can *see* with their noses. You must hide near the cliff until we can find a way to help you.' As she spoke Clio appeared by her side, sniffing the air.

'*The Implacable One cometh, O Promised One. His scent I learned on our journey to this place. It is fearful as no other.*'

And her words were true. Even as she uttered her warning there was an ear-shattering roar and through the trees the enormous shape of a massive carnivore could be seen.

'It's a giganotosaurus!' said Helen in astonishment.

'Yes,' said Julian. 'I'd forgotten we haven't told you about our adventures yet. This place is teeming with creatures from the middle to early late Cretaceous.'

He turned to the others. 'God help them down there.

That dinosaur is probably the largest and fiercest predator that ever lived on earth.'

'Shouldn't we try and tranquillize it?' Richard asked urgently, looking round for where Julian had put the rifle.

'Or *them*,' Clare said grimly, with true medical detachment. 'If only we could see them it would be quicker and easier to put them out than that thing. They'd never know what happened.'

But they never had to resolve the philosophical dilemma that they might have faced for, before a tranquillizing dose of any size could have been loaded into the rifle, the colossal creature burst into the clearing. For a creature of its size it moved remarkably quickly and headed straight for the rifle, which was all the horrified onlookers could see of the doomed pair. The gun was now once again in mid-air; it was as steady as a rock Julian noticed, with reluctant respect for Chopper's courage, and pointing straight towards the oncoming leviathan.

The massive rifle boomed out once again but if it had any effect whatsoever it wasn't apparent. The awesome monster made a sudden swinging movement and it was as though a rent had appeared in the very air itself, through which Chopper was partly visible. The half figure turned and ran back towards the cliff base like some bizarre cartoon character with only one arm and one leg. The creature bent down and the speechless onlookers heard a blood-curdling shriek from the object it swept up in its clutches. It then held the figure in its front paws like a squirrel eating a nut and the shrieks died abruptly in a single sickening crunch that those watching would remember for the rest of their days. Chopper was a big man, but that fearful creature ate him in just two mouthfuls. Then the distraught audience saw another surreal sight. Two disembodied feet and lower legs appeared as the pilot pulled up his robe to allow him to run. The screaming legs ran across the clearing looking for all the world like a half-eaten gingerbread man. The giganotosaurus set off after the apparition with a gigantic bound and the final, inevitable act of the drama was hidden from view as victim and pursuer disappeared into the conifers.

A scream that gradually rose to an appalling crescendo ascended from the woods and then stopped abruptly, as if an electric switch had been thrown.

The shocked silence on the ridge was eventually broken by Clare.

'That was truly, truly awful,' she said. 'How are we ever going to forget what we've just seen?'

'We won't,' said Richard. 'All we can do is to remember that they came to this pass because of their own selfishness and greed.'

'And don't forget,' added Helen, 'that as far as they knew they had just left us to die of thirst and starvation.'

'I know you're right,' said Clare, '– but somehow it doesn't make it seem any better at the moment.'

'Well,' said Richard briskly, 'we should try to get back to camp before nightfall and it's a long way. Where's the ladder into the other valley?'

He turned and looked along the crest of the other side of the ridge.

'It's not there,' said Clare, 'that's why Chopper and the pilot thought they had marooned us.'

'Well, they were right; we *are* marooned, aren't we?' said Richard, frowning.

'No,' said Clive. 'I've still got the original rope up here – the one I pulled the rope ladder up with. We could let it down again and you could go down it to get some of the spare ladders. I say *you* because I can't do anything with this wrist.' He held up his injured arm. 'Mind you, I don't fancy even going down a ladder with it, so it's just as well I don't need to.'

'The screaming legs ran across the clearing looking for all the world like a half-eaten gingerbread man.'

'Why not?' asked Richard. He looked puzzled. Clive grinned.

'It's a long story, but your clever daughter found her way up here through a network of caves inside the cliff. We're going back the same way.'

'Well,' said Clare quickly, 'it wasn't really me. It was Sophie, but I don't know how she knew about it.' Lucy looked interested and sat down with Sophie. After a moment or two she told the others.

'Sophie met a Pleistocene monkey down in the valley who told her about the caves. Apparently there were two routes, one of them very dangerous.' She paused and smiled at Clare. 'She didn't like to slag you off to me, but

I got the distinct impression that you didn't do exactly what she advised you to do.'

'Ah yes,' said Clare. 'That's another whole story which I'll tell you on the way down. I need to, to prepare you all for what you're going to see. All in all, it's been a pretty horrendous day!'

She then told them about the dreadful cave with its colony of spiders. The three scientists were fascinated, and on their descent through the cavern they took photographs and made notes of all they could see of the spiders' lair through the fissure in the ceiling of that sinister grotto.

On their way back to the camp Helen told them what the professor had said about the villains' plane.

'From what I could make out,' she said, 'the plane itself is intact but it's stuck in some kind of marsh at the bottom of a steep bank. Having seen what Lucy can achieve I think we may be able to do something about it, though I didn't tell him that, of course. He thinks that we're all now trapped in the valley and is presumably hoping that we've got some contingency rescue plan that will include him. He's clearly very clever but I still can't decide whether he's genuine or not.'

'Time will tell,' said Julian. 'We'll obviously have to pretend to believe his story for the moment, but we'll need to keep a very close eye on him.'

Clare, who was walking behind the others with Lucy and the monkeys, said quietly to Lucy: 'They can pretend all they like, but I don't trust him an inch!'

'Well, I've not met him yet but I trust your instincts,'

Lucy replied. 'I think I'll take out a little insurance.'

She turned to her loyal monkeys:

'I have yet another favour to ask. We think the Bearded One may wish us harm,' she explained, *'so you must take it in turns to watch him and let us know his movements. Sometimes he may put on a special skin and then you will not see him, but you will still be able to smell him.'* She had noticed during the walk that Queenie was limping slightly and Clare explained what had happened up on the cliff top.

'What ails thee?' Lucy asked the monkey. *'Did a buzzithorn or a fellfang injure thy leg?'*

'Nay. One of the evil ones hurt me. I could not see him but I knew from his awful smell that it was the one like a great snortikin.'

As they crossed the fallen tree that bridged the central river Clare stopped to look down into the limpid water and pointed out a shoal of large fish to Lucy.

'I don't know what they are,' she said longingly, 'but I bet they'd be jolly tasty. I'm already fed up with all that stuff out of tins and cartons.'

'What dost thou seek?' asked Queenie, who always kept Lucy under close observation.

'My sister, Clarekin, looks at the gillifin and wonders if they are good to eat,' Lucy replied. The monkey turned to Clio who immediately left the group and disappeared beneath the trunk of the tree on her way down to the river bank. The girls were intrigued.

'I didn't know monkeys could catch fish,' said Clare, after Lucy told her what had been said, 'but I bet that's what she's up to.'

When they got back to camp Helen introduced the professor to Julian, Richard and Lucy. Luke was agog for news about his erstwhile companions. He expressed remorse when he heard they were all dead and his face adopted appropriate expressions of grief as Helen told him how three of them had been bitten by poisonous spiders and how Chopper and the pilot had been attacked by wild animals in the other valley after tricking the explorers with the invisibility suits. If the professor was disconcerted that they had found out about the invisibility suits he showed no sign of it. He was actually rather pleased about the way things had turned out. The fact that Chopper and Biggles had stolen the suits only corroborated what he had told Helen about his suspicions.

After Luke had returned to his cabin, followed a few seconds later by Queenie, Helen went to get some tins for their supper from the food stack.

'I don't think you'll need all those, Helen,' said Clare cheerfully, inspecting the labels. 'Maybe just the peas and carrots. If I've learnt anything on this trip it's that when Queenie gives orders, things happen. I think fresh supper's on the way.' Helen gave a puzzled smile but obediently started putting some tins of meat back, just as Clio bounded into the camp with a fish in her mouth which she laid proudly in front of Clare.

'Told you so!' said Clare triumphantly.

'It's a trout!' exclaimed Richard. 'And what a whopper!' He turned to Julian, doubtfully. 'At least I think it's a trout.

Did they exist in the Pleistocene, or am I exposing my ignorance?'

'They certainly did,' laughed Julian. 'In fact trout are among the most primitive of all bony fishes. They've been around for a *very* long time.'

Meanwhile, Clio had turned to Lucy.

'I sought the aid of the gillilance, who caught this at once. She now catches more and has been joined by other marshiquills. As we spoke the gillibane drew nigh; when he learnt that we serve thee he went to seek a special crustakin he says is fit for the Promised One. I shall return with Sophie to help me bring what they have caught.'

Lucy went to get a bag for Clio who then sped off again, accompanied by Sophie and her baby.

'What's going on now?' asked Helen with an amused smile as she picked up the magnificent fish.

'The monkeys have gone to get some more fish and some shellfish. Clio says she's got a heron, other waders and an otter doing all the fishing.'

While they waited for the monkeys to return Richard examined Clive's wrist. He was relieved to see that the bones didn't need setting and adroitly replaced Clare's temporary splint with a proper military field splint from his first aid supplies. Meanwhile, Julian went off to retrieve part of the engine grille from the wreckage of the plane in which he and Helen had first come to the crater. From this he constructed a makeshift barbecue and a fire was blazing merrily beneath it by the time Sophie and Clio returned, carrying the bag between them. Everybody smiled at the sight: the monkeys looked for all the world as if they had just returned from a trip to the local supermarket, the domestic picture completed by the presence of Sophie's baby.

Eager hands pulled several glistening fish from the bag and there at the bottom was a large pile of beautiful crayfish, the otter's gift to the Promised One. Soon the fire had turned to glowing charcoal and Julian cooked the most delicious barbecue that any of them could ever remember.

Over supper they discussed the professor's reaction to receiving the news of his companions' gruesome fates.

'Well, I think he was just a good actor pretending to be sorry,' said Julian. 'I'm sure that, underneath, he was pleased and relieved to hear they were all dead.'

'But that wouldn't be surprising even if he's innocent,' said Clive, 'considering how they treated him. It's a truly incredible discovery he's made and they were going to exploit it for their own benefit – and now we know what they are really like I've no doubt they would have killed him once they had everything they needed from him.'

'But the whole thing seems very odd,' said Clare. 'How could a bunch of thugs like that possibly get to know about research going on in a university and contrive to kidnap the professor without a tremendous hoo-ha in the media? Can't you imagine the headlines: "Top Professor Engaged in Earthshattering Research Disappears Without Trace".

'Yet we never heard or saw anything in the news. I think it's all very fishy – excuse the pun,' she added with a smile, as she forked up a generous portion of trout.

'Maybe he was far cleverer than we think and was actually using the thugs for his own purposes,' said Helen.

'Maybe he would eventually have killed *them*. It would be easy enough to do with his invisibility suit. But then, if he's not innocent, why would he have had anything to do with that lot in the first place?'

'He must have had something to hide,' burst in Lucy. 'Maybe it's not his invention at all. Maybe he pinched the idea and could only develop it in secret with their help.'

'In that case he and the thugs were probably using each other', said Clare slowly. 'It was only a question of time before he would kill them or they would kill him. We must have precipitated a final crisis by our unexpected arrival. Without realizing it, we set in motion a series of events and accidents that have resulted in the prof coming out on top.'

They all fell silent for a moment. If their analysis was correct they had a ruthless criminal in their midst – one who in all probability had been prepared to commit serial murder to achieve his ends and who, almost certainly, had another invisibility suit and weapons at his disposal.

'We'll have to watch him like hawks,' said Clare, 'or we might all get murdered in our beds. That invisibility suit is really spooky – he could even be here now, listening to everything we say.'

It was an uncomfortable thought, and they looked around uneasily.

'I think you've all forgotten something,' Lucy said calmly. '*We* can't see him but the animals know exactly where he is all the time. That's why I've got the monkeys keeping a twenty-four-hour watch on him. He's asleep in his hut at the moment.'

They all looked relieved and slightly foolish at having forgotten the continuing protection that Lucy's power provided.

Richard was impressed by his daughter's forward planning.

'But why were you watching him before we had our discussion?'

Lucy laughed. 'Clare and I were discussing him on the way back across the crater. We both think he's a crook and I've had him on CCMW ever since we got back.'

'CCMW?' asked Richard.

'Crater Camp Monkey Watch,' said Lucy, and they all laughed.

'I think it's great we've got him under surveillance,' said Julian, 'but he's still a danger. If he's armed he may not care whether we can see him or not.'

'Well, at least *you're* safe, Dad,' said Clive. 'You're the only one who can fly so he needs you to escape from the crater. The rest of us are dispensable!'

'We don't know that,' said Helen, and the others looked at her. 'I mean, we don't know he can't fly. We don't know anything about him. He could be a flying ace for all we know.'

There was silence again. What she said was true.

'Does he know our plane's bust?' asked Julian. Helen thought for a while.

'Yes,' she said. 'He came to talk to me just after I'd got your note. I was very upset and worried about you and, as I had no reason to suspect him, it was only natural to tell him what had happened. I even thought they might be able to rescue you in their plane but, of course, he had come to tell me it was unusable.'

'Well, even if he can fly a plane, we're safe for the moment,' said Richard, 'because he knows both planes are out of action which means he can't escape. He'll expect us to have emergency rescue plans in place, and without having the details he won't make a move until a rescue plane is actually on the ground.'

'Talking of which, it's a pity we *don't* have a contingency rescue plan in place!' said Julian. 'The plan I made with José depends on our radioing him. I know we had trouble using a radio near the cliffs last time we came, but for some reason I never imagined it wouldn't work *anywhere* in the valley. Maybe it's something to do with the funny ore the professor's been so interested in; it must affect all electromagnetic radiations.'

'Actually, we *do* have a contingency rescue plan,' interjected Lucy, and Richard suddenly remembered the note she had made him write for José's dog. She explained the arrangement to the others and they all felt greatly relieved.

'But,' Lucy continued, 'we only need to use it if we can't get their plane out.' She nodded her head to the villains' camp where the professor slept. 'From what Helen says, the plane isn't damaged, it's just stuck, so we should be able to get it out with the help of the animals.'

'If and when we do, though,' said Clare, 'we'll have to be extra careful of the professor because he'll then have a means of escape if he can fly. And another thought has just struck me. Am I right in thinking, Helen, that Chopper and the pilot didn't leave the camp yesterday until *after* the prof had spoken to you?'

'Yes,' said Helen. 'They were still there when I left – they had to be, because they followed me to the cliff.'

'Well that proves the professor is either a completely innocent victim – as he claims – or is working strictly to his own agenda; he certainly wasn't acting in collusion with the other villains.'

'How come?' asked Clive. He was beginning to find the whole thing rather bewildering.

'Because he let Chopper and the pilot go off looking to steal an aeroplane that he already knew had crashed. Helen had just told him.'

'Clever girl,' said Richard. 'You're absolutely right – but it still means we've got to watch him, so keep the CCMW going, Lucy.'

'So,' said Helen, 'our next task is to look at their plane and see what state it's in. If we can't get it working, or Julian doesn't think he can fly it, we'll use Lucy's brilliant dog plan. Meanwhile we'll all behave as normally as possible to the professor, but watch him for the slightest sign of suspicious behaviour. What will we do, incidentally,' she added, 'if he does try something?'

'Leave that to me,' said Lucy with a grim smile and on that note they all went to bed. Despite the fact that their minds were buzzing with everything that had taken place that day they were all physically exhausted and soon they were fast asleep, while the monkeys took turns to sit, silent and watchful, around the professor's cabin.

20

Spider Speak

The next day they woke to the sound of a tropical thunderstorm. Peals of thunder reverberated round the valley and lightning streaked through the sky every few seconds. The rain was torrential and soon the ground around the tents was turning to mud.

The men splashed their way through the downpour over to the girls' tent. Clare and Helen were getting some breakfast ready on a camp table and Lucy was talking to Queenie.

'The Bearded One is still asleep, even though the jagged skyflashes crash so loudly,' the monkey told her.

'Thank you,' said Lucy. *'Tell me when next he leaves his wooden den and whether he is carrying a firestick.'* The monkey disappeared and Lucy joined the others for breakfast.

Over the meal the conversation turned back once again to the cave in the cliff and Clare's terrifying encounter with the giant spiders.

'One thing still puzzles me,' said Clare. 'Lucy had instructed the animals in this valley to do us no harm; that's why Clive and I – and Helen, of course – were able to cross the valley safely to the cliff. That's right, isn't it?' She looked questioningly at her sister who nodded in agreement.

'Well, I don't think I would ever have been brave enough to go into that dark cave unless I knew that nothing would harm me – even though Sophie here was tugging me to go in.' The monkey was crouching by her side and she stroked her affectionately. 'But when we came up against the spider, I had no doubt whatsoever that it would have attacked me. It attacked Sophie and, as you know, it killed the others –' her voice faltered slightly as she remembered those sinister grey cocoons dangling in the cave. 'But we know that they were *also* protected by Lucy because the animals thought all the humans in the crater were linked with her – even before we arrived the animals in the valley didn't harm the villains.'

'What are you saying?' asked Richard.

'What I'm saying is that the spider didn't seem to know what every other animal in our valley knew. I was wondering if the spider caves go right through to the other side and that the spiders are actually from the *dinosaur* valley – where the animals don't know about Lucy.'

The others were impressed. 'What a fascinating thought,' said Helen.

'Did spiders exist in the Cretaceous?' asked Richard.

'Oh yes,' she said. 'In fact I've got a fossil amber paperweight on my desk at home in which there's a spider web dating from the early Cretaceous period – about 110 million years ago.'

'The only problem is,' said Julian, who had been following the conversation intently, 'that we know that there *can't* be a communication through the cliff because the valleys have completely separate populations of animals, separated in time by millions of years.'

This was so obviously true that the group was silent for a moment.

'Just say . . .' said Helen thoughtfully, 'just say that there *is* a communication, but that it's only small enough to let small animals through – and of course giant spiders. Once the spiders had colonized the caves during the Cretaceous period, nothing could ever have passed from one valley to the other. Large animals would have been prevented by their size, and anything small enough to get through would have been eaten by the spiders. They and their progeny have just sat there for millions of years gobbling up anything from either side that came through.'

'What an intriguing thought,' said Richard. 'Just imagine, a colony of giant spiders sitting in the dark, there since time immemorial, acting as the unconscious custodians of the isolation that has preserved these unique habitats.'

As they thought over Richard's words, Lucy noticed that Clare was looking nervously at Clive and winked at the others. Since they had been tiny she had teased her big sister about her fear of spiders.

'Well, there's only one way to find out if Helen's right,' she said briskly. Everybody looked at her expectantly. 'Before we leave the valley I'm going to the cave – Clare can show me the way to the spiders' den – and I'll see if they know I'm the Promised One.'

'What a great idea!' said Helen.

'Fantastic scientific information,' said Julian.

'Well, as long as you're careful,' said Richard gravely, 'I can think of nothing that could be of greater value to our knowledge of natural history.'

There was a long silence in which they all looked at Clare, struggling to keep their faces straight.

Clare looked extremely uncomfortable.

'Well,' she said, 'to be honest . . .' She suddenly saw that everybody was laughing.

'You rotten swines!' she said. 'Just because I don't like spiders!'

'Sorry to wind you up,' said Lucy with a grin. 'You should've seen your face – I wish I'd had my camera. But about the spiders: I could go back, but there's a quicker way to find out.' She looked down at Sophie:

'Did you speak to the great arachnopod in the cave of the great rock?'

The monkey gave a visible shudder at the memory.

'I told it that we were on the service of the Promised One. It knew her not. It had . . .' she faltered *' . . . it had a terrible voice . . . it was high like the screech of the arboribane, and dark like a sunsleep without the Great Silver One, and cold like the water that comes from deep in the rocks.'*

Lucy told the others what she had said.

'That settles it!' she continued. 'I'm definitely not going back, not for all the science in the world. Anyway, we've got our answer. The spiders must have come through from the Cretaceous valley and have been lurking in that ghastly place for millions and millions of years.'

At that moment Queenie pushed her way through the tent flap.

'The Bearded One approaches. He carries nothing. He wears a special skin but I see him still!'

'He's on his way over,' Lucy told the others. She looked puzzled. 'Queenie says he's got a skin on but she can still see him, whatever that means. And he hasn't brought a gun,' she added with a wry smile, 'so maybe it's just a social call.'

Soon they heard him outside the tent.

'Knock, knock!' he called. Clare was tempted to shout 'Who's there?' but thought better of it.

'Come in, professor,' Helen called, and the flap opened to admit Luke in a plastic raincoat.

'Good morning,' he said. He raised his voice to make himself heard over the drumming of the rain on the tent. 'It's a little damp this morning, and I wondered if you might all be more comfortable in one of our cabins. I've put some coffee on.'

Their plan had been to examine the stuck plane that morning but there was no prospect of doing that in these conditions, so they accepted his invitation. As they got their macs and umbrellas out Lucy spoke to Michelle on her shoulder. She knew from the recent conversation that the professor probably wouldn't make a move until his means of escape was assured, but she wasn't taking any chances.

'*Soon we enter the den of the Bearded One and he will give us something to drink. You have smelt many times the hot, black, water that is drunk by the Tailless Ones and you must warn me if this smells different from any you have smelt before, or if the Bearded One's drink smells different from ours. Be cautious, the drinks will be very hot!*'

'*It shall be done as you wish,*' replied the little monkey.

As she saw her sister communing with the tiny creature Clare smiled to herself; she knew exactly what her sister was up to. Just before they left the tent Lucy turned to Luke.

'Do you mind if my pet monkey comes with me, professor?' she asked, putting on her sweetest smile. 'She's very curious and she'd love to see inside your cabin.' Luke welcomed the opportunity to appear to be a genial father figure.

'Of course I don't mind, my dear.' He smiled. 'I've already seen how cute she is.' As they walked across to the other camp, Lucy spoke to Queenie who immediately disappeared into some nearby trees. Within a few moments she was back.

'*I have spoken to the drumquill,*' she told Lucy, '*and she will do as thou desirest.*'

Soon they were all sitting round the table in the mess hut, which was the communal dining area for the villains. Luke poured them all coffee and, just as he turned away to make a new pot there was a sharp tapping on the door. He stopped and stared at the door, pale with fright. As he watched, Lucy winked at the others. Then the tapping was repeated; this time much louder and more insistent.

'Who . . . who in God's name can that be?' he whispered. 'I thought they were all dead.' He looked questioningly at the others, who shrugged their shoulders in apparent bewilderment. The professor went slowly to the door and opened it a crack. Seeing nothing he gradually opened the door wider and then stepped out and looked around. As he did so Michelle scampered round the table sniffing at the mugs, gave a favourable report to Lucy, and was back on her shoulder before he came back inside, looking totally perplexed.

'There's no one there!' he muttered with his hand on his forehead. 'I could have sworn . . .' his voice faded off as he saw the others seemed completely uninterested in his mystery tapping.

'Funny thing, the wind,' said Clive cheerily as the rest struggled to keep straight faces. Lucy glanced out of the window as if to check on the wind, and was just in time to see the woodpecker disappearing into the woods.

In the event the coffee was delicious.

Talk soon turned, inevitably, to the invisibility robes. As his visitors already knew about them Luke saw little point in being secretive about 'his' invention, especially as he intended to kill them all anyway. They were naturally fascinated by the discovery and he patiently answered all their questions.

'Changing the subject,' he said after a while, 'you must all lead charmed lives. I still find it scarcely credible that four vicious, heavily armed thugs, five if you include the pilot – I was never quite certain about him – have all met with fatal accidents and the six of you have emerged completely unscathed.'

'Well, we intended them no harm,' said Richard, truthfully, 'in fact we tried to save them. I don't think anyone would have wished upon them the terrible fates that they suffered but their greed led them to steal your amazing discovery and they've now suffered the consequences – speaking of which,' he continued, 'I thought you should know that they had a computer disk which presumably contained your invisibility data. We couldn't retrieve it, but at least you can be sure nobody else will ever see it. I presume,' he added casually, 'that you've got back-up data?'

The professor paused slightly before replying – a little too long, Clare thought, for a completely innocent victim. She was sitting opposite him, and had been watching him intently for any sign that might indicate his innocence or otherwise. He decided, again, that he should appear completely open. He had nothing to lose for they were never going to speak to anyone again outside this crater.

'Yes, of course,' he said. 'And thanks for your concern. The disk they stole had already been degraded, as it happens – I always suspected they would steal it – I have all the original data on the hard drive of my computer and a summary of it on another back-up disk.' They all paused for a moment as they reflected on the irony of Chopper and Biggles having sacrificed their lives for a worthless piece of plastic.

'One thing that has puzzled me since you first told me about your kidnap,' said Helen, the first to break the grim silence, 'is why they brought you here. I know it's remote but surely there are dozens of places they could have hidden you while you worked – the basement of a disused warehouse in a city would have been ten times easier and cheaper than coming here.'

'Ah,' said the professor with a smile. 'That's because of the rocks.' He went on to explain about the pilot bringing rocks to the university and how they had come here to obtain the raw materials to make the suits. As he did so Helen suddenly interrupted with a gasp.

'Of course!' she said. 'The pilot. He picked up those rocks for ballast when he rescued us from the crater. After Lucy and Richard left and it was safe for us to move about in the evening –' She stopped and corrected herself, just in time, before mentioning Lucy's instructions to the animals – 'when we began to get more *adventurous* about moving about in the evenings, we occasionally noticed some glowing at dark and we thought that we were looking at glow-worms. From what you've told us though, we were obviously seeing the same phenomenon as the pilot.'

'At least it explains why we couldn't find any glow-worms,' said Julian with a wry smile. 'I wanted a specimen to take back with me and was mystified by their absence, even in places where the glow was very strong.'

The conversation moved back to the extraordinary events of the previous twenty-four hours and the deaths of the villains. 'Can you easily make a new suit?' asked

Richard. 'Helen told me that Chopper and the pilot took the only two in existence and I'm afraid they are now giving some wild animal indigestion.' Again, there was a brief but unmistakable pause before the reply, and Clare was now certain the man was lying.

'I can of course,' replied the professor. 'As I said, I have all the relevant data, but it's a long and difficult job and I'll probably wait now until I'm back in my own lab with proper facilities.' He stopped for a few seconds and then continued. 'Which brings me on to the question of getting out of here. I presume that you've got some contingency plans for being rescued and I was hoping that you might be able to include me in the arrangements.'

'Of course,' said Julian. 'As you probably now know, radios don't work in this crater – we now think it may be something to do with your special rocks and I'd be interested to hear your expert views on that later. Because we'd been here before, we were already aware of the transmission problem so our back-up plan is rather complicated. But before we start getting everybody involved in a great deal of worry and expense I thought I'd take a look at your plane if I may. If we can get it going and it's a model I can fly, it'll save a great deal of time and trouble.'

'Well, the plane's nothing to do with me,' said the professor. 'They just bunged me in it and brought me here. As far as I'm concerned you do anything you want with it! The only thing is,' he continued, 'the pilot was adamant it can't be moved. I haven't seen it myself, but apparently it's stuck in some kind of bog and he said it would take at least fifty men to shift it.'

'Or a team of large horses,' said Lucy suddenly, with a disarming expression on her face. The professor looked at her in some surprise. It was the first time she had contributed to the discussion.

'Well . . . yes, my dear,' he said with a patronizing smile. 'If there were any here, I suppose they would be as good as a tractor. But this isn't a farm, you know.' He then added: 'I wish it was, I haven't had any decent grub for weeks.' He suddenly turned to Helen.

'I don't suppose you've . . .?'

'Yes,' she laughed, 'we do have some supplies as it happens. It's all longlife or tinned but it's probably a change from what Chopper and co. fed you.' She looked out of the cabin window. 'It looks as if it's beginning to clear up. Let's all have lunch together and then we'll go and look at the plane.'

She and Julian went back to their own camp to get some of the food they had brought. On the way they discussed how they could conceal Lucy's power from the professor during the plane removal.

'I think,' said Helen, 'that the truth is something so unlikely that he won't even think about it. We'll just say she's got a way with animals – he's already seen Michelle, and he'll find that it's surprisingly true.'

After a lunch of pasta and Bolognese sauce followed by chocolate-chip cookies they went to look at the plane. The rain had stopped and a watery sun had appeared. As they walked its warmth grew steadily stronger and steam began to rise from the water-logged ground. As it happened, the professor decided to work in his laboratory. He wasn't particularly interested in the operation as he was certain it wouldn't succeed.

The plane was steeply angled down a grassy bank with the nose just short of the cliff. Its tail stuck up in the air but the front half of the fuselage was embedded in a marsh with the wings just resting on the surface. The marsh itself was fed by water running down a gulley between the bank and the cliff. Rivulets of water streaming down the cliff fed into the gulley and after the recent heavy rain torrents of water were gushing down it. The marsh itself was higher than the river beyond into which it ultimately drained. A ridge of fallen rock formed a natural boundary to the marsh and water streamed through cracks in this down to the river itself.

'The good news,' Julian announced as they stood on the bank looking down, 'is that I can fly the plane. It's the same model as our own which isn't really surprising, I suppose – it's far and away the best aircraft for this kind of work.'

'Can we get it out?' said Richard.

'That depends on you and Clive and Lucy,' said Julian. 'You and Clive because we need rope and I seem to remember you and Clive having had quite a lot to do with rope in the last couple of days. And Lucy, of course . . .' He turned to her with a smile, 'because we need her to find that team of horses she was talking about.'

They all laughed at the memory of the professor's

reaction to her suggestion.

'First the rope,' he continued, turning back to Richard. 'Do you have any strong enough for the job?'

'Certainly,' replied Richard confidently. 'Climbing ropes are made of braided polyamide filament – a sort of nylon. They're incredibly strong – have to be; our lives depend on them. The only problem is that the strongest ones we brought were the ones we used on the cliff.'

Lucy had been looking at the plane and listening.

'So you want the ropes from the central escarpment. The ones you were throwing from the plane?'

Richard nodded.

'I missed a couple of times, so there should be two lying around. We left the one Clive used on top of the cliff.' Lucy spoke to Queenie then turned back to the others with a smile:

'She says they'll easily find them with the help of the local monkeys.' As she was speaking Sophie and Clio scampered off towards the central escarpment. Lucy looked puzzled and spoke to Queenie once more.

'Go thou not with thy kin?' she asked the monkey.

'My duty is here, with the Promised One,' Queenie replied gravely. 'I must keep watch on the Bearded One.'

'I thank thee,' said Lucy. 'Thou art right.'

She told the others what had passed, feeling amused and slightly ashamed that a monkey had been able to sort out its priorities better than she had.

21

Search for a Subterranean Slitherkin

While the monkeys were finding the ropes the others stood on the bank looking down at the trapped plane.

'Now,' said Julian to Lucy. 'Let's talk about your "horses". What do you suggest?'

'I think the best things would be those things that look like a cross between a camel and an elephant.'

'That sounds like the animal Queenie got for us yesterday!' exclaimed Clare. 'What's it called?'

'Macrauchenia?' said Julian.

'Yes,' said Lucy, 'I'm sure that's what you called them before. Let me call one and you can see if it'll be OK.' She started to walk away towards the plain and then stopped and turned back to Clare.

'What do you think I should say? I can't really talk about their long noses, but that's what's different about them. The easiest thing would be to send Queenie to get one but she's back keeping an eye on the professor and I think she'd be reluctant to go. I'd hate to force her as she's being so loyal and dutiful.'

'Considering you're meant to be the queen of creation, or whatever, you're being really stupid,' said Clare, smiling. 'Just because we humans think their hose-like noses are incredibly ugly doesn't mean they do. They probably – in fact certainly – think a nose like that is the best thing since sliced bread!'

Lucy grinned. 'You're right, as usual. I'll give it a try.'

She left the others and wandered away to get clear of the trees round the camp. There were no animals that she could see, but she knew from her previous experience with condors that her 'voice' could carry for an incredible distance and she projected her thoughts across the great expanse of savannah.

'Hear me O great grazers of the plains; ye with the noses that put all others to shame. The Promised One is in need of your aid!'

She returned to the others and only moments later a macrauchenia trotted out of the undergrowth. It must have been grazing in the bushes nearby all the time.

The gentle herbivore, a female, stood placidly beside them, occasionally stooping to browse while she waited for further instructions. Her head was ten feet from the ground when she raised her long neck and her nose ended in a short trunk that gradually got smaller towards the tip – rather like a conical hose pipe.

'She seems perfect for the job,' said Julian. 'Can you get another five, do you think? One horse is equal to twelve men and these things look a lot stronger than horses. That should give us some serious muscle power, probably more than twice what the pilot estimated was necessary. I won't ask you if you think they mind helping us because I already know the answer!'

'I think all we have to do is wait!' laughed Lucy. 'I sent out a bit of a general call.' Sure enough, within a few moments a herd of about fifty of the creatures appeared. Lucy thanked all of them for coming and, after Julian had selected the individuals of his choice, let the others know, as kindly as possible, that their services would not be required that day. She also sent out another call to prevent any more of the creatures appearing.

Julian spoke to Clive and Richard.

'We'd better knock up some kind of yoke and harness – like you see on carriages and Wild-West wagons. There must be plenty of tools in the crooks' camp – they built all those cabins.'

As they went off to collect the tools Lucy turned to the six remaining animals and pointed to the stricken plane.

'The thunderquill's hooves are trapped in the watery earth. We require your great strength to make it free. There will be lianas around you for a while, but soon ye shall be free once again.'

Soon the men returned and set to work. The macrauchenia stood patiently as they were harnessed. While this work was in progress the monkeys returned with the ropes, assisted by some very savage-looking monkeys from the valley. They were accompanied by a wolf-like creature with massive teeth that had apparently been recruited to bite the grapnels off the ropes.

'The wolf-fang helped us,' Sophie explained to Lucy, *'and now comes so that he can tell his kin that he has seen thee.'*

Julian said he was a protocyon – a primitive canine.

The men tied one end of each rope to their makeshift harness and the other to the tail-wheel of the plane. Under Lucy's instruction the macrauchenia started forward and took the strain. The ropes tautened and began to pull on the plane. Soon the ropes were tense but the plane didn't budge an inch. The animals began to paw at the ground to gain better purchase and strained at their harness.

'Stop!' said Julian, and Lucy asked them to stop.

'I think they're OK for a bit more,' she said after speaking to them, 'or do you think the ropes are going to snap?'

'Neither,' said Julian. 'I think the force we've already applied should have started to shift the plane at least a bit. I'm worried that it's actually jammed on something we can't see in the marsh. If we carry on pulling we might rip the tail-wheel off or even damage the whole tail section.'

'I've got an idea,' called Clare. She was sitting with Helen on the bank a few yards from the plane and had been watching the whole operation.

'Any ideas welcome!' said Julian good-naturedly. 'As long as they leave the plane intact.'

'Why don't we drain the bog,' said Clare. 'Then we can see what's going on and maybe fix ropes to the front wheels as well.'

Julian looked sceptical at first but then looked at the bog and the river beyond, several feet lower.

'I like the idea,' he said, 'but the labour involved is immense, even with all six of us at it. We'd need to cut a drainage channel through or round that rocky ridge separating the bog from the river –' he pointed, '– and stop any more water coming in at the top end by diverting the flow coming down from the gulley.'

'Maybe we won't need to do anything ourselves,' said Lucy quietly. 'Let me just make some enquiries; though I think I need to speak to something more intelligent than our hosenoses, begging their pardon.'

She turned and spoke to Queenie. A moment later Sophie and Clio went off and soon returned with a very large, fierce-looking monkey, obviously from the same group that had helped them earlier.

'*Greetings, O great agile one,*' said Lucy to the newcomer. '*I thank thee for coming once again.*'

'*Greetings, O Promised One,*' came the reply. '*How may I be of service to thee?*'

'*We wish to free the thunderquill from the watery earth, –*' she pointed – '*and we wish to take the water away. There are many creatures in this valley that are unknown to us. Are there any that can help us in this task?*'

The monkey examined the bog, then turned back to Lucy. The others watched this silent interchange with fascination.

'*The great shieldkin with the tail-that-batters can dig the earth and will come to serve thee at my bidding,*' he said slowly, '*but . . . but there is another within my ken who is mighty in the ground.*'

He sounded doubtful.

'*What is this creature?*' asked Lucy, to prompt him. She

264

wasn't sure of the reason for his hesitation.

'He looks like a giant malevolent one or a giant earthkin – and yet he is neither. We call him the slitherkin. He speaks but rarely and never to us arborikin. I think he will only come to serve thee if he hears thy voice.'

'Let us try both creatures,' said Lucy. 'The arborikin by my side –' she indicated Clio, '– can seek out the shieldkin while thou leadest me to the slitherkin.'

'As it pleases the Promised One. The slitherkin is hard to find and we may have to search far yonder until the Brilliant One goes to rest.' He indicated towards the centre of the valley.

'I will come,' said Lucy, 'and some of my kin will accompany us.'

She turned to the others and explained what the monkey had said.

'I've no idea what the "slitherkin" is,' she said, 'but no doubt we'll soon find out.' She turned to Clare and Clive.

'Do you fancy an adventure, you two? It'll make a change; it's been a boring couple of days, after all!' They all laughed and the three young people set off with the Pleistocene monkey while Clio set off with Sophie to look for some glyptodonts.

As they left the men returned with Helen to their own camp, after unhitching the macrauchenia who wandered off to browse nearby.

The monkey led Lucy and her companions towards the centre of the valley. After half a mile or so he crouched and put his ear to the ground, and then did this at similar intervals as they walked.

Eventually, after listening intently, he tensed then turned his head and put his other ear to the ground. He grunted and stood up.

'*The slitherkin is near,*' he said simply. Lucy thought he looked somewhat apprehensive. He then set off in a new direction and they all followed, wondering what on earth they were going to see.

Soon the monkey stopped, sniffed and peered ahead. Then he spoke again.

'*There is the spoor of the slitherkin. There is none other like it.*'

Lucy followed his gaze and saw some fresh earth banked up on the surface. As they grew near they could see that it was the edge of a giant trench, a yard wide and a yard deep that ran along the ground for about fifty yards. Bushes, rocks and small trees that had obviously been in its path, lay thrown or pushed aside outside the giant furrow. They walked along the trench until they saw it disappear into a hole, like a giant mole hole. The monkey, who had become progressively more nervous, stopped again.

'*The Promised One should speak,*' he said, '*for the slitherkin draws nigh and we are in great danger until he knows it is thee who comes.*'

Lucy spoke; she had learnt that most animals seemed to respond best to a direct request or command:

'*Greetings, O Master of the Earth. The hour has come for thee to serve the Promised One.*'

There was no reply. She waited and repeated the message.

'Look!' said Clare suddenly, and pointed to a spot thirty

yards or so away. The earth was agitated by something underneath and then a slightly raised mound appeared and extended towards them. Something was moving along just underneath the surface. Suddenly the ground broke and a head appeared. It looked like the head of a giant snake but as it emerged from the soil two small horns appeared, like the retractile antennae of a snail. These protruded above two pitted depressions that might have been eyes. The head was followed by a long, black, scaly body with a yellow zigzag stripe along its back. It continued emerging for so long that the frightened onlookers began to think it must be endless. Eventually the entire creature slid out from the ground. It was about twenty-five metres long and over a metre in width. It looked incredibly sinister.

'What on earth . . .' began Clare. She glanced at Lucy, but Lucy was preoccupied and looking distinctly worried. Clare moved closer to Clive.

'I can't believe this . . . this *alien* creature can possibly know about Lucy and obey her,' she whispered. 'Have you got a gun?'

'No,' Clive whispered back. He put his arm round Clare protectively. 'Stay still. I'm sure it'll be OK.'

The monkey left Lucy's side – she was standing at the forefront of the group – and went to stand behind Clive and Clare, which Lucy didn't find particularly reassuring. The creature looked at Lucy: it still hadn't spoken. For a terrible, almost unendurable moment Lucy thought that her power was useless with this animal and that she had brought her sister and Clive into terrible danger. Then, at last, it responded. Its voice was slow and cold and made Lucy think of dark, awful, underground caverns and icy sepulchres.

'It is many aeons since my kin were told of thee, and I had to come and smell thee before I spoke.' He sounded both primitive and arrogant, and Lucy felt less comfortable with him than almost any creature with whom she had ever conversed. Then, to her great relief, he continued in a more positive vein.

'Thou art indeed the Promised One. I never thought my kin would need to serve thee: what dost thou desire?'

Clare glanced at Lucy. Her sister's face had relaxed and she was clearly managing to converse with the beast. She squeezed Clive's hand and said, 'I think it's going to be all right.'

He returned her squeeze and didn't seem in any hurry to let go as they watched Lucy speaking to the extraordinary creature lying before them.

'I need thy skill to make tunnels in the ground.'

'In which place. Here?'

'No, a league hence. We will show you the place.'

The creature glanced to the sky, now overcast once again. *'I can come above the earth for the Brilliant One hides this day and will soon descend to his sleep. With the Promised One by my side the deathquills will not molest me.'* He paused, then added by way of explanation: *'All other creatures go in terror of me but the deathquills fear naught that moves, save the greatfang and the Mighty One, and they sometimes attack me.'*

Lucy turned to the others.

'It's OK; we're off. He's coming above ground because it'll be quicker. He says he doesn't usually do that because of the sun, but it's cloudy today. He's also not too keen on the terror birds: they sometimes have a go at him but they won't if he's with me.'

Even as she spoke two enormous terror birds approached. Clare and Clive had seen them at a distance and remembered Helen and Julian's account of their terrifying encounter with one of these creatures on their previous expedition, but it was only at close quarters that they fully appreciated how large and fearsome they were. Three metres tall, like giant ostriches with massive hooked beaks and formidable claws, the birds stalked menacingly towards the group.

'I hope you can talk to these guys,' said Clare to Lucy. 'They look like the nightmare birds from hell.' So saying, she felt it was a good excuse to squeeze Clive's hand a little tighter again.

Lucy didn't answer. She was already talking to the birds. Soon she turned to the others.

'It's OK, they're desperate to help so they're going to accompany us back. There's no animal in this valley that will attack us, but they say they'll protect us. It seemed rather ungracious to refuse so they're tagging along. I expect it gives them massive street cred with their mates.' She looked at them again as they moved even closer. 'Scary, aren't they? Helen told me last time we were here that they were probably the top predators when South America was still an island and you can see why. The big cats and dogs came down later when it joined up to North America and that's when the sabre-tooths started to rule the roost.'

'Talking of which . . .' said Clive, pointing behind Lucy. She turned to see four sabre-tooth cats majestically stalking towards them.

'Word is obviously round,' he continued with a smile, 'that the Promised One is out and about in the crater and everyone wants a piece of the action.'

And his analysis just about summed it up, for a moment later Lucy confirmed that the cats were coming along as well 'to give us added protection,' she laughed. As she spoke the largest smilodon, a female, came right up to Lucy and nuzzled her. For a moment Clare thought she was going to attack her sister and the thought of what those massive eight-inch fangs might do made her blood run cold. But Lucy stroked the animal and tickled her behind the ear.

'Would you believe it!' she said. 'This is the very cat that I used to show Dad and Helen and Julian that I could really speak to animals! She heard I was here and came to see us.'

The party made their way back to the camp. It was clear that the valley monkey was not entirely at ease in the presence of various hostile creatures who would, under normal circumstances, have torn him limb from limb, but he gradually adjusted to the fact that, within the magic, protective umbrella of the Promised One, he was invulnerable. As they drew near, Helen, who had been looking out for them, started to laugh, and pointed out across the valley.

'Just look at what she's collected this time!'

The men turned to see the bizarre spectacle consisting of three humans, one with a marmoset on her shoulder, a monkey, a pack of sabre-tooths, a pair of terror birds, miscellaneous small attendant creatures and, slithering along behind, what looked like a giant snake. A thought suddenly struck her and she turned quickly to Julian.

'Where's the prof? If he sees this circus it's going to take some explaining.'

'Relax,' said Julian chuckling. 'He didn't go to his lab. He went for a nap after that lunch you cooked us and has been out cold ever since. I've just been across to his cabin to check – though I knew it would be OK as Queenie didn't come and alert us to any trouble. The wine was a brilliant idea, by the way, where on earth did you dig that up from?'

'I brought it with me,' said Helen. 'It was meant to be a surprise for our last day here, hopefully to celebrate a successful expedition. But when I thought about keeping the prof out of the way while Lucy did her stuff with the animals it seemed to be a much better use for it – and, as you saw, I made sure he drank more than anyone else.

'And now,' she said, looking once more at the approaching spectacle, 'I must get my camera. This is definitely one for the family album!'

As she ran across to her tent Richard and Julian gazed once more at the approaching pageant and now as it drew near they could see that the immense creature in the rear

'What on earth is that – it must be over 80 feet long!'

was not a snake, but something that looked as if it belonged in an anthology of mythical and legendary animals.

'My God!' exclaimed Richard. 'What on earth is that – it must be over eighty feet long!'

Julian gazed fascinated at the approaching monster. 'I really don't know,' he said eventually. 'It looks more like a giant worm than anything else. They do exist – in Australia there are still worms up to ten feet long – but I've never heard of anything like this. I'll look it up later.'

Richard was intrigued. He had always been impressed with Julian's phenomenal knowledge of ancient animals and this was the first time he had seen him nonplussed.

Helen reappeared with her camera, and they went to

meet the others; they were joined by Sophie and Clio who were accompanied by two glyptodonts, giant armadillo-like creatures, each the size of a small car. Their vicious, spiked, mace-like tails were obviously the 'tails-that-batter' referred to by the crater monkey.

By now it was almost sunset and they decided that if the animals could start draining the bog overnight then they might be able to free the plane in the morning. While the animal search party had been gone, Richard and Julian had worked out exactly where the drainage and diversion channels should be dug, and now explained their plans to Lucy. The animals who had simply accompanied her for the kudos of being in her company now dispersed and they were left with the glyptodonts and the giant 'worm'.

Lucy soon set the glyptodonts to work scrabbling at the rocks and soil above the marshy area, to divert all the water that flowed into it. She then spoke to the burrowing monster, pointing to the raised ledge that prevented the bog draining into the river below.

'We want all the water surrounding the thunderquill to go down to the Flowing One. Can you help in this task?'

'Yes,' was the simple reply, and the creature slithered into the bog itself. Soon over half its prodigious length was under the surface and half remained, draped languidly across the bank and extending back into the nearby bush in gentle, sinuous curves. Soon, powerful eddy currents began to appear in the marsh from the direction of the head of the creature, and within a few moments several square metres of the surface were seething and swirling and bubbling, as though it were a giant, mud-filled jacuzzi.

'We don't know how long this will take,' said Richard as the sun disappeared behind the western rim of the crater, 'and the animals seem to be happy to continue in the dark, so I suggest we all go in and have some supper.'

'Well, I've got good news for you there,' said Lucy who had just spoken to Queenie. The monkey had approached her as they all stood watching the drainage operation. 'Sophie and Clio went for a little forage and they've just found a dead pig at the base of the escarpment – it must have fallen down from the jungle above. If we can grab it before the terror birds and the jackal-things we can have a pork barbecue. Sophie says she'll take you.'

Twenty minutes later the men returned with the fresh carcass. In the meantime the others had lit a fire. They all decided it would take too long to roast the pork on a proper spit, so Richard cut some steaks which they barbecued on the grill they had used for their fish supper the previous evening.

After supper, while the young ones talked to the professor about the endlessly engrossing subject of invisibility, Richard asked Julian once again about the strange creature engaged at that very moment in draining the marsh.

'I think I know what that is,' said Helen at once; she had missed their previous discussion. 'At least, I know something that's *said* to look like it, but most orthodox scientists don't really believe it exists. Have you heard of cryptozoology?'

She looked at Richard enquiringly.

'Ye-es,' he said slowly. 'Isn't that all about animals that are rumoured to exist but which mainstream science doesn't recognize?'

'Exactly,' Helen replied. 'Typically, there'll be an animal that has been seen – often by very credible witnesses – but for whose existence there is no conclusive proof. The sort of creatures we're talking about include the Loch Ness monster, Bigfoot, and the Yeti. They're also called cryptids or UMAs – unidentified mysterious animals. Conventional scientists are mostly sceptical about these kinds of animals but cryptozoologists point out that many creatures we now know *do* exist were originally thought to be myths or hoaxes. These include the gorilla, the giant squid and the Komodo dragon.'

Richard nodded. He was listening intently.

'And where does our big worm fit into all this?' he asked.

'It's a creature called a Minhocão. In the nineteenth century there were several reports of sightings of a giant worm-like animal over seventy feet long. The reports came, interestingly, from South America, mostly from Brazil but also from Uruguay and Nicaragua. The animal gobbled up livestock and dug enormous trenches which were said to cause houses and roads to collapse, to divert rivers and to destroy orchards and plantations. Eyewitnesses described a creature very similar to the one we've seen today. Since the end of the nineteenth century there have been no further sightings, though mysterious trenches are still said to appear from time to time in various places. Those who believe in the creature think it may now be extinct; others say it never existed at all and that villagers had simply mistaken anacondas for something much longer and larger.'

'But if it did – or does – exist, what actually is it?' asked Richard.

'Some people think it is a giant worm, some suggest it is a descendant of a creature like an armadillo – the glyptodonts you saw today. Others think it is a kind of giant salamander or a species of lungfish – which might account for the fact that our specimen seemed perfectly happy under water.'

'Do you believe in it?' asked Richard. Helen laughed.

'Not until a few hours ago. This thing is so like the descriptions given by eye-witnesses, it's difficult to believe it's not the same creature.'

'We must ask Lucy to get some scales or saliva from it,' said Julian, who had been listening with great interest. 'If we can analyse its DNA we might at least be able to establish what kind of animal it really is.'

'Whatever it is,' added Helen, 'it seems to have been a brilliant choice for the job by that monkey. It seems tailor-made for what we're trying to do.'

The professor had finished his conversation with the others and twisted his camp chair to face Julian across the embers of the barbecue.

'How did you get on today? I'm sorry I didn't come and help, but I felt it was important to get back to the lab and construct another invisibility suit as soon as possible.' Helen winked at Julian, who managed to suppress a smile.

'Not very well,' he replied. 'As you warned us, the plane is stuck pretty tight. We're trying something different though. We've dug some channels to try and drain the marsh overnight and we'll see if that helps in the morning.'

'Well, I wish you the best . . .' he stopped and gaped. The others followed his gaze. While he had been speaking Queenie had reached up and taken a tissue from a box on the table. She had now taken her glasses off and was carefully rubbing the lenses, just as she had seen Lucy do on countless occasions. Helen laughed at his expression.

'She hates them being grubby,' she said without further

explanation and the others managed to hide their smiles as the professor nodded but looked even more bewildered.

Tired by the labours of the day they turned in; the monkeys resumed their watch over the professor and soon there was nothing to be heard other than an occasional crackle from the dying fire, and the calls of the hunters and the hunted in the Pleistocene night.

22

The Mighty Ones Get Stuck In

The next day dawned bright and clear and by the time the group assembled for breakfast the equatorial sun was already evaporating the remains of the previous day's rain. All except Clive breakfasted on the delicious fruits collected that morning by the monkeys, who seemed indefatigable. Clive ate his favourite breakfast cereal that his indulgent mother had brought over four thousand miles for him.

After breakfast they went to see the plane. The whole area had been transformed overnight. The plane now stood, completely exposed, on a bed of mud that was already drying and cracking in the baking heat of the sun. At the lower end of the former marsh two enormous tunnels could be seen, through which the water had obviously drained down into the nearby river. In two or three places there were depressions in the former bank of the marsh which ended in solid rock – places where the burrowing worm had obviously failed to create a channel. At the top end the rivulets of water streaming down the cliff from the rainforest above were now diverted into a channel that carried the water down to a different part of the vast plain. The animals had obviously worked as a team: the glyptodonts had created a barrier of rocks and earth that prevented any water entering the marsh area, but the metre-wide channel that now carried the flow hundreds of yards in the opposite direction on to the plain was unmistakably the work of the giant worm.

The cause of the problem in shifting the plane the previous day was now apparent. The wheels were jammed in front of a rocky ledge which was now protruding from the mud. Julian had been absolutely right: the macrauchenia could have pulled all day and would have succeeded only in snapping the ropes or ripping off the tail of the plane.

'A brilliant idea, Clare, draining the marsh,' Julian acknowledged graciously as they surveyed the scene. 'There's no way we could've pulled it out without knowing about those rocks.'

'And now it's easy,' said Lucy. 'I'll be back soon. Oh, and get the harness ready again – please,' she added over her shoulder as she disappeared off into the bush.

Within a few minutes the obliging team of macrauchenia appeared, but there was no sign of Lucy.

'We may as well hitch them up,' said Julian. 'We're obviously expected to use them again.'

They assembled the team once again under the watchful eye of Queenie, who was obviously instructing the animals in Lucy's absence. As they were all engaged in their task they were suddenly aware of giant shadows passing over them. Richard, puzzled by the fact that the sky had been completely clear of clouds, turned and found himself facing two giant ground sloths. Lucy was standing in between the giants, looking very pleased with herself.

'Sorry to be so long,' she said cheerfully, 'but they were miles away. Oh, well done,' she added, seeing the macrauchenia all hitched up to the tailplane. 'You've got everything ready.'

Helen, who was standing behind Clare and Clive, put her arms round their shoulders as they stared in wonder at the size of the animals.

'Hulking great things aren't they? They're giant ground sloths – their scientific name is megatherium. They look to be just what we need for this job.'

Lucy asked Julian where the sloths could best hold the plane without damaging it and he showed her. The giants then lumbered into the drying mud and each got hold of the front of a wing just where it was attached to the main body of the plane. At Lucy's command they lifted the plane so that the wheels were in the air, completely clear of the rocks. The sloths had now sunk about a foot into mud under the combined weight of their massive bulk and the aeroplane. As the macrauchenia team started pulling, the sloths managed to drag their feet out to the accompaniment of loud sucking and slurping noises and the plane immediately started to move backwards. As soon as the wheels were clear of the mud Lucy instructed the sloths to lower the plane so that the wheels were on firm ground and the macrauchenia then hauled the plane steadily up the steep incline back to the level plain on which it had originally been parked. Then they pulled it round so it was facing in the right direction to take off along the airstrip.

'Now for the moment of truth,' said Julian. 'Is the engine still OK?' He retrieved the safety chocks, still on the ground nearby where Biggles had hurriedly thrown them before hiding the plane, fixed them under the wheels, and clambered into the cockpit. The key was in the controls – there had been no point whatsoever in the previous pilot removing it – and Julian tentatively started the engine. As it sputtered encouragingly and then roared into life everybody clapped and cheered in relief.

That evening they all ate together again with the professor, who was astonished at their success in retrieving the plane.

'Draining the marsh was a brilliant idea,' he said. 'It obviously made it so easy to get the plane out. I wonder why the others didn't think about it. They actually had a lot more muscle power than you did.'

The others winked at each other and smiled, but said nothing.

After the professor had retired to his own cabin for the night, Helen pointed out that, now the plane was in working order, they had to be even more careful, just in case the professor was able to fly.

'I think it's OK,' said Lucy, smiling broadly. 'Take a look.'

They all looked out and Clive put out the light in the hut so they could see better what was going on outside.

Gradually their eyes adjusted to the dark and, helped by the fact there was a full moon, they could see the silvery outline of the plane. Lying around it some dark shapes could be made out and as they watched one of them yawned and turned its head and its massive sabre teeth glistened in the moonlight.

'Well,' said Richard, 'I think we can go to bed without worrying about the plane suddenly starting up and disappearing in the middle of the night.'

They all agreed, and made their way to their tents, happy in the knowledge that they would soon be heading home.

The next morning they had breakfast before the professor appeared. The monkeys, as usual, were keeping a discreet watch on him. The sabre-tooths had faded away in the early morning, their nocturnal duties over, and had been replaced by some venomous-looking snakes that just happened to be in the grass between the professor's cabin and the plane.

'I've been thinking about the professor and his invisibility research,' said Clive. 'He'll probably try and wipe his computer before he leaves so, if we decide at some point he's definitely a baddie, we'd better try and stop him doing so. There may be all kinds of stuff on there that would be invaluable to the police.' They all agreed.

'Talking of which,' said Julian, 'I have a plan to decide once and for all whether or not he's genuine. I'll just run through my thoughts with you: if he really is an innocent victim he's going to be happy with any reasonable rescue plan that we come up with.' They all nodded. 'If, on the other hand, he's a crook, we're all in great danger, especially if he can fly a plane. We know about the invisibility suit and if, as Lucy suggested, he pinched the research idea from someone else, he knows that his crime will be exposed as soon as we reach civilization.' They all nodded again. 'What he won't allow if he *can't* fly,' Julian continued, 'is for me to leave the crater without him. He needs to accompany me so that, once he's forced me to take him where he wants to go, he can dispose of me before I can speak to the police. My plan is aimed at exposing us to the least danger possible, on the assumption that he *is* a villain.' He then outlined his idea.

During the morning Julian tinkered with the plane to make sure he was happy with it for the forthcoming flight from the crater. At lunchtime they all sat down with the professor. Julian ate hurriedly and, before the others were finished, stood up and said: 'I want to fly in daylight so I'll get off as soon as possible. I've got one or two final things to check but I hope to leave in about ten minutes. You guys finish your lunch and I'll see you in a day or so. Cheerio!'

He walked round the table to bend over and kiss Helen; the others said goodbye and waved, and then, trying to behave as normally as possible turned back to carry on with their lunch. As the families carried on chatting Helen stole a glance at the professor. His face was white and he was fidgeting as if desperately thinking what to do. In that instant she knew that he was not the innocent victim he had claimed to be. Lucy caught her glance and, without moving or looking, spoke to Queenie who was sitting on the floor beside her.

'I have already spoken to the deathtails about the magic window. Go now and tell them that their time has come. Then, watch the Bearded One. If he leaves my sight, follow him and tell me in haste what he does.'

The monkey quietly got up and wandered out of the open door. Her disappearance went unnoticed by the professor who was looking progressively more agitated.

'What's happening!' He suddenly blurted out. 'Where's Julian going?' He was trying to sound casual but his voice was trembling.

'Oh, he decided that he didn't want to risk taking the whole family in a plane which has just been hauled out of a swamp,' said Helen lightly. 'He's worried there could be concealed stress damage to the tail section where we fixed the cables. If there is, a lighter load would be much safer. Besides, there wouldn't be enough room to take you as well as all our lot. So he's going on his own and will come back with a bigger plane, or accompanied by a bigger plane from Richard's company, and pick us all up as soon as it can be arranged.'

'That makes good sense,' said the professor. He had recovered his composure. He stood up. 'Excuse me a moment. I have a number I'd like him to call to reassure my relatives.'

He left hurriedly, and shut the door of the mess hut behind him. They all rushed to the window and peeped out cautiously. They saw him hurry over to his cabin and shut the door. Queenie emerged from the lab nearby and jumped onto his hut roof. She bent down so she could peer in through the window. Soon she sprang down and bounded back to the mess hut.

'The Bearded One has taken up a flat tree from the floor and there is a small cave under there. From this cave he has taken a firestick, a special skin, and some little, hard leaves that look like the Great Silver One. He now wears the skin and I can no longer see him, though he still has a bad smell.'

'Thank you,' said Lucy. *'You have done well. Now I must ask a further favour.'* She spoke again and then turned to the others as the monkey hurried off, obviously on a new mission.

'She says he took a floorboard up in his hut and removed a gun, some cloth and what sounds like some CD disks. Then he shook open the cloth and disappeared.'

She looked at Helen, who had turned pale.

'Don't worry, it's no more than we expected. I'm following our plan. All we have to do is wait and we'll be safer in here, as Julian said.'

They clustered round the window again just in time to see the professor's cabin door swinging shut and the laboratory door opening and closing. Clare turned to Clive.

'You were right! He's trying to wipe the computer before leaving.' A few seconds later the laboratory door burst open and slammed against the wall of a hut. Somebody was obviously leaving in a hurry.

'Whatever you did, Lucy, seems to have done the trick!'

laughed Clive. As he spoke the plane engine started up and they rushed over to the other window from which they could see the plane. The propeller had spun into life, its blades already turning so fast as to be invisible, but with their pitch feathered so the plane would not move, and Julian got down from the cabin to remove the safety chocks from under the wheels.

At that moment a sabre-toothed tiger bounded out from the bushes near the plane and stood in front of Julian who was now climbing back in. The great cat sniffed the air and suddenly fell to a predatory crouch with eyes peering intently forward, seeking an invisible prey, shoulders low to the ground and hindquarters bunched up like tightly coiled springs. Its intentions were unmistakable to the onlookers who had seen this behaviour a thousand times before at home, watching a cat preparing to spring on a bird or mouse.

Suddenly a pistol appeared in mid-air. As it did so, a hawk which had been sitting on the roof of the plane took off and flew straight towards it. There was a single shot an instant before the powerful talons of the raptor tore the gun from the professor's grip and the sabre-tooth rolled over on to its side. There was a moment when nothing seemed to happen. The hawk had disappeared with the gun. Julian stood in the door of the plane looking bewildered and the onlookers waited, gazing anxiously at the scene in which this drama had so suddenly unfolded. As they watched the big cat grunted, struggled to its feet, sniffed again at the air, then started to limp purposefully towards something it could clearly identify but which was still completely invisible to the humans.

Suddenly there was a thud, and the professor's head appeared in the air. It fell to the ground and, as the sabre-tooth lurched towards it for the kill, Lucy ran out of the cabin and called to the animal. The sabre-tooth stopped short of the head and looked up at Lucy, just as its fearsome jaws were about to sink into an invisible form lying before it. Then it relaxed.

'Stand still Lucy!' Julian shouted, 'For God's sake don't do what he did.' She froze as he went back into the cockpit and switched off the engine. The propeller slowed and finally came to a stop. The crisis was over.

The others all poured out of the cabin and rushed over. Richard gave Lucy a quick hug, then bent down to examine the professor's head. To his relief, it was still attached to his body which was invisible under the robe. With the help of the others he removed the robe and carefully examined the inert man. He was alive, but deeply unconscious and there was an ugly wound on the back of his head.

'As he stepped away from the cat he walked back into the propeller,' explained Julian. He looked down at the prostrate form on the ground. 'It must've hit him a glancing blow – he's lucky he didn't lose his head.'

Richard looked up. 'He's seriously injured, just the same. He's almost certainly fractured his skull. We must get him to hospital as soon as possible if he's to have any chance of survival.' He thought quickly. 'We should go right now, the three of us. I can do my best for him while you get us somewhere suitable as soon as possible. We'll come back for the others tomorrow.'

'OK,' said Julian, 'But,' he added grimly, 'everything depends on what the prop looks like.'

He went over and inspected the propeller which was now stationary. To his relief it was intact.

'The invisibility helmet must have helped to soften the blow for both him and the prop,' he said. 'Let's go.'

They laid the professor across two of the seats with Richard just behind. They waved to the others and once again the engine roared into life. The plane gathered speed across the plain, lifted off and disappeared over the rim of the crater.

'Well,' said Lucy. 'That's one patient sorted out. Now for the other. We've lost the proper doctor but I'm sure you two medics can do something. Come and help me with the cat.' They walked over to where the sabre-tooth lay.

'The evil one has hurt thee with his firestick,' said Lucy. *'We have come to help. Do not harm those who touch thee now.'*

She nodded to Clive and Clare who knelt beside the cat to examine it. There were two wounds, an entry wound near the top of the shoulder and an exit wound a few inches further back.

'At least there isn't a bullet in there,' said Clare. 'Surely that must be a good thing.'

'Yes,' said Clive, 'but we don't know what damage it's done inside. It could have fractured the shoulder blade. I haven't done much orthopaedics yet, but I doubt if that would need any treatment. We actually saw her limp on it, so I don't think anything really dreadful has happened to the bones. In nature of course, she couldn't hunt or defend herself, and probably wouldn't survive but I'm sure Lucy can sort those problems out. The main thing is whether she's got serious internal bleeding or not. We wouldn't be able to do anything about that.'

They made the cat as comfortable as possible, gave her a large dish of water and Lucy arranged for her fellow cats to feed and defend her.

'I should've asked Dad to bring a vet,' said Lucy, as they walked back to the camp. 'I just didn't think about it.'

'You didn't have time,' said Clare comfortingly, 'and his main concern was the professor.'

'And,' said Clive, 'what's a vet going to think about being asked to look at a sabre-tooth? Your secret would be out.'

'Good Lord!' exclaimed Clare, looking at Lucy who gave an embarrassed grin. 'You're right of course. We'd completely forgotten that.'

Clive blushed. He had come to realize that it wasn't often anyone scored over the Bonaventure sisters. They were a formidable combination. It was bad enough trying to keep up with Clare (whose suggestions throughout the trip had invariably turned out to be the best ones), but when the smart girl you fancied also happened to have a little sister who could *talk to animals* . . . He rapidly changed the subject.

'And now,' he said, 'I'm dying to know if the professor

managed to wipe the computer.'

'Ooh yes! I'll come with you,' said Clare. Clive turned to Lucy. 'Can you come too, so that its custodians don't attack us!'

She laughed. 'Of course.'

And they all made their way to the lab.

The first thing they saw as they entered the hut was a crate just inside the door.

'What on earth...' said Clive, as he bent down and inspected the pile of stones it contained.

'It's ore!' exclaimed Clare. 'The ore that's only found here. He was planning to take some back so that he would be sure to have a future supply of the stuff that makes invisibility suits. He was obviously going to force Julian and you to load it into the plane at gunpoint but was overtaken by events.'

The others agreed – there was no other explanation – and then made their way past the crate to the desk. The computer was turned on and a screensaver composed of a series of endlessly changing Newton's rings was on the monitor.

'Looks clear,' Clive said, and moved towards the keyboard.

'Stop,' said Lucy, 'unless you want a nasty surprise. I told them only to come out if somebody started tapping on the keys. Watch.'

He stopped and she stepped forward and tapped the keyboard a few times at random. A few seconds later three enormous black scorpions appeared, from under the keyboard one on each side and one from the front. They raised their claws and their tails curled up with the stings in a menacing pose. Lucy looked at them for a moment and soon they relaxed and scuttled away. Clive watched until they were safely under the door of the cabin before he could relax.

'Cripes!' he said, 'No wonder the prof left in such a hurry!' Then he sat in front of the computer and started to operate the keyboard, rather clumsily with his splinted wrist.

'Your security plan was a brainwave,' he exclaimed. 'He'd just had time to tap in his password before the scorpions drove him out. What a bonus!' He pointed to the screen where the word MORIARTY was displayed.

'I wonder what it means,' said Lucy. 'I'm sure I've heard of it before.'

'Probably his mother's maiden name,' said Clive. 'Usually is. Whatever it is, knowing it is going to save some police computer nerd quite a lot of time.' He sat and started flicking through the computer folders as the girls went back to check on the injured sabre-tooth.

23
Another Invisible Surprise

The next day the big cat was alive, and though she wasn't moving much, she had drunk all the water and was eating heartily the food brought to her by the others. 'I think if she was bleeding seriously she wouldn't have survived the night,' Clare reassured Lucy, 'so she's already past the most dangerous period.'

By mid-morning they were all sitting in the mess hut drinking coffee and wondering what time the plane might return. The sky was overcast and there was the occasional rumble of thunder. Suddenly there was a sound like a gunshot nearby. They all looked at each other in consternation. Clive got up and looked out cautiously.

'That wasn't thunder. Sounded as if it came from the lab,' he said. 'I suppose I'd better go and investigate.'

'No!' said Lucy. 'It sounded like a gun. There might be other crooks we don't know about. I'll send Queenie.' Clive looked relieved at this suggestion as he felt very vulnerable with one arm out of action, and soon the monkey was on the lab roof peering through the lab window. As she jumped down and scampered back they saw a wisp of smoke drifting out through the window netting.

'*The magic window has been struck by a jagged skyflash and is dead,*' she reported. '*There are no tailless ones.*'

Lucy told the others and they rushed over to the lab. The computer was a smoking hulk and the lab floor was covered in shards of shattered screen and electronic fragments. Everything else in the room looked undamaged. Lucy looked up. The roof was intact.

'Queenie said it had been struck by lightning,' she said, puzzled, 'but I don't see how it can have been.'

'It wasn't a thunderbolt,' said Clive. 'It was a bomb.' The others looked at him. He was consulting his watch.

'Yes,' he murmured. 'It would have been about this time yesterday.'

'What on earth are you rambling about?' said Helen.

'Sorry, I was just working it out. I think the professor had a small explosive device fitted inside the computer which could be triggered by an electronic time clock. It was a self-destruct mechanism: a way of ensuring that his data wouldn't fall into anybody else's hands if he was taken ill, locked up, or whatever. He had a safety lock which he would reset every day as long as he was OK. He reset it at exactly this time yesterday morning when he was in the lab. He couldn't, of course, reset it today so it's gone off, just as he intended.'

'So, after all our clever planning,' said Lucy, 'there's nothing left for the police after all.'

'No-o,' said Clive. Helen glanced at him. Her son looked

thoughtful but she said nothing.

They looked out for a plane all afternoon, but it wasn't until the following day that two planes appeared in the sky. Julian and Richard were in one and the other was a police plane, containing a pilot, a detective and a forensic technician who immediately set to work examining the professor's cabin and laboratory. The remains of the computer were carried to the plane, together with all kinds of files, rock samples, chemicals and strips of cloth impregnated with test mixtures of metamaterial.

The detective was Captain Colarinho, the same police officer who had been involved in the arrest of Chopper and his gang eighteen months earlier. He was astonished to see Richard and Lucy again.

'You two seem to have a talent for finding villains in remote places. Had you thought about joining our police force? Lucy is a little young but I'm sure she could be called a "special juvenile rainforest consultant" or something.' They all laughed and Richard was relieved that the investigation was in the hands of someone he knew and trusted.

Captain Colarinho was particularly interested in the professor's pistol which Lucy had retrieved and given to Julian.

'You did well to get this off him,' said the detective with genuine admiration in his voice. 'You must have been watching him –' he was proud of his excellent English and paused to search for the correct idiom, '– like a hawk.'

'Er, yes,' said Julian. 'I suppose that's a pretty accurate

way of putting it.' The detective was puzzled as everyone smiled at this remark, but put it down to post-traumatic stress. They had, after all, been through quite an ordeal.

The following day, at the request of the detective they took him to the escarpment where Sam and his companion villains had met their deaths and described how they had been attacked and eaten by wild animals. They told him of their plane crash and how Chopper and the pilot had been killed while trying to steal their plane. The detective looked up at the forbidding crags of the escarpment and decided he'd investigated far enough.

'These were all jail-birds,' he said, 'and you are respected scientists. I think a statement that you witnessed their deaths will be enough at this stage. If we need anything else we'll come back to you but,' he nodded to the cliff, 'I can't see any police team wanting to crawl over that lot looking for non-existent clues. Talking of savage animals –' He looked around nervously. 'Shouldn't we be getting back to the camp?'

'Yes, I suppose we should,' said Richard nonchalantly, looking at the setting sun. 'It'll be dark very soon.'

The detective couldn't help but be impressed by his quiet courage.

'I thought my job was dangerous,' he said, 'but you guys must have nerves of steel to explore in places like this.'

'Oh, it's just part of the job,' said Richard modestly, 'and we start young. Lucy here is only thirteen,' he put his arm round her and she smiled innocently at the detective, 'and yet we wouldn't go anywhere without her!'

They planned to leave the next day. The police had finished their tasks and Julian, Helen and Richard had sorted and filed all their precious scientific data about the valley of the dinosaurs, as they now referred to it.

Lucy was up at dawn and went to the spot where she had climbed down a makeshift ladder into the crater eighteen months earlier. There, a hundred feet above her sat the great eagle, waiting patiently, tearing now and then at the carcass of a monkey lying at his feet.

'I thank thee O master of the jungle skies. Thy task is now fulfilled. Fare thee well.'

'I have been honoured to serve thee twice in my life. Fare thee well.'

Lucy wiped a tear from her eye and walked back to join the others.

Over breakfast, their last meal before leaving, Julian pointed out that it was exactly a week since they had arrived.

'I just can't believe all that's happened in a week,' said Helen. 'It seems more like a month.'

'– Or a lifetime for most people,' said Richard. 'Aircrashes, dinosaurs, surgical operations on dinosaurs, invisible villains, giant spiders, people eaten by animals – it's like living in an adventure story.'

'– And not just an adventure story,' added Lucy with a sly glance at Clare, '– a love story too.' She put on the dramatic voice of a TV critic. 'Let's not forget the tale of steamy and secret passion that has run like a golden thread through this week in the crater!'

She ducked under the table as Clive went scarlet and Clare threw a banana at her. Queenie pounced on it and gave it to Lucy, thinking she had been meant to catch it.

They all had final jobs to do and while Clare and Clive went off to shut down the generator Lucy spoke to the others and they laughed and nodded. 'You're really mean!' said Helen, but she had to smile.

When the time came to get in the plane Clare got into one of the two back seats and Lucy climbed in quickly beside her. As Richard and Helen made to get in next, Julian said to Clive: 'I thought you'd like to sit in the front on the way back. You said you wanted to learn to fly and you can watch me at close quarters.'

'Well, it's kind, Dad but . . . but wouldn't Lucy rather sit up here and . . .' he was obviously thinking very fast, '. . . and then she can wave goodbye properly to all her animals,' he ended rather lamely. 'I'll just sit in the back with . . .' He was interrupted as everybody except Clare burst out laughing. Red-faced, he looked back and saw that she was blushing too.

'What a wind-up!' said Lucy. 'And they walked straight into it. Come on, Clive, get back here next to Clare – I'll sit in front so I can – what was it?' She gave a wicked giggle. 'Oh yes, wave to the animals.'

Clive and Clare had to laugh as he came and sat next to her.

'Your sister gets worse,' he said good-naturedly, 'but I'm very fond of her really.' Then he leant over and whispered in her ear. 'But not as fond as I am of somebody else.' They squeezed hands as the little plane bumped across the plain, gathered speed and flew east, back into a world that had moved on millions of years earlier than the one they were leaving.

They returned to the airstrip at Cayman Creek where they had stayed on their outward journey as Lucy wanted to restore the monkeys to their home territory. As soon as they had landed, and Julian had opened the door, Queenie jumped out and scampered into the trees. She returned a few minutes later while they were pitching their tents.

'*I have told those in the forest that the Promised One is safe,*' she explained to Lucy. '*Since none can pass in or out of the Valley of the Mighty Ones the animanet has been silent about thee, and all creatures have been waiting to hear of thy return. Soon the Great Ones will take the news hence across the Great Salt to the Isles of Albion.*' Lucy thanked her and explained the interchange to the others.

'Just a minute,' said Clare with a frown. 'If we've been shut off from the animanet how could you have got a message to that dog?'

'Good thinking,' laughed Lucy. 'I wasn't going to bore you with it, but I had a little arrangement with a monkey eagle, just in case.' As she was explaining herself the bushes parted and a black panther stalked majestically onto the airstrip.

'Melanie!' shouted Lucy, and rushed to embrace the great cat. She brought her back to the group and introduced her to Clare and Clive who, of course, knew how she had helped Lucy before, but were now lost in admiration at her beauty and lithe power.

Later that evening as they sat and chatted round the camp fire Clive looked over at Lucy who was sitting with Michelle on her shoulder, Melanie stretched at her feet, and Queenie and Clio sitting on either side. Sophie, who had formed a special attachment to Clare since their adventure in the cave, was sitting with Clare and, as was now her habit, had the earbud of Clare's iPod in her ear.

'The animals certainly look after you,' said Clive. 'I must confess, until I saw your power in action I really had no idea just how important you are to them and the absolute sway you hold over them.'

'Talking of which,' added Julian, 'your idea of bringing the monkeys along was absolutely brilliant. I thought it was a bit of a gimmick when you first mentioned it, but they almost certainly saved our lives. Please thank them on our behalf for all they did.' There was a chorus of agreement and Lucy told the monkeys, who went round the group and gave an affectionate lick to everybody in turn.

'Sitting here again,' said Clive, looking across at Richard, 'reminds me of our greenhouse discussion over the campfire last week. We never really came to any conclusions and I've been thinking about it a great deal. What are we actually going to do about global warming?'

'A good question,' replied Richard, 'because it's something that scientists and governments can't agree about.'

'What do *you* think we should do, Richard?' asked Helen who had followed the previous discussion with interest, 'because I should tell you that Julian and I argue endlessly about this.'

'Oh, dear,' said Richard with an apologetic smile, 'I'm bound to upset one of you then. Make yourselves comfortable because it's a long story.'

They made some more coffee and then sat talking long into the night about the future of the planet.*

The next day Lucy spoke to the monkeys with Clare by her side. She was holding the earbud of Clare's iPod in her hand.

'We now return to the City of the Great Clock in Albion. Without your help we would not have survived the many dangers that have threatened us since we last stood in this place. I will return one day and speak once more to the arborikin, but I know not whether it will be to thee or to those that follow thee.' She then turned and spoke to Sophie, giving her the earpiece. *'Clarekin bequeaths this to thee in return for thy loyal service.'* The monkey whimpered in delight. She put the bud into Kai's ear, but the little creature took it straight out and started to suck it, much to the girls' amusement. Sophie then spoke:

'Fare thee well O Promised One – and give my special thanks to Clarekin; but for her courage my son and I would surely have been devoured by the great arachnopod.' Lucy gave the message

* *Readers who are interested in this subject will find an account of the campfire discussion in the appendix on page 322.*

to Clare who burst into tears as she hugged Sophie and Kai.

The sisters then turned and walked sadly back to join the others who were preparing to board the plane. Soon Cayman Creek lay far below as the plane climbed and then banked to follow the glistening thread of the river tributary back towards the mighty Amazon.

That night they stayed once again with José and his family in Macapá, who were enthralled to hear of their astonishing adventures. Cerberus was inseparable from Lucy and Francesca said that since their previous visit he had been much more even-tempered and had even started wagging his tail at strangers. Lucy retrieved the message she had left with him; as she explained to Richard, it would cause endless complications if it were discovered sometime in the future by an enthusiastic gardener.

Before they went to bed, Julian, who had spent most of the evening on the phone, asked José if he could possibly take him into town the next day.

'I need to go to the Achilles Insurance offices and fill in some forms about the plane crash,' he explained. 'I spoke to a clerk in London called Underwright who didn't sound very happy with my "broken by wild animals" story, so I'd like to go and sort it out as soon as possible.'

'That's fine,' José replied. 'I've got some business to do with Richard at the company offices so we can drop you off on the way.' He turned to the others.

'We'll be gone all day, so I suggest the rest of you go off on an interesting little trip that Rio has planned.'

They all looked at his son who blushed at this sudden attention.

'We'd love to go on a trip,' said Clare kindly, though she did wonder what trip could possibly be interesting in comparison with the one they had just completed.

'Where to?'

Rio was learning English as school but was a little nervous about speaking.

'It is a – a surprise,' he said haltingly. He stopped, then went and whispered to José who obviously supplied him with a word in English. He turned back to the others and continued:

'It is an *invisible* surprise.' He grinned as he saw their perplexed expressions.

'An invisible surprise,' said Lucy. 'That means it's something we can hear, then.'

'No,' said Rio. He was now relaxed and enjoying being the centre of such intrigued attention. 'No, you cannot hear it or . . .' he consulted José again, '. . . or even feel it.'

The others clustered round, firing questions at him but he just smiled and told them to wait until tomorrow.

The next morning the three men went into town and Francesca set off in her large pick-up truck with the others. Her passengers were, if anything, even more curious than the night before, having all tried in vain to work out what Rio planned to show them. After forty minutes they came to a little town where Francesca stopped the car and they all got out.

'The tourists are all over there,' she said, pointing to a busy café at the end of the road, 'but we are going to the garden of a friend. Just follow Rio.'

Helen suddenly began to have a suspicion of what was going on, but the younger ones still looked completely mystified as they followed Rio through the iron gates of a large villa which swung open automatically after Francesca had rung the bell and spoken on an intercom. Helen took her camera out as Rio guided Clive, Clare and Lucy across the lawn while Francesca went up to the house to see her friends.

'Stand there,' he said, lining them one behind the other. They looked more puzzled than ever.

'No, not there, *there*!' He laughed and gently pushed them a little to one side. Lucy looked down and saw that the three of them were standing along a straight line of red bricks crossing the lawn. The line wasn't nearly wide enough for a path and it wasn't where one would expect a little path to go – it ran diagonally from the middle of the garden wall across the lawn and a flower bed, and ended under a corner of the house.

'Now stand with your legs apart, one on either side of the bricks.' Lucy obediently followed instructions and Helen grinned. She knew that her suspicions had been correct. She started taking photographs of Lucy who was standing with a look of amused perplexity on her face.

'Will somebody please tell me what's going on!' said

Clare in a tone of mock exasperation, 'because I certainly haven't a clue.' Clive turned and spoke to her over his shoulder.

'Whatever it is, I think we're having a trick played on us. Let's move!'

They left the line and joined Helen.

'Spoilsports, wimps and cowards,' said Lucy, laughing. 'I'm staying; there might be a prize for all you know.'

'You are now standing . . .' said Rio with mock solemnity – he had obviously been practising this phrase in English for several days – 'with your right foot in the northern hemisphere and your left foot in the southern hemisphere.' Lucy looked puzzled and then smiled as enlightenment dawned.

'The equator!' she exclaimed, clapping her hands in delight, 'I'm actually on the equator! This is so cool. I can't wait to tell my new geography teacher, Miss Atlas; she starts next term and this should get me off to a good start with her!'

Francesca reappeared, accompanied by her friends, a middle-aged couple. They were just in time to see Clare push Lucy off the line, stand astride it herself and strike a dramatic pose. She put her sunglasses to her mouth as if speaking into an imaginary microphone and put on her best imitation of a masculine voice.

'And now, ladies and gentlemen and viewers round the world, I am pleased to announce the winner of the Miss Latitude and Miss Longitude competition. As you know, most of the competitors have been eliminated by *degrees* during the contest, leaving us today with just our four finalists. Of these, Miss Tropic of Cancer has been disqualified by our judges because of her persistently sideways gait in the deportment final; Miss Tropic of Capricorn resigned because of a tummy ache and, though we've now learnt that she was only *kidding* she remains out of the competition because of her capricious behaviour. In the *meantime*, Miss Meridian Greenwich has been eliminated because of her age, even though she maintains that she is still in her *prime*. It therefore gives me great pleasure to present to you this year's winner – Miss Equator!'

Clare then changed position so as to now face the imaginary compère, fluffed up her hair and pretended to accept a heavy trophy. Clive looked on open-mouthed; he had never seen this side of Clare's personality before and he loved it. She now pretended to put the trophy on a nearby garden table and spoke into the microphone again, this time adopting the high-pitched, squeaky voice of a feather-brained contestant with an American accent.

'Thank you! Thank you! Thank you all!' She blew kisses to a vast, imaginary audience. 'In view of my central position in the world I feel well placed to use my new, incredible fame to work even harder for my favourite causes. These include the very young, the middle-aged, the old, the very old, hospitals, schools, sports clubs, religious organizations, humanists, charities, commerce, the arts, politics . . .' the others were now helpless with laughter but she hadn't finished, 'wild animals, sick animals, pets, foreigners, motorists, cyclists, pedestrians and the environment. My amazing success today was, of course, achieved largely through my own talent and charisma, despite my lack of *degrees*. However, I would like to mention one or two others who did help me a tiny bit. Up in the north . . .' she gesticulated to Lucy with her left hand . . . 'my little sister – from whom I've always, well – nearly always, well – sometimes, been able to borrow make-up when I needed it and, in the south . . .' she included Rio in an expansive sweep of her right arm . . . 'a friend, without whom I certainly wouldn't be standing here today. And from now on . . .' she continued, twisting round to face Helen who was standing behind her on the line of bricks taking photographs of the performance . . . 'I do not wish to be pestered by the paparazzi – especially those trying to improve their career at a late stage by switching their attention from old fossils to beautiful young women!'

They all clapped enthusiastically, especially Clive, and Clare ignored Lucy's exaggerated wink as he carried on longer than anyone else.

Francesca's friend stepped forward.

'That was fantastic,' she said, 'you should be on the stage! I'm Dacey, by the way,' she said in perfect English, shaking Clare's hand and then those of the others in turn. She pointed to the line.

'As you can see it runs right through our garden – that's why we bought the house. Norman –' she nodded to her husband – 'laid the bricks for fun and it never fails to fascinate our guests. Now Francesca warned me you were coming for Rio's surprise and I've got a little one of my own.'

They followed her round the corner of the house to a large patio where a magnificent buffet lunch awaited them by the side of a swimming pool. Rio, blushing with pleasure at the success of his mission, told them the names of the local delicacies spread before them, and over lunch they gave their hosts a carefully edited account of their crater adventures.

On the way home Clive complimented Clare on her performance in the garden.

'I just can't believe how you could make all that stuff up on the spur of the moment,' he said, admiringly. 'I couldn't do that in a million years.'

Lucy sniggered and Clare gave her a sharp poke in the ribs to shut her up.

Later in the day the girls were in the bedroom they were sharing, getting ready for dinner.

'Clive was really impressed with you, wasn't he?' said Lucy, innocently. Clare looked at her suspiciously. She always knew when her sister was up to something.

'It would be such a pity if someone happened to tell him that your class once did a little show about the equator for your year group, wouldn't it?' Lucy continued. She thought that Clare turned a little pale.

'You . . . you wouldn't . . .!' she stammered.

'That all depends,' said Lucy with a wicked smile. 'I've been under a lot of stress recently and when I'm talking

I feel as if anything might pop out. Perhaps if I knew I was going back to a nice new bedroom I might feel more relaxed and more in control of what I say.'

'So that's what all this is about!' exclaimed Clare. As the eldest of the three daughters in the family she had the biggest bedroom. It had windows on two sides and an *en suite* shower. Since Clare had gone up to university and was now away from home for much of the year, Lucy had been pestering her to swap rooms but Clare had so far resisted her request.

'This is nothing short of blackmail,' Clare continued, 'and I've got some seriously bad news for you, you little toad.'

'What?' said Lucy in alarm.

'It just so happens that I was embarrassed about Clive thinking I was so clever and I've already told him about the school show. He didn't seem to care – he just said how clever I was to remember all the jokes so quickly.' She gave a modest blush, but Lucy had now lost all interest in what Clive did or didn't think about Clare.

'What . . . what's the bad news?' she asked.

'The bad news is that I'd already decided to give you my room, but now you've turned out to be such an underhand little sneak I've changed my mind.'

They looked at each other for a moment. Lucy looked completely deflated, then Clare suddenly burst out laughing.

'Got you!' she said. 'And you deserved it!'

Lucy smiled and gave her sister a big hug.

'Thanks for swapping. I really love your room and you can leave anything behind that won't fit in mine.'

And with that, they went off down to dinner.

24

A Final Surprise

The morning after the trip to the equator, while they were all sitting chatting after breakfast, the phone rang. José picked it up, spoke to the caller, and then handed the phone to Richard.

'It's the police. For you,' he said. Richard looked puzzled for a few seconds, then remembered that he had given José's number to Captain Colarinho, the detective who had come to the crater, in case the police required any further information from them before they left the country. To his surprise it was a detective in Rio who spoke. He was called Poirot, the inspector who had assisted Lucinda Angstrom after the professor had attempted to murder her. He explained that she now knew the professor had been captured, and that the police would be arresting him if he ever recovered.

'Don't tell me,' said Richard, 'she's a brilliant scientist doing research into the physics of light.'

'Well . . . yes,' replied the astonished detective. 'But how on earth did you know that?'

'Oh, just a hunch,' Richard replied.

'I know you must all want to get home as soon as possible,' the inspector continued, 'but this young scientist has been through a great deal since her boss attempted to murder her – allegedly,' he hurriedly added. 'She knows the crucial role that your families played in bringing the professor to justice and she would love to meet you all in person to thank you. If you are flying out from Rio would it be possible for you to spare a few hours to see her?'

Richard explained that, as the rest of their families were still on holiday in the Pantanal, they had intended to spend a few days in Rio to do some sightseeing and that they would love to meet Dr Angstrom.

'LA! Of course, that's what it means!' exclaimed Clive, when Richard told the others what the inspector had said. They all looked at him in bewilderment, and he carried on. 'LA kept appearing in the professor's computer data. I thought it was some physics abbreviation – "light activation" or some such thing – but it isn't. It stands for Lucinda Angstrom. He was her boss and must have pinched all the invisibility stuff from her!'

'Which is why he tried to murder her,' said Helen.

'Exactly,' agreed Clive. 'The whole thing fits together.'

'Don't you think it's time to tell us the rest now?' asked Helen. Clive looked at her in guilty surprise. 'Come on,' Helen went on, 'you don't really think I've been your mother for over twenty years without knowing when you're holding out on me?' He gave a rueful grin.

'You're right. When I checked through the professor's computer while you two were away,' he glanced at Julian and Richard, 'I realized that the material in there was absolutely unique. It struck me that if the police lost the computer, or it got damaged, or whatever, all that precious information would be lost for ever, so I copied it on to a CD, intending to give it to the authorities. After the computer was destroyed I began to think about what I should do. The invisibility invention had already killed five people – six if the prof doesn't make it – and until a minute ago we still didn't know if the professor had pinched it. If he hadn't, that meant we were the only people left alive who knew about the invention, and I seriously wondered whether it might be better for the world to keep it that way.' He smiled, 'We're certainly all experienced at keeping incredible secrets. Anyway, I was going to discuss it with all of you before we left the country, but the problem seems to have resolved itself. Once we know for certain that this Lucinda is the rightful owner of the material it clearly belongs to her and she can handle it in whatever way she originally intended.'

A few days later they visited a small house in one of the poorer suburbs of Rio where, for her protection, Lucinda had been staying incognito until the professor was caught. The door was opened on a chain by her older sister. She knew the professor was now effectively in custody, and the visitors were expected, but she found it difficult to throw off the habits developed over weeks of caution. As she peered through the gap at the group on the doorstep she gasped. The door slammed shut as she unhooked the chain and then was thrown wide open. Then Lucy gasped and threw herself into the woman's arms.

The others looked at each other in bewilderment. Helen turned to Richard.

'What on earth's going on?' she asked. Richard shrugged his shoulders.

'I've absolutely no idea,' he said with a bemused smile. 'All I know is that, wherever I go, there's some person or animal greeting Lucy like a long-lost friend!'

By now Lucinda and her niece and nephew had emerged and appeared just as perplexed as the others by the doorstep scene. Eventually Lucy broke away from the embrace and turned to Richard.

'This is Maria, Dad. She's the lady who was so kind to me when I was kidnapped by Chopper.' She turned to Clare. 'She gave me the pencil I wrote your note with.'

'But why are you here?' asked Richard. Maria just smiled and, shrugging her shoulders, looked round at her sister.

'She doesn't speak any English, Dad!' said Lucy.

'Hello. Perhaps I can explain. I'm Lucinda Angstrom and this is my sister Maria.' Lucinda stepped forward and held out her hand. 'I invited you here to meet you and thank you,' she continued after they had all introduced themselves, 'but it looks as if Maria already knows one of you! Come and sit down and let's start from the beginning, shall we?'

Over coffee the whole extraordinary story was disentangled. Maria, whose married name was Arrumadeira, was the eldest of four sisters, Lucinda being the youngest. Maria had been a maid in Chopper's villa at the time of Lucy's kidnap and had helped her in her ordeal.

Lucinda was fascinated to hear about the professor's activities in the crater, how the families had gradually got more suspicious about him during their stay, and how effective the invisibility suits had proved to be in practice.

They, in turn, were appalled to hear Lucinda's story and learn the true extent of the professor's depravity.

Eventually it was time to go. Maria's daughter was the same age as Lucy and it was agreed that she would come and stay with the Bonaventures for a holiday and to improve her English. Lucinda said she could accompany her when she next came to a scientific conference in London.

'Before you go, there's one more thing I need to ask you,' said Lucinda as they prepared to leave. She sounded hesitant and looked somewhat embarrassed. 'I really don't know how to put this; you've all been so kind.'

'Carry on,' said Helen smiling. 'I think we've all got a pretty good idea what you're going to say. In fact, I'll say it for you. You can be quite certain that none of us will ever tell anybody about your invention unless you give us permission to do so, or you publish it. Was that your question?'

Lucinda looked relieved. 'Yes it was, and thank you for being so understanding.'

'Well, as a family of scientists we're all used to keeping secrets, aren't we?' She looked at the others who all smiled and nodded. 'And now,' she continued, 'I think Clive has got a little surprise for you.' Lucinda looked puzzled as Clive went over to his bag and pulled out a package. When he told her what it was she flung her arms round him.

'You have absolutely no idea,' she said through tears of joy, 'how much this means to me. The professor stole or destroyed all my original data and I was dreading the thought of getting back to my lab and starting again from scratch.'

They all said goodbye and, after Lucy had given Maria a final extra hug, they returned to their hotel where they were reunited with the rest of the two families who had just returned to Rio, relaxed and suntanned after their holiday in the Pantanal. The rest of the day, and most of the night, was taken up with them all swapping stories of their respective adventures. The younger children were fascinated by Clare's account of the spiders' cave but their favourite story was the one about Lucy's ride on the dinosaur. Little sister Sarah and cousins Ben, Henry and Christopher, listened wide-eyed as she told them for the third time that it was:

'The biggest and best elephant ride you could ever imagine!'

The next day they returned to England to pick up the threads of normal life once again. It was just two weeks since they had come to Brazil.

'This has to have been the most action-packed fortnight in my life,' said Richard as they sat in the airport lounge, waiting for their flight to be called. 'I thought the last trip to the crater was bad enough, but in comparison with what we've just been through it now seems like a rest-cure. After living on pure adrenaline day in, day out, I really don't know how I'm going to settle back into a humdrum everyday existence.'

'Don't worry, Dad,' said Clare. 'In this family I shouldn't think things will stay too quiet for very long.'

How right she was!

Epilogue

Thirty-five thousand feet above the Atlantic, the plane flew steadily towards Heathrow above the ocean clouds in brilliant sunshine. During the long flight Richard was making some scientific notes about the flora and fauna of the new valley and Joanna was sitting next to him reading the newspaper. Suddenly she nudged him and pointed to an article she had just read. He glanced over then, seeing the heading to the article, dropped his work, took the paper from her and started to read.

SECOND SIGHTING OF 'MONKEY GIRL'

from our correspondent in the
Democratic Republic of Congo

Two weeks ago in this column I reported that villagers in a remote area close to the Salonga national park claimed to have seen a girl of about thirteen foraging with a small group of bonobos (pigmy chimpanzees). On being approached the group disappeared immediately into the forest, accompanied by the girl who seemed to move through the undergrowth with extraordinary agility. As there have been no reports of missing children in the area no further action was taken. Wildlife experts are anxious that the few remaining groups of this threatened species should be left as undisturbed as possible and, as the sighting occurred shortly after a somewhat boisterous tribal wedding party, no further credence was given to the villagers' tale. Yesterday, however, the story took an intriguing turn. Two (alleged) poachers arrested in the reserve said that they had not been after bush meat but had seen a child in the forest and had gone into the reserve to rescue her. When they called to her she climbed a tree at an astonishing speed, joined several small apes and then made off with them in the trees through forest so dense that the men were unable to follow.

These sightings inevitably raise the question as to whether this is a feral child – one who, by being lost or abandoned, has become separated from human society and has been reared by wild animals. Stories of such children have been around for thousands of years and many of them are clearly the stuff of myth or legend. Famous fictional feral children include Romulus and Remus, the founders of Rome; Mowgli, from

The Jungle Book by Rudyard Kipling; and Edgar Rice Burroughs' Tarzan. There are, however, approximately one hundred reports in the literature of real feral children. Some of the most famous of these include the Hessian wolf children (1341);Wild Peter of Hamelin (1724);Victor of Aveyron (1797), portrayed in the film *L'Enfant Sauvage* by François Truffaut; Kaspar Hauser (1828), found near Nuremberg in Germany; and the Indian Wolf Girls (1920) aged eight and eighteen months, who were discovered in the care of a she-wolf in Godamuri, India.

Researching these cases has proved to be one of the most fascinating assignments ever undertaken by this correspondent but it has also been, it must be said, a somewhat depressing one. Most of these children, isolated from all human contact from a very early age, never become satisfactorily reabsorbed into society. They usually never learn to speak properly, and many die at an early age. It is to be hoped that, if the present stories turn out to be true, and the girl is restored to the community, modern psychological rehabilitation techniques will prove to be more successful than those attempted in previous cases.

Richard lowered the paper, frowning. He looked at Joanna,

then turned to see what the others were doing. Clare was studying her medical books and Lucy and Sarah were watching the in-flight movie. He looked back to Joanna. Her eyes were moist.

'Is it possible?' his voice came out in a whisper.

'I just don't know,' said Joanna, her voice trembling. 'I just . . . don't . . . know.'

Richard picked up the paper and together they read the article again.

'It's the right place . . . and the girl's the right age . . . but how could she possibly have survived that hell?' said Richard.

'It would have been a miracle,' Joanna agreed. She paused. 'But we've got to go and check. Otherwise we'll never sleep easy again for the rest of our lives.'

They both lay back, held hands and wrestled with their tormented thoughts as the plane thundered on into the evening sky.

Appendix

Coping with Carbon: the Campfire Discussion on Energy Resources

When everyone had settled down again with their fresh drinks, Richard took up the thread of the previous conversation. His expression had become more serious.

'I believe very strongly,' he started, 'that we must move as quickly as possible to nuclear power: nuclear fission in the short term, and nuclear fusion as soon as it becomes possible. Nuclear energy is simply the cleanest and safest energy form that is capable of meeting the world's energy needs without destroying the planet.'

The young people all looked surprised.

'But what about all the cars and lorries and ships and planes? How can they use nuclear power?' asked Clare.

'Once you have a cheap and unlimited source of energy you can convert it into other forms. Nuclear energy, for instance, could power electric cars, trains and trams very easily. Even more likely, though, for transport, is the possibility of using fuel oil derived from current crops such as rape-seed and sugar cane or produced by genetic engineering. Although this still involves putting carbon into the atmosphere, the crops remove it as they are growing so the whole process is practically carbon neutral – far different from digging mineral oil out of the ground and adding the carbon it has had trapped in it for millions of years into our current atmospheric load.'

'But ever since I've been a little girl,' Clare continued, 'I've heard about nothing but the dangers of nuclear power: about nuclear accidents causing radioactive fallout, about terrorists stealing uranium or plutonium and making bombs, about the problem of nuclear waste which doesn't become harmless for hundreds or even thousands of years. How can it suddenly be OK to use nuclear power?'

Julian nodded in agreement and added, 'Yes, you've got to admit there are a lot of problems.'

'But they are nothing to the problems we now face if we continue to use fossil fuels,' said Helen. 'Carry on, Richard – at last I have an ally!'

'OK,' he replied. He turned and looked at the younger ones. 'I'm afraid that during your lifetimes it has been fashionable to talk only about the *dangers* of nuclear power. But, in my view, you have been given a distorted view of the situation. Let me give you some facts: more people die

every year from accidents in the fossil fuel industries than have *ever* died in the entire history of the nuclear power industry.'

With the exception of Helen, his listeners looked sceptical.

'What about the Chernobyl disaster?' asked Julian. He was referring to the catastrophic accident in a Russian nuclear power station in 1986.

'I'm sure you will be astonished to learn,' said Richard, 'to pick just one example from thousands, or possibly hundreds of thousands, that the Aberfan disaster in Wales, in which a tip of coal waste collapsed on a school, killed three times as many people as did the Chernobyl fire.'

'Only so far,' said Julian passionately. 'The same UN report from which you've taken the figures you've just quoted also said that another four thousand people are likely to die in the future from the delayed effects of Chernobyl radiation.'

'True – and tragic,' replied Richard calmly. 'But Chernobyl was a one-off accident in an out-of-date reactor that is never likely to be repeated. Six thousand people die *every year* from accidents in Chinese coalmines alone, but how much publicity does that receive in our news media? And in addition to these accidents, which occur, of course, in every country that mines or drills for fossil fuels, there are thousands of workers who die every year in both accidents and from the long-term health effects of mining: illnesses such as respiratory diseases and cancers. And as if that wasn't enough, just think of the staggering numbers of ordinary people who have died or suffer prolonged respiratory ill-health as a result of breathing in the *pollution* caused by fossil fuels. All those fogs and smogs caused by the burning of coal in our towns and cities have killed untold numbers of people, and that has been going on for hundreds of years. The London smog of 1952, for instance, just one of an incalculable number of fogs in the preceding hundred years, killed over four thousand people, more than the most pessimistic predictions about Chernobyl.'

There was a long silence as they thought about what he had said. It was broken by Clive.

'I must confess I'd never thought about it in those terms before, and your arguments are very persuasive, but I still feel uncomfortable about nuclear energy. What about wind and wave energy?'

'They're fine,' said Richard. 'There's only one problem: they can't remotely provide us with the amount of energy the world needs to keep going. Despite the billions of pounds spent on them, for example, not a single wind turbine in England currently produces more than a quarter of its energy capacity. There are successful prototype experiments such as the focusing of the sun's rays by giant mirrors. These hold great promise but putting them into practice universally presents serious practical difficulties and would require the massive use of space and resources. Remember that the whole universe runs on nuclear power: our own sun is just a giant nuclear reactor – and we've done very well out of that so far. In fact . . .' he gave a wry smile . . . 'everything we've mentioned in this conversation – coal, oil, peat, wind ,waves, solar power – is the product of the dreaded nuclear energy: it all came from the sun, which is using what the universe regards as the basic and infinite energy source.'

'Well,' said Julian, 'there are a lot of scientists who would disagree with almost everything you've said, and my own views are somewhere in between theirs and yours. I do agree that while wind and water are very useful clean sources of energy they can't solve the energy crisis facing the world. I'm still not sure about nuclear power but I do agree that we should be developing biomass fuels from crops as quickly as possible for all forms of transport, and solar energy for houses.'

'I know I've expressed a strong point of view,' replied Richard, 'but all I'm really saying is that we have to do something that is quite fundamentally different from what we have done so far, which is tinkering about with fossil fuel emissions in completely ineffective ways, and talking about wind and wave power which can't possibly meet our future energy needs. When we think about countries such as India and China with their vast populations starting to use as much energy per person as we do – a process that is already happening – we will quite simply destroy the planet if we don't change to nuclear energy, and a lot sooner than anyone dares to tell you at present.'

'What about carbon offsetting?' said Clive.

'What's that?' asked Lucy.

'Well,' he replied, 'there are all kinds of ways of balancing out the carbon dioxide we produce. You can work out, for instance, how much is generated by a flight on an aeroplane and then pay for enough trees to be planted somewhere to offset it.'

'That sounds great,' said Lucy.

'Actually, not that great,' Clare interrupted. 'We did a project on all forms of carbon trading in year thirteen and there are lots of problems. The system is unregulated for one thing, so people often have no idea if what they've paid for has actually happened. Many people think carbon offsetting is just a way of allowing rich people or rich countries to carry on in just the same way as before, but with easier consciences.'

'A bit like the sale of indulgences in the Middle Ages,' interjected Helen. 'I think the whole thing is a massive gimmick.'

'I completely disagree,' said Julian passionately. 'I think it is a tremendous way of getting people to concentrate on

the actual amount of carbon they are producing during their work and leisure activities. It's going to be a vital tool in the battle against global warming.'

'But what are we to think when sensible and clever scientists around the world can't agree?' asked Clare. 'And . . .' she looked apologetically at Helen and Julian, '. . . even husbands and wives who are scientists?' She looked very confused.

'All you can do,' said Richard, 'is to keep an open mind. Don't think that everything you see on the telly, or learn at school, or read in the newspapers is necessarily the whole story. What you read or are told may be true, but it may be only part of a much bigger picture. Learn as much as you can about the facts related to nuclear power and fossil fuels and renewable sources of energy, then make up your own mind on the basis of informed knowledge rather than on emotional hype or ideology. This problem is so large and so urgent that it *has* to be solved. Who knows, it could be the only universal problem actually capable of making all nations talk and cooperate. That has never happened before in the whole of history, so some good may yet come out of all this.'

On this more optimistic note they all went to bed. They were exhausted after the excitement and traumas of the day and soon all were fast asleep under the watchful, protective eyes of Lucy's friends.

Lucy's Lexicon

(The suffix -kin is both singular and plural)

Agile One	Tina's name for Clio
Albion	England
animanet	animal communication network
arachnopod	spider
arboribane	harpy eagle
arborikin	monkey
Bearded One	Professor Strahlung (see 'Notes on the names in the book')
Black Furriclaws	Tibbles
Brilliant One	the sun
buzzibane	lizard
buzzikin	fly, bluebottle, etc.
buzzithorn	bee, wasp, hornet, etc.
CCMW	Crater Camp Monkey Watch
changekin	chameleon (see Glossary)
City of the Great Clock	London

Clarekin	Clare
coneybane	stoat, weasel, etc.
coneyhop	rabbit
crawlipod	any crawling insect
creepipod	caterpillar
crustakin	crustacean: crayfish, prawn, shrimp, etc.
deathquill	terror bird (see Animal Anthology)
deathtail	scorpion
Dreadful One	cayman, crocodile, alligator
dreykin	squirrel
drumquill	woodpecker
earthkin	earthworm
fellfang	any species of venomous snake
firestick	any handgun: pistol, revolver, etc.
fledgiquill	bird
Flowing One	river
forkiquill	red kite
furriclaws	cat
gillibane	otter
gillifin	fish
gillilance	heron
Great One	whale
Great Pterokin	aeroplane
Great River of the Junglefangs	Amazon River

Great Salt	the sea
Great Shieldkin	glyptodont (see Animal Anthology)
Great Silver One	the moon
Greatfang	sabre-toothed cat (see Animal Anthology)
Hedgiquill	hedgehog
Helenkin	Helen
Henbane	fox
Hippophant	tapir
House of the Little Tailless Ones	Wendy house (see Glossary)
Implacable One	giganotosaurus
jagged skyflash	lightning
Little One	pigmy marmoset
magic window	visual display unit (computer monitor)
malevopod	primitive snake with lizard–like hind legs
Malevolent One	snake
Merciless One	any predatory dinosaur
marshiquill	wading bird
Mighty One	giant ground sloth (see Animal Anthology)
minikin	shrew
nosekin	macrauchenia (see Animal Anthology)

paterpromise	Lucy's father (see the 'Notes on the names in the book')
peckosaur	ceratopsian dinosaur (see Animal Anthology)
Prodigious One	argentinosaurus (see Animal Anthology)
pterokin	pterodactyl
raspihop	grasshopper, cricket, etc.
Relentless One	dromaeosaur (see Animal Anthology)
Savage One	carnotaurus
scurrident	agouti
scurripod	rat, mouse, vole, etc.
shieldkin	tortoise, turtle, terrapin
sleepikin	dormouse
slitherkin	Minhocão (see Animal Anthology)
snortikin	peccary, pig
stripeybrock	badger
sunsleep	night
Tailless One	human being
thunderquill	aeroplane
thunderstick	rifle
Timid One	herbivorous dinosaur
velvetkin	mole
wolf-fang	protocyon
wolfkin	dog, wolf

Notes on the names in the book

Many of the names that appear in the book tell you something about the character they belong to. Some are very obvious, others much less so, and some are in Portuguese, the language of Brazil. Here is a list describing them, giving the chapter or section in which their name first appears. See how many hidden meanings or associations you spotted as you read the story.

Unusual words or abbreviations used in this section are explained in the glossary.

Achilles *Chapter 23* Achilles was one of the great warrior heroes of Greek mythology and an obvious name for an insurance company wishing to portray strength and protection. As an infant, Achilles was dipped into the river Styx by his mother; its magical waters conferred protection and this proved useful in his many battles. She held him by the heel to dip him, however, and he was eventually killed by a poisoned arrow in the heel – his only vulnerable point. The term 'Achilles' heel' is now used to mean a weak point. This insurance company's *Achilles' heel* is Julian, who has now lost two expensive aeroplanes smashed up by pre-historic animals.

Algy *Chapter 4* Algy is Biggles's partner. In the famous stories about Biggles by W. E. Johns, Algy (short for Algernon Montgomery Lacey) is Biggles's second-in-command and close friend.

Angstrom *Preface* The angstrom is a unit of length equivalent to 0.1 nanometre. It is used to express wavelengths in the electromagnetic spectrum and is a very appropriate name for Lucinda.

Arrumadeira *Chapter 24* This is the Portuguese word for maid. Maria *Arrumadeira* is Lucinda's widowed sister and was one of Chopper's maids.

Atlas *Chapter 23* The name of Lucy's new geography teacher. An atlas is a book of maps. The name comes from the Titan in Greek mythology who carried the heavens on his shoulders.

Barker *Chapter 4* Before going to jail for drug offences Barker was a lumberjack and cut *bark*.

Biggles *Chapter 4* Biggles happens to have the same name as the famous fictional pilot hero who appears in the books by W. E. Johns. Major James Bigglesworth, known always as *Biggles*, was a fighter ace who featured in numerous flying adventures.

Bonaventure *Preface* Bonaventure is Lucy's surname. Saint Bonaventure (1221–74) was a mystic and philosopher who was the author of *The Life of St Francis*.

Cerberus *Chapter 2* In Greek mythology Cerberus was the three-headed watchdog that guarded the entrance to Hades, the underworld. In this story *Cerberus* guards the

message from Lucy that he has buried underground.

Chopper *Chapter 2* Before going to jail, Chopper ran a logging company which *chopped* down trees.

Colarinho *Chapter 23* Captain Colarinho is one of the Brazilian policemen. *Colarinho* is a Portuguese word for a person who catches someone.

Constante Subornos *Chapter 4* The crooked governor of the prison. His name in Portuguese means 'frequent bribes'.

Crack *Chapter 4* 'Crack' is Barker's nickname. Barker's criminal activities include drug peddling. *Crack* is a slang term for a highly addictive form of processed cocaine.

Dacey *Chapter 23* A Gaelic name meaning southerner. *Dacey* lives on the equator with her husband, Norman (*qv*) but, presumably, on a different side of the house.

Darwin *Chapter 16* Charles Darwin (1809–82). A British naturalist renowned for his theories of natural selection and evolution. *Origin of Species* is the shortened title of his most controversial and famous book.

Einstein *Chapter 5* Albert Einstein (1879–1955). A US citizen born in Germany. He was a famous physicist and mathematician who formulated the special theory of relativity in 1905 and the general theory of relativity in 1916. He was awarded the Nobel Prize for physics in 1921, and his work has had a profound influence on modern scientific thought and practice.

Fossfinder *Preface* Helen and Julian Fossfinder are palaeontologists who look for *fossils*.

Gyges of Lydia *Chapter 5* In Greek mythology, Gyges of Lydia is a shepherd who finds a golden ring that makes him invisible. The ring is referred to by the famous philospher Plato in *The Republic* where he argues that no man can be so virtuous as to remain uncorrupted by its power.

Hades' cap *Chapter 5* In Greek mythology, Hades is the king of the underworld. He possesses a 'cap of darkness' which makes the wearer invisible.

Heathrow Airport *Chapter 1* London's famous international airport. It is built on the site of a hamlet called Heath Row. Archaeological excavations at the site of the new Terminal Five have revealed stone-age artefacts. Humans were active here when terror birds, giant ground sloths and sabre-toothed cats were still roaming the plains of South America (even outside the lost crater).

Lucinda *Chapter 5* The name Lucinda means *bringer of light*: an appropriate name for this scientist. The Roman goddess of childbirth, Lucine, gave first light to the newborn.

Lucius *Chapter 5* The name Lucius comes from the Latin word *lux*, meaning *light*, the subject in which the professor is an expert. Lucius comes from the same root as *Lucifer*, which means *light-bearer*, and was the name of the highest angel in heaven. He led a rebellion against God and was cast down to hell where he is identified with Satan. His fall from grace is reflected in the life of

Professor Lucius Strahlung.

Lucy *Chapter 1* The name Lucy means light, a perfect name for the Promised One who is a beacon for all animals.

Melanie *Chapter 3* This is the name of Lucy's panther. It comes from *melas* – the Greek word for dark or black.

Meridian Greenwich *Chapter 23* The Greenwich Meridian is the prime meridian of longitude in the world (0 degrees) and the point at which Greenwich *Mean Time* is determined (see Glossary). It passes through the Royal Observatory at Greenwich, near London. In the beauty competition, Miss Greenwich is said to be in her *prime* (see Glossary).

Moriarty *Chapter 22* Professor James Moriarty appears in the famous fictional detective stories about Sherlock Holmes by Sir Arthur Conan Doyle. Moriarty is Holmes's arch enemy and is commonly regarded as being the first 'supervillain' in literature. Holmes refers to him as 'The Napoleon of Crime'. In the present book *Moriarty* is the maiden name of Professor Strahlung's mother so, appropriately, the two evil professors are presumably related.

Napoleon (above) Napoleon Bonaparte (1769–1821). Emperor of the French (1804–1815). A brilliant general, he was eventually defeated at the battle of Waterloo (1815) by the British Duke of Wellington, later to become Prime Minister. Napoleon died in exile on the island of St Helena.

Newton *Chapter 22* Sir Isaac Newton (1642–1727), an Englishman, was one of the world's greatest mathematicians and scientists. He is famous for his work on calculus and on the physics of gravitation and optics.

Norman *Chapter 23* An Old German name meaning northerner. *Norman* lives on the equator with his wife, Dacey (*qv*) but, presumably, on a different side of the house.

Paterpromise *Chapter 3* The Paterpromise is Richard, the Promised One's father. *Pater* is the Latin word for father.

Peter Flint *Chapter 5* Lucinda's boyfriend. He is a geologist with very appropriate names. *Peter* comes from the Greek word *petros* meaning stone, and *Flint* is a type of rock called quartz.

Photogyraspar *Chapter 5* This is not a real substance but is the name Lucinda coined for the ore discovered by Biggles. *Photo* comes from the Greek word *phos* meaning light. *Gyrate* means to rotate or spiral from the Greek word *guros* a circle. *Spar* is a transparent or translucent microcrystalline mineral. Thus *photogyraspar* is a crystalline mineral that twists or distorts light.

Poirot *Chapter 5* The original Hercule *Poirot* is a famous Belgian detective who appears in many of the detective stories written by Agatha Christie.

Pollard *Chapter 4* The name of one of Chopper's lumberjacks. To *pollard* a tree means to cut its branches in such a way as to stimulate bushy growth.

Ray *Chapter 5* Lucinda's technician. Presumably he brings a *ray* of light into her laboratory.

Rio *Chapter 2* Rio means 'river' in Portuguese. José and Francesca live at the mouth of the Amazon and named their son accordingly.

Sawyer *Chapter 4* This is Chopper's surname. Before going to jail, Chopper ran a timber company and *sawyer* means one who saws timber for a living.

Shortshanks *Chapter 4* Bert Shortshanks is Chopper's diminutive associate. The shank is another word for the shin, so *shortshanks* means short legs.

Sapientia *Chapter 16* St Sapientia's is Lucy's new school. *Sapientia* is the Latin word for wisdom.

Strahlung *Chapter 5* *Strahlung* is the German word for radiation. The professor studies light, which is a form of electromagnetic radiation.

Tropic of Cancer *Chapter 23* An imaginary line of latitude encircling the earth approximately 23.5 degrees north of the equator (0 degrees). *Cancer* is the Latin word for crab, which is why Miss Tropic of Cancer was disqualified from the beauty competition on account of her sideways gait.

Tropic of Capricorn *Chapter 23* An imaginary line of latitude encircling the earth approximately 23.5 degrees south of the equator (0 degrees). *Capricorn* comes from the Latin word *capricornus* meaning goat-horned. A young goat is called a kid, and one of these must have been the cause of Miss Tropic of Capricorn's tummy ache.

Underwright *Chapter 23* Mr Underwright works in Julian's insurance company. An *underwriter* assesses insurance risks and determines the premiums (payments) that are due.

Verdade *Chapter 2* José Verdade turned out to be one of the few honest men in Chopper's company and took charge after the villains were arrested. *Verdade* is the Portuguese word for truth.

An Anthology of the Animals of Antiquity

(mya = million years ago; tya = thousand years ago.
Difficult words are explained in the glossary.)

Argentinosaurus *Chapter 10* Scientific name:
Argentinosaurus huinculensis, meaning: 'Argentine lizard'. A
herbivorous sauropod dinosaur that, on current evidence,
was one of the largest land creatures that ever lived.
Length: 35 metres; weight: 80–100 tonnes; lived:
approximately 100–90 mya.

Bigfoot *Chapter 21* A cryptid, also known as
'**Sasquatch**'. A large, hairy, bipedal, hominoid animal
that is believed by some to inhabit the remote forests of
North America. Height: 2–2.5 metres.

Carnotaurus *Chapter 11* Scientific name: *Carnotaurus*
sastrei, 'carnotaurus' meaning 'carnivorous bull'. A fierce
carnivorous dinosaur with tiny arms that walked on its
hind legs. It had bull-like horns – hence its name (*taurus*
is the Latin word for 'bull'). Length: 7–8 metres; weight:
1 tonne; lived: uncertain – probably 110–90 mya.

Ceratopsian dinosaur *Chapter 12* Meaning: 'horned
face'. Any of a large variety of quadrupedal, herbivorous

dinosaurs having horns and/or frills and beaked skulls. Lived: Cretaceous period (142–65 mya).

Dromaeosaurid dinosaurs *Chapter 12* Meaning: 'running lizards'. Various theropod dinosaurs closely related to birds. Small to medium-sized, fast-running carnivores that probably hunted in packs. Length: 1–7 metres; lived: Cretaceous period (142–65 mya).

Giant ground sloth *Chapter 2* Scientific name: *Megatherium americanum*, 'megatherium' meaning 'large beast'. A massive bear-like mammal with large claws, related to the tree sloth. It walked upright on the ground and was mainly herbivorous. Length: 6 metres; weight: 3–4 tonnes; lived: 2 mya–8 tya.

Giganotosaurus *Chapter 12* Scientific name: *Giganotosaurus carolinii*, meaning: 'giant southern lizard'. Probably the largest carnivorous dinosaur that ever existed. Length: 13–14 metres; weight: 8 tonnes; lived: 110–95 mya.

Glyptodont ('grooved or carved tooth') *Chapter 21* Scientific name: *Doedicurus clavicaudatus*, 'clavicaudatus' meaning: 'pestle tail'. An edentate mammal related to the modern armadillo, with an armoured carapace and a spiked tail. Herbivorous. Length: 3 metres; weight: 1.4 tonnes; lived: 2 mya–15 tya.

Loch Ness Monster *Chapter 21* A cryptid, also called '**Nessie**' (Scottish Gaelic: *Niseag*). Its (disputed) scientific name is: *Nessiteras rhombopteryx,* meaning: 'The wonder of Ness with the diamond-shaped fin'. The name was given

by the late Sir Peter Scott and sceptics point out that the 'scientific' name is an anagram of 'monster hoax by Sir Peter S.'

Loch Ness is the largest body of fresh water in Britain (by volume) and the monster is claimed to be one of a colony of lake creatures similar in appearance to the (long-extinct) plesiosaurs. The first reported sighting of the creature was said to have been by St Columba on 22 August AD 565.

Macrauchenia *Chapter 14* Scientific name: *Macrauchenia patachonica*, meaning: 'long llama/long neck of Patagonia'. An herbivorous, hoofed mammal looking like a cross between a camel and a horse, with a long, hose-like nose. The last member of a group of extinct South American animals known as litopterns. Head height: 3 metres; lived: 7 mya–20 tya.

Minhocão *Chapter 21* A cryptid, also known as **'Surubin-Rei', 'Sierpe'** and **'Mboi-assu'** (big snake). A huge earthworm-like creature said to destroy plantations, orchards and livestock in South America.

Cryptozoologists believe it may be a giant member of a species of caecilian or a lepidosiren. Others think it may be an anaconda, or a hoax.

Najash rionegrina Meaning: 'serpent from Rio Negro' *Chapter 12* A fossil of this creature has been recently discovered in Patagonia. It is a snake with hind legs, and is believed to represent a primitive form in the evolutionary progression from lizards to snakes. The name

is derived from the Hebrew *Nachash*, the snake that tempted Eve to eat the forbidden fruit in the Garden of Paradise. God punished the snake by commanding it to crawl thereafter on its belly (Genesis 3.14). Some interpret this line as meaning that, before God's command, snakes had legs. Length: 1 metre; lived: 90 mya.

Notoceratops *Chapter 12* Scientific name: *Notoceratops bonarelli (nomen dubium),* 'notoceratops' meaning 'southern horned face'. A horned, frilled, ceratopsian dinosaur with a beak. It was an herbivorous quadruped. The exact identity of the animal is dubious and based only on a single jaw bone. It probably lived 80−70 mya.

Protocyon *Chapter 21* Scientific name: *Protocyon scagliarum* A wolf-like carnivore, now extinct, that hunted on open plains during the Pleistocene period. It probably lived 1− 0.5 mya.

Psittacosaurus *Chapter 12* Scientific name: *Psittacosaurus mongoliensis,* 'psittacosaurus' meaning 'parrot lizard'. A small, primitive, ceratopsian dinosaur with a tough, hook-like beak. It was herbivorous, could walk on two or four legs and was probably a fast runner. Length: 1−2 metres; weight: 25−80 kg; lived: 120−95mya.

Pterodactyl *Chapter 9* Meaning: 'winged finger'. Any of a large variety of flying reptiles belonging to the order *Pterosauria*. The wings were covered in thin membranes of skin, like a bat, and the animals ranged in size from that of a small bird to monsters with a wing span of 14 metres. Pterodactyl species existed over an immense span

of time: 228–65 mya.

Sabre-toothed cat *Chapter 2* Scientific name: *Smilodon populator*, 'smilodon' meaning: 'knife tooth'. Often referred to as sabre-toothed 'tigers', these animals are not true tigers but they are similar to our modern big cats. The cat gets its name from its massive (20 cm) canine teeth. It fed, like the modern lion, on large herbivorous animals. Length: 1.2–1.5 metres; weight: 200 kg; lived: 1.5 mya–10 tya.

Sauropod *Chapter 12* Meaning: 'lizard foot'. Herbivorous, quadrupedal, long-necked dinosaurs that were the largest creatures ever to have lived on land. Well-known examples include Apatosaurus (Brontosaurus), and Diplodocus. Sauropods first appeared in the late Triassic period (approx. 215–200 mya) and their last representatives, the titanosaurians, died out in the great Cretaceous-Tertiary extinction event, 65 mya.

Stegosaurus *Chapter 11* Scientific name: *Stegosaurus armatus,* meaning: 'armoured roof lizard'. A large, quadrupedal, herbivorous dinosaur with a double row of armoured plates along its back and long tail spikes. The mouth was beak-shaped and the front teeth were absent. The brain was among the smallest among dinosaurs – the size of a walnut. Length: 9 metres; weight: 4–5 tonnes; lived: 155–145 mya.

Terror bird *Chapter 21* Scientific name: *Phorusrhacos longissimus,* meaning: 'rag bearer'. A large, flightless bird with a massive beak – large enough to swallow a cat in

one mouthful. The terror bird was carnivorous and could run very fast – possibly up to 60 kph. The wings were adapted into sharp claws that could catch prey. Height: 3 metres; weight: 130 kg; lived: 27 my–10 tya.

Triceratops *Chapter 11* Scientific name: *Triceratops horridus*, 'triceratops' meaning 'three-horned face'. A large, quadrupedal, herbivorous dinosaur with a massive head, large bony frill and a horned appearance somewhat reminiscent of a modern rhinoceros. The frill and horns may have been used for defence but it is now thought more likely that they were used in display for dominance and courtship behaviour, similar to some modern deer. Length: 9 metres; weight: 6 tonnes; lived: 70–65 mya.

Tyrannosaurus *Chapter 10* Scientific name: *Tyrannosausus rex*, meaning: 'tyrant lizard'. A giant, bipedal, carnivorous, theropod dinosaur. Its massive head and thorax were balanced by a heavy tail, but its arms were relatively small. Its powerful jaws had the greatest bite force of any dinosaur. Scientists are still uncertain whether T. rex and other active dinosaurs were warm-blooded or not. Length: 12–13 metres; weight: 6–8 tonnes; lived: 85–65 mya.

Velociraptor *Chapter 12* Scientific name: *Velociraptor mongoliensis*, 'velociraptor' meaning 'swift thief'. A turkey-sized, bipedal, theropod dinosaur. It was carnivorous and, in common with other dromaeosaurids, had a large, sickle-shaped claw on the hind foot. Velociraptors achieved popular awareness through the 1990 novel

Jurassic Park by Michael Crichton, and the 1993 film of the same name directed by Steven Spielberg. Length: 1–2 metres; weight: 20 kg; lived: 83–70 mya.

Yeti *Chapter 21* A hominoid cryptid reported principally from the Himalayan mountains. The name derives from Tibetan roots meaning 'rock bear' and the creature has many other appellations, including **'The Abominable Snowman'**, '**Meh-teh'** (man bear) and '**Mizo'** (wild man). Himalayan folklore is steeped with traditions about a man-like creature leaving footprints in the snow and occasionally glimpsed among the trees or snow-covered rocks in remote mountain sites. Some cryptozoologists believe it may be an extant example of the ape *gigantopithecus*, the largest ape that ever lived, but this is thought by mainstream science to have been long extinct (100 tya). Sceptics think that the yeti sightings may actually be those of the langur monkey, the Tibetan blue bear, or the Himalayan brown or red bear.

Glossary

The explanations in this glossary give only the meanings of words as they are used in the book. Many of the words have other meanings as well, and if a full description of a word is required the interested reader should consult a dictionary.

(abbrev. – abbreviation, adj. – adjective, adv. – adverb, conj. – conjunction, Idiom. – Idiomatic, interj. – interjection, n. – noun, pl.n. – plural noun, prep. – preposition, v. – verb)

abate *v.* to diminish; to make or become less in intensity or degree
abbreviation *n.* a shortened word or phrase
abominable *adj.* horrible; loathsome; detestable
abrupt *adj.* sudden; immediate; unexpected
abundance *n.* plenty; large amount; copious supply
access *n.* the right or ability to enter, use or approach something
accomplish *v.* to achieve; to succeed; to complete
accusation *n.* an allegation that someone is guilty of a crime, misdemeanour or offence; an imputation or charge

acknowledge *v.* to recognize the truth of something; to admit a reality

acronym *n.* a pronounceable word made up from some or all of the initial letters of a longer title; e.g. *laser* (*qv*)

activate *v.* to set in motion; to start off; to make active

ad nauseam adv. very boringly or tediously. Latin phrase meaning 'to the point of sickness'

adamant *adj.* determined; having an unshakeable opinion about something; impervious to pleas

adapt *v.* to change or adjust to new conditions

adaptation *n.* a modification that makes something better suited to its environment or situation

address *v.* to deal with; to sort out; to get on with; to confront

adjacent *adj.* next to; near; adjoining

adjust *v.* to change; to adapt, especially to cope with some new circumstance or situation

adjustment *n.* a change or modification

admiration *n.* high regard; esteem; respect

ado *n.* fuss; delay; bother

adopt *v.* Chapter 2: to take responsibility for; to take into the family; Chapters 19, 23: to assume a different voice or expression

adrenaline *n.* a hormone associated with excitement, stress or activity

adroitly *adv.* dexterously; skilfully

aeon *n.* an unimaginably long period of time

aerial *adj.* to do with the air or aircraft; in or of the air

aerobatic *adj.* able to perform complicated or spectacular aerial manoeuvres

aeronautical *adj.* to do with aircraft or pilots

agenda *n.* a list of things to be attended to; a schedule; a plan of action

aggression *n.* hostility; offensive activity

aggressive *adj.* hostile; quarrelsome; belligerent

aghast *adj.* filled or overcome with horror; appalled

agile *adj.* nimble; athletic

agility *n.* speed and skill in movement; nimbleness

agitated *adj.* excited; disturbed

agog *adj.* very curious; intensely attentive

ail *v.* an old-fashioned word meaning to feel unwell. An *ailment* is another word for an illness

aimlessly *adv.* without purpose or direction; having no goal

ajar *adj.* slightly open

alacrity *n.* liveliness; speed; briskness

alert *adj.* Chapter 11: attentive; vigilant; *v.* Chapters 13, 21: to warn; to put on guard

alien *adj.* foreign; strange; unfamiliar; from another world

alleged *adj.* described as such; presumed to be; not proved to be

alliance *n.* an agreement or pact; a union to achieve a purpose

allocate *v.* to give to; to assign; to allot

Alsatian *n.* a large wolf-like breed of dog, often used as a guard dog. Also called a German Shepherd

amateur *n.* a non-professional person; one who engages in an interest for enjoyment or sport, rather than for remuneration

amber *n.* fossilized pine resin

ambient *adj.* to do with the immediate surroundings or conditions

amidst *prep.* amid; in among; in the middle of

ammonia *n.* a very pungent gas. Chemical formula: NH_3

ample *adj.* more than enough; easily sufficient; abundant

anaesthetic *n.* a substance capable of producing loss of consciousness (general anaesthesia), or loss of sensation in a specific area of the body (local anaesthesia)

analyse *v.* to study in detail; to examine; to discover specific information, meaning or composition

analysis *n.* the results obtained from examining something, or determining its composition

anchor *v.* to fix; to fasten securely

anguish *n.* severe pain; misery; intense grief

annihilate *v.* to eradicate; to destroy completely; to extinguish

anon *adv. (poetic or archaic)* soon; in a short time

anonymity *n.* the state of being unknown or unidentified

anonymous *adj.* from or by an unknown person

antenna *n.* one of two (or more) mobile tentacles or appendages on the head of an insect, mollusc, etc. They are usually sensory organs

anthology *n.* a collection of literary pieces or articles on a specific subject

anticipate *v.* to expect or foresee

antiquity *n.* the distant past; the quality of being ancient

apologetically *adv.* in a contrite manner

appal *v.* to horrify; to shock; to dismay

apparent *adj.* easily seen; obvious; evident

apparently *adv.* seemingly

apparition *n.* something that appears, such as a ghost or spectre

appellation *n.* name; title

apprehensive *adj.* anxious; fearful

appropriate *adj.* Chapters 2, 5, 8, 23: suitable; fitting; *v.* Chapter 4: to take; to acquire

aptitude *n.* ability; skill

archaic *adj.* out of date; ancient; antiquated

archaeology *n.* the study of the past by the examination of materials, buildings and artefacts from ancient cultures

arduous *adj.* strenuous; difficult; requiring great effort

Argentinosaurus *see* Animal Anthology

aroused *adj.* awoken; stimulated

arrogant *adj.* conceited; boastful; proud

artefact *n.* a man-made article

arthritis *n.* inflammation of the joints

artistic licence *n.* a deviation from conventional rules to achieve a desired effect

asap *abbrev.* 'as soon as possible'

ascent *n.* climb

ascertain *v.* to discover; to determine; to establish

assailant *n.* an attacker

assess *v.* to judge; to evaluate

assets *pl.n.* possessions; property

assiduously *adv.* conscientiously; perseveringly

associate *n.* a colleague; a partner in an enterprise; a companion; a friend

association *n.* a friendship or companionship

astounding *adj.* amazing; impressive; bewildering

atmosphere *n.* the layer of gases surrounding the Earth or other celestial body

audible *adj.* loud enough to be heard

authoritative *adj.* having a commanding or assertive manner; wielding authority

avert *v.* to prevent something happening; to ward off

avidly *adv.* greedily; eagerly; with great desire

avow *v.* to admit openly; to affirm; to declare or assert

awe *n.* wonder; respect; admiration

awesome *adj.* very impressive; amazing; outstanding

awestruck *adj.* filled with awe

babble *n.* chatter; incoherent or meaningless speech

backlit *adj.* lit from behind

back-up *n.* a support; a contingency plan or arrangement

bade *v. (archaic)* a past tense of the verb *to bid*, meaning to instruct or command

bafflement *n.* bewilderment; perplexity; puzzlement

balaclava (helmet) *n.* a close-fitting hood covering the ears and neck, used to provide warmth or anonymity

baleful *adj.* menacing; hostile; vindictive

ballast *n.* heavy material providing stability or weight

balmy *adj.* pleasant; mild; soothing

bank *v.* (of an aircraft) to tilt to one side while making a turn in the air

bastard *n.* a person born of unmarried parents. In this story it is used in its informal sense as a swearword, meaning an unpleasant or obnoxious person

bay *n.* an assigned parking space; a marked-out area

batter *v.* to beat heavily and repeatedly

beacon *n.* a signal; a light or fire to attract attention

bead *n.* Chapter 10: *beads of sweat* means small drops of sweat

beckon *v.* to summon with a gesture

befall *v.* to happen to; to take place

behemoth *n.* a monstrous beast

behest *n.* an order; a serious request

belligerent *adj.* aggressive; truculent

bellow *n.* a roar; a loud deep sound, usually emitted in pain or rage

bemused *adj.* confused; bewildered; baffled; confounded

benefit *v.* to be the recipient of something good; *n.* an improvement or advantage; something that does good

bequeath *v. (archaic)* pass on; hand down

bereft *adv.* parted from; deprived (of)

berserk *adj.* in a violent rage or frenzy

bestow *v.* to confer a privilege or honour

betrayal *n.* treachery; deceit; disloyalty

bewildered *adj.* confused; puzzled

bidding *n.* order; command; summons

bide *v. (archaic)* to stay in a place

bifurcation *n.* division or fork into two branches

Bigfoot *see* Animal Anthology

billiards *n.* various games played on a material-covered table with pockets into which hard balls are struck with a long cue

bind *v.* to tie; to secure

biomass *n.* vegetable material containing, or used as, a source of energy or fuel

bipedal *adj.* having two feet; walking on two feet

bird *n. (slang)* an informal term for a girl or young woman

bitch *n.* a female dog or other canine animal. The word is also used (as in Chapter 19) as a slang term of abuse

for a female person meaning she is spiteful or malicious

black panther *n.* a melanistic (black) variant of a big cat such as a leopard or jaguar

blackmail *n.* the use of threats (usually of disclosure) to obtain money or, as in Chapters 4, 23, to influence the actions of another

blind eye *phrase* to 'turn a blind eye' to something means to pretend not to notice it

bloody *adj.* *(slang; swearword)* a strong imprecation used to lend particular emphasis to a phrase or statement

blotchy *adj.* having irregular patches of discoloration

blunder *v.* to stumble in a clumsy fashion

BMW *abbrev.* Bayerische Motoren Werke: Bavarian Motor Works – a famous German car company

bog *n.* spongy wet ground; marsh; quagmire

boisterous *adj.* lively; unruly; unrestrained

bonhomie *n.* (from French) jovial friendliness; cheerfulness; goodnaturedness

boon *n.* a favour

booze *n.* *(slang)* any kind of alcoholic drink

botanist *n.* one who studies plants

boundless *adj.* limitless; endless; vast

bounty *n.* reward; generous gift

bowels of the earth *phrase* very deep underground; down in the depths

braided *adj.* interwoven; plaited

brainwave *n.* a sudden good idea; an inspiration

brash *adj.* showy; tasteless

bravado *n.* a show of courage (sometimes unfounded); a display of great self-confidence

brawl *n.* a noisy fight

break *n.* a brief holiday. To *take a break* means to have a short period of leave or vacation. In the title of Chapter 7 this meaning is punned with another meaning, that of breaking out of prison.

breakaway *adj.* describing a group or faction that has separated from a main body or organization

breaker *n.* a large white-crested wave breaking on to the rocks or shore

breakthrough *n.* a significant discovery; a ground-breaking development

breathtaking *adj.* exciting; awesome; very impressive

brew *v.* to prepare a drink by boiling or infusing

bribe *n.* a gift of money or goods in exchange for a favour

brisk *adj.* quick; lively; energetic

brood *n.* the young in a family; offspring

brow *n.* the forehead

browse *v.* to feed (usually on vegetation) in a calm and leisurely manner

budge *v.* to move; to shift

buffet *n.* a meal at which guests help themselves from a variety of dishes

buffoon *n.* a fool; a stupid or ridiculous person

bugging device *n.* concealed electronic spying
equipment for recording or acquiring information

bulk *n.* size or volume (especially when large or massive)

bung *v.* *(slang)* to throw; to chuck; to sling; to push in

burden *n.* a load or cargo, especially one that is heavy or
onerous. A 'beast of burden' is an animal carrying such
a load

burdensome *adj.* difficult to put up with; hard to bear;
onerous

bush meat *n.* the flesh of wild animals killed for food
(often illegally)

cache *n.* a hidden store

caecilian *n.* a tropical limbless amphibian resembling an
earthworm

calculus *n.* a branch of mathematics

camouflage *n.* colouring, appearance or shape designed
to hide or conceal

cancer *n.* a malignant growth; a tumour

canine *n.* a member of the dog family; a canid

cannibalism *n.* eating the flesh of one's own kind

canopy *n.* the highest general level of foliage in a forest,
formed by the crowns of trees and penetrated by only
the tallest species

canyon *n.* a ravine; a gorge

capacity *n.* ability; power

capricious *adj.* unpredictable; fickle; impulsive

captor *n.* one who captures and holds another captive

carapace *n.* shell or shield, made of bone or chitin

carbon offsetting *n.* the averaging out of carbon (dioxide) production and consumption

carcass *n.* a dead body

caress *v.* to touch or stroke affectionately

carnivore *n.* meat eater

Carnotaurus *see* Animal Anthology

cartel *n.* an association of separate groups having a common aim or purpose

cause a stir *phrase* attract attention; get things moving

cautiously *adv.* with great care; warily

cave racer *n.* scientific name: *Elaphe taeniura*. A cave-dwelling snake that lives mainly on bats and swiftlets in the wild. Length up to 2.5 metres. Similar snakes would have lived in the Valley of the Mighty Ones

cavern *n.* a cave, usually large and often underground

cayman *n.* an American species of crocodile, similar to an alligator

CCTV *abbrev.* closed–circuit television

ceratopsian *see* Animal Anthology

ceremony *n.* ritual; formal service

cf. *abbrev.* compare; see *(Latin: confer)*. Used to guide the reader to another source of information, in this glossary to another word

challenging *adj.* demanding; difficult; hard in a stimulating way

chameleon *n.* a type of lizard having the ability to change colour so as to blend in with its surroundings

channel *n.* groove; furrow; ditch; a specific path or course

charade *n.* a pretence; a travesty

charisma *n.* a personal quality giving its owner the power to inspire or influence others

charred *adj.* burnt; scorched; blackened by fire

charter business *n.* a company providing transport for lease or hire

chased *adj.* decorated or ornamented by engraving or etching

chasm *n.* a very deep split or cleft in the ground

cheroot *n.* a type of cigar with both ends cut off

chimera *n.* a creature made up from parts of different animals

chock *n.* a block or wedge used to prevent movement

chore *n.* a boring, routine job; an unpleasant task

chorus *n.* the sound of a group of voices

circumvent *v.* to go around; to bypass

cistern *n.* tank in which water is stored for a WC

claw-hammer *n.* a hammer with a cleft on one side of the head, used as a lever to extract nails

clearing *n.* an area within a wood that is free of trees or large shrubs

cleft *n.* a split; a fissure; a crevice; a crack

clench *v.* to grip tightly; to squeeze together

clog *v.* to block; to impede or obstruct

close a deal *v.* to complete a transaction successfully

close quarters (at) *pl.n.* very near; in close proximity

cluster *v.* to gather round in a close group

clutch *n.* a hatch or cluster of eggs

clutches *pl.n.* hands; paws; claws; talons; things that take a grip

coatimundi *n.* an omnivorous mammal from Central and South America, related to the raccoon family

cockpit *n.* the pilot's compartment in an aircraft

cockup *n.* *(slang)* a mess-up; a mistake

cocoon *n.* a protective covering or wrap, usually made from a silky substance

coin *v.* to make up a new word; to invent or fabricate a neologism

coincidence *n.* the simultaneous chance occurrence of events that are apparently connected

cold blood (in) *adj. or adv. phrase* without remorse; ruthlessly; deliberately

collide *v.* to bump into violently; to crash

collision *n.* the impact between two crashing objects

colloquial *adj.* informal; conversational; idiomatic

collusion *n.* secret agreement, often to do something wrong; conspiracy; connivance

colonize *v.* to take over or settle; to inhabit; to establish a colony

colony *n.* Chapters 12, 19, 20: a group of animals inhabiting a particular place

colossal *adj.* huge; gigantic; immense

combustible *adj.* capable of being burnt

commercial *adj.* to do with buying and selling; connected with business

committee *n.* a group of people chosen to make decisions about a particular subject

communal *adj.* shared or used by everybody; belonging to the community

commune *v.* to communicate closely

communication *n.* Chapters 1, 9, 10: the exchange of information; the imparting of knowledge, thoughts or feelings to another or others; *n.* Chapter 20: a connecting route or passage

commute *v.* to reduce the length or severity of a prison sentence

comparison *n.* judging or comparing one thing against another

compere *n.* the person running a show; the master of ceremonies

complex *n.* a building or institution made up of a number of interconnected parts or components

complicated *adj.* composed of different parts that are

difficult to understand; intricate; problematic

comply *v.* to agree with or submit to rules, conditions or requirements; to be obedient

compost *n.* decomposed organic material (e.g. rotting vegetation)

composure *n.* calmness; serenity

compound fracture *n.* a fracture of a bone that communicates with the air through a break in the skin

conclusive *adj.* not in doubt; decisive; final

condor *n.* a species of large vulture found (principally) in the South American Andes

conference *n.* a meeting for the exchange of information on a particular topic

confer *v.* to bestow upon; to endow; to grant

confess *v.* to admit to something; to acknowledge responsibility or guilt

confident *adj.* being sure about something; being certain

confidential *adj.* secret; private

configuration *n.* the arrangement of different parts

confined *adj.* limited; enclosed; restricted

confrontation *n.* the coming face to face of opposing individuals or groups

congealed adj. changed from fluid to solid; coagulated; clotted; curdled

conical *adj.* cone-shaped

conifer *n.* a species of tree or shrub that, typically, is evergreen and bears cones

conjunction *n.* coming together; union; coincidence

connive *v.* to plot with another, often in secret; to conspire

conscience *n.* the feeling of what is right or wrong; a sense of morality

consequence *n.* something that follows, or results from, a previous action or occurrence

consolation *n.* a source of comfort; something that gives solace

console *v.* to comfort; to bring solace

conspirator *n.* one who plots in secret with another or others

conspiratorial *adj.* to do with secret plots and plans

consternation *n.* worry; concern; anxiety

constraint *n.* an inhibition or restraint; a prohibition

consultant *n.* an expert who gives specialist advice on a particular subject

consume *v.* to eat or drink

contaminate *v.* to pollute; to spoil; to make impure by mixing

contemplate *v.* to think about intently; to consider

contemptuous *adj.* scornful; disdainful

contentious *adj.* controversial; arguable; the subject of dispute

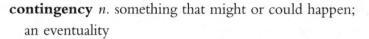

contingency *n.* something that might or could happen; an eventuality

contractor *n.* an individual or firm that supplies a service or materials

contrite *adj.* remorseful; sorrowful

contrive *v.* to manage to do something, especially by using a trick; to engineer a desired result

conventional *adj.* following regular standards of behaviour or thought; orthodox; conforming to accepted norms

converse *v.* to communicate (with); to engage in conversation

conviction *n.* a firmly held belief; a fixed opinion

cooperation *n.* assistance; willingness to help or collaborate

coordinates *n.* sets of numbers that define an exact location

copse *n.* a small wood or thicket

corpse *n.* a dead body; a cadaver

correspondence *n.* the exchange of letters

corroborate *v.* to support or confirm a fact or opinion

corrosive *adj.* something that eats away or destroys, such as an acid or alkali

corrupt *adj.* crooked; dishonest; depraved; open to bribery

cough up *v. (slang)* to pay, usually reluctantly

countermeasure *n.* an action that neutralizes or opposes an action by another

courtesy *n.* politeness; good manners. In Chapter 4 the word is used ironically

crack shot *n.* someone who shoots with great accuracy

crackdown *n.* a policy of strict enforcement; the imposition of severe measures

crag *n.* a peak; a rugged point on a rock

crater *n.* a bowl-shaped geographical feature, typically associated with volcanic activity or meteorite impact

crave *v.* to desire greatly; to yearn; to plead or beg for

crayfish *n.* a freshwater crustacean resembling a small lobster

credence *n.* belief (in); acceptance

credible *adj.* believable; trustworthy

crescendo *n.* an increase in loudness

crest *n.* the top of a hill; the highest point along a ridge

crestfallen *adj.* disappointed; disheartened; dejected

Cretaceous period *n.* the last period of the Mesosoic era, between the Jurassic and Tertiary periods, 144–65 million years ago

Cretaceous–Tertiary extinction event *n.* a major geological and palaeontological landmark. The event, which occurred 65.5 million years ago and caused the extinction of the dinosaurs and many other species, may have been due to the impact with the Earth of a

massive asteroid. Also known as the K–T extinction or the Cretaceous–Paleogene (K–P) event

crevice *n.* a crack; a fissure; a cleft

cripes *interj.* *(slang)* an expression of surprise or dismay

crisis *n.* a crucial stage in a sequence of events; a turning point; a critical point

critical *adj.* crucial; decisive

criticize *v.* to judge something disapprovingly; to censure

crooked *adj.* *(slang)* corrupt; dishonest; lacking integrity

crouch *v.* Chapters 12, 16, 20, 21: to bend low; to stoop; *n.* Chapter 22: a position adopted prior to a pounce

crucial *adj.* decisive; critically important

crumpled *adj.* collapsed into a twisted or distorted shape

crustacean *n.* one of a class of animals having a carapace or shell

cryptid *n.* a cryptozoological term for a creature rumoured to exist but not recognized by mainstream science

cryptozoology *n.* the study of creatures whose existence has not been scientifically proved

crystal *n.* a substance with a characteristic regular shape that results from the specific internal arrangement of its atoms or molecules

culture *n.* artistic, literary, dramatic and similarly refined pursuits

cumbersome *adj.* unwieldy; (of an object) awkward to carry because of its shape, weight or size

currency *n.* money

curtly *adv.* abruptly; rudely

custodian *n.* one who guards

custody *n.* arrest; the state of being held by the police

cycad *n.* a tropical or subtropical plant, which has an unbranched stem and fern-like leaves

dab *v.* to touch or mop with small light movements

dashboard *n.* instrument panel; fascia

data *pl.n.* facts; measurements; observations; recordings

daunting *adj.* frightening; disheartening; intimidating

dawn *v.* to start to become apparent (to); to become comprehensible

dean *n.* a senior official in a university or college

decay *n.* rotten or decomposed tissue

decrepit *adj.* worn out; broken down; dilapidated

deferentially *adv.* with respect

deflect *v.* to turn something aside from its course; to cause something to swerve

deforestation *n.* the clearing of trees

deftly *adv.* dexterously; nimbly; skilfully

déjà vu *n.* *(French)* the sensation that a current event has been experienced before

delicacy *n.* a choice food; a delicious titbit

delivery *n.* manner of speaking

delve *v.* to rummage; to feel around or search (in)

demise *n.* death

denizen *n.* a person or animal living in a place; an inhabitant; a resident

dense *adj.* thick; crowded; impenetrable

deportment *n.* behaviour, particularly in respect of physical bearing or carriage

depravity *n.* moral corruption; debasement; perversion

depression *n.* a dent; a depressed or sunken place

deprive *v.* to take away from; to prevent from possessing or enjoying; to dispossess

derive *v.* to obtain; to draw (from); to get (from)

dermestid beetle *n.* member of a family of various beetles in which the larval and adult forms are destructive to a wide variety of organic materials. They are so effective as carnivorous scavengers that they are used in museum laboratories to clean flesh from bones.

descendant *n.* a person or animal descended from an earlier ancestor or form

deserted *adj.* desolate; remote; empty; uninhabited

desolate *adj.* uninhabited; deserted; barren

despondent *adj.* dejected; downcast; hopeless; disheartened

destination *n.* the end-point of a journey; the place to which a voyage is directed

destined *adj.* decided in advance; pre-ordained

destiny *n*. the fate determined for a person or thing; their future or fortune

detachment *n*. indifference; aloofness; disengagement

deteriorate *v*. to get worse; to diminish in quality; to depreciate; to disintegrate

device *n*. a piece of equipment or tool for a specific task; a contrivance

devise *v*. to plan; to work out; to contrive

devoid *adj*. without; free from; lacking; destitute

devote *v*. to allocate time or energy to some undertaking or enterprise; to dedicate oneself to a cause or pursuit

devour *v*. to eat greedily or voraciously; to consume

dialect *n*. a form of speech used in a particular geographical area, or by a particular group or social class

dictate *v*. to impose one's will on another or others; to tyrannize

dilemma *n*. a quandary; a situation requiring a choice between two apparently equal but (usually) undesirable or unpalatable alternatives

dim *adj*. poorly illuminated; not well seen; indistinct; obscure

dimensions *pl.n*. measurements of size, e.g. length, height, width, etc.

diminutive *adj*. small; tiny

dire *adj*. fearful; disastrous; ominous

disarming *adj.* neutralizing, reducing, or counteracting hostility or suspicion

discard *v.* to throw away; to get rid (of)

discern *v.* to see; to perceive

disclosure *n.* revelation; the unveiling of hidden or secret information

disconcert *v.* to upset; to unsettle; to frustrate

disconsolate *adj.* very sad; dejected; inconsolable

discreet *adj.* tactful; behaving so as to avoid embarrassment

disembark *v.* to get out of, or down from, a means of transport

disembodied *adj.* without a body; lacking a body

disentangle *v.* to free; to unravel; to release

dislodge *v.* to remove; to get something out that was stuck or fixed

dismal *adj.* saddening; gloomy; depressing

dismantle *v.* to take apart

dispensable *adj.* not essential; expendable; disposable

dispense (with) *v.* to manage without ; to dispose (of); to do away (with)

disperse *v.* to leave a gathering; to break up; to scatter

displace *v.* to move out of position; to replace; to supplant; to take the place (of)

disposal *n.* the opportunity to use something or someone; to have the use (of)

dispose (of) *v.* to kill; to get rid (of); to throw away

distort *v.* to twist out of shape; to deform; to contort

distract *v.* to draw attention away from something

distracted *adj.* confused; attention taken away by something

distraught *adj.* very upset; agitated; distracted

diversity *n.* the quality or state of being varied or different

divert *v.* to change the direction of someone or something; to turn aside

DNA *n.* deoxyribonucleic acid. The substance in cells of which genes are made and which can be used to identify species and individuals

dodgy *adj.* *(slang)* risky; dangerous

dominant *adj.* principal; predominant; ruling; overriding

don *v.* to put on (clothes)

donate *v.* to give (usually as a present or gift; the use is ironic in Chapter 19)

double take *n.* a repeated, delayed, or exaggerated reaction to a given event or situation

downpour *n.* heavy rain

downside *n.* the bad aspect of a situation; the disadvantage

drape *v.* to hang or cover, especially casually or loosely

draw *v.* (on a cigarette) to suck air through; to take a puff

dromaeosaurid *see* Animal Anthology

drone *n.* a continuous low sound

drug trafficking *n.* the illegal trading of drugs

earthshattering *adj.* *(slang)* momentous; enormously important; 'earthshaking'

eavesdropping *v.* listening secretly to the conversations of others

ecological *adj.* related to environmental matters; to do with ecology

ecosystem *n.* a system comprising various living and non-living elements; the interactions between the organic and non-organic elements of a given environment

eddy *n.* a current in water or air that has a whirling motion

edentate *adj.* belonging to an order of mammals lacking teeth (e.g. anteaters)

e.g. *abbrev. exempli gratia (Latin).* This means 'for example'. Now frequently simplified to eg

eggshells (walking on) *metaphor* 'to walk on eggshells' means to proceed with the utmost care

egotism *n.* concern with oneself; self-centredness; conceit

elaborate *v.* Preface: to give more detail in a story or account; to expand upon; *adj.* Chapters 8, 16: detailed; complex; complicated

elapse *v.* (of time) to pass by

elation *n.* extreme happiness; joyfulness

elect *v.* to choose; to select by vote

electromagnetic radiation *n.* a range of energy
emissions in a spectrum ranging from the longest radio
waves to the shortest gamma radiation. Visible light is
part of the spectrum

element *n.* part; component

eliminate *v.* Chapter 23: to remove; to take out; *v.*
Chapter 8: *(slang)* to murder

emanate (from) *v.* to come from; to originate from

embed *v.* to fix in firmly; to stick into

ember *n.* glowing fragment of wood (etc.) in a dying fire

emblazon *v.* to make obvious with bright or splendid
letters, colours, insignia. etc.

emissary *n.* messenger; agent; representative

emission *n.* a substance that is given out or emitted. In
Chapter 3 the word *emissions* refers to polluting
substances, particularly gases, produced by the burning
of fossil fuels

emit *v.* to send out; to utter

emphasize *v.* to stress; to give prominence to

enacted *v.* played out; performed

energize *v.* to provide with energy; to stimulate

engaged *adj.* involved (in or with); occupied; busy

engrossed *adj.* completely absorbed in; occupied; taken
up with

engulf *v.* to surround completely; to overwhelm; to
swallow up

enlighten *v.* to instruct; to provide information

enlightenment *n.* sudden understanding; knowledge

enlist *v.* to engage support or service for a task or venture

en suite *adj. (French)* built as a single unit; part of a set

enthral *v.* to enchant; to spellbind

enticing *adj.* attractive; tempting; alluring

envisage *v.* to imagine; to visualize; to foresee

epic *adj.* having heroic or legendary qualities

epilogue *n.* a short postscript

epoch *n.* a particular period of time in history

equator *n.* an imaginary circle around the middle of the Earth at 0 degrees latitude. It divides the Earth into the northern and southern hemispheres

equatorial *adj.* to do with the equator

equivalent *adj.* equal in size or significance

escarpment *n.* a long, broad, very steep slope

establish *v.* Chapters 2, 5, 21: to determine; to confirm; to validate; to ascertain; *v.* Chapters 4, 10: to set up; to create

etc. *abbrev. et cetera (Latin).* This means 'and the rest'; 'and so forth'; 'and the others'

ethos *n* distinctive culture, spirit, or attitude

euphemism *n.* an inoffensive word or phrase used instead of an offensive, rude or vulgar one. Also, an indirect expression rather than a direct one

euphoric *adj.* extremely happy; elated

evaporate *v.* to turn a liquid into a vapour

evade *v.* to get around; to dodge; to avoid

evasive *adj.* avoiding trouble, difficulty, danger etc.

even-tempered *adj.* calm; not prone to anger

exasperation *n.* anger; irritation

excavate *v.* to dig out; to unearth, especially at an archaeological site

exclusive *adj.* catering for a privileged group; fashionable

excrement *n.* droppings; dung; faeces; 'poo'

exert *v.* to apply with great effort; to use forcefully

exhilaration *n.* pleasurable excitement; elation

existence *n.* the state of existing; the state of being (inanimate) or life (animate)

exotic *adj.* possessing strange beauty or quality; having unusual allure

expanse *n.* something extending over a wide area

expansive *adj.* wide; extravagant; all-inclusive

exploit *v.* to use for one's own advantage

exquisite *adj.* particularly beautiful; attractive with delicate, refined qualities

exquisitely *adv.* with extreme skill and delicacy

extant *adj.* still existing; still living; surviving

extent *n.* size; scope; area; range

exterminate *v.* to destroy completely; to wipe out; to annihilate

extort *v.* to obtain money (or favours) by threats,

intimidation or violence

extraction *n.* taking out; removal; withdrawal

extravagant *adj.* spending money excessively or
. wastefully; unrestrained

exude *v.* to give out

eye-opener *n.* *(Idiom.)* something surprising, unexpected,
or revealing. In the title of Chapter 11 it is used as a
pun on this sense and its literal sense

fabulous *adj.* based upon a fable or myth

facilities *pl.n.* the equipment and buildings required to
conduct some activity

fag *n.* *(slang)* cigarette

fascination *n.* awe; curiosity; intense interest

fashion plate *n.* a person dressed beautifully and
fashionably; the personification of elegance and fashion

fatal *adj.* causing death

fathom *v.* to work out; to get to the bottom of; to
penetrate or solve a mystery

fauna *n.* all the animals living at a particular time, or in a
particular place

feat *n.* an outstanding action or accomplishment; a great
achievement; an exploit

feather *v.* to change the pitch (angle) of the blades of an
aircraft propeller so as to reduce or abolish their
propulsive force

feather-brained *adj.* silly; forgetful; frivolous

felon *n.* one who has committed a serious crime (felony); a villain

fence *n.* *(slang)* one who deals in stolen goods

feral *adj.* wild or savage, especially after being previously tame or domesticated

ferocious *adj.* extremely fierce; savage

fertile *adj.* highly productive; rich

fervent *adj.* intense; heartfelt; ardent

fibrous *adj.* material containing strands or fibres, often tough in texture

fidget *v.* to make repeated restless, agitated or uneasy movements

filament *n.* a strand of fibre, thread or wire; a fibril

first-hand *adv.* directly; from an original source

fish to fry *metaphor* to have *other fish to fry* means to have other things to do, usually more important or interesting

fissure *n.* narrow crack or cleft

fitful *adj.* occurring in irregular spells. A *fitful* sleep (Chapter 6) is broken and restless

flank *n.* the lower part of the side of an animal or person

flinch *v.* to draw back in a sudden movement; to wince

flippancy *n.* frivolity; inappropriate levity

flora *n.* all the plant life living in a particular place or at a particular time

fluent *adj.* written or spoken with ease and facility

flurry *n.* a sudden burst of activity; a commotion

flying ace *n.* an expert pilot, often famous

foe *n.* enemy

foetid *adj.* foul-smelling; smelling of decay; nauseating

foil *v.* to frustrate or defeat an attempt by another; to baffle

foliage *n.* the leaves of plants

folklore *n.* the unwritten traditions, stories or legends of a particular group or culture

forage *v.* to search for food

forbidding *adj.* frightening; ominous

foreboding *n.* a feeling of impending trouble; a sense of forthcoming malice or evil

forefront *n.* the very front; the vanguard

forensic *adj.* related to law. In Chapter 23 the forensic technician is gathering evidence that might be used in legal proceedings

foresight *n.* insight into future needs; anticipation of problems or requirements

formidable *adj.* awesome; impressive; threatening; something inspiring fear or dread because of its size, strength or ability

formulate *v.* to arrange in order; to organize; to devise

forthcoming *adj.* about to happen or appear

fossils *pl.n.* the remains or impressions of animals or plants that lived in a previous age

fracture *n.* a break or crack, often, as in Chapters 2, 22, of a bone

fray *v.* to fall apart; to wear; to tatter

freak *adj.* very unusual; unpredictable; unexpected

free agent *n.* a person or animal who is free to behave or operate at will; one who is unconstrained

from scratch *adv. phrase (slang)* from the very beginning

frustrate *v.* to stop; to prevent; to hinder; to thwart; to annoy

fulfil *v.* to achieve; to complete a task; to attain an ambition; to carry out a mission successfully

full-scale *adj.* all-out; complete in every detail

fumble *v.* to grope blindly; to search awkwardly or clumsily

fundamentally *adv.* basically; primarily

funding *n.* money; finance

furrow *n.* a groove; a wrinkle; a trench. In Chapter 13 *her brow furrowed* means her forehead wrinkled in puzzlement

fuselage *n.* the main body of an aircraft

gait *n.* manner or style of walking or moving

game *adj. (slang)* prepared to have a go; willing to try; plucky

gaol *n.* a somewhat old-fashioned spelling of jail

gargantuan *adj.* giant; enormous

gastrolith *n.* a stone in the stomach

gear *n.* equipment; supplies

general relativity *n.* the theory of gravitation proposed by Einstein in 1916

generate *v.* to cause; to create; to produce; to bring into being

generator *n.* a machine for producing electricity from mechanical energy. In Chapter 8 it would be an engine driven by petrol or diesel

genial *adj.* easygoing; cheerful; pleasant

genuine *adj.* real; authentic; not fake

genus *n.* one of the taxonomic groups into which a family is divided. A *genus* contains different species

geology *n.* the study of the history, structure and composition of the Earth

geological fault *n.* a fracture in the Earth's crust causing displacement of its layers

geologist *n.* a scientist who studies geology

gesticulate *v.* to send a message or signal by using body movements (usually of the hands or head)

gesture *n.* something done or said to make a point or to emphasize something

ghoulish *adj.* morbid; disgusting; malevolent

giant ground sloth *see* Animal Anthology

Giganotosaurus *see* Animal Anthology

gimmick *n.* something designed to attract attention or publicity (especially when having little or no real substance)

ginger tom *n.* most (not all) ginger cats are male (tom), so *ginger tom* is a common expression

gingerly *adv.* in a timid or cautious manner

girder *n.* a beam, usually steel or iron, used in construction

gizzard *n.* part of a bird's stomach having a thickened, muscular, wall

glade *n.* a clearing or open space in a wood

glance *v.* to strike at an oblique angle so as to bounce off

glean *v.* to obtain in small pieces; to gather gradually; to garner

glimmer *n.* a faint glow or twinkle of light

gloom *n.* darkness; dimness

glow-worm *n.* a firefly; a beetle or larva of the family *Lampyridae* having a luminescent organ

glyptodont *see* Animal Anthology

gore *n.* coagulated blood; exudate from a wound

gorge *n.* Chapters 17, 18: a ravine; *v.* Chapter 12: to eat ravenously; to stuff oneself with food

gouge *v.* to dig out; to scoop; to make a hole

GPS *n.* global positioning system. A worldwide location and navigation system based upon satellite signals

graft *n.* *(slang)* work

grapnel *n.* a device with multiple hooks which is attached to a rope and thrown to secure a firm mooring

grapple *n.* Chapter 9: a hook by which something can

be secured; *v.* Chapter 18: to struggle in close combat; to come to grips with someone or something

grappling hook *n.* a grapnel

grating *n.* a metal grille

gravitation *n.* the attracting force between bodies, caused by their mass

grille *n.* a grating of metal bars that admits cooling air

grimace *n.* a twisted or contorted facial expression

grisly *adj.* horrible; gruesome

ground-breaking *adj.* novel; making a new advance

grub *v.* to dig the surface in order to search

gruelling *adj.* extremely tiring; punishing; exhausting

guano *n.* the dried excrement of sea birds, bats or seals

guise *n.* appearance; pretence; semblance

gully *n.* a small valley; a channel; a fissure between rocks

gumivore *n.* a creature that eats sap or gum

hack *v.* to gain unauthorized entry to a computer system

hacksaw *n.* a saw for cutting metal

half measure *n.* something inadequate

halfway house *n.* *(metaphor)* the midway point of a progression; a transition point

haltingly *adv.* hesitantly

hamlet *n.* a small village; a group of houses

hangar *n.* a large building for the storage and maintenance of aircraft

hapless *adj.* unfortunate; wretched

harness *n.* an arrangement of straps that fit around the body and to which things can be attached

harsh *adj.* rough; coarse; grating

hatch *v.* Prologue: to devise a plot or scheme; to contrive; *n.* Chapters 10, 11 and 12: short for *hatchway*, meaning an opening for access in a vessel or aircraft

hawser *n.* a strong heavy rope or line

hence *adv.* Chapter 11: therefore; for this reason; Chapters 3, 18, 21, 23: from this time or place *(archaic)*

henceforth *adv. (archaic)* from now on

hindsight *n.* the understanding of the true state of affairs after the event; insight after the truth has been revealed

histrionic *adj.* excessively dramatic; melodramatic

hitch *v.* Chapters 14, 21, 22: to connect; to harness; to fasten; Chapter 19: to pull up; to adjust

hither *adv. (archaic)* towards this place; to here

hither and thither *adv.* here and there; this way and that

hitherto *adv.* until now; up to this point

hoard *n.* a hidden store; a cache

Holy Grail *n.* the bowl or chalice used by Jesus Christ at the Last Supper. The phrase is now often used to describe something that is very highly sought after or aspired to

hominid *n.* a primate of the Hominidae family which includes man and extinct precursors of man

hominoid *adj.* manlike

Homo sapiens *n.* the scientific name of modern man

hone *v.* to sharpen

hoodwink *v.* to trick; to deceive; to dupe

hoo-ha *n.* a fuss; a commotion

hormone *n.* a substance produced by an endocrine gland and transported (usually) in the blood to have an effect on a distant organ(s)

horsetail *n.* a plant of the genus Equisetum. A notorious garden weed

hostile *adj.* very unfriendly; antagonistic; inimical

hot-wire *v. (slang)* to start an engine without a key by bypassing the ignition switch

hulk *n.* the abandoned body or frame of a vessel, usually a ship

hulking *adj.* large and ungainly

humanist *n.* one who believes in the advancement of humanity through its own efforts rather than through religion

humdrum *adj.* dull; ordinary; routine; boring

hunch *n.* an intuition; a guess

hybrid *n.* something of mixed origins

hydraulic *adj.* operated by fluid pressure

hype *n.* exaggeration; hyperbole

ideology *n.* a set of beliefs or ideas

idiom *n.* linguistic usage that is characteristic of the native speakers of a language, or peculiar to a particular group or culture

idle threat *n.* a vain threat; one that will not be carried out

i.e. *abbrev. id est (Latin).* This means 'that is' or 'in other words'. Often shortened to ie, and often used incorrectly instead of e.g. (*qv*)

ilk *n.* a type or sort

illicit *adj.* illegal

illuminate *v.* to make light

imitation *n.* mimicry; the act of copying

immaculate *adj.* without blemish; completely clean; unspotted

immeasurable *adj.* incapable of being measured; limitless

immemorial *adj.* very ancient; from a time too long ago to be remembered

immensity *n.* enormity; vastness

impassable *adj.* incapable of being traversed

impassively *adv.* calmly; serenely; uncaringly

impenetrable *adj.* not possible to get through

imperceptible *adj.* too slight or subtle to be noticed

imperial units *pl.n.* standards or definitions legally established in Great Britain for distances, weights, measures, etc.

implications *pl.n.* effects or results that might not at first be obvious

implicitly *adv.* unreservedly; absolutely; unquestioningly

imply *v.* to suggest or infer an outcome or consequence

impose *v.* to enforce; to require another or others to comply with something

impregnable *adj.* unable to be broken into

impregnate *v.* to soak; to permeate; to saturate; to imbue

impress *v.* to make an impression on; to have a strong effect on

inaccessible *adj.* not reachable; unapproachable

inanimate *adj.* without life

inappropriate *adj.* unsuitable; unfitting; untimely

incalculable *adj.* incapable of being determined; beyond calculation

incline *n.* a slope or gradient

incognito *adj.* unknown; in disguise; under an assumed name or identity

incongruous *adj.* an unexpected or inappropriate mixture; unusual; bizarre; ill-matched; having disparate elements

inconspicuous *adj.* not easily seen

incredible *adj.* unbelievable; beyond belief

incur *v.* to bring something on oneself

indefatigable *adj.* tireless; unflagging

indefinite *adj.* uncertain; unsettled

indicate *v.* to give a sign; to point out or show

indifferent *adj.* unaffected; unconcerned; uncaring

indispensable *adj.* essential; absolutely necessary

indulge *v.* Chapter 22: to pamper; to coddle; to spoil

indulgence *n*. Appendix: a remission of temporal punishment for sin

ineffectual *adj*. without effect; without success; inadequate; useless

inert *adj*. not moving; still

inevitable *adj*. certain to happen; unavoidable

inevitably *adv*. unavoidably; without any doubt

inexorably *adv*. relentlessly; unstoppably

inextricable *adj*. not able to be disentangled

infinite *adj*. endless; limitless

inflammation *n*. redness, heat and swelling, usually painful, in an injured or infected part of the body

inflict *v*. to cause to suffer; to impose on

informant *n*. one who provides information

informer *n*. one who informs on another or others; one who *(slang)* 'sneaks'

initial *adj*. first; at the beginning; early; preliminary

initiative *n*. will; drive to act. In Chapter 12 *on her own initiative* means that Clio acted on her own without being prompted

innovative *adj*. new; inventive; novel; imaginative

insatiable *adj*. incapable of being satisfied; continually greedy

inseparable *adj*. incapable of being parted or divided

insuperable *adj*. insurmountable; incapable of being overcome

insurance policy *n.* a protection against a possible contingency

intensify *v.* to increase; to become more evident

intercept *v.* to interrupt the passage of something or someone from one place to another

interchange *n.* the exchange of information; communication

intercom *n.* *(abbrev.)* short for *intercommunication system.* An internal telephone system

interject *v.* to throw in; to interrupt; to interpose abruptly

interlude *n.* an interval; a period of time for rest or activity separating longer periods of different activities or events

interminable *adj.* unending

intermittent *adj.* now and then; periodic; occurring at regular or irregular intervals; occasional

interpretation *n.* explanation; understanding; elucidation

interrogation *n.* asking somebody questions

intimate *adj.* (of knowledge) deep; extensive; detailed

intimation *n.* hint; suggestion

intimidate *v.* to frighten; to scare; to subjugate

intoxication *n.* poisoning

intricate *adj.* involved; difficult; complex

invaluable *adj.* priceless; having a value that is too great to calculate

inveterate *adj.* fixed in a habit; having ingrained behaviour; hardened

invulnerable *adj.* incapable of being hurt or wounded

iron rations *pl.n.* basic, life-preserving foods for use in an emergency

ironic *adj.* surprising or incongruous in a slightly amusing or sarcastic way

irresistible *adj.* incapable of being refused or denied; overpoweringly desirable

jail-bird *n.* one who has spent time in prison, especially repeatedly

jargon *n.* specialized vocabulary or language associated with a particular profession or group

jaunt *n.* a short outing or excursion, usually pleasurable

JCB *n.(trademark)* a large construction machine with a shovel at the front and an excavator arm at the back. Named after its English manufacturer **J**oseph **C**yril **B**amford

joyrider *n.* one who drives a car for pleasure and excitement. The car is usually stolen, and the driving reckless

juddering *adj.* shuddering; vibrating; shaking

Jurassic Park *n.* a famous novel about dinosaurs written in 1990 by Michael Crichton. It was adapted into a film in 1993 by Steven Spielberg

jut *v.* to stick out; to protrude; to project; to overhang

juvenile *adj.* youthful

kaleidoscope *n.* a toy which produces an endless variety of symmetrical optical effects by means of internal reflecting mirrors

ken *n.* range of knowledge

kilonewton *n.* symbol kN. A derived SI unit of force equal to 1000 newtons. One newton imparts an acceleration of 1 metre per second per second to a mass of 1 kilogram

kin *n.* relatives; kindred; a group related by blood ties

kinsman *n.* a member of the same family, tribe or race

kite *n.* a bird of prey with a long, forked tail

knock off *v. (slang)* to kill

know-how *n. (slang)* knowledge of how to do or make something

kudos *n.* status; prestige; glory; acclaim

laceration *n.* a wound with torn or jagged edges

lackey *n.* a servile follower; a hanger-on

lance *n.* a long, straight, pointed weapon

languid *adj.* inactive; lacking energy

laser *n.* a device for creating an intense, narrow, monochromatic, beam of light. The word is an acronym, representing **L**ight **A**mplification by **S**timulated **E**mission of **R**adiation

latitude (line of) *n.* an imaginary line, parallel with the equator, used in geography, navigation, etc. A line of latitude is expressed in terms of the number of degrees it lies north or south of the equator (which is latitude 0 degrees). The degrees give the angle subtended at the centre of the globe between the equator and the line of latitude described, in a plane at right angles to the equator

latrine *n.* a lavatory; toilet; WC. The term is usually applied in an institution (camp, barracks, prison, etc.)

lead *n.* a clue; something giving guidance or direction

league *n.* an old unit of distance equal to 3 miles (4.8 kilometres). *'In league with'* (Chapter 4) means working with; planning with; conspiring with

leer *n.* an unpleasant, suggestive look or smile

leg *n.* a section of a journey

legitimate *adj.* legal; lawful; authorized

lepidosiren *n. Lepidosiren paradoxa.* An eel-like South American lungfish

lest *conj.* in case; for fear that

leviathan *n.* a huge, powerful monster

liana *n.* a tropical climbing plant; a woody vine

liberation *n.* freedom; liberty

limpid *adj.* clear; unobscured; transparent

literate *adj.* able to read and write; educated

loathsome *adj.* disgusting; abhorrent

locality *n.* an area or neighbourhood

Loch Ness Monster (see Animal Anthology)

log *v.* to cut down trees for timber; to fell

longitude (line of) *n.* an imaginary line (meridian) passing at right angles to the equator and used in geography, navigation, etc. The prime meridian, 0 degrees, passes through Greenwich, near London. The position of any other meridian is expressed in degrees to the east or west of this line, i.e. the angle between the plane of the prime meridian and the one being described

loom *n.* Chapter 8: a machine for weaving yarn into a fabric or textile; *v.* Chapters: 10, 14: to approach with a threatening or ominous aspect; to come close; to overhang

lucrative *adj.* profitable; financially rewarding

lumber *n.* Chapter 8: sawn timber; wood for construction and carpentry; *v.* Chapters 3, 17, 18, 22: to move in an awkward or ungainly fashion

lumberjack *n.* one who cuts down trees

luminescence *n.* light emitted at low temperatures as from phosphorescence or chemical processes. The context in which the term is used by the professor in Chapter 8 is nonsense; he is just using a big word to do with light to impress the villains

lungfish *n.* a freshwater fish with both gills and an air-breathing lung

lurch *v.* Chapter 13: to pitch suddenly forwards or to one side; Chapter 22: to stagger or stumble

lurk *v.* to move or lie in wait in a concealed way, usually for an evil purpose

mace *n.* a medieval weapon consisting of a spiked club

Macrauchenia (see Animal Anthology)

macroscopic *adj.* visible to the naked eye (cf microscopic)

magnitude *n.* size or extent

maiden name *n.* a woman's surname before marriage

mainstream *adj.* in agreement with current thought or attitudes; conventional; orthodox

makeshift *adj.* something found or put together to use when a proper tool is unavailable

malevolent *adj.* wishing evil on others, or appearing to do so

malignant *adj.* causing harm or evil

malodorous *adj.* foul-smelling

manipulate *v.* to handle or control, often skilfully

manoeuvre *v.* to move into a suitable position

maraud *v.* to roam or wander in search of spoils; to raid; to harry

maroon *v.* to abandon; to leave isolated

materialize *v.* to appear; to take shape; to become visible

matter-of-fact *adj.* without apparent emotion or excitement

mean (time) *n.* in Chapter 23 the mean time referred to is Greenwich Mean Time (GMT). This is the solar

time at the Greenwich meridian (0 degrees longitude). Because of the Earth's tilt and elliptical orbit, the position of the sun at noon at Greenwich may vary in time, which is why the value is calculated as an average or *mean* time

medic *n.* (informal) a doctor, medical student or medical assistant

menace *v.* to threaten with violence or danger

menagerie *n.* a zoo

mentor *n.* a trusted adviser

meridian *n.* a line of longitude

mess hut *n.* a dining hut (usually for soldiers etc.)

metamaterial *n.* a material with properties that depend upon its structure rather than on its composition. The term is used particularly to describe artificial materials with properties not found in naturally occurring substances

metaphor *n.* a figure of speech in which a word or phrase is used in a non-literal sense, to denote a resemblance to the situation described, e.g. 'She froze with fear' (compare with *simile*)

metric units *n.* the decimal units used in measurement systems based upon the metre

miasma *n.* an unwholesome or noxious atmosphere

microscopic *adj.* only visible under a microscope

Middle Ages *n.* a period in history commonly regarded

as lasting from the end of classical antiquity in AD 476 (the deposition of the last western Roman emperor) to the Renaissance in AD 1453 (the fall of Constantinople). The sale of indulgences alluded to in the Appendix occurred from about the twelfth century onwards

midst *n.* *in their midst* (Chapter 19) means 'in the middle of them'; 'among them'

midwife *n.* a woman who assists in the delivery of a baby

migration *n.* the movement of animals between different habitats

millennium *n.* a period of one thousand years

mind-blowing *adj.* *(slang)* stunning; psychedelic; overwhelming

minder *n.* *(slang)* bodyguard or protector, especially of a criminal

Minhocão (see Animal Anthology)

miniature *adj.* small; minute; reduced in size

minimize *v.* to reduce to the smallest possible amount or to the least possible degree

miscalculation *n.* a wrong judgement

miscellany *n.* a miscellaneous collection; a mish-mash; a hotch-potch

miscreant *n.* a villain or wrongdoer

misfortune *n.* bad luck

misleading *adj.* deceptive; confusing

mission *n.* a task to fulfil; an objective; a quest

mock *adj.* Chapter 23: pretend; sham; *v.* Chapter 19: to ridicule; to treat with contempt or scorn

modest *adj.* self-disparaging; unpretentious; understating one's achievements or ability. The word is used in its true sense in Chapter 23 and in an ironic sense in Chapters 8 and 23

mole wrench *n. (trademark)* An adjustable tool which can be locked into a vice-like grip

molest *v.* to disturb for an unpleasant or evil purpose; to accost; to attack

momentarily *adv.* for a very short period; temporarily

momentous *adj.* having great significance

moon (time) *n.* a lunar month (i.e. 28 days, being the time from one full moon to the next)

morose *adj.* unhappy; gloomy; peevish; ill-tempered

mortal *adj.* deadly

mortar *n.* a bowl in which substances are ground or pulverized with a pestle

mould *n.* type or character. He *'fits the mould'* in Chapter 13 means that he conforms to a particular type

mull *v.* to ponder

municipal *adj.* to do with a town, city, borough, etc.

mutual *adj.* in common; shared

myriad *adj.* very many; innumerable

naïve *adj.* innocent; credulous; ingenuous

Nature *n.* a famous scientific journal

naught *n.* *(archaic)* nothing

navigate *v.* to plot the position and direct the path taken, during a journey

Neanderthal man *n.* *Homo neanderthalensis,* a primitive man who lived in the late Palaeolithic period

neologism *n.* a new word

nerd *n.* *(slang)* a stupid person or, in more recent usage, an intensely focused or dedicated person, with few interests outside a narrow field

New World *n.* the transatlantic countries of the western hemisphere; the Americas

Newton's rings *pl.n.* an interference pattern caused by the reflection of light between two surfaces differing in shape. *See* 'Notes on the names in the book'

niche *n.* a particular and suitable position or space

nicotine *n.* an alkaloid found in tobacco that causes yellowish–brown stains on the fingers and teeth of heavy smokers

nigh *adv.* *(archaic)* near

nimble *adj.* quick; agile; moving neatly

Nobel prize *n.* a famous international prize named after the Swedish scientist and philanthropist, Alfred Nobel. It is awarded for outstanding contributions in a number of

fields, including physics – Professor Strahlung's subject

nocturnal *adj.* to do with the night

nomen dubium *n. (Latin)* This means 'doubtful name'. It indicates a name that is not recognized by mainstream science

nonchalant *adj.* casual; unconcerned

nonplussed *adj.* stuck for an answer; at a loss; confounded; perplexed

northern hemisphere *n.* that half of the Earth lying north of the equator

nostalgia *n.* desire or yearning for past events, places, etc.

Notoceratops *see* Animal Anthology

notorious *adj.* famous for something bad; infamous

nuclear fission *n.* the splitting of an atomic nucleus with (usually) the release of energy

nuclear fusion *n.* the combination of two nuclei with the release of energy

nuclear waste *n.* waste radioactive material resulting from nuclear processing

obliging *adj.* helpful; ready to assist; agreeable

oblivious *adj.* unaware (of); taking no notice

obscured *adj.* hidden; covered

obsessed *adj.* completely absorbed in or preoccupied by something

obstacle *n.* something in the way; a blockage

oedema *n.* an excess of fluid in body tissues or a body part

Old World *n.* the world as it was known before the discovery of the Americas

opaque *adj.* not transmitting light

optics *n.* the study of light and vision

optimistic *adj.* hopeful; confident; expecting a good outcome

opulent *adj.* wealthy; plentiful; abundant; extravagant

ordeal *n.* a stressful experience

ore *n.* a mineral from which valuable constituents such as metals can be extracted

orthodox *adj.* conventional; conforming with mainstream standards or norms

orthopaedics *n.* a surgical speciality concerned with bones and joints

ostensibly *adv.* to all outward appearances; apparently; seemingly

outcrop *n.* a protruding section of rock

outlandish *adj.* conspicuously or grotesquely unconventional; bizarre

overburden *v.* to overload with weight or work

overcast *adj.* cloudy; obscured; covered over

overhang *n.* part of a formation that protrudes beyond or hangs over, the rest

pageant *n.* a parade; an elaborate procession

palaeontologist *n.* one who studies fossils

panorama *n.* an extensive, unbroken view

Pantanal *n.* a vast area of wetlands in South America, famous for its flora and wildlife

paparazzi *pl.n.* photographers who invade the privacy of celebrities to obtain compromising or 'candid' shots

paracetamol *n.* a pain-relieving drug; an analgesic

parallel *adj.* separated equally at every point

parole *n.* freedom given prematurely to a prisoner which is conditional upon good conduct

partial *adj.* incomplete

patronizing *adj.* condescending; in a superior manner

pax *interj. (Latin).* Peace

peal *n.* a long, loud sound

pecking order *n.* the hierarchy in a flock of birds. The phrase is commonly used metaphorically, as in Chapter 4

peddle *v.* to deal in illegal drugs

peeping Tom *n.* one who hides and spies on another or others; a voyeur

peg it *v. (slang)* to die (also: *peg out*)

penetrate *v.* to enter; to pierce; to find a way into or through something

pensive *adj.* deeply thoughtful, often with an element of sadness

perfidious *adj.* treacherous; deceitful; faithless

perfunctory *adj.* cursory; superficial; without great attention

perilous *adj.* very dangerous; extremely hazardous

periphery *n.* the outer edge of an area or group; the boundary

perish *v.* to die

pernicious *adj.* seriously harmful

pertain *v.* to relate (to); to have reference or relevance (to)

perturb *v.* to disturb; to trouble; to discomfit; to discompose

pervade *v.* to spread throughout; to permeate

pessimistic *adj.* expecting the worst; anticipating trouble

pestle *n.* a club-shaped implement for pounding or grinding. Often used with a *mortar (qv)*

phenomenal *adj.* outstanding; extraordinary

phenomenon *n.* an unusual or remarkable occurrence

philosophical *adj.* learned; wise; relating to philosophy

phosphorescence *n.* a light that persists after the radiation causing it has ceased, or a light produced at low temperatures by a chemical reaction

pick-up *n.* a truck with an open rear body and low sides

piece of the action *phrase* in Chapter 21 *everyone wants a piece of the action* means that everyone would like to join in and participate

pinch *v. (slang)* to steal

piton *n.* a metal spike that is driven into rock or ice to secure a climbing rope

placate *v.* to pacify; to calm; to appease

placid *adj.* calm; unexcited

plateau *n.* a flat area on raised land

plausible *adj.* believable; credible; apparently reasonable

Pleistocene epoch *n.* the first epoch of the Quaternary period. It lasted from 1.8 million years ago to 10 000 years ago

Pliocene epoch *n.* the last epoch of the Tertiary period. It lasted from 5 to 1.8 million years ago, the start of the Pleistocene epoch

pliers *pl.n.* a gripping tool with hinged arms and serrated jaws

plight *n.* a situation of danger or great hardship

plutonium *n.* a toxic, metallic element that is used as a reactor fuel in nuclear weapons and nuclear power stations

poignantly *adv.* sadly; distressingly

policy *n.* Chapters 2, 3: a plan of action; Chapter 19: an insurance document or contract

polyamide *n.* a synthetic polymeric material such as nylon

poncho *n.* a South American cloak consisting of a piece of material with a single hole through which to put the head

ponderous *adj.* slow; laborious

pool *n.* billiards

port *n.* the left side of a ship or an aircraft (when looking

forwards). Also known as *larboard*

portable *adj.* easily carried

post-traumatic stress *n.* stress or worry following an
unpleasant or damaging experience

potent *adj.* very strong; powerful; forceful

potential *n.* unrealized capacity; latent possibility

potentially *adv.* possibly

precaution *n.* safety measure; an action taken to prevent
or ward off trouble

preceding *adj.* foregoing; former; coming before

precipice *n.* a sheer, steep cliff face

precipitate *v.* to cause to happen; to bring on earlier
than expected

precipitous *adj.* very steep

predation *n.* predatory behaviour

predator *n.* a carnivorous (meat-eating) animal; a
hunter–killer

predicament *n.* a very difficult situation

prehensile *adj.* adapted for grasping

preliminary *adj.* preparative; introductory

premature *adj.* happening before the expected time

pretence *n.* make-believe; a false or misleading display

pretty pass *n.* a sad or bad state of affairs

primate *n.* a mammal belonging to the order Primates
which includes anthropoids and prosimians. Primates
are characterized by advanced binocular vision, large

brains and specialized digits for grasping

prime *n.* the period of life in which one has maximum power and vigour

primitive *adj.* early; crude; undeveloped

primordial *adj.* existing from the earliest time; primeval

priority *n.* something that requires early attention, that takes precedence

privilege *n.* a special benefit; an advantage

problematic *adj.* posing or constituting a problem; questionable

proceeds *pl.n.* profits or returns from a venture or transaction

prodigious *adj.* very great; vast

profound *adj.* deep; extensive; far-reaching

progeny *n.* descendant(s)

progressively *adv.* increasingly

project *n.* Chapters 5, 8, 13 and Appendix: a task; a plan; a job; *v.* Chapter 21: to throw one's voice (or, in Lucy's case, a thought) so that it can be heard at a distance

prologue *n.* an introductory section to a story, play, speech, etc.

prompt *v.* to urge to start or continue

prong *n.* a projecting point

proposal *n.* plan

prospect *n.* Chapter 4: a view or sight; Chapters 9, 17, 20: an expectation

prostrate *adj.* lying flat

protocol *n.* code of behaviour; etiquette

prototype *n.* a preliminary or experimental version of something

protrude *v.* to stick out; to project beyond a surface

proximity *n.* nearness; closeness

Psittacosaurus *see* Animal Anthology

psychological *adj.* to do with the mind

pterodactyl *see* Animal Anthology

pterosaur *see* pterodactyl

pulverize *v.* to reduce something to fine particles or dust by pounding, grinding or crushing

pun *n.* a joke that relies on a play on words; usually words that sound the same but have different meanings

pungent *adj.* having a very strong or acrid smell or taste

punctuate *v.* to interrupt frequently

purchase *n.* Chapter 5: the act of buying; *n.* Chapter 21: a firm foothold (in this case 'hoofhold'!)

purist *n.* one who insists on a correct style

putrefactive *adj.* having a disgusting smell of decomposition

pygmy marmoset *n. Callithrix (Cebuella) pygmaea.* The world's smallest monkey, weighing approximately 130 g. It lives in the forests of South America

quadruped *n.* an animal that walks on four legs

quandary *n.* a puzzling situation; a predicament

quarry *n*. something hunted or pursued

quartz *n*. a colourless mineral with an hexagonal crystalline structure that is found in rocks. It is composed of silicon dioxide

quick on the uptake *phrase (informal)* quick to understand; smart

qv *abbrev. quod vide (Latin). This* means 'which see' and is used to denote a cross reference

rack (one's brains) *v*. to try very hard to remember something, or to think of a solution to a problem

radioactive *adj*. emitting radiation spontaneously from atomic nuclei (includes alpha, beta and gamma radiation)

radioactive fallout *n*. the descent of radioactive particles from the atmosphere to Earth

ramble *v*. to speak or write in a disorganized way

random (at) *n*. not in any particular order; in a purposeless fashion

range *n*. a chain of mountains

rank *adj*. having a disgusting smell or taste

rapt *adj*. totally engrossed; spellbound

raptor *n*. a bird of prey

raucous *adj*. hoarse; loud; harsh

ravine *n*. a deep, narrow valley

reabsorb *v*. to take back (into)

realm *n*. field or area of interest

reassert *v.* to re-establish

reassure *v.* to comfort; to restore confidence; to allay fears

recess *n.* a space that is set back; an alcove; a niche

reconnoitre *v.* to inspect; to survey; to examine; to explore

recount *v.* to tell; to describe; to narrate

recumbent *adj.* lying down; reclining

redundant *adj.* unnecessary; surplus to requirements; superfluous

refine *v.* to improve; to make more suitable or elegant

reflect *v.* Chapters 3, 5, 18: to bounce something back (usually light or heat); Chapter 20: to think; to ponder

reform *v.* to improve; to give up a bad habit or bad conduct

refuge *n.* a place of safety; somewhere providing shelter or protection

refuse *n.* rubbish

relentless *adj.* without stopping; sustained; unremitting

reluctant *adj.* unwilling; disinclined

remnants *pl.n.* remaining pieces or parts

remorse *n.* sorrow; regret; compunction

rendezvous *n.* a pre-arranged meeting place (*from French*)

rend *v.* to tear forcefully; to rip

renewable *adj.* capable of being replaced or replenished

renowned *adj.* famous

rent *n.* a tear; a slit

repellent *n.* a substance that wards something off or

drives it away

replenish *v.* to re-fill; to replace what has been used

repulsive *adj.* disgusting; repugnant; loathsome

research *v.* to obtain information or collect facts about a subject; to study in detail

reservation *n.* an emotion, attitude or fact that prevents the wholehearted acceptance of something

reserve *n.* Chapter 1, Epilogue: an area of land set aside for the conservation of animals, plants, etc.; *n.* Chapters 3, 4: spare or replacement stock for contingency use; *v.* Chapters 4, 12: to retain for a particular use

resolve *n.* Chapter 13: determination; resolution; *v.* Chapters 19, 24: to settle; to sort out; to solve; *v.* Chapter 2: to plan; to determine; to decide

resonant *adj.* resounding; echoing

resort *n.* a means of help or action; a recourse

resourceful *adj.* capable; ingenious; having the ability to deal with difficult situations

respectable *adj.* having good standing in society; well thought of; worthy; estimable

respective *adj.* relating separately to two or more different things

respiratory *adj.* to do with breathing

rest-cure *n.* a break taken to rest for medical reasons; an undemanding, unstressful period

restore *v.* to return something to its original or previous state

restrain *v.* to hold back

resume *v.* to start again

retch *v.* to heave as if to vomit; to vomit ineffectually

retractile *adj.* capable of being withdrawn

retreat *n.* Chapter 12: a refuge; a safe, secluded spot; a sanctuary; *v.* Chapter 10: to withdraw; to retire; to recede

retrieve *v.* to recover something; to get something back

reverberate *v.* to resound; to echo and re-echo

revere *v.* to hold in deep respect or awe; to venerate

reverie *n.* a daydream; a state of absent-mindedness (from French)

review *v.* to re-examine; to reassess

revolutionize *v.* to bring about a fundamental change

revolver *n.* a handgun with a revolving chamber that allows several shots to be fired in succession, without the need to re-load

revulsion *n.* extreme disgust; loathing

ricochet *v.* to bounce off; to rebound (usually with a whining noise)

ridge *n.* a long, narrow range of raised land

rig *v.* to set up; to arrange; to prepare for use

rim *n.* the raised edge of a curved or circular object

ringleader *n.* the organizer or leading person in a group engaged in mischievous or illegal activity

ritual *n.* ceremony

rival *n.* a competitor

rivulet *n.* a small stream

rogue *n.* scoundrel; villain

Rolex *adj.* *(trade name)* an expensive brand of wristwatch

romp *v.* to make rapid and easy progress

roost *n.* a place to rest or sleep

roost (to rule the) *v.* to be in charge; to be the boss

roster *n.* a list showing people's turns for duty; a duty rota

Rottweiler *n.* a species of robust dog with a reputation for being fierce

round the corner *adj. phrase* soon; imminent

rueful *adj.* sorrowful; repentant

rugged *adj.* jagged; very uneven; rough

rule the roost *see* roost

rummage *v.* to search carelessly or untidily

rumour *n.* hearsay; uncertain information

ruthless *adj.* hardhearted; merciless

sabre-tooth 'tiger' *see* Animal Anthology

sacrifice *v.* to give something up; to forgo; to surrender (for the sake of something or someone)

safeguard *n.* a protection against danger or damage

sagely *adj.* wisely (the word is used ironically in Chapter 8)

sag *v.* to fall; to sink down

salamander *n.* a terrestrial amphibian of the family

Salamandridae that returns to water to breed

sanctuary *n.* somewhere safe from danger; a refuge; a place of asylum

satisfaction *n.* pleasure in having fulfilled a desire; contentment through achievement

saunter *v.* to stroll at a leisurely pace

sauropod *see* Animal Anthology

savannah *n.* open grassland, studded with trees and bushes

scam *n.* *(slang)* a swindle; a method of cheating

scarce (to make oneself) *phrase* to leave; to disappear from view; to make oneself inconspicuous

scavenger *n.* an animal that eats the flesh of dead creatures, or other decaying organic matter

sceptical *adj.* disbelieving; doubtful; mistrustful

scholarship *n.* an award of financial aid for academic achievement

scope *n.* capability of action; capacity; opportunity

score over *v.* to come out on top or ahead of another or others

scornful *adj.* contemptuous; disdainful; derisory

Scotland Yard *n.* The world-famous police headquarters in London

scrabble *v.* to scratch, scrape or grope with hands, feet or claws

scratch *n.* the very beginning; the start

scree *n.* a heap of rock fragments

scrutiny *n.* close observation

scuba diver *n.* 'Self Contained Underwater Breathing Apparatus', one who dives with the aid of a breathing apparatus consisting of one or more compressed air cylinders

scuttle *v.* to run using small, rapid steps

seam *n.* a linear deposit or stratum of rock, ore, etc.

seamless *adj.* without an apparent break or join

seething *adj.* moving in an agitated state, as though boiling or foaming

semblance *n.* outward appearance

sentence *n.* punishment; term of imprisonment

sentiment *n.* a feeling; an emotion

septicaemia *n.* blood poisoning

sepulchre *n.* a tomb; a burial vault

sequence *n.* things happening one after the other; a succession of events

serendipity *n.* accidental good fortune

serenely *adv.* calmly; peacefully; in a state of tranquillity

serrated *adj.* toothed; notched; jagged

serial *adj.* in a series; several

severity *n.* harshness; rigorousness

shard *n.* a broken piece or fragment of pottery, glass or similar substance

SI units *n.* The *Système International d'Unités* is an international system of units used in science and technology

shoal *n.* a group of fish

short circuit *n.* an accidental (or, as in Chapter 7, deliberate!), low-resistance connection in an electric circuit that permits the passage of excessive current

shoulder blade *n.* the scapula, a large flat bone in the shoulder

sidle *v.* to move sideways

silhouette *n.* the flat outline of a solid figure

silo *n.* an underground chamber or tunnel in which missiles are kept secret or safe from attack

simile *n.* a figure of speech drawing a resemblance between things that are different in kind, e.g. 'She was as quiet as a mouse'

sinister *adj.* threatening; suggestive of evil; ominous

sinuous *adj.* winding; twisting

sitting duck *metaphor* an easy target

skewed *adj.* at an oblique angle; slanted

skysill *n. (Anglo-Saxon)* the horizon

slag (off) *v. (slang)* to slander; to disparage

slang *n.* a word or phrase that is not standard language but is used informally; jargon

sleazy *adj.* sordid; seedy; disreputable

slippage *n.* a fall (of rock, in this instance)

slipstream *n.* the stream of air behind a moving vehicle

smite *v. (archaic)* to strike forcibly

smog *n.* a mixture of fog, smoke and pollutant chemicals

sneer *v.* to utter something in a scornful or contemptuous manner

solar energy *n.* energy from the sun

sole *adj.* only

solemnity *n.* seriousness; formality

souped-up *adj. (slang)* modified so as to have increased power

source *n.* origin; starting point

southern hemisphere *n.* that half of the Earth lying south of the equator

sparse *adj.* scanty; scattered; small in number

specific *adj.* relating to a particular thing; definite; explicit

specimen *n.* an object of interest, collected and kept for future study or display

spectacle *n.* an unusual or interesting sight; a phenomenon

speculate *v.* to guess; to conjecture

spider monkey *n.* a New World monkey of the genus *Ateles* having a very long, prehensile tail

spit *n.* a long rod on which meat or a carcass is skewered for roasting over an open fire

spook *n. (slang)* a spy; an undercover agent

spoor *n.* the trail left by an animal or person

sputter *v.* to give out a succession of disjointed, explosive sounds

stabilize *v.* to steady; to keep in equilibrium

stable *adj.* steady; firm; balanced

stalk *n.* Chapters 10, 12: the stem of a plant; *v.* Chapter 14: to approach stealthily; Chapter 21: to walk in a threatening way; Chapters 21, 23: to walk in a haughty, imperious manner

stammer *v.* to speak hesitantly

stance *n.* position; attitude

stand in good stead *v.* to prove to be useful; to be of good service

starboard *n.* the right side of a ship or an aircraft (when looking forwards)

stationary *adj.* standing still

statistics *n.* facts and figures; quantitative data on a subject

stay *n.* a structural support

steal a march *v.* to get ahead; to obtain an advantage (especially by an underhand ruse)

Stegosaurus *see* Animal Anthology

stifling *adj.* oppressive; stuffy

stipulation *n.* a condition, usually one upon which an agreement depends

strand *v.* to leave helpless; to desert; to maroon

strand *n.* a thread or fibre

strata *n.* the plural of stratum which means a layer (especially of rock)

strategy *n.* a plan of action

streak *v.* to move very rapidly

street cred. *n. abbrev. (slang)* street credibility. The display or possession of the style, behaviour, knowledge, etc., that is currently fashionable within a peer group

strew *v.* to spread; to scatter

stricken *adj.* severely damaged

strut *n.* to swagger; to walk haughtily or pompously

stuck in (to get) *phrase (slang)* to start work energetically. The phrase in the title of Chapter 22 is also a pun

stupefaction *n.* bewildered amazement; astonishment

stupendous *adj.* wonderful; amazing; astonishing

submissively *adv.* humbly; in a servile fashion

subsequently *adv.* afterwards; later

subterranean *adj.* underground

subtle *adj.* not very obvious; difficult to detect

suburb *n.* a district on the outskirts of a town or city, usually residential (where people live)

succulent *adj.* juicy

succumb *v.* to give way; to be overcome; to be overwhelmed

suffix *n.* something added to the end of a word

sullenly *adv.* morosely; gloomily; sulkily

summit *n.* the top; the peak; the highest point

supernatural *adj.* inexplicable by the ordinary laws of nature; miraculous

superstitious *adj.* having an irrational belief in omens, charms, etc.

supreme *adj.* being the most important; having the highest status or greatest power

surge *n.* a strong rush; a powerful increase

surmise *v.* to conjecture; to infer

surmount *v.* to rise above

surreal *adj.* having an unreal or dreamlike quality

surveillance *n.* watching; observation; scrutiny

survey *n.* Chapter 13: an analytical inspection; *v.* Chapter 22: to take a comprehensive view

swarm *n.* Chapter 13: a large group of small animals, especially bees and other insects; *v.* Chapters 17, 18: to climb rapidly

sway (to hold sway) *v.* to wield power; to rule

swiftlet *n.* a swallow-like bird of the order *Apodiformes*. The cave swiftlet is unusual among birds in that it can use echolocation to navigate in total darkness. The nests of some species are collected for the famous Chinese delicacy of bird's-nest soup

swirling *adj.* spinning; whirling; twisting

symbiotic *adj.* interdependent; mutually beneficial

symbol *n.* a sign or logo

symptom *n.* the manner in which an illness affects a patient

tack (to change) *v.* to change direction; to adopt a different course or approach

tactics *pl.n.* methods; plans; approaches

tag along *v.* to accompany; to trail behind

tailor *v.* to make suitable for a specific purpose

tailor-made *adj.* perfect for the purpose

tapir *n.* a mammal of the genus *Tapirus* which is found in Central and South America, and South-East Asia

taut *adj.* stretched tight; tense

taxi *v.* (of an aircraft) to move along the ground

technique *n.* method; skill; knack

temptation *n.* an attraction; an allure; an enticement; a desire

tenacious *adj.* sticky; adherent

tentatively *adv.* hesitantly; cautiously; uncertainly

terrain *n.* ground (when describing the geography or topography of an area)

territory *n.* Chapter 9: an area defended as being its own by an animal; Chapters 9, 23: a particular area or region

terror bird *see* Animal Anthology

tersely *adv.* shortly; curtly; abruptly

tether *n.* a tie; a restricting rope, wire, etc.

thee *pronoun (archaic)* you, the objective form of thou

theoretical *adj.* not actually tried in practice; possible in theory or thought

theory *n*. an idea; an hypothesis; a conjecture

theropod *n*. any bipedal carnivorous dinosaur of the suborder *Theropoda*

thicket *n*. an area of dense vegetation composed of small trees, bushes, shrubs, brambles, etc.

thine *adj. (archaic)* belonging to you; yours

thou *pronoun (archaic)* you; the one addressed

thrall *n*. the state of being in another's power; enslavement

thunderbolt *n*. a flash of lightning accompanied by thunder

thus *adv.* therefore; it follows

timorous *adj.* timid; fearful

Titan *n*. one of a family of primordial gods in Greek mythology

titanic *adj.* possessing or involving colossal strength

toil *n*. a net

token *n*. a symbol

top *v. (slang)* to kill

tortuous *adj.* twisting; turning; winding

toxins *pl.n.* poisons

traces *pl.n.* straps on a harness

trafficking *see* drug

tranquillize *v.* to calm; to settle

tranquillizer *n*. a calming drug

translate *v.* to convert from one language into another

transmission *n*. the transfer of information

transmit *v.* to pass on; to transfer; to impart

transversely *adv.* crossways

traverse *v.* to cross; to go over

treacherous *adj.* betraying; disloyal

trench *n.* furrow; ditch

trepidation *n.* anxiety; fear

tributary *n.* a river or stream that joins a larger one

Triceratops *see* Animal Anthology

tropic *see* 'Notes on the names in the book'

truculently *adv.* aggressively; obstreperously

turbine *n.* a machine with blades or vanes that rotates in a current of water, gas, etc., to generate energy

turbulence *n.* gusty air currents

twig *v. (slang)* to understand suddenly; to work out what is going on; to catch on

Tyrannosaurus *see* Animal Anthology

ultimate *adj.* final; last

unassailable *adj.* irrefutable; undeniable

underlying *adj.* basic; fundamental

undertake *v.* to promise to fulfil a task or mission; to commit oneself

underworld *n.* criminals

undeterred *adj.* not put off; not dissuaded

undiminished *adj.* not any smaller

undisputed *adj.* unquestioned; accepted

unearthly *adj.* weird; eerie

unendurable *adj.* unbearable; intolerable

unerring *adj.* consistently accurate; without any mistakes

unfurl *v.* to unroll; to unfold

ungracious *adj.* impolite

unhesitatingly *adv.* unwaveringly; without pausing

unhitch *v.* to untie; to disconnect; to unfasten

unimaginable *adj.* beyond comprehension

uninhabited *adj.* unlived in; unoccupied; without inhabitants

unkempt *adj.* untidy; ungroomed; dishevelled

unmolested *adj.* left alone; not attacked; not interfered (with)

unperturbed *adj.* not bothered; unagitated; undisturbed

unregulated *adj.* uncontrolled; not subject to rules or regulations

unsavoury *adj.* unpleasant; distasteful; disagreeable

unscalable *adj.* not possible to climb; insurmountable

unscathed *adj.* unharmed

unswervingly *adv.* constantly; without deviating

untold *adj.* incalculably great in quantity or number

uproariously *adv.* loudly; boisterously

uranium *n.* a radioactive, metallic element used as a source of nuclear energy

usher *v.* to show in; to escort

vanishingly remote *phrase* extremely unlikely

vantage point *n.* a position giving a favourable view of a scene or situation

vein *n.* a quality or trend in speech; writing; etc. 'In a more positive vein' means 'on a more positive note'

Velociraptor *see* Animal Anthology

venture *v.* to set out on a possibly hazardous undertaking; to set forth with caution or trepidation

vertical *adj.* perpendicular; upright

vertigo *n.* dizziness

vet *v.* Chapter 13: to check up on; to appraise; *n.* Chapter 22: an animal doctor (an abbreviation for veterinary surgeon)

vibrate *v.* to shake; to quiver; to oscillate

vice-chancellor *n.* a senior official in a university

vicinity *n.* neighbourhood; surrounding or adjacent area

vigorously *adv.* energetically; robustly

vindicate *v.* to justify; to prove something to be right or necessary

virtually *adv.* almost; practically; in effect

virulent *adj.* extremely infective

vista *n.* an impressive view

voracious *adj.* eager to devour

wader *n.* a long-legged bird that lives in or near water

walking on eggshells *metaphor* this phrase is used as a metaphor for very careful or cautious behaviour. In the title of Chapter 10 it is used in both its metaphorical and literal senses

wallaby *n.* an herbivorous marsupial similar to a small kangaroo

wallow *v.* to roll about or become immersed in mud or water

watercourse *n.* a route along which water flows

whence *adv. (poetic)* from; from what place

white lie *n.* a fib; a minor untruth

whither *adv. (poetic)* to what place; where

wince *v.* to move or grimace suddenly because of a pain or injury; to flinch

witness *v.* to watch; to see; to observe; *n.* one who has seen an event

wrath *n.* extreme anger; rage leading to retribution or vengeance

wry *adj.* twisted; contorted (facial expression) as an indication of quiet amusement

ye *pronoun (archaic)* form of address to two or more people

Yeti *see* Animal Anthology

yield *v.* to produce; to reveal; to bring forth

yoke *n.* a frame for linking draught animals together

yonder *adv. (poetic)* over there – often far away

Unit conversion table

1 inch = 2.54 centimetres
1 foot = 12 inches = 0.3 metres
1 yard = 3 feet = 0.91 metres
1 mile = 1760 yards = 1.61 kilometres
1 league = 3 miles *(archaic)*
1 pound = 16 ounces = 0.45 kilograms
1 ton = 2240 pounds = 1016 kilograms

1 centimetre = 0.39 inches
1 metre = 3.28 feet = 1.09 yards
1 kilometre = 0.62 miles
1 kilogram = 2.2 pounds
1 tonne (metric ton) = 1000 kilograms = 2204.6 pounds